The Edge of Us

Zoe Chauvel

Contents

Prologue

The sun disappeared under the heavy, dark gray clouds - a sign that a storm was approaching on the vast horizon. It would hit Fairhope in an hour tops judging by how angry the sky looked. The wind howled in mourning, like a widow at the bedside of her husband in passing. I listened to the sounds around me - the swings moved back and forth in a screech by their own accord. The trees rustled in the wind, while a few cars passed by with a honk or two. It was desolate, standing here in the vacant park; the sudden chill in the air bit at my skin. My breath fogged up in the air as I breathed out in slow steady breaths. Shivers ran down my spine as the temperature began to drop in an alarming rate.

I should be home under the warmth of my covers, curled up in bed reading a book as I got lost in the pages written in black and white. Or maybe I would be practicing the piano as mom always instructed me to do so. Even if she didn't I would still play on my own will. I loved the piano just as much as it was necessary to breath. It was a part of me, a part that had grown since I was seven.

But today had been different.

Today hadn't been an ordinary day filled with dungeons and dragons or damsels in distressed being rescued by the love of their lives. No, today was the day I had gone to the doctors, while mom and dad told me what they had been hiding from me since I was born. Today everything changed as the knowledge I'd gained swept into the very core of my existence, settling there like a turtle and its shell; it was part of me – it always had been.

I shook my head, trying to forget about today and just focused on waiting here in eye of the storm. There weren't many people I would do this for, especially when a storm was brewing, threatening to hit my home any minute. But I was waiting because I had promised and I seldom broke a promise.

I was waiting for my best friend.

He was supposed to be here at three o'clock sharp. Looking down at my wrist watch I read that that had been twenty-three minutes ago. I don't know what I was still doing here in light of the storm. Maybe, it was the fact that he needed me right now. His mom had just passed away after years of fighting cancer. We all knew her time was coming as she began to go to the hospital more often than usual. It was hard as Mrs. Rowely had been like my second mother. She was kind and nurturing to all the kids in the neighborhood as she knew most of us from her daycare center. Many of her kids from the past and present showed up the day of her funeral with tear streaked faces and red roses to be set on her coffin as we all took turn to say goodbye.

Tomorrow would mark the third week since her death – twenty one days to the letter. Thinking of Mrs. Rowely sent a pang through my chest and my eyes to water at her memory. No one deserved to die from a terrible illness like cancer. Why did some people have the privilege to live life without any harm, while others died unexpectedly from sickness?

It wasn't fair.

Life isn't fair, Anya.

I gulped back my father's words. He was right and I knew that life wasn't fair, but sometimes I wished there was a reason for why things happened. Why this was happening to me or why it was going to happen.

It was inevitable.

I looked down at my wrist watch again as I read 3: 47. He was almost an hour late. I wondered what was keeping him so long. Part of me wondered where he was, while the other part began to form the words I would say to him when he arrived. He would hate me – of that I was sure of. He would never talk to me ever again.

But isn't that what you want?

Yes, but it's complicated. I sighed,replying back to my conscious.

Life is complicated.

I sighed as the internal battle raged on inside of me with no sign of levying any time soon. There were just so many different ways that my news would affect him. He could choose to stay by my side with the new development or he could choose to leave. Part of me wanted the latter because I didn't want him to go through any sort of pain again, not after what he just went through with his mother. The other part   the stronger and righteous part wanted him to stay because I knew that he would never leave me no matter what. Through thick and thin we would be friends forever. It was a promise we had made each other back in second grade.

I began to walk towards the playground, my feet dragging on the grass. I felt the coldness of the ground as the grass poked my sandal covered feet, sending a slight prickle up my leg. I took every step warily, counting how many paces it took from my spot to the swings.

Fifteen...seventeen...twenty-one...

Nothing else existed beside the steps in front of me as I made my way towards the playground. It was as if time froze, and took all my thoughts away with the wind as they flowed freely in the sky. It was exactly forty-three steps when I got to the swings as I took my seat, and pushed myself off the ground. The air around me burned my skin, gnawing at it like fire ants – leaving a trace of their brutality behind. I didn't care, though. I felt numb. The fear of a cold didn't scare me as it used to. Everything was different now and I felt fearless because nothing could hurt me; nothing but this one thing.

I heard footsteps as my heart thudded in my chest only to fall as I saw that it was only an officer. Disappointment sank into my stomach and I realized how much I wanted to see him – how much this meeting meant to me. He had always been my rock when the waves came crashing on the shore. He never let me wash away, holding me intact when life got rough. Even when his mother was dying he had been strong, holding down the fort while everyone around him sank deep down into their grief.

There was only once when I saw him breakdown, and I held him as his tears soaked my shirt through, and heart wrenching spasms racked his body.

"You need to get on home, kid. The storm will hit any second and you don't want to be caught in it."

I looked up, the voice cutting through my thoughts as the memories slowly faded. I saw clear blue eyes looking at me with concern as I recognized who he was.

"Anya, did you hear me?"

"Yes. Sorry, Mr. Weatherly! I'll go home right now." I said, hopping off the swing.

"Good," he said, giving me a knowing sly smile. "Tell your folks I said hi. Get home safe, kid."

I turned back and yelled, "Will do!" and began to run as the wind became fiercer, making it hard to run or even walk for that matter.

As I made my way home I didn't see him and the disappointment was too hard to ignore as it made my heart sink. I had needed him today more than ever and he hadn't been there. Maybe, he didn't want to be friends anymore. Summer was almost ending and that meant starting high school in just a few weeks. He probably had found new friends to hang out with – cooler people than me. He probably had better things to do now.

The boy I knew as my best friend would never leave me waiting for an hour for him to show up. No. Things were changing – he was changing. In the midst of all that had happened today I had hoped that he would be the only thing in my life that would remain the same. I now saw that it couldn't be, as much as I didn't want to admit it. Everything was changing from this day forward.

Nothing would ever be the same way again.

Chapter 1

First Day of School

> 4 years later...

"Anya! You're going to be late for school!"

I sighed, taking one last look in the mirror before I grabbed my bag, and rushed down the stairs – almost tripping on the last step. I caught myself on the banister, and looked menacingly down at my untied shoe lace. Kneeling down I quickly tied my shoe and checked the other, making sure that it was also tied. Tripping would not be the best thing to do on the first day of my senior year. It would mostly likely deem me as a klutz along with the many other names I'd gained throughout the years.

"Anya!" My mother called again from the kitchen. "You're going-" She stopped mid-sentence as soon as she saw me standing in the foyer, her shoulders relaxing in relief. "All set?" She asked as she continued to wash the remaining dishes from last night.

I sighed, "Ready as I'll ever be."

She smiled. She put the dishes away in a clatter and turned on the dishwasher to run its cycle. Her eyes were warm and joyful as she enveloped me in a hug. "Look at you! You grow more beautiful each year like the roses in the garden."

"And that is a fact," my father chimed in kissing me on the forehead.

I smiled. They never tired of giving me compliments no matter how much I protested. That's parents for you; They loved you, suffocated you, annoyed you, but at the end of the day they were still family. They were my family and I loved them nonetheless.

My father grabbed his thermal full to the brim with coffee and gave my Mom a quick peck on the lips before he was out the door. A second later he said, "C'mon, bug. Don't want to be late to school, now do we?"

"Nope," I said, popping the 'p'. Dad was always running late, but we got me to school safely even if he did have to break a few traffic laws here and there. He used to be a 'daredevil' as my mom called it before he settled down to have a family of his own. He traded in his motorcycle for a sensible Ford Taurus and his leather jacket was now tucked away in the back of the closet, covered by his suits and ties.

I draped my messenger back over my shoulder and gave Mom a quick kiss on the cheek. I turned; ready to leave when she grabbed my elbow, her eyes assessing mine. "Did you take your medicine?"

I nodded. How could I forget? It's a pattern that I'd been adapted to my whole life, but I've been taking it on my own for the past four years – ever since I found out that stormy day. It wasn't entirely a bad thing. There was still hope, and that is what I'll always have – no one could ever take that away.

Hope is what made people stronger everyday; sometimes, it was all that people clung to.

"Anya! Now, we're really going to be late for school!" My father called from the garage breaking through my reverie. I shook my head from my thoughts and quickly gave Mom another kiss before shooting out the door in frenzy.

The cacophony of voices, lockers being shut, and the occasional shriek of shoes scrapping against the linoleum pierced my ears as I walked through the halls of Velmont High. I treaded carefully through the hallway, weaving my way through my peers as I made my way towards the end of the hall where a list of homerooms was taped outside the theater.

I accidentally bumped into someone - my shoulder colliding with a girl's. I winced from the contact – certain that I would have a bruise the next morning. I muttered a quick "Sorry!" and continued onward. But my apology wasn't accepted as she called, "Watch where you're going, vampire!"

"And the fun begins," I muttered.

There were a few cackles of laughter around me, but they were drowned by the buzz of people's conversations. I kept walking and was almost to my destination when I saw a kid being slammed into the lockers. The sound was loud like thunder as it echoed throughout the hallway. Conversations ceased as silence filled the atmosphere in a heavy, tense manner reminding me of the subtle tranquility before a storm hits. My heart stopped beating for a second when I realized who was causing the trouble.

The kid (my guess was that he was a freshmen) was cowering before him – his hands held up to cover his face as fear radiated from him in perpetual waves. Liam leered down at him, while his friends backed him up and snickered. A strange feeling overcame me, and before I knew it I was weaving my way towards him.

My hands were shaking when I said, "Count on Velmont High's infamous bad boy Liam Rowely to cause a scene on the first day of school." My voice came out surprisingly brave without a tinge of fear. How I was feeling was an entirely different matter. I wasn't feeling brave at all, but instead nervous at standing this close to him.

He slightly turned his head at the sound of my voice, his eyes shining brightly with malice. "Back off, Vanchester."

"No. Leave him alone."

He snickered, his lips twisting up in a smirk. "What? Is he your boyfriend?" He searched my eyes, scrutinizing me. I wanted to back away, but held my ground. I wasn't going to show him that I was weak even though it is what I felt inside. He shrugged. "Thought you could do better; guess I was wrong."

I rolled my eyes. "Leave him alone, Liam. Or are you that much of a coward that you can't find someone your own size to harass?"

There was the distant sound of gasps and low murmuring from my peers at my words. For the first time since I'd confronted Liam I looked around my surrounding and noted that our peers had enclosed a small perimeter around us, watching the spectacle unfold in front of their eyes. My eyes flickered from one face to another until I found the eyes of my best friend, Gemma. Her brown eyes shined with admiration and fear all at the same time, and I saw her slightly nod to show that she had seen me.

The bell rang; signaling the start of the school day. Everyone began to scatter like deer trying to get away from their predator. Guess who was the predator?

I knelt down and offered my hand to the kid – Liam's slate blue eyes watching me intently. The kid grasped my hand without hesitation, his brown eyes shining with gratitude. He mumbled a quick "Thank you" and ran to the other end of the hallway into a classroom. Liam's crew was long gone by now and there were only a few bodies lingering in the hallway, grabbing last minute items before morning classes officially began. Smoothing down my dress, I hurriedly walked to the end of the hall to the list, ignoring Liam on my heels, and read that I was in RM 818, my dad's room.

I sighed, hastily walking towards the other end of the hallway where the room was located. Liam was still on my heels and I refrained from turning around and telling him to leave me alone. He would have to get to his class eventually. There was only three minutes left until the late bell rang.

My father greeted me with a nod as I entered his classroom. He was writing his name on the whiteboard and I took a seat in the second row next to Gemma. It was a blessing that she and I had a last name close in alphabet or else I'd be doomed to spend the hour with no one to talk to as the tedious paperwork was prepared and finished.

As the final bell rang, Liam casually strolled in and took the unoccupied seat on the other side of me. There were plenty of other empty seats scattered throughout the classroom, but he just had to sit next to me.

I felt the brush of Gemma's hand on my forearm, her face etched with worry. Her hand went up to her hearing aid, pushing a button to turn it on, and disappeared behind her straight jet black hair. Her eyes gleamed with mischief as she glanced at Liam and then at me. She signed, "What do you think he wants?"

I shrugged signing back, "Probably wants to make my life miserable."

She tilted her head in thought then signed, "Maybe he's drawn to you like moth to a flame because you stood up to him and it was the first time you've talked to him in years."

I scoffed. That was absurd. Liam Rowely didn't care about me or anyone else for that matter. The only thing he cared about was himself and the so-called reputation he steadily obtained since he stepped through these halls.

"You're joking, right?" I asked aloud.

She shook her head, smiling. "No joke."

Liam cleared his throat loudly; gaining the attention from the students surrounding us. "Why don't you take your secret language somewhere else. Some of us are trying to learn."

Anger boiled inside my veins at his petty remark. It was a low blow to make fun of Gemma's disability. He knew better than to laugh at other people's expense. "You can move if you like. That will solve all our problems."

He grinned, leaning in to me; his face only inches away from mine. His slate blue eyes danced with amusement as he said, "I always liked them feisty. Want to go out sometime?"

My cheeks flamed at his remark and I turned my head slightly, hiding my face with my hair. I heard him chuckle, satisfaction ringing in his laughter. I sighed in frustration and reached into my bag, grabbing my notebook.

He always made me so angry! I didn't understand the sudden outburst of annoyance whenever I saw him or heard of his endeavors. Maybe it was the fact that I once knew a boy who was merely a shadow to the one sitting next to me. My pencil began to sketch on its own accord as my thoughts drifted to the past, where the boy sitting next to me was my best friend instead of a stranger.

Chapter 2

"So, I heard you had an interesting morning," Hayden said sliding into the bench next to Gemma. He kissed her forehead in greeting and she smiled, tenderly and lovingly.

I sighed slumping down into my seat, feeling small. "I should have just stayed invisible." The dark clouds loomed overhead, covering the edge of the sun as the world turned gray. It was going to rain. In any other given day I would welcome the rain with open arms, but not today as I was wearing a dress and would be walking home. Dad had a first day of school meeting, and I imagined that they would throw a grand old party filled with confetti, balloons, cake - the whole shebang. They'd probably celebrate the first day of school, and the very fact that no teacher committed murder or strangled a kid.

I took out my peanut butter and banana sandwich from my bag taking a huge bite of it as the growling in my stomach ceased. The sticky peanut butter stuck to the roof of my mouth, while the sweet taste of banana added an extra hint of yumminess. There was nothing better than peanut butter and banana sandwiches for the first day of school. It was tradition, a custom that was presently only celebrated by one.

"I think it's too late for that." I heard Hayden say bringing me back from my thoughts. I looked at him and saw his eyes flickering back and forth between me and something behind me. I furrowed my eyebrows and looked at Gemma to see if I could detect any trace of what Hayden was looking at. I had no such luck. Gemma was finding her container full of fruit seemingly more interesting than the conversation at hand. She glanced at me, but quickly averted her eyes.

I looked back at Hayden to see the smirk on his face. Curiosity got the best of me and I turned around to lock my brown eyes with cold slate blue ones. He was leaning against the stucco wall of the art building. His arms were leisurely crossed over his chest and his eyes were calculating as he watched me.

There was no wave. No smirk. No way of indicating that he saw me looking back at him, curiously. He reached into his pocket and pulled out a cigarette and lit it in one swift motion. I shook my head, disappointment washing over me like a giant tidal wave crushing me under its might.

"Looks like he's taken an interest to you."

I turned around and glared at Hayden. He was amusing himself with this new piece of information and I kicked him under the table. "Ow, hey! I'm just messing with you. Relax, will you? You don't need to be violent."

Gemma stifled a laugh and I smiled. She spoke as she signed, "Shouldn't have said that."

Point one for Anya. Score! Hayden was going down. I smiled and said, "Exactly. Listen to your girlfriend. Jerk."

He shook his head. "Women."

Hayden was so difficult sometimes. But I liked him. He was a good guy for Gemma and saw past her disability. He even started to teach himself how to sign with the help of Gemma and I on a daily basis. At this very moment, Hayden was trying to sign, but wasn't getting anywhere by the confused expression on Gemma's face. Her brows were drawn together, making a crease on her forehead. Hayden became animated – waving his hands in the air in frustration as neither one of us understood what he was trying to say.

It was quite amusing.

Eating my delicious sandwich made me thirsty and I reached inside my bag for my soda, but ended up empty handed. I rummaged through my bag as panic rose up like bile in my throat. "Dammit," I muttered. This could not be happening. Could this day possibly get any worst?

"Hayden?"

"Hmm?"

"Will you go grab me a soda from the vending machine?" I asked pushing the money across the table. "Please?"

He looked at me like I was a pest that he was examining under a microscope. In an instant his expression changed to amusement as he casted a glance behind me. "Are your legs not functioning?"

God, how I really detested him sometimes. "Please?" I asked sweetly.

"No, Anya." He said firmly. Gemma gave him a loaded look and he sighed being reprimanded for his harsh tone. Score! Two points for me, while Hayden sat at a whopping zero. Maybe he'll go and get my soda out of guilt. "Look, you can't avoid him. You know him. He's not going to back off until he gets what he wants, Anya."

"So that's a definite no?"

He raised his brow and motioned me to go. I did but I sulked my way there. This was ridiculous! Some so-called friends that I have; Hayden was definitely going to get pushed down the stairs today. That was a fact; unless Gemma tried to stop me then it wouldn't be that good of a plan. I chuckled and it made this walk a bit more bearable. When Liam saw me coming towards him he raised an eyebrow, continuing to smoke his cigarette leisurely like a still black and white fram of Hollywood actor from a 50's film. I ignored him as I put the money into the machine and pressed E3 for my Coke.

"You think you're better than me?"

I stiffened at the sound of his voice. My soda had been dispensed, but I made no move to grab it and go. Instead I risked the chance and looked at him. A burning sense of familiarity made its way into the very fiber of my being. I remember that same look...years ago. It was the kind of look that asked me to implore him with understanding and answers. It was the latter that I could not give.

Even if it had been years it didn't mean that I had lost my ability to read him like a newly written novel. Every chapter was a mystery as the words hid a deeper meaning than anyone else could ever understand. Yet, he was still a stranger to me. I didn't fully know him any longer.

"No," I answered in a whisper. "That isn't true."

"Then what is it?" He asked, taking in a breath of the cigarette and drawing out the smoke towards me. I tried not to notice how his lips gingerly curved around it, or how he held it gingerly pinched between thumb and third finger as he drew it almost reverently to his mouth.

"Wasting away your life is my problem, Liam."

He chuckled but it wasn't friendly. He stepped towards me and the smell of smoke assailed my nostrils, making me take a step back. He leaned in close to my face, while the cigarette was now in his hands, letting the ashes fall on the ground.

"What I do with my life is none of your concern."

It used to be, I thought but instead in one swift motion I took the cigarette from his hand and dropped it on the ground, stomping it with my foot.

"Hope that was your last one." I said, raising my eyebrow in a challenge.

"If I knew you were this feisty I would have asked you out years ago. How about now?"

I scoffed. "I'd rather spend time with my mother's cat."

Amusement flickered in his eyes as he ran a hand through his ashen blond hair. "You always liked that cat better than me." He laughed, crossing his arms over his chest. "How's Mr. Cuddle's these days?"

"Is this your way of trying to be on my good side? 'Cause if it is," I leaned in to him and stood on my tippy toes to whisper in his ear, "It's not working."

A bemused expression settled on his face as I crouched to grab my soda from the machine. No matter how much I wanted to see his expression as I walked away I willed myself not to turn around. It was a monumental step of epic proportions. I had talked to Liam Rowley for more than five minutes, while holding a semi-civil conversation. It was an accomplishment nonetheless, seeing as he and I haven't spoken a word to each for four years.

As I sat down at the table and rejoined my friends as they high-fived me, I couldn't help but notice the gnawing feeling at the pit of my stomach. There was no telling what was going to happen next, and it frightened me.

With Liam Rowely there was no telling what the next day would bring.

It was always unknown territory, a place that I had not ventured in a very long time, and was uncertain if I ever wanted to return. It was dangerous to associate with him because of who he was now. It was irrational to even be in the same vicinity as he was.

But I had done it, and somewhere a can of proverbial marbles had spilled.

Chapter 3

Thunder roared overhead as the cracks of lighting followed after as if there was a war above unseen by human eyes. I knew that I should have gone home straight after school as Dad had suggested. Hayden offered to drive me home, but I had declined – wanting to take a walk down town and go to the music store. It had been a few weeks since I'd last seen Mr. Edison and I missed his stories of the war and the beautiful sheets of music that he'd compose in his earlier years.

I could spend hours in his music store, and it was exactly what I had done. It was nearly six when I headed out into the cold, frigid air. The rain quickly covered me, drenching me from head to toe. Silently, I prayed that the sheets of music Mr. Edison gave me would not be ruined by the rain. They were too precious and valuable to have the ink smeared, making the pages unrecognizable and weathered.

The streets began to flood with the drastic pouring of the rain. I cursed myself for forgetting my cell on top of my vanity this morning. Mom and Dad would be worried sick when I got home, and I'd probably get grounded. Not to mention that I'd probably have a wicked cold tonight; I could already feel my bones begin to ache deep down to the marrow. It hurt.

The loud roar of an engine startled me as it stopped beside me, and the driver cut off the engine. I kept walking, wondering where he was heading. All the stores had closed due to the sudden storm – well, all the stores I had passed. As I looked down the street I saw the other owners begin to close up shop; Open signs were switched to say Closed, lights switched off, and cars whizzed by in a hurry to get home.

"Anya!"

I turned around at the sound of my name, needing proof that it was who I thought it was.

"What are you doing here?" I asked.

Liam gave me a bewildered look and grasped my hand as he began to pull me towards his motorcycle, or bike as I liked to call it; a bike with an engine. "You're going to catch your death. Take the favor."

I snatched my hand from his grasp, digging my heels to the ground. He stopped, eyeing my warily. "I don't need your help. I'm not a lost puppy. I know my way home."

"I also know that you get sick easily. Stop being stubborn and hop on," he said motioning to his bike. "I won't bite."

Really, I thought, could have fooled me. I watched Liam's expression change from wariness, to irritation, to pleading all in a matter of seconds. "How did you know I was here? This is nowhere near your house. Have you been following me?"

He scoffed. "Stop thinking of yourself so highly, Anya." He ran a hand through his matted blond hair that looked more like a dirty blond soaked from the rain. "Will you just listen for once?"

I eyed the bike suspiciously and then glanced back at Liam. He was going out of his way to take me home, why? Four years of silent reproach had been broken this morning when I stood up to him, but that was because he was being a jerk - terrorizing an innocent kid on the first day of school. Talk about a horrible nightmare coming true for a freshmen. It wasn't enough reason for Liam to begin to talk to me. Even when I went to the vending machine, I pointedly ignored him. He could have done the same, but instead he talked to me – he actually talked to me.

And now this?

It was strange and uncommon. Like an eclipse; it only happened rarely and after years of it being dormant.

"Are you coming or not?" He asked, impatiently. He was already straddled over his bike, the engine loud in the silence and emptiness of the street. I bit my lip, weighing my options. I could politely decline his offer and go home only to get sick for a week. Or I could go with him and make him hate me less and complete number 9 on my list.

I chose the latter.

It was selfish and hoped that I wasn't wrong.

I ran forward and saw the small smile forming on his lips. "Do you have an extra helmet?"

He grabbed his and tossed it at me. "Your house is just over the bridge. I'll be careful."

Gnawing at my bottom lip, I suddenly felt queasy. "No, I-what if something happens? It's raining and the road is dangerous." I took a step back, thinking twice about my decision. "You could lose control and you-"

"Will you just get on?" He said annoyed.

I huffed in agitation and strapped on the helmet. Hiking up my dress I climbed on and shivered at the coldness of the leather on my skin. "Hold on tight."

He revved up the engine and gently pushed off the curb – the action made me veer to the left and without another thought I snaked my arms around his waist like a vice, fearing that if I let go it would cause my untimely death.

Liam chuckled and I had a smartass retort at the tip of my tongue, but my voice caught in my throat as we began to zoom through the streets. I gasped at the velocity and tightened my hold around Liam's waist. The air whipped around me and I pressed the side of my cheek to his back, making myself small in the space given between us. I was hyper aware of my surroundings, and of my body. My thighs ached by how clenched together they were around Liam's hips; holding on for dear life. My arms were tightly clasped around his waist where I could feel the hardness of his abs underneath his leather jacket. Then there was the strong scent of his musk that strangely smelled of cinnamon as I breathed him in. It reminded me of warm winter nights sitting by the fire drinking eggnog, while we talked about everything and nothing...

What in the world was I doing?

I mentally slapped myself and closed my eyes, blocking away all my thoughts - concentrating on the rain and wind as it bit my skin. The roars of thunder made me shudder as its angry cries filled the vast plane. I looked up at the sky to catch the crackle of lighting breaking through the dark gray atmosphere. Slowly, I began to count in my head as I did when I was younger.

One Mississippi...two Mississippi...three Mississippi...four Missississ-

Another wave of lighting broke through the sky and I cringed. The storm was only four miles away.

We began to slow down as the familiarity of my neighborhood came into view. Liam came to a stop on the curb of my house and killed the engine. I climbed off the bike ungracefully; almost tripping over my own feet as the feel of gravity came crashing down on me. Liam caught my forearm, sending a burning fire coursing through my veins as he steadied me.

"Thanks," I muttered as I averted my eyes to look at my feet. I was suddenly nervous to be around him, and I was afraid to see what I might find when he looked at me. This was unprecedented. I wasn't very good when it came to dealing with things out of my comfort zone, and he was definitely one of those things.

"I think I see your dad at the window," I heard him say. I turned on my heel and saw that his observation was true. Dad disappeared, drawing the curtain back as I saw his shadow move towards the direction of the kitchen on the thin white curtains. I was so dead. Dad was going to blow a gasket.

I sighed, dreading the uncomfortable conversation that would ensue once I stepped inside. The roar of the engine made me whirl around, and before I could thank him for the ride – Liam was already down the road with only the glow of streetlights to illuminate his way home as the sun set.

Later that night, as I laid in bed, I heard my parent's muffled voices through the paper thin walls. My father's voice was low and had an edge that I'd never heard before.

"She was on the back of his bike, Charlotte. It was dangerous and reckless! She shouldn't have been on it in the first place. Not with this kind of weather and not ever in her life until she's thirty!"

I heard my mother giggle and said in a tone that I could only guess as teasing, "I never thought to see the day you'd be acting this way."

Pause.

"Oh, God...I've become my worst nightmare: the overprotective father."

A smile tugged at the corners of my mouth at my father's realization. It couldn't have come at a better time. There was a small part of me that feared he would talk to Liam tomorrow before homeroom. I would die of humiliation or better yet, I'd silently pray for the ground beneath me to open up and swallow me whole.

Either one would be great.

"It happens to the best of us. You wouldn't be a good father if you didn't care about your little girl's well being," my mother said soothingly.

There was a long pause and I waited for what seemed like hours for more words to be spoken between them. I glanced over at my clock and read 10:47 in big neon purple numbers. I sighed, feeling the heavy wave of exhaustion wash over me like quicksand. But I willed my body and mind to stay awake for just a bit longer.

Finally, I heard my mother say, "We need to let her make her own decisions. It's her life and if she wants Liam back into her life we have no right telling her otherwise. You know how these kinds of decisions are precious to her."

I sighed in relief. If I could I would jump out of bed and hug my mom. She always understood when it came to factors of my life. If I told her I wanted to go and jump off a small cliff she would support me. Dad would also support me after he tried to reason that it was dangerous. He was always concerned about my well-being, and I didn't blame him.

"I know," dad said. "You're right. I'll just have to grin and bear it, won't I?"

"That's right, honey."

I had to hand it to Mom. She was the best negotiator on the planet! With my mind at ease I let my body rest and hoped that aching in my bones would subside by morning. My mind was a different matter as they were filled with thoughts of Liam.

He had entered back into my life, and now it would be difficult to extract him from my mind like it had been in the very beginning.

It had taken two years to let him go, and watch as his life slowly unraveled from the seams.

Could I do the same thing again?

Chapter 4

Liam

She looked like shit today.

Her skin was abnormally pasty like the color of a blank sheet of paper. I watched from the other end of the hall as she stared at her locker mirror, pinching her cheeks to add a bit of color into them. There was a sheen coat of sweat matting her skin as the small hairs on her forehead clumped together in disarray. She was also acting more like a klutz than usual - dropping her books when she meant to put them in her bag, tripping over her own feet as she took a seat in Calculus, and stopping in the middle of the hall as if she was a lost puppy.

I knew that I shouldn't have been watching Anya, but something had changed.

Everywhere I turned she was there at the end of the hall or in my line of sight. During homeroom, from the corner of my eye I had caught her attention towards me - her lips parted, as if she wanted to say something to me, but no words were every uttered. In the last four years I hadn't seen or heard a squeak out of her, and now she was EVERYWHERE. She was like the plague - no matter how hard I tried to rid myself of the disease it would always inflict its torture wherever I was.

The past is always difficult to forget; the scars would always remain.

"So you took Anya Vanchester home yesterday?" My best mate Collin inquired, leaning up against the wall next to me. "What gives?"

"Since when did you begin to question my decisions," I remarked flippantly, tapping the pack of Methol's against my palm. I took three steps to my locker and punched the top of the metal, making the door swing open.

"Don't jump my dick, man" he said raising his hands in surrender. "I was just asking. Everyone is talking about it. Karla is pissed."

Great. Karla was going to give me hell for giving Anya a ride on my bike. She was probably seething in anger and riling up her cult of blond dimwits to go and-

Shit!"

"Looks like Karla is going to start trouble with vamp girl," Collin said as I spun around to see Karla and her groupies surround Anya and her best friend, Gemma. Anya's back was turned to me, hindering her facial expressions, but I did see her back stiffen when Karla leaned in close to her face.

My feet began to involuntarily make their way towards the scene, but someone caught my shoulder. Collin.

"Don't. They'd just see it as her being your next slam-piece if you go and get between that."

He was right. I shouldn't even be concerned. Why did I care? I shrugged off the thought and turned to Collin, nodding in agreement. "You're right. It's her problem," I said through clenched teeth.

Collin eyed me warily as if silently asking, "What's with you?"

I turned back to my locker, stuffing miscellaneous items into my backpack. It's not like I was going to use any of this crap. But I needed to do something to mask what I really wanted to do. I shut the locker and the sound resonated throughout the now empty hall. Collin was gone - actually everyone was gone. The only person who remained was Anya, slumped down on the linoleum floor - banging the back of her head repeatedly on the lockers.

Swiftly, I turned on my heel but something stopped me. Maybe it was guilt, perhaps pity or it might have been curiosity - that made my direction change towards her. Logically, I knew this was a bad idea. If one of Karla's bimbo lacheys saw me word would spread faster than wild fire through these halls. Putting it out would result in damages being done in return, and that was something I would not take part in.

"Forget to take your medication this morning? I'll go get the nurse if you-"

"Shut up, Liam." Her voice was hard, cold. I don't ever recall her sounding like that. She must have been really peeved. "Go away. I don't need you or your pity."

I rolled my eyes. She had some nerve. It seemed like my presence brought out the worst in her. I wasn't even sure what the hell I was still doing here. I heard her sniffle and it made my steps halt from retreating. The image of a long ago memory flashed through my eyes, remembering a time where I had come across Anya in this very position.

We were nine and this kid name Ronnie Jenkins was teasing her on the playground. He kept on harassing her about her pale skin and sickly appearance that day. He made her cry and I found her at the playground (one of our favorite haunts back in the past) after school. The memory was freshly embedded in my mind as if it was yesterday. I remember finding Ronnie later that day and giving him a piece of my mind.

He was outside of the ice cream parlor when I found him. I wasted no time with small talk and punched him in the face. I felt the curve of a smile slide on my lips at the memory. People rarely change once they grew up into adults. I was a living, breathing example of this very concept. I was still that little boy who defended their best friend from the trivial and demeaning angst of immature and condescending people. Didn't I want to defend her just a couple of minutes ago from Karla's claws?

Anya always had it rough growing up but I was always there, until I wasn't anymore.

"Can you just please leave?"

Her voice snapped me out of my reverie - it was soft, pleading; resigned. I looked down and met her red-rimmed brown eyes and the wavering of her bottom lips. Tears threatened to spill from her eyes like a flowing waterfall cascading over a ridge. She wanted me to leave immediately before it happened.

My jaw clenched as I debated on what to do.

In the end, I walked away from her like I had all those years ago.

The smell of alcohol and smoke assailed my nostrils as I walked through the door. Nothing but those two scents mixed in the air would have made it Home Sweet Home! as if it was the embodiment of some semblance of a happy home. There was nothing cheerful about this house. It was a shadow of its previous glory. Nothing has been the same since Mom died.

Dad was probably slumped on the couch in front of the t.v - oblivious to his surroundings as he drowned his sorrows and grief with cheap beer. The sound of an announcer's droned voice reached my ears as I passed the living room towards the hall and into my room. I dumped my backpack by the door and flopped on my back onto my unkempt bed, feeling the stab of the remote on my back. In one swift movement I grabbed it and threw it on the floor, closing my eyes as the smell of grease and oil lingered on my skin.

It had been a long day down at Jimmy's Automotives. Today wasn't one of my best days as thoughts of Anya clouded my brain. I couldn't erase the sullen look on her face from this afternoon. Guilt washed over my mind like a shattered dam rapidly spilling all the water supply from its reservoir.

I should have never taken her home last night. If I hadn't stopped when I saw her walking home - none of this would have transpired. We could both pretend like we never knew each other, and keep on going with our life on different sides of the social anarchy of high school. She was no one to me - not anymore. That is how it should stay for the rest of our lives. Anya and I had nothing in common. She was the social reject with her deaf friend and former "bad" boy. I was the type of guy that made men want to lock up their daughters and send them to an all girl's Catholic school. One look at me reeled their own judgment that I was indeed that boy that would nab their chastity belts on the back of my Ducati and leave them crying in my midst. Which was stupid, by the way. Sex on a motorcycle wasn't comfortable, if not nearly impossible.

A loud crash made me jump out of bed, towards the living room where Dad laid on the floor - broken glass from our family portraits scattered around him. I knelled down beside him and lifted his armpits to pull him up, laying him gently on the sofa. There's a blanket discarded on the floor and I drape it over him.

I sighed, knelling down once again to pick up the jagged edges of glass. They were remnants of a lost family in each broken fragment like some kind of ancient Chinese civilization waiting to be discovered once again. As if that would ever happen - stuff like that doesn't exist in reality. Maybe in something like Star Wars when Luke finds that Darth Vadar is his father. One of the most epic known lines in movie history: "Luke, I am your father."

Must have been a big blow for Luke finding out that his arch enemy was his dad.

After I cleaned up the mess Dad made I began to throw away the empty beer cans that graced our living room floor, and pretty much every surface in the vicinity. It was the same routine every night. He'd come from work and drink away his pain until he passed out from the overwhelming amount of alcohol in his system. Next morning he'd be sober, ready for work as if the night before never happened.

But that was Dad for you.

Emptying the last cans into a black trash bag, I glanced at his heavily intoxicated demeanor as his light snoring filled the quiet space. I reached forward, grabbing the ends of the blanket and brought it to his chin - tucking him under the wool's warmth.

I whispered, "Night Dad," and left him on the couch to sleep the effects of being inebriated. It was half past eleven when I made it back to my room, crashing from the exhaustion overwhelmingly poignant fitful sleep.

Chapter 5

"How is operation "Avoiding Liam" going?" Gemma signed - a conspirator gleam in her brown eyes.

I shut my locker door a little too forcefully and turned to face the wickedly giddy look on her face. She found amusement in my dilemma, and concluded that once the year was over Liam and I would be friends once again. It would be a story that would be told for decades of lost friendships and new found land; full of unlikely compromises.

Yeah, right.

That was as likely as hell freezing over, which wasn't ever going to happen.

She was such a hopeless romantic. Her ideology always made me feel better in times where I gave up hope in finding my one true love. Okay, so maybe I was also a hopeless romantic. But who could blame me? I had dreams of finding someone to love me for who I am considering my unique circumstance.

When it came to her hopeful outlook of Liam and me, I couldn't help but feel annoyed. She had this idea that Liam would turn out to be just like Hayden. That was an unlikely juxtaposition. Hayden and Liam were entirely two different people on the color spectrum.

For one, Hayden once held a pretense to be a part of the "in crowd"; while Liam was the embodiment of what Hayden tried to be.

Luckily, Hayden saw the error of his ways – thanks to Gemma's sweet nature. At the beginning there was a language barrier between them, but when two people loved each other – words were not needed. It was all about body language and the actions that one committed to the other and vice versa.

Hayden's declaration of love – per se – was when he sat with us one day at lunch a year ago. He blatantly walked up to our table, asked if he could join us, and when we agreed he took a seat next to Gemma – acting as if that moment of perpetual defiance never occurred.

"Anya…earth to Anya…Anya!" I startled, focusing on Hayden's face hovering a few inches from mine. His hands grasped my shoulders, shaking me out of my thoughts.

"What," I snapped. "Is. Your. Problem? You're hurting me."

His brow creased as a flicker of confusion and recognition flashed across his slate green eyes. "Sorry," he muttered bashfully. "Gemma has been trying to garner your attention for the last five minutes, but you weren't even on this planet, let alone here. You alright?"

My eyes settled on Gemma's worried eyes and back to Hayden's in a matter of seconds. "Why wouldn't I be fine? I was just thinking," I said, shouldering my messenger bag and taking a few steps down the hall. When I heard Gemma and Hayden's steps gather beside me, we made our way towards the theater for the winter play auditions.

It has been three weeks since school had officially begun with all extracurricular activities undergoing a brand new season. The theater department's first show of the year was going to be a modern adaption of Beauty And The Beast. Every year I would play the piano music that accompanied the school plays. Dr. Devino (who was the school's drama and music teacher) believed I was the finest pianist he knew in town and thus, chose me every year as the pianist to play. I begged to differ. I wholeheartedly believed that Mr. Edison had superior and finer piano skills than I would ever have. But Mr. Edison hadn't played the piano for ten years; ever since he developed chronic arthritis, ailing him to never play the beautiful instrument ever again.

I felt the soft tap of fingers gracing my bare shoulder and turned to see Gemma signing, "We'll see you later tonight?"

Nodding, I said while signing, "Of course. It's movie Friday!"

"Just to remind both of you," Hayden added smugly. "It's my pick of the movie and I'm thinking of a badass action movie. Maybe Death Race or Death Race 2."

Gemma and I crinkled our noses in disgust. "No way," she said. "Romance."

He threw his hands up in exasperation one moment, then crossed his arms the next. "Ha! I love you, but not enough to sit through the third straight week of lovey dovey scenes!"

Gemma laughed, dragging a bewildered Hayden in tow. Poor guy. His masculinity was being ripped from underneath his feet! Of course, we were just giving him a hard time. Knowing Gemma she'd probably tease him until tonight. He'll get his movie, but not until we see his tears.

Ha ha.

Pulling on the door to the theater, I entered meeting the brightness of a spotlight, shining brilliantly on center stage at Karla.

Everyone turned at the sound of the traitorous door clanging shut behind me. Karla gave me a death stare that could only be perceived by me, making my skin crawl like she'd dump a bucket of a thousand live spiders all over my body.

This was going to be an exceedingly long afternoon.

"Well, I think that's the last one for today," Dr. Devino called out from his seat in the audience. "Whoever thought of having the first round of auditions on a Friday must have been delusional."

I stifled a laugh, "Um…it was your idea, Dr. Devino. Your logic for it – if I recall – was that the kids who showed up to audition on a Friday were the ones who will take their roles with determination, diligence, and great ambition."

"Is that right?"

I nodded, stacking up the pieces of sheet music together in one pile, setting it on the edge of the piano's weathered wooden surface. Gingerly, I ran my finger tips on the piano keys – mindful of not to press the keys hard enough, erupting a sound from Old Betty Lou. It was not the name I chose, but one that Devino had taken the liberty to calling the old beast. It had seen better days when the school had opened in 1978, but she still emitted beautiful notes.

"Kid, are you going to stay a while longer?" He asked from the side exit. Dr. Devino was ready to leave with top hat and coat at the ready! He was one of my favorite teachers because of his flamboyant nature, but also because he reminded me of one of those cool cat's from the 50's. Those were the days – filled with snapping jazz numbers and beautifully played music that made the 50's vibrant and enticing.

"Just a bit. You don't have to wait up for me," I said waving him off. "I know the drill. I'll turn the lights off, lock up, and all that other jazz."

He eyed me warily, but couldn't manage to hold down his serious expression as a smile made the corners of his eyes crinkle and light up with merriment. "Alright, kid. Say hi to your folks when you get home!" With those final words he was off faster than a gal could say, "Monkey's with well worn threads act bananas".

Liam

It was a quarter past five as I walked the empty dark halls of the school. Karla had forgotten her leather jacket earlier and had persuasively asked me to retrieve it. I couldn't say no after she'd promised me something in return. Knowing Karla it would be something we'd both enjoy.

How anyone could still be enclosed within the school's doors was beyond me. But as I walked towards the theater I heard the sound of music resonating from inside in delicate, passionate lulls. It was music weaved especially for a person to be utterly captivated by the melody. It was entrancing and spellbinding as the melody seeped into the marrow of my bones, spreading through my veins.

The sound of the music drew my curiosity closer, my steps softly padding down the hallway, afraid of fracturing this dream – if it was one. My hand never wavered from the doors hinges as I pried them open as quietly as I could to not disturb the flow of the harmony. It opened with a slight creak on its hinges, but it wasn't loud enough to break the connection. The theater was dark and empty with only the single glow of the spotlight illuminating the vast space. Turning the corner, my eyes fell on a girl wearing a royal blue dress seated on a bench, leaning over the old school piano where the sweet, caressing music emitted.

My breath caught in my throat as I realized who the girl was.

I should have known.

If anyone could put her heart and soul into music it was Anya. The piece she was playing moved in a slow inclining motion to only increase in a burst of fervor. I leaned back on the wall, listening intently as I watched her body move to the melody she played. Under the low light she looked like an unearthly being; like an angel sent from above to indulge mankind with her gift. Her slender, delicate fingers danced over the keys in a secret whisper, each note indulging me in a bittersweet nostalgic feeling.

There was a time, long ago where I would sit beside her on the piano for hours on end – listening to the music she played. None of those moments could ever compare to the one right now. It was different in the way that her music wasn't fragmented or broken because of the unfamiliar territory. She knew the ivory keys before her like she knew the contours of her hand.

Suddenly she stopped, her shoulders sagging as she slumped in her seat. Silently, I watched and hoped that she'd continue to play without her knowing I was here. There was something about her music that struck a dead cord inside me, awakening it from its slumber. After a few seconds she began to gather the sheets of music in front of her, carefully tucking them away in a folder, and finally into the safety of her bag.

I stepped out of the shadows toward her and said, "Don't stop."

She startled; turning around and meeting my gaze. Her hand clutched the small pendant that hung from her unblemished neck. "You scared me to death! What are you doing here?"

"I-I," At a sudden loss for words, I folded my arms beneath my chest – generating a semblance of assurance in the gesture. "I forgot something earlier and I was-"

"Karla's jacket is right over there," she pointed to the far side of the stage where I saw a jacket hanging from a hook. "That's what you're here for, right?"

How she could be so perceptive I didn't know. Anya didn't spare a glance at me to look if she had been right. She resumed packing her belongings as the stab of indifference hit me like a bucket of ice water. What the hell was her problem? I gave her the impression of a compliment and she sneered at me. Maybe sneer isn't the right word – haughty would suffice.

"Why did you stop?"

"It's late and I have plans."

"Well, don't make me stop you," I muttered.

Anya shouldered her bag over her head, safely securing it against her hip. Her brown eyes bore into mine, quizzically – trying to read my intentions. Luckily for me, I wasn't even certain why I was still standing here.

"Don't you have plans of your own? Like maybe getting back to your blond bimbo?"

I felt the smirk slid into my face at her flippant manner. "Are you jealous, Vanchester?"

She scoffed, "Maybe in your dreams, Rowely." She took a step to her left, heading towards the exit but I blocked her path. "What do you want now?"

"You've gotten better," I said. Her face twisted into confusion, her brows knitting together. I rolled my eyes, deciding to elaborate. "You've gotten better at playing."

"That's what happens when you practice."

"I see."

She sighed, "Well, if that's all. I have somewhere to be." Anya took a slow hesitant step to the left that I matched, blocking her path once again. "What," she snapped. Her eyes were cold and unyielding, causing a rift to run through my body. "Do you want? If you want to play a cat and mouse game be my guest, but I will not subject myself for your own amusement."

Churning her words in my mind for a moment I wondered what she could possibly mean by them. There was something in her clear brown eyes that was accusatory; she blamed me for something that had happened recently. Searching her eyes, I tried to find what her problem with me was. Throughout the years we had stayed clear of each other's paths, but in light of recent events that had become difficult to do.

For starters, Anya and I had five out of seven classes together. It was virtually impossible to ignore her. We would sit on opposite sides of the classroom, but I would often find myself gazing in her direction wanting to know her every thought. The next moment I would mentally slap myself for thinking such notions. I found my-self also caring about what she thought of me, which is something I haven't allowed myself to consider.

"What did Karla tell you that day in the hall?" The thought was out of my mouth before I could mull it over.

Her head snapped up, meeting my gaze, her shoulders tensing under my inquiry. A flash of recognition crossed her features in an instant, settling to a guarded stance. "Nothing," she said quickly. "Liam, I really have to go. I don't have time for this."

She moved curtly to the right, walking briskly towards the exit and out the doors. I followed, catching up to her small strides in a matter of seconds. I was curious to know what had been exchanged between Karla and Anya that afternoon to make her dislike towards me grow in disdain.

I follow her out of the school doors and into the empty parking lot. My bike was parked near the north side of campus where Anya was heading. Taking a wild guest she was probably going to meet up with her makeshift group of friends to do God knows what.

"Tell me," I demand. "What did she tell you?"

She kept on walking; ignoring me like I was some sort of pest she wanted to be rid of. Finally, she abruptly stopped a few feet from my bike and says, "You forgot her jacket."

My brows furrow in confusion. "What are-"

She nodded to the direction of the school. I turn my head, remembering that the only reason I was here was to grab Karla's stupid jacket. Seeing Anya had made me forget about everything except her. Turning back around I say, "Has anyone ever told you that you're-"

My words stop in my throat as I see Anya's small distant figure down the street, leaving me dumbfounded with more questions than answers.

Chapter 6

"Wrooks wrike the writtle Anya bug has an admirer," Hayden teased with his Scooby-Doo imitation. A sucky imitation, if I may add. "That's so cute," he continued, pinching my cheeks.

I slapped his hand away. "Stop being annoying! You're not five."

"Aww," he ruffled my hair playfully like if I was a puppy. "It's not my fault you're in denial."

"Gemma!" I called. She was in the kitchen refilling our snack bowl and drinks. I prayed that her hearing aid was on so she could hear my holler. "I'm going to beat your boyfriend up if he doesn't stop being an ass!"

"I'm simply stating the facts," he said defiantly. "Should I refresh your memory?"

"I don't really-"

"Shh, Anya," he said interrupting me. His eyes were deadly serious as he held out a finger and began to count out his points. "One: He gave you a ride home when he saw you. He didn't need to do that. But he did it of his own accord. Two: He's been watching you for the past few weeks. Why is he suddenly interested in you?" He asked with raised brows. I shrugged and he smirked – indulging in the moment that he was right. Ugh he was such a jerk! "Three: He was watching you play for-who-knows-how-long except God," he said, his voice rising as he went on.

I rolled my eyes at his theatrics. Hayden was like the big brother I never wished for, but apparently received one Christmas morning. "He was probably there for a solid ten minutes! Then when you stopped he wanted more...Why? Oh!" Hayden exclaimed, remembering to add more to his list of reason. "He was being persistent about the whole Karla fiasco and he forgot her jacket, didn't he? Doesn't this all mean something to you?"

"I don't know," I said burying my head in my hands. "Leave me alone. You're giving me a headache."

"Hayden, leave her alone," Gemma said coming into the den. Her voice was fragmented, her syllables not pronounced correctly as a "normal" person's. She was much more open to talk when it was only the two of us instead of where there were people who would laugh at her expense because she was different. After years of knowing her I understood what she'd said. Even Hayden comprehended Gem's warning by the wounded look on his face.

"But, babe-"

"No buts honey."

A wickedly sly smile spread on my lips. So she had heard everything. Thank God! She'd take my side for sure. "She needs time to come to terms with this "new" Liam," she said using air quotes. "In time she'll be swept of her feet."

"Ugh," my smile was quickly wiped of my face, replaced by a scowl. I grabbed a pillow from the futon and buried my head into its softness. "Not you too!" My words were muffled, but I knew that they had heard because of Hayden's low chuckle.

I felt Gemma sit in between me and Hayden on the old futon that wheezed under her weight. She shook my shoulder mercilessly until I looked up and met her soft pleading eyes. "We're just kidding," she said, tucking a stray curl from my face. "But in all seriousness – there has been a slight change in his behavior. Maybe, he found you alluring since you stood up to him on the first day of school. Guys like that sort of thing, right?" She looked at Hayden and he shrugged, a smile tugging on his lips.

"Well, I don't want anything to do with him. Have you forgotten what Karla said?"

"No, but you shouldn't let that blond crone tell you what to do. Since when have you let someone stop you?"

She was right. But it wasn't as black and white as she believed it to be. Liam and I were all shades of gray mixed in with years of treaded land and unknown terrain. Some days, like today – felt familiar. Liam had always been persistent, and when he wanted to know something he was relentless, like today. It was only my unconventional form of a distraction that I was able to flee from his sight. Then there were days when I hardly knew him at all; he was a mere shadow of his former self. The Liam I knew would never freely bully an innocent kid just for the sake of a "good time". The only time I've known him to throw a punch at someone was Ronnie Jenkins back in the fourth grade! Liam's act of chivalry was justified because Ronnie had been picking on me, making me feel like I was a waste of space.

On the first day of school, I saw and later found out that Harry (the innocent kid) had mistakenly opened Liam's locker as his own. On those grounds alone it wasn't a concrete reason for Liam to go all Hulk on the poor kid. There were no justifications for a tremendous amount of his actions the past few years. That was the guy who I had come to know from afar. I didn't believe that a person could change in a matter of seconds. It took time. If Liam continued to progress into the boy I had known then maybe I could picture Gemma's hopeful image of Liam and I.

"What's next on the list?" I heard Hayden's distant voice, snapping me back from my thoughts. My gaze flicked to where he knelled in front of the rack full of dvd's. "C'mon...don't you have anything other than romantic comedies, babe?" He whined.

I stifled a laugh and grabbed my bag, pulling out a copy of The Evil Dead. "Here," he turned around and hesitantly took the movie from my hands. "Its horror and a supposedly a cult classic – so I hear. Now, will you stop being a girl?"

He rolled his eyes and popped in the movie, curling up on the futon with Gemma. As the movie commenced I found myself sick to my stomach. The movie wasn't even scary. It was gory and perverse with demonic trees and lots and lots of fake blood. Gemma was not having a grand o' time either. Her face was nestled in Hayden's chest as she covered her eyes with her hand. Hayden's eyes were fastened to the t.v. screen never wavering by the vicious display of the demonic characterization.

I didn't know when I stopped watching the movie, and began to lose myself within my thoughts. I reflected upon what both Gem and Hayden had said about me and Liam. Was I really in denial? Could Liam possibly be interested in me? Or was I merely a game like Karla had insinuated?

He was just so...unpredictable. Liam had always been that way – that hadn't changed at all as we grew apart. In a way he was like a piece in a score. There were harmonies and melodies that fitted perfectly within a composition. Then there were single moments within the piece that were unlike the rest of the music. It was passionate and beautiful and exhilarating kind of like how Liam was.

Even though I saw the person he became I never gave up hope that there was some good left inside of him. Sometimes, I would kick myself for having that glimmer of hope residing in me because it left room open for disappointment. With Karla's threat I felt insignificant like an ant scurrying in the dirt, making that small space grow into a gaping hole.

You think he wants to be friends with a pathetic loser whose only friend is deaf? Think again honey. He doesn't want anything to do with you except to get in your pants, and even that I'm not sure. Who'd want to even to touch you? You're disgusting. An abomination to the human race...

"I'll be right back," I said to Gemma and Hayden quietly getting up from my seat.

The memory brought fresh tears to brim in my eyes. I didn't want to cry in front of my two best friends. I needed to be strong, and couldn't show them that I was weak although it was exactly how I felt. Crashing into the bathroom, I closed the door hastily behind me. I caught my reflection in the mirror and saw my red-rimmed eyes as a salt tear cascaded down my cheek. Many followed afterwards like the slow sprinkling of rain falling from the sky, relentless once it began. Karla's words shouldn't have affected me as they did, but what she said was true.

It was what everyone saw in me.

My eyes were rimmed with purple shadows from lack of nutrition and sleep deprivation. I tried to reduce my intake of sleeping pills because I didn't want my body to become immune to them. I wouldn't get any sleep if that happened, and I'd become an insomniac. My skin was abnormally pale, but on rare and fortunate days I had a bit of color to my skin like a creamy soft tan. Even when I looked healthy I wasn't inside. I was sick, fragile like a beautifully crafted glass vase. One wrong move and I would shatter with no hope of putting the pieces back together.

My eyes swept down to my shoulders where I saw the bluish tint of a bruise beginning to form. I sighed in resignation as I sat down on the corner of the tub. There were days when I had my suspicions about Hayden knowing my secret. Hadn't his eyes flashed with recognition when he saw how hard he was shaking my shoulders earlier?

His dad was a doctor and had possibly asked about me. Knowing Dr. Novak I doubted that he would have divulged his son with his patient's personal records and information. No one knew of my predicament except for my parents and Gemma.

I came close to telling one other person the day I found out of what my life had always consisted of but never knew the extent of my "special care." The only reason I told Gemma freshman year was because we kept bumping into each other in the hospital parking lot. She was in the building next to the hospital where she had her monthly hearing check-up. Later, I learned that she was gathering information about possibly receiving a cochlear implant so that one day she could be able to hear again.

It was late February when Gemma and I first talked to each other in the hospital caf. She came right up to me and began to talk about my pins on my bag. She thought they were beautiful and unique (at least that's what I thought she said). Her words were harsh and incoherent, but I was polite and could understand certain things she said.

She was really sweet, and even though I could only understand parts of her words I knew she was talking about my pins because she kept pointing and glancing at them. In turn I unpinned a music pin and handed it to her. She was humble and hesitant in taking it, but I insisted. In the end she took it gingerly from my hand and pinned it to her collar.

That was the day where are friendship began. It was difficult at first talking to Gem because she sometimes didn't catch what I said. She had to rely solely on reading my lips when her hearing aid couldn't pick up certain things. I had to learn to decipher her estranged dialect in the words she spoke. It must have been the fifth or sixth time after I began to talk to Gem that I asked my parents if they could buy me a book about sign language.

My parents were inspired by my willingness and passion that they also embarked on their own journey to learn the strange-new language. After months of practice I finally succeeded in the hand gestures that would give spoken words meaning. Gemma was so amazed and ecstatic that she began to cry. The first words that I ever flawlessly heard her say were, "Thank you. No one has ever done something like this for me. Thank you so much, Anya."

Her words had been cut and difficult to decipher like always, but she had signed while she spoke and I understood every word perfectly. That same day I told her the reason for my frequent doctor appointments. When I finally got the courage to share my secret with her she looked at me with understanding and compassion instead of pity.

"No one is perfect," she had said. "You are strong for it."

I took a deep shuddering breath as I remembered my reply to her. "I don't feel strong."

There were days where I felt weak and worthless like Karla had said. Her words about Liam had cut through the very fiber of my being because of our past. He had been my best friend and the only person in the world who I wanted to tell my secret to that cold and stormy day where everything had dissolved into nothingness.

He had left me all alone for the remainder of that summer. I've waited for days for him to show up at my house, but he never came. I thought of so many reasons for his abrupt cold demeanor towards me. The only logical explanation was that he was tired and fed up with having to defend me. He was sick of being vamp girl's friend. Liam got what he wanted that summer; new skin and friends. When we began our freshman year of high school Liam treated me like a ghost. He never once acknowledged my presence, and it was then that I realized that I had lost him.

A fresh wave of tears flowed down my cheeks as my breath hitched in my throat. I blamed him for two years before I learned about forgiveness, hope, and God. My heart had been a cold and dark place for so long that when I finally let go my resentment towards him I felt light. Like a burden had been lifted from my shoulders.

Grabbing some tissues from the counter I wiped my tears from my face and blew my stuffy nose. I've forgiven Liam for abandoning me when I needed him most for almost two years. But my heart would always remain cautious like a girl treading through the forest, alert in case of a wild tiger ready to strike. I couldn't let someone get that close to me again – fearing that they would desert me as he once had.

Chapter 7

A nya

I reached into my locker, searching for my government and English textbooks that were buried somewhere in the chaos of graded assignments, sheet music, and gym clothes. A desolate flyer escaped the clutches of my cluttered mess, gingerly landing near my feet. I picked up the light blue paper, my eyes scanning its content before crumbling it in my hands and discarding it. The flyer was a reminder from the student council of the upcoming Winter Formal.

It was two months away and already it was the talk of the school. Rumor had it that it would be the most extravagant Winter Formal Velmont High had ever seen. The theme was kept under lock and key until the two weeks leading up to the dance. I heard from Taylor Kingly that the dance was being sponsored by one of the student's father, who was generously donating a hefty sum. My guess was that it was Karla's dad and was giving his little girl the best senior year ever.

"You're breaking up with me?" Speak of the devil.

"You cannot be breaking up with me!" Karla shrieked, her voice resonating along the metal walls.

Everyone stopped what they were doing; turning their attention to where Liam and Karla stood in the middle of the hallway. The atmosphere was eerily still, waiting for the next sound to break through the intensely filled silence. I leaned my hip against the metal locker, tugging my cardigan around my cold body as I perked my ears to listen in on their conversation.

"I am," he said.

"You can't just break up with me," she said again, stomping her foot like a petulant child. She huffed and puffed like the big bad wolf himself. "Is it because of her? Is that why? You're seriously dumping me because of that disgusting piece of-"

I sucked in air, filling the stab of her words. She couldn't be talking about me, could she?

"Save your breath," he said. "It has nothing to do with anyone. We were never anything to begin with."

"But we were beginning...I thought that you-"

He held up his hand, silencing Karla's plea on her lips. "Stop groveling, you look pathetic."

His words were sharp like a knife struck right through her heart. Her bottom lip began to quiver, the tears that brimmed in her eyes threatening to spill. It was no secret that I disliked Karla, but no one deserved to be publicly humiliated. My heart swelled with pity as I saw the walls she'd built slowly cave in, while Liam stood stoic like a Greek statue, cold and distant.

What was wrong with him? Why was he acting like this? Didn't he have a heart?

"No, you're pathetic," she spat. My jumbled thoughts seized as I turned my attention back to them. "You think that sleeping with girls will make you numb. Well, you go it, Liam! You are a heartless bastard who will never be fully satisfied. Go find some other girl who will put it up with your daddy issues."

Liam's shoulders tensed, her words shattering the disinterested demeanor he'd so carefully constructed. There was a shift in his behavior like a pot of boiling water bubbling over the rim when it was left on the stove for too long. His gaze was no longer careless but guarded. They held each other's intensely fused stares, neither folding.

Karla's eyes burned a deeply rich evergreen that possessed the power to kill anyone that stood in her path by just a blink of her perfectly primed eyelashes.

Amber, one of Karla's cronies, leaned into her leader – whispering something that caused Karla to slightly nod. She gave Liam one last deathly glare before turning on her heel – sauntering off towards the restroom with Amber and Whitney in tow; their heels clicking loudly on the linoleum floor.

The bell's shrill ringing startled everyone out of their daze, signaling the start of first period. Locker doors were shut hastily as everyone began the familiar path to class. I quickly scavenged my books from beneath a pile of old newspapers clippings and shut my locker, running past Liam.

Liam.

I skidded to a stop, turning back to look at him. He hadn't moved an inch since the breakup occurred. He looked like he was in a daze, lost in his own thoughts. My steps were deafening in the emptiness of the hall, and proved to be the only sound that snapped him out of his reverie.

"You okay?" I asked as he blinked his slate blue eyes into focus.

His brow furrowed in confusion that lasted for only a flicker of a second, his infamous crooked smile replacing his bewilderment.

"Peachy," he said. "I didn't know you cared after you stood me up."

"I don't," I lied. "And I did not stand you up. We weren't on a date or anything." The nerve of him! Here I was trying to be a good person, and he turns the tables around to something of insignificance. What did he even mean about 'standing him up'?

"Well," he stalked forward, closing the gap between us. It was like he was a prowling lion and I was a poor antelope, waiting for his teeth to tear into my flesh. I stepped back, shivering at the thought.

He wouldn't really do that, would he? I shook the thought away; it was preposterous.

"How about dinner Friday," he offered. "We could catch up over some Mexican tamales down at-"

"Are you insane?" I gaped. Did he hit his head somewhere between the last ten minutes? "You just broke up with Karla, and you're asking me out?" I rolled my eyes, turning on my heels at his audacity.

"Anya, wait!"

The shrill bell rang again, letting me know that I was late. I cursed myself for letting myself care about him. I should have known that he would only treat me as a joke.

A hand curled around my elbow, making me stop. He turned me to face him, his eyes laced with seriousness. "There wasn't anything between Karla and I. Ever."

I pulled my arm from his grasp and stepped back. "That's good to know, Liam. Thanks for that enlightening piece of information."

He let out a long breath, running his fingers through his blond locks in exasperation. "Forget it," he finally said. "Forget I said anything."

My lips parted in astonishment at the sudden shift in his mood. His eyes no longer held any trace of amusement, but instead masked...disappointment? He turned sharply on his heels, his long strides taking him down the hall in a matter of seconds. His name was stuck in my throat as I watched him push the double doors with more force than necessary, disappearing into the cool autumn day.

Liam

I killed the engine, my anger dissolving once I had time to clear my head. I needed a breather – riding was the only thing that could make me forget about the mess of thoughts that were too entwined to understand. I would worry about it later.

I looked up at the old weathered sign of the music shop, feeling nostalgic as memories surfaced in my mind like a river flowing downstream. I saw Mr. Edison's clear silhouette behind the shop window. He was sitting on a stool, hunched over as he peered at something in front of him.

Taking a deep breath, I walked into the shop –the small bell jingling its delicate cheerful tune as I entered, alerting Mr. Edison of my arrival. He looked up from the mass of sheet music that covered the glass counter. His glasses sat on the bridge of his nose, almost sliding off as he did a double take.

"Liam! What in heaven's name are you doing here, boy?" He eyed me suspiciously, coming around the desk to take a good look at me.

He stopped short, faking a hard cold stare that turned in warm smile. He grasped my shoulders and enveloped me in a one arm hug. "Haven't seen you in ages, kid! You've grown five inches and have left me to bite the dust."

I chuckled. "It's good to see you old man."

He stepped back, tilting his head in thought. "Golly, I haven't heard that in...years. You have to come by more often."

"Will do."

I moved towards the black polished piano, remembering long summer afternoons spent indoors drinking lemonade, while I listened to Anya's piano lessons. The pearly white keys remained pristine and unmarred by age underlining the wooden finish. My eyes lingered to a score that vaguely looked like it was written in Anya's hand. It was titled Lucia Mia.

It wasn't Spanish, but looked like it was Italian. If I wasn't mistaken I believe it translated to "my light".

"So, what can I do for you kid?" Mr. Edison asked. I turned to see the confusion flicker in his old gray eyes as realization flashed across his face. "Wait...Aren't you supposed to be in school?"

I waved away his worry. "School can wait. I was wondering if you could do me a favor."

His eyebrows rose in curiosity, "What do you have in mind?"

Chapter 8

I leaned back on the metal wall and watched the numbers of the elevator slowly crawl to their appointed destination. There was a lady with a baby hanging on her hip who looked peeved at the man standing next to her. My guess was that he was her husband and probably forgot to bring the diaper bag. It would also explain the foul smell of baby poop that swirled around the small metal contraption.

The elevator came to a steady stop, the doors clattering open in a loud ear splitting shriek. Maintenance really needed to fix that set of metal doors before it became a hazard. I stepped out into the corridor, letting out a breath that I was not aware I was holding. I walked down the hall of the hospital's children's ward, smelling the strong pungent smell of rubbing alcohol and antiseptics.

Theater practice had been canceled for today by Dr. Devino. There was a rain check with the dentist that had been long overdue and something about a pie waiting afterward – at least that's what he said. Gemma and I just exchanged a glance when he told us 3rd period. Devino then proceeded in doing a pantomime, which made us rush out of the room in a fit of giggles.

I turned the corner and stopped dead in my tracks, my mouth gaping open. The memory of Dr. Devino faded along with the smile on my face. He was leaning over the counter, his elbows propped on the receptionist desk. There was a smile on the young woman's face as she twisted a lock of her hair around her finger thrice. High pitched giggles reached my ears as she laughed at a cheesy pick up line he uttered, enjoying the amount of attention he was giving to her. Liam in turn wore a charming smile that was familiar when he flirted.

What on earth was he doing here?

"Anya!" I turned around to see Dr. Wong's warm smile, rushing to greet me. She was one of the doctors at the pediatric ward who managed special cases such as mine along with Dr. Novak.

I glanced towards Liam and saw that his eyes were trained on me, capturing his full attention. Oh how I wished the floor would crumble beneath my feet and send me to my perilous doom. God, why couldn't I escape him? As if I didn't get enough of him at school. What could he possibly want to land him here of all places?

"How are you dear?" She put an arm around me, leading me towards the receptionist desk where Liam commenced his flirtation with his new prey.

"I'm good. How are Maddie and Jon?"

She smiled. "They are doing well. They both have been asking about you – wondering when you'll go and visit them...which reminds me," we finally come to a halt in front of the desk where Liam straightens up and flashes one of his signature dazzling crooked smiles. "We have a new volunteer today. I thought you could get him acquainted with the other patients and show him around since you are our star volunteer."

Dr. Wong winked and flashed an appraising smile that surprisingly made me sulk. Any other day I would be thrilled to have a new volunteer, but it was Liam. Did I need to say more? Looking over her shoulder I saw the amusement shining in his eyes at my discomfort. I kept my cool even though I wanted to demand why he was here on my turf. With a tense smile on my face I said, "Sure, I'd be happy to."

His dazzling smile turned into a grin that made the receptionist swoon. Pitiful.

"Excellent," Dr. Wong said not noticing my odd behavior. "I will leave you two then." She turned on her heels, heading down the corridor towards the lab. "Have fun," she called back.

Liam chuckled, his eyes shining a bright baby blue. "Oh we most definitely will."

We spend half an hour on dreaded paperwork in the small cramped file room. Liam listened intently as filled him on what we did, while having an annoying smirk on his face that was surprisingly charming. Ugh. No...don't think like that Anya. It's just a game; a stupid and immature game he's playing.

"So what's next boss?"

I gave him a pointed look, folding my arms. "You could murder someone with that look."

"Yeah, like you," I muttered.

He chuckled. "You're cute when you get angry."

I rolled my eyes. He was really getting on my last nerves. I don't know what it was with Liam that caused me to be so...violent. He just irked me to the bone, but at the same time made my curiosity pique. What was he doing here? Was this all a game like Karla had said? What were his intentions? Why was he becoming a constant in my life?

But I didn't ask any of those questions – how could I?

I sighed.

At least...not yet. You can't ask yet, but maybe you can ask eventually.

"Finally," Liam says. "I got you to smile."

I scoffed. Was that an attempt at flirting with me? "I wasn't smiling at what you said. Egotistical much?" I snatched the papers from his hand and turned my back to him, not wanting him to see the traitorous blush staining my cheeks. With trembling hands I flipped through the papers; everything was properly done down to the letter.

"We're good here," I say tucking away his information in the volunteer folder to keep on file. I open the door to the small office, filling the room with the cacophony of voices from the corridor. "Follow me."

We walk down the corridor until we come to the closed door leading to the children's playroom. From the clear glass windows I see little Maddie and Jon in a corner playing with a puzzle. A smile formed on my lips as they saw me and waved, excitement lighting up in their eyes.

"Friends of yours?"

I nodded. "You sure you're ready for this? If you aren't its perfectly understandable."

An easy going smile slid unto his lips. "I'm always ready," he said and winked.

God, please help me.

I turned the knob to the room and was attacked by Maddie and Jon, squealing with joy. "Anya, we missed you! – Where have you been? – Who is this? Is he your boyfriend? – Oooh can you read to us too?"

"One at a time guys," I turned around and see Liam genuinely smiling. Maybe this wouldn't be a total disaster. I take Maddie and Jon's hand and lead them to a table where I pick up The Real Story Of The Big Bad Wolf.

Liam moved to the other side of the room and began to play with Gracie. I hear his voice change as he orchestrated the puppets, creating a scene with a damsel in distress and a dashing knight. If he had three hands he would probably use it for a horse.

"Is he your boyfriend?" Maddie asked again, her green eyes sparkling in the light. Her freckled cheeks were slightly hollow due to the intense treatment for her osteoporoses. I looked over at Jon and saw the expectancy in his crystal blue eyes. He was a year younger than Maddie and was frail from the Leukemia treatments. Even though they were sick it didn't stop them from living their life, just like me. Being sick wasn't a death sentence but an obstacle we needed to conquer.

We were all fighters.

"So is he?" Jon asked.

I smiled, ruffling Maddie's hair. Scrunching up my nose in distaste I said, "No way."

She giggled while Jon wore a serious expression too old for his six year old self. "You're lying. You like him and he likes you."

I put a finger to my lips and signaled them to be quiet. They did as I said and leaned forward to hear what I had to say, their eyes gleaming with interest. "Shh...it'll be our little secret."

Their eyes widened in excitement and they nodded their heads like bobble heads. "Okay, we pinky swear!" they said simultaneously.

I reached out my pinky finger and we all interlace our pinkies as best we could. "I trust you guys – you have to guard this secret with your lives." They nodded, sharing a conspirator smile with one another. "Now, do you guys want me to read the real story of the big bad wolf?"

"Yes! Yes! Yes!"

My audience at first only consisted of my two little munchkins, but as I began to read it grew to the entire room's children sitting around me, listening intently to my storytelling. At one point while I read I saw Liam standing by the door, his arms crossed as he listened with a wishful expression on his face. I wondered what was on his mind that caused him to be thoughtful and oddly pleasant to behold. The image of a Greek statue once again entered my mind as I imagined him sitting on a platform while Myron or Phidias began to chisel Liam's image into a marble sculpture.

Two nurses entered the room a few minutes before I finished the story to a round of applause. They were there to usher the children back to their beds for dinner. After a few minutes of coaxing and whining, the children one by one began to shuffle out of the room. Peering up at the clock I read that it was 6:54.

"Bye Anya! Promise to come back soon?"

I kneeled down and hugged both Jon and Maddie in turn. "I promise. I have to come Saturday so I'll stop by after...."

They nodded, knowing what I could not say. Their eyes flitted to Liam and I slowly nodded, telling them that he did not know in that simple gesture. "Be good and eat all your vegetables." They wrinkled their noses and smiled.

"Okay, little ones. Time to go," the nurse said, ushering them out of the room.

I waved to them one last time until they disappeared down the corridor with the rest of the children. Since I was already on my knees I began to pick up all the scattered puzzles and put them in their rightful place. Liam also helped me tidy up the room until everything was picked up and back on the shelves in order. There were no words exchanged between us through the twenty minute it took us to leave the room spotless.

The silence was comfortable and familiar. It wasn't filled with meaningless banter that seemed to have become a familiarity on its own. It was just the two of us again like when we were kids. Every now and then I glanced at him and saw his strong hands curled around the small toys like a giant roaming the farmlands, carefully trying to handle everything with gentleness. It was nostalgic seeing Liam today like his old self, carefree and lovable – like that part of him was never truly gone, but dormant. He just needed to be reminded of who he was and not what he had become.

"Ready to go?" he asked.

"Mhm...I have to call my dad to come get me. I'll see you around."

I turned around and inspected the bookshelf to make sure that every book was put back into its place. There was a reason for turning my back to him. I didn't want him to see the longing in my eyes as he left. It was a feeling that I couldn't deny no matter how many times I told myself that it was wrong. But I saw hope in Liam – something that I hadn't seen all these years, and it was surfacing like a newly found piece of treasure from the sea.

"I'll take you home. It's on the way."

"No, it's okay. I can manage."

The sound of his footsteps reached my ears and I turned around to see him walking over to me, his eyes intense as he held my gaze. "So can I."

"It's not you. I appreciate the offer, but your bike scares me." I laughed uneasily, trying to lighten the mood. "Besides, it didn't turn out so well the first time."

He chuckled, the corners of his mouth quirking up in a dazzling crooked smile. "Second times a charm. Trust me." He reached out his hand, waiting for my answer.

My eyes lingered to his outstretched palm, warm and inviting. There were so many things wrong with this moment, but they became minimal in the one good thing that I saw in his eyes.

Hope.

It's the only reason I took his hand.

Chapter 9

The next few days were a daze.

My head was constantly spinning like a dancing table top, while my stomach was having an acrobatic show that I was not aware of until the very last minute. I felt like a lion tamer in the middle of the stage as everyone's cool gaze watched my every move; waiting for me to have my flesh mauled by the lion's paws.

There was only one reason – or should I say person – that had gotten me into this predicament: Liam.

The new rumor that surfaced the day he dumped Karla was that he did for me. Me. Out of all the girls at Velmont High he did it for me? Yeah, right. That was just a vicious rumor started by none other than Karla, who was jealous that Liam had suddenly taken a keen interest in me. Oh and it wasn't only her doing – it was also his. Liam didn't even take the time to correct the rumors; instead he fueled them by proving everyone's thoughts and deliberately stirring the gossip mill.

The night he drove me home I thought that he was changing, but I had been extremely wrong. He was just doing this because it was a game. It was always a game to him.

It was finally Friday and I couldn't wait to go have my usual movie night with Hayden and Gemma. It was my turn to pick this week's movies and I had decided on thrillers/horror films. It definitely would not be a repeat of last week with those demonic trees and perverse demons. I picked Dear Mr. Gacy and A Haunting In Connecticut. Both were based on a true story, which automatically made a movie ten times scarier – it was a proven fact.

I was positive that Hayden would enjoy my picks and thank me for not having another chick flick night. Poor guy – he had to have more guy friends. He couldn't complain though, seeing as AHIC is more horror than thriller and Gemma would mostly likely curl up against him.

He could thank me later.

It was days like these that I wished I had someone who'd love me for me just like Hayden loved Gemma.

I sighed as I dislodged two of my textbooks from a piece of old bubble gum that glued them together. Okay, that was definitely not my doing. That was beyond disgusting. I bet the gum was there since last year!

"Hey, precious."

I froze, my shoulders tensing at the sound of his voice. After momentarily being taken aback I continued to organize my locker as if his presence hadn't fazed me. I didn't turn to look at him when I said, "Who are you, Gollum? You seriously need to brush up on your pick up lines – something that doesn't sound creepy."

He chuckled and said, "It's Smeagol. C'mon Anya, don't tell me I need to brush you up on the Lord Of The Rings."

I rolled my eyes and continued to ignore him until I couldn't take the feeling of his eyes watching me any longer. I turned to face him with the intention of telling him to go away. But when I met his cool gaze it made my heart leap inside of my chest. No, stop it Anya. Get a grip. You've forgiven him, but that doesn't mean you have to fall for him like every other pathetic girl.

Liam leaned his body against the lockers, crossing his arms over his chest. His voice was casual when he asked, "What are you doing this weekend?"

Well, this was new. He was actually taking the time to ask me instead of assuming I'd go out with him. I shut my locker and said in a cool voice, "Just the usual weekend lounging around with Mr. Cuddles and knitting sweaters."

A warm smile curved his lips as amusement danced in his eyes. It made him appear...approachable and carefree. "Has anyone ever told you that you're a smartass?"

My eyes looked skywards as I thought for a moment. "Nope," I said popping the P. "You are the first. I'll definitely have to remember that."

Shouldering my bag I began to walk towards the theater. I didn't expect for Liam to follow, but he was right on my heels – a smirk displayed on his curved lips. "Well, I'd hate to take you away from your stimulating weekend, but how about I take you down to the pier instead."

My face twisted into confusion as his words settled on the floor of my mind. I sighed in resignation and turned to him. "What do you want Liam?" It was tiring trying to get rid of him. He was so persistent and determined when he was passionate about something. It was just the way he was ever since he was a kid.

My stomach began to twist into familiar knots as my mind tried to find reason in his actions. If he was hell bent on going out with me did that mean he really wanted to? Or was it still part of a game that he needed to win or else face social suicide?

"So what do you say?"

I looked up to see a glimmer of hope and anticipation twined in his eyes. I must have missed his answer to my previous question and now he was waiting for my answer on his invitation. He didn't appear malicious or cruel, making me second guess my recent judgment of him in the past few days.

"Anya?"

My voice was came out in a whisper when I said, "You'll have to ask my father."

There was no way Dad would allow me to go out with him. He already thought that Liam was a bad influence, and pried over dinner about the rumors at school. Dad wasn't oblivious and knew what everyone said about me. It was one of the reasons that he was so protective, while Mom gave Liam the benefit of the doubt.

"I see," he said pensively tapping his forefinger against his lips.

"Anya!" I turned my head at the sound of my name and saw Janie Graymore rushing up the hall. "Where have you been? Practice has begun and Devino needs you on the piano," she said in a huff.

Janie's eyes flickered to Liam and she suddenly straightened her slack form as a flirty smile began to curve her lips. "Hey, Liam. H-how ar-are you?"

Oh, for the love of all that is good in this world! Did every girl that came in contact with him turn to mush?

"Janie," I said taking her arm and dragging her away from Liam before she made a fool of herself. "I'll see you later," I called to Liam over my shoulder as the distance between us grew.

He says something underneath his breath at the same time Janie exclaimed, "Bye Liam! See you Monday!"

As we make our way down to the theater Janie sighed dreamily and said, "He's so mysterious. What I would give for him to talk to me."

"Trust me. You wouldn't. He's so...aggravating."

"I like passionate as a better term for him."

I rolled my eyes. "You are just blinded by his good looks. Also, aggravating and passionate are two completely different things!"

She shook her head with a teasing smile on her plumped lips. "Nope. If he frustrates you then there is pent up fiery-"

"Oh, please...stop," I muttered.

Jane nudged my arm and laughed. "Oh girl. You have no idea what every other girl would give for just one look from him and you get it 24/7."

"I do not," I protested even though I knew her words were true.

She sucked in a whoosh of air and relented. "Fine. But he's still a nicely piece of..."

By the time I got home I was exhausted and alone in my vacant house. Watching movies was more tiring than I had anticipated and I had fallen asleep through most of AHIC. The sound of Gemma's surprised squeal woke me from my slumber, and I only saw the last twenty minutes of the film. A wave of vertigo overwhelmed my senses, making me stumble in the darkness.

No, no...not now, please...

I gripped the door fame to the kitchen, willing the dizziness to fade. I took deep calming breaths until my vision cleared and I was no longer in a haze. When I finally found the light switch I turned on the lights in the kitchen and noticed a bright pink sticky note on the fridge saying:

Went out to Coco's.

We'll be back around midnight.

There's frozen pizza and mashed potatoes in the fridge.

Love you bug!

-Mom & Dad

P.S. There's a letter for you :)

I rushed over to the mail holder, almost tripping in the process as I locked sight with a huge manila envelope with my name printed in blocked letters on a label. On the left hand corner Juilliard was printed in big bold letters with the mailing address stamped beneath. My heart beat increased in my chest as I stared dumbfounded at the package. The envelope was marked as First Class Mail from New York and was classified as priority mail from the postal service.

What was this? It couldn't have been an acceptance letter – it was too soon and I wasn't planning to apply. Juilliard was my dream since I was a little girl; a dream that I had come to accept I couldn't have.

It'd be a miracle if she even graduated. We can prevent the sickness as we have all her life, but these next years are crucial. She doesn't have much time.

The memory of Dr. Novak's words surfaced in my mind, crisp and fresh like it was just yesterday. It had made me so angry that Dr. Novak was talking about my life like I wasn't even in the room hearing his diagnostic. I knew I was sick and fragile unlike the other kids, but I hadn't known how sick I really was until that summer day. I was angry that my parents had kept this from me all my life, but as the years went by I realized why they kept this vital piece of information from me. They wanted me to live a strong and healthy life for as long as I could without having to worry about dying.

After Dr. Novak ran a few more blood test I was free to go. I stormed out of his office and headed down to the parking lot in a fury of anger. Each step I took diffused my resentment towards Dr. Novak and my parents. Anger was soon replaced by the heart wrenching reality that I was given a countdown.

On the car ride home that day I was quiet, lost in my own thoughts as I stared out the window. My parents were also quiet that it soon became awkward. By that point all I wanted to do was get out of the car and run to Liam, telling him everything that had happened that day.

He would have told me that everything would be okay. He would have said that I would prove the doctors wrong; that I would be a miracle.

I bit the inside of my cheek to stop the tears that brimmed in my eyes. With trembling fingers I began to break the seal as I heard my heart thud loudly in my ears. I was curious and nervous to read the contents the envelope contained.

When I finally got the nerve to begin to read I was rendered speechless.

Dear Miss Anastasia Vanchester,

We are pleased to inform that you have captured the attention at our esteemed institution with your extraordinary and artistic talent. Throughout the years we have kept a watchful eye on your accomplishments and look forward to seeing your application on our desks by 2011, December 15th. You were one of ten artists out of the entire country chosen for this introductory notice by scouts that specialize in finding astonishing and potential young students with the gift and passion in music. This is a great honor that you should be extremely proud of as it marks the beginning of wonderful and aspiring journey to others who pursue the dream of becoming a Juilliard student.

I scanned the rest of the letter as it listed a variety amount of scholarships and information that I could contact if I had any further questions. I must have read the letter twenty times before the realization of it all finally sank in. My feet made their way to the couch as I curled my legs beneath, clutching the letter in my hands.

This was surreal and something that I never imagined beyond my wildest dreams. It was Juilliard. Juilliard! They were amazed by my incredible gift that they had personally written me a letter to fill out an application to their school. I was one of ten students out of the entire country to stand out in their eyes. Ten! How could this have happened? It was a blessing – a possible sign that God wanted me to do this; that there was a certainty that I would live beyond eighteen.

Tears spilled down my cheeks in a never ending wave of gratitude. My heart swelled at this new found hope given to me as I clutched the letter to my chest as if my life depended on it. It was like a life raft that I clung to, fearing if I let go I'd be lost in the ocean's dark abyss.

When my parents came home a few hours later they found me on the couch with swollen red rimmed eyes, a red stuffy nose, and the wrinkled letter in my hands that contained the possibility of my dreams coming true.

Chapter 10

The sun's brilliant warm rays seeped through the curtains as I opened my sleep crusted eyes. Pulling the coverlet over my head to block the gleaming sunlight I peek over my nightstand and read 8:37 in bright purple neon numbers. I groaned into my pillows and after a long minute unwilling emerged from my warm cocoon.

I stretched feeling the muscles in my body stronger – well stronger than they normally were. I breathed in the distant smell of batter in the air as I slipped on my favorite pair of pink fluffy pig socks. As I bounded down the stairs there was a bounce to my step. For once in weeks I felt great and not at all weak or sick. In the entrance hall I glanced at my reflection and saw that there was a little color to my cheeks.

I was fortunate to have a blood transfusion every month. It was expensive, but my parents did everything that they could to keep me stable and alive. I would feel great and lively for a few days after the blood transfusion until my body began to regress once more, and I became pale and weak.

Stop being negative, a voice coaxed inside my head. Enjoy the day while you have it. Go frolic in the sun.

I shook my head and smiled. Like I would really go out and spend the day in the sun. I would do what I always did on Sunday and that was practice my piano and lounge around with Mr. Cuddles with a book. What I had told Liam wasn't so far-fetched from the truth.

The smell of chocolate chip cookies assailed my nostrils as I walked into the kitchen to find Mom baking. There was a smidge of flour on her cheek, while strands of hair escaped her messy ponytail. When she saw me enter her brown eyes lit up with joy. "Want to help, sweetie?"

I nodded and ran to grab an extra apron of the hook and draped it over my neck. It was Dad's white apron that said Kiss The Cook in large blocked red letters. Mom had gotten it for his birthday last year. I was tying the apron around my waist when the sound of doorbell rang.

"Anya!" Dad called from the den. "Will you get that?"

"Yeah, Dad!" I called back. I turned to Mom and asked, "Are you having company over?"

"Not right now. It's too early."

My eyebrows furrowed as I wondered who could be at the door. The door bell rang again, breaking through my thoughts and I dashed out of the kitchen to answer it quickly. I was expecting one of Mom's friends from the restaurant or Ms. Berkert. She was always paying us a visit on Sunday morning's and had a cup of tea with Mom.

But my guesses were wrong when I opened the door to find an uncanny visitor.

My eyes widened in shock and I shut the door in his face. My heart was beating erratically in my chest as I realized what he was doing.

You'll have to ask my father.

I see.

Shoot!

He was here because of me! He was here to ask my Dad for permission! No, no, no, no. This could not be happening. It was absurd to think that he was here because of me. He probably just wanted to get a cup of sugar for his dad because....he was also making chocolate chip pancakes. Yes, that was it!

Who was I kidding? That was the epitome of pathetic excuses every created on earth. Why would he want sugar from us when he could ask Mrs. Davis, his neighbor for some instead of walking down the street to my house? Yeah, that made sense.

There was a light knock on the door that jolted me from my thoughts. Taking a deep breath, I slowly opened the door to find Liam grinning.

"Is that how you greet all your guests?"

I felt the heat rise to my cheeks as I hid my face behind my hair. "What are you doing here?"

"I think you know which is why you shut the door in my face. That wasn't very polite. It kind of hurt my feelings."

I scoffed. "As if you have any. Seriously, what are you doing here? If my Dad finds you out here he's going to have your head on a platter."

His smile widened making his eyes shine a luminous blue gray. "As intimidating as that sounds I am not afraid of a challenge."

"So I'm a game to you?"

His smile dropped and his eyes were intensely serious as he said, "No. Is that what you think?"

"I-"

"Anya? Who's at the door?"

Shoot. Liam was definitely dead now.

Dad appeared behind me and cracked the door open to reveal Liam's lone figure on the porch. I saw Dad's jaw clench and the muscles on his hand and back stiffen in utter shock. If I could I would run upstairs and hide but I couldn't leave Liam alone to fend for himself. That would be like leaving a poor little defenseless bunny rabbit with a wild coyote. Except Liam wasn't a defenseless bunny rabbit. He was more like the roadrunner to Will. E. Coyote.

"Good Morning, Sir."

"Liam."

Liam cleared his voice and asked, "May I come in?"

I stepped back and leaned my frame against the opposite wall and watched as my father's eyes calculated Liam until he opened the door and gestured for him to come in. I saw Liam walk into the living room with Dad on his heels. There was no time to improvise and I ran into the kitchen and told Mom what was going on. Her eyes widened as she quickly washed her hands in the sink and joined me in the living room with Dad and Liam.

Dad had already taken his shot gun out and was "cleaning" it. Oh, goodness. Kill me now.

"Why should I allow you to take her out?"

"Phillip!" my mother chastised. She turned to Liam and said, "It's nice to you Liam. How have you been?"

Liam flashed one of his signature dazzling smiles. "Thank you, Mrs. Vanchester. I've been good."

"That's good. Would you like to stay for breakfast?" Dad glared at Mom, muttering something underneath his breath that she ignored.

Liam flickered his eyes to me and smiled. "I was actually wondering if I could take Anya out today. If that is okay with both of you."

"Oh," Mom perused her lips trying to hide the grin on her face. "I think it'll be good for her to go out."

"Mom," I said through clenched teeth.

She ignored me and turned to Dad. "Don't you agree Phillip?"

He muttered something that sounded like, "No, not at all," but said loud and clear, "Yes, I suppose. But I don't necessarily believe that going out-"

"Phillip! Kitchen. Now."

Dad gave Mom a loaded glance before getting up from the couch and walking into the kitchen. I watched as the kitchen door swung close and they disappeared, leaving me alone with Liam. I stared at my feet until I got the nerve to go and sit across from him on the couch.

"Your dad hates my guts."

"Yeah, he does. Can you blame him?" I asked.

He sank back into the plush velvet cushions, his hand reaching into his breast pocket of his leather jacket. "No. But people can change for the worst and redeem themselves."

He sighed and looked down at the floor, a crooked smile forming on his lips. "I never took you for a fluffy pink pig socks kind of girl."

I blushed and tucked my feet underneath me. "They are very comfortable and warm. I never took you for a smoking kind of guy."

He chuckled. "So you think I'm smoking, huh?"

"No! That's not what I-"

The door to the kitchen opened and I saw my parents shuffle back into the living room; Mom beaming while Dad sulked. I guess he had lost the battle – that was not a surprise. The moment that she had called him into the kitchen was when he lost his ground.

"So," Mom began. "Liam, you have our permission to take Anya out.

"But," Dad interjected, "have her back at nine and not a minute late. Got it?"

Liam stood up from the couch and smiled. "Yes, sir. Will do." He turned to me and asked, "Have breakfast with me?"

I stood up from my perch and looked over to Mom slightly nod and Dad's hard gaze on me. He wanted me to say no and reject his offer. That's what I should have done. I should have stopped Liam's pursuit then and there, but I couldn't because of what he had said earlier.

People can change for the worst and redeem themselves.

I folded my arms over my chest and looked into his beautiful slate-blue eyes, trying to read him like I once was able to those many years ago. There was nothing that I could see and I wished that I was able to know his every thought that flashed in his eyes like when we were kids. But we were kids anymore and as time passed we both changed.

Sighing I uncrossed my arms and said, "Sure. I'll be ready in ten minutes."

Having breakfast with Liam was like a cosmic even that only happened once in a blue moon.

We barely engaged in conversation and I mostly spent my time staring out the window at the beautiful scenery all around me.

Fairhope was simple yet an exquisite little town located on the coast of Alabama. There were only a few tourists out today as they walked the streets with cameras in their hand and their Roll Tide tee and houndstooth caps. A little boy who was wearing a bear harness walked hand in hand with his mother as she stopped in front of an ice cream vendor. It was just another ordinary day filled with daily routine. Well, maybe it was for everybody else, but definitely not for me.

After we finished breakfast Liam paid the bill and we headed out towards the pier. I noted that it was barely eleven from The Clock on the corner of Fairhope Avenue and Section Street. I dreaded the next few hours with him. Who knows when he'd even take me home! It would be just my luck if he took me home exactly at the time my parents told him too. That would be pure agonizing torture.

"You don't have to do this," I said as we walked downtown. "We can both pretend we went on," I waved my hand around trying to explain what this was. "Whatever this is...we can even split up and meet at The Clock after a few hours. Then you can drop me off home. Sound good?"

He remained striding down the street while only taking a moment to glance in my direction. "You won't get rid of me that easily. Plus," he added grinning wickedly. "I've got a few tricks up my sleeve."

"That can't be good."

We walked for hours saying as little as possible to each other. It seemed like he was taking me around town doing nothing at all. If this was his grand master plan, well, it was a particularly good one. Liam had certainly changed. When we were kids he always kept me on my toes and was always very secretive and spontaneous when planning something. He might have been the town's bad boy, but he had lost all sense of creativity.

What he hadn't lost was his gull.

The thought of Liam actually going to my house and asking my father for permission to take me out never crossed my mind. He was calm, cool, and collected while Dad probably set him under a microscope to examine. I only heard what Mom heard when we came into the room, but it all stopped there because Mom was obviously on Liam's side. She always believed that he'd come around after he left me. She called it Being-A-Teenage-Boy. I called it Being-An-Ass-And-Trading-Your-Best-Friend-For-Popularity.

I was such a hypocrite. I had decided to forgive Liam entirely, but here I was judging him when I shouldn't have. The past needed to stay in the past and we both needed to make a fresh start and move forward. It was all we could do, right?

We must have walked for hours until we came to the pier and sat on the edge of the wooden walkway. There weren't many people around us with the cool breeze in the air it was too cold to take a swim in the freezing water. Even with my light green cardigan and jeans it was chilly and the sun was beginning to be covered by light gray clouds.

I was shivering when Liam draped his leather jacket over my shoulders.

"Thanks," I said. "Won't you be cold?"

He shook his head. "I'm fine."

We sat in comfortable silence for a long while and soon the sun began to set over Mobile Bay. Time felt like it was frozen when I was with him and I didn't realize how much time had truly gone by until the world's beauty brought me back to earth. The sun touched the ocean setting it ablaze in a wondrous kaleidoscope of soft purples and pinks. It was always a beautiful blessing to see a sunset in Fairhope.

My breath caught in my throat as I stared in awe at the massive amount of deep dark ocean water. The breeze was a sweet caress upon my skin as I closed my eyes and took a moment to appreciate the beauty of this moment. Closing my eyes made me connect with all the sounds around me that I was oblivious too when my eyes were opened. I heard the sound of the waves slowly crashing on the shore. There was the distant sound of a song bird chirping merrily as it flew over head. I felt the last few rays of sunlight on my skin for only a couple of seconds before the sun was gone, and darkness consumed the sky.

I slowly opened my eyes to see Liam watching me closely, his eyes soft and dark without any light to shine in them.

"What?"

"Nothing...you just looked...peaceful."

I smiled feeling the sincerity of his words. "I was. Thank you for bringing me here. I haven't been here in a while and it was nice."

He leaned back on his hands and stared out at the water. "I haven't been here since..." His words trailed off as he lost himself in his own thoughts. I leaned back on my hands and kicked my feet back and forth over the edge, waiting for him to break the silence. There was something about Liam that intrigued me. Like the fact that he was an entirely different person when he was with me. Sure, he was infuriating and cocky, but he had his moments – moments like these that made me forget about how irritating he could be.

"Want to get some ice cream? I think Billy's is still open." He stood up and offered me his hand. I took it and he pulled me up in one swift motion, seeing his muscles flex by the effort. I quickly turned my head before he saw the blood pool to my cheeks. God, what was wrong with me?

Billy's was only ten minutes away from the pier and we walked under the florescent street lamps. We were almost to the shop when we rounded a corner and bumped into Karla and Collin, Liam's best friend. Liam's back tensed as he stepped in front of me to block my view of them.

"Where the hell have ya been man?" He asked. His words were a little slurred and by the smell of alcohol on his person there was no doubt in my mind that he had been drinking. Collin clasped a hand around Liam's shoulders and steered him away from. "I've been calling you all day and nothing. There's a party at Karla's tonight, her rents are outta town. You down?"

He glanced back at me and I saw a single command in his slate-blue eyes. Go.

Go? Go where?

Liam flicked his eyes toward the ice cream and immediately understood that he wanted me gone from the vicinity. I take a step towards the shop as I hear Collin offering Liam a joint. Karla's attention immediately turns to me and she stalks forward to meet me.

"You know," she said reaching out to finger a lock of my hair. I cringed and stepped back, feeling trapped against the glass window of Mrs. Davis' flower shop. "Liam isn't as lost a soul as you think he is. He knows what he's doing. He pretends to like you and make you feel special, taking you out to the pier or to dinner. Then beds you and breaks up with you in a school hallway." Her last words were laced with vile as an image of a cobra ready to strike entered my mind.

Were her words true or was she just trying to get under my skin?

I looked up to see Collin and Liam heading back towards us, Collin's voice ringing loud and clear when he said, "She's good with her fingers. I wonder if she's good with her mouth."

My face must have turned scarlet because Collin came around and put his arm around me. He smelled like cigarette smoke and cheap alcohol. "Chill. I'm just having some fun. That's why you like her, cause she deep throats?"

I cringed away from him and wrapped my arms around myself, feeling tainted and disgusted.

"Stop, man. Just stop," Liam said in a low commanding voice. "Go home."

Collin laughed cynically. "I'm just having some fun. Maybe we can both get a hit on that. You know how I like the innocent ones," he winked at me and I shivered.

I needed to get out of here. This was getting out of hand. As if things couldn't possibly get worst, Liam punched Collin straight in the jaw. He fell backwards and Karla ran to his side, tending to the blood gushing from his nose.

"I said go home."

I backed away at the sound of his voice. It was cruel and predatorily like he was fighting claims over land, but instead he was fighting for me.

The thought was frightening as I realized how violent he could be.

I ran. My feet slapped against the pavement as I bolted down the street, despitethe agonizing protest of my lungs. I could hear Collin's harsh voice saying, "Fuck you man!" in the distance.

"Anya!" Liam called. I rounded the corner, refusing to turn back.

I don't know for how long I ran until my chest burned from the exertion and my breathing became shallow that I could barely stand up straight. I shouldn't have ran – I know shouldn't have, but I needed to escape. There were mixed feelings tumbling in my head as I saw what Liam did. I felt proud and thankful for him standing up to me, but I also felt scared at seeing him lose his temper like that.

I didn't even know what time it was and knew that I was a long way from home. I was probably thirty minutes to an hour away from home. I was guessing an hour as I felt my body begin to shut down and it began to physically hurt to walk, but I kept on moving no matter the protest from my aching body.

I heard the distant sound of an engine rev and soon found that it was Liam's motorcycle down the street. I straightened my posture and pretended that I was fine when it was the opposite of what I felt. He pulled up beside me and said, "I'll take you home. There's no need to walk home in the dark."

"No," I said defiantly. "This was a mistake. I can find my way home."

"Anya."

I stopped walking and threw my hands up in the air in exasperation. "Those are your friends Liam, what does that make you?"

"Fuck them. They're all assholes."

I shook my head. "Then why do you pretend to be something that you aren't? You obviously aren't like them. Why do you wear a mask every day of your life since you abandoned me?"

The truth was out before I could think, and I clasped a hand over my mouth – horrified at my words. Hot angry tears threatened to spill and show the vulnerability that I felt. I took a step forward and continued to walk down the vacant street. After a few minutes I heard Liam pull up beside me once again, but this time he killed the engine. I didn't stop and I soon felt the warmth of his hand on my elbow, turning me around to face him.

"You abandoned me, Anya. Like everyone else in my life."

My anger diffused as I stared at his face, dumfounded. I saw a flicker of pain flash in his eyes like electricity in the sky before his jaw tightened and he pulled the familiar mask over his features. "Forget it. Sorry for wasting your time."

He turned on his heels and hopped onto his bike, revving up the engine in a fury that echoed in the still empty night. I stepped forward and said, "Liam, wait!" but I was too late as my voice was lost in the roar of the engine as it zoomed down the street and disappeared under the pitch black veil of the horizon.

Chapter 11

Liam wasn't at school on Monday, and I couldn't hide the complete and utter dejection I felt without his presence.

I was usually at school earlier than anyone else because Dad had to clock in early, and I liked the hour before school to practice the piano in the music room when no one was around. Sometimes I would go to the library and linger in the rows of books until students began to surface from the weekend. At exactly 7:35 was when I went into the caf. and meet Gem and Hayden to have breakfast.

Today was nothing like my normal day to day routine.

I stayed by my locker all through the morning, even when the hall was empty and the only sound was the vibrating heater above my head. I watched and waited for him to show, and when the first bell rang there was a sinking feeling gnawing at the pit of my stomach. I told myself that the only reason I wanted to see him was to give him back his jacket that I had secretly stashed inside my locker from prying eyes. But who was I kidding? I was only trying to fool myself and even that wasn't working.

I missed him.

I missed his annoying charming smirk and his brilliant slate-blue eyes that had a mind of their own like the every changing seasons.

I missed his infuriating cocky, arrogant self, and the way he'd cross his arms over his chest when he had a mischievous glint in his eyes.

He had become a constant – an annoying constant – but someone who had become part of my life and it was strange and almost foreign not having him around.

As the day passed by I found myself holding my breath whenever the door would open to a class we shared. That split second of hope would only end in sheer disappointment that I found myself drowning in. Gemma noted my strange behavior, and I lied to her about why I was on edge – coming up with the pathetic excuse that Julliard was causing me to have anxiety attacks. Gemma didn't believe me, nor did Hayden. At lunch they both eyed me suspiciously as I tried to enjoy my delicious turkey and cheese sandwich.

When the final bell rang I couldn't be more relieved that the day was finally over. I didn't need to keep that small piece of hope that he'd show up twenty minutes before school ended. No one would ever do that if they were of right mind.

Theater practice began twenty minutes after school ended with no real change except for Karla's terrible singing, but it was more like screeching nails on a chalkboard. Mr. Devino had no idea that she couldn't carry a note to save her life, and was mentally killing himself for not testing her voice before he casted her as Belle. Everyone in the play had decided unanimously that Karla needed to lip sync. It was too late to change the cast, so we would just have to grin and bear it with this small set back. The only questions that remained was: Who would be singing Belle's song?

That question was answered the next day as soon as practice was over.

As everyone was packing up to go home, Devino went up to Janie and asked her to sing. At first she was shy and modest , refusing to sing even when Devino praised what Mrs. MacMillian (the choir teacher) said of Janie's talent. When she conceded and opened her mouth to let beautiful harmonious melodies ring from her voice, it was decided in that moment that she would sing Belle's song.

With one problem settled there still needed to be another explained.

It was no mystery that Liam Rowely skipped school on a normal basis. It was a miracle that he was even graduating by all the absences that were marked on his record. There was a time last year that I remembered he missed an entire week, and when he came back it was like he was never gone in the first place. But considering the fact that he left pissed off at me on Sunday night – I concluded that it was my fault he was absent. What are the odds of him not showing up to school two days in a row after we had gotten into an argument. It was all water under the bridge for all I cared. I just wanted to see him and felt guilty that the reason he was avoiding school was because the thing he was avoiding was me.

As I walked home, I thought about what he said that night; the words kept repeating in my mind like a broken record player that I desperately wanted to smash with a hammer. I hated feeling guilty when that was the furthest emotion I should be feeling. What was there to feel guilty about? He was the one who left me. He was the one who found new friends, while I had to fend for myself for months until I found a friend in Gemma.

Maybe the reason I felt guilty was because of the wounded hurt in his eyes when he said: You abandoned me, Anya. Like everyone else in my life.

I hugged his jacket close to my body, the scent of cigarettes mixed with cologne swirled in the air around me. What could he have meant by me abandoning him? I was always there for him, always. Not a day passed by that I didn't wish things were different between us. But then at the same time I knew that everything happened for a reason. If it wasn't for me and Liam's diffused friendship, then I never would have met Gemma or Hayden for that matter, and I wouldn't trade them in for all the gold in the world.

The street lights flickered to life above me, and ahead the sun gently fell behind the building tops and the vast crystal blue ocean in the distance. Down the street I saw Liam's bike parked in his driveway as the sleek black shined in the fading light.

There was nothing that could explain the draw that pulled me into the direction of his house, but it was too late to figure it out when I stopped in front of his door. I contemplated for a moment, wondering if this was the right thing to do, and decided that it was. I needed answers. We both did.

I knocked on the door, quietly at first and when I heard nothing on the other side, I knocked again – beating my hands against the dark wood until there was the distinct sound of footsteps echoing through the wooden frame.

There was the sound of bolts and chains rattling from their place before Liam swung the door opened. His brows furrowed together as he assessed me with stormy gray eyes.

"What are you doing here?"

I gulped, looking down at my feet and then at his exposed muscular torso as his only other item of clothing was a pair of old worn gray sweats that held a worn hole at his waist.

"I-I," I bit my lip and focused my eyes at a spot above his head. "I came to return your jacket. You haven't been at school and I-"

A loud crash (that sounded like broken glass) rang from within the open doorway. Liam flinched, shutting his eyes tightly as he leaned his head on the door. I stepped forward as he turned and called, "You alright, Dad?"

I heard the distant sound of grunting and a slurred voice yelled, "Fucking great! Get me another beer!"

Liam turned back to face me with a distressed look on his face. "You need to leave."

My eyebrows shot up in surprise as I heard another loud crash and an angry grunt. He began to steer me away from the porch like I was a sheep without a shepherd, needing to be lead in the right direction. Too bad he wasn't a shepherd or else I would have done what he asked. I dug my heels into the floor and spun around to face him. "Is this how you treat all your guests?"

His brows rose in surprise as he eyed me warily. There was another shout from the house that traveled to our ears like leaves in the air on a windy day. Liam's back tensed as he walked back up the porch steps with me trailing behind.

"Where is my God damn beer?!"

He sighed, his shoulders becoming slack as he entered back into his house and turned back saying, "It's your choice," and disappearing down the hall towards the kitchen.

I stood transfixed, contemplating on whether stepping foot into his house or turning back and going home. There was another crash, and I could only imagine that the living room was now destroyed or the floor was covered in razor sharp glass. It all piqued my interest no matter how volatile the scene might be.

There's a saying that immediately popped into my head as I stepped over the threshold and shut the door softly behind me: Curiosity killed the cat.

My steps were wary and light on the cherry wooden floorboards as I headed towards the living room to wait for Liam. Everything looked exactly the same as I remembered, from the family portraits that filled the walls to the furniture that didn't look out of place. I picked up a picture frame and grazed my thumb over the happy toothless little boy in the picture. He was proudly holding a fish by its tail as Mrs. Rowely ruffled his hair playfully and Mr. Rowely had a loving hand clasped around his son's shoulders.

I remember the day when Liam had lost his two front teeth. It was mid afternoon with the sun beating down on my back. I was playing in the yard where I was squishing ants and rollie pollies to a bloody pulp.

"Look, Anya! Look!" Liam exclaimed running up the driveway and into the yard.

I rubbed my dirt caked hands on my dress and stood up to see two shiny brand new quarters in his hands. "It's from the tooth fairy! She's real and she left me money!" His eyes were beaming a bright sky blue that matched the cloudless June day.

The memory faded into the recesses of my mind, leaving me to wonder where the boy who believed in the tooth fairy had gone.

He grew up, I thought sadly. Just like you did.

"Ah," I snapped my head up and saw Mr. Rowely looking at me with feigned curiosity over the sofa. His eyes that mirrored Liam racked my body from the top of my head to my toes. It sent a chill down my spine and I pulled my sweater around me to cover up, feeling suddenly naked under his scrutiny.

"What do we have here? Liam didn't tell me he was having company over. Want a beer sweetheart?"

I shook my head. "No, thank you."

"Pretty little thing, aren't ya? Just like my wife. Too bad women are all liars and whores," he spat. I stepped back at the harshness of his voice and bumped into something hard and solid. I felt Liam's hand graze my shoulder, stepping forward to drop the six pack of beer near his father's feet.

"What took you so long, boy? Are you so useless that you can't even get your old man a beer?" He grabbed the pack and ripped the plastic rings in frenzy, almost desperately. In one quick motion Mr. Rowely popped the cap off and guzzled down the alcohol like it was the last available drop of water in a scorching desert. I stared incredulously at the man who had once been kind, lively, and loving. There seemed to be no trace of those qualities in the man I was looking at now.

"If there's nothing else I'll be in my room," Liam said.

"Just one thing," his father looked back at me with a leer on his face. "Fuck her and get out. That's all women are good for these days."

Liam turned on his heels, his jaw clenched as he gently pushed me down the hall towards his room. He shut the door behind him in anger and I flinched. I was too numb and disoriented from the scene to process Mr. Rowely's demeanor. It was like he had lost himself in the ocean and no one had saved him. No one.

"So now you know," Liam said softly, almost like a whisper. "He's..."

My eyes flickered to him as he sat on the edge of his unmade bed. He propped his elbows on his knees as he leaned forward with a vacant look in his eyes. I had no idea that this is what had become of Mr. Rowely. Fairhope was a small town and surely I would have heard rumors of the downward spiral that had made its way into his life. But there was nothing – not even a speck of dirt to come to this conclusion: His father was an alcoholic.

A hard shuddering tremor went through my chest as I slowly moved to sit directly across from him on the hard, cold wooden floor. I looked at Liam with his head in his hands, looking down at the floor. I wanted to make him feel better. I wanted to make him forget about what his father had said, but at the same time I was curious of the things Mr. Rowely had said. My curiosity would have to wait for another time where the subject wouldn't make Liam look so...drained.

"So," I began. He lifted his head and looked at me quizzically as if he wondered what I was still doing here. "How about we watch some Lord Of The Rings? I know you're a closet dork and probably have them stashed somewhere from prying eyes."

A crooked smile began to quirk on the edge of his lips as the familiar glint of mischief formed in his mind. "Usually girls don't keep their clothes on very long in my room."

I scoffed. "Well, this girl is and would you mind putting on a shirt, please? That's seriously disturbing."

"That's a first."

I smiled as the awkward run-in with Mr. Rowely quickly became forgotten. I stood up and walked to the small bookshelf that used to hold all of his dvds, cd's, and books. His walls were a bare and solid white, with only the trace of glow stars sticking to the ceiling.

"I don't really know what entertainment to provide that involves clothes. You'll have to coach me." I rolled my eyes and kept rummaging through his shelves looking for the first movie in the trilogy when I stumbled into a pile of porn magazines.

"Ugh. That is disgusting." I pinched the corner of one of the mag's and dropped it on the floor. "Do you have no shame?"

He pursued his lips, contorting a thoughtful look on his face. After a few long dramatic seconds he said, "Nah."

"That's sick." I stepped back from the shelf and asked, "So, um…where's your dvds? I do not want to find any more of your dirty little secrets. I think one is enough for today."

He pushed himself up from bed and brushed past me towards his closet, flicking the light on to shed a dim glow inside the space. I sat down on the bed, grabbed a pillow, and made myself comfortable as I leaned my back against the wall. Liam came back out with the dvd in hand a black fitted t-shirt that still showed his muscular toned arms.

He loaded the movie into the player and left the room silently as the previews played. My eyes roamed around his room at the cluttered desk that faced the tightly blinded windows to the dirty pile of laundry at the corner of his room. When Liam came back into the room the movie was starting and he handed me a can of coke and the bowl of popcorn he had made.

Its sweet buttery deliciousness melted in my mouth as I savored every piece. Sweets weren't a luxury I could relish in, but I would make an exception just this once. Liam flopped onto the bed beside me, grabbing some popcorn in the process. He was such a guy, unaware of the social displays of eating like a gentleman – not that those existed anyways.

Half way through the movie I sent Mom a quick text of where I was and specifically told her not to tell Dad. He would have a coronary and march right down to Liam's house the minute he found out. He would bang on the door relentlessly until he had me in his line of sight.

By the time that the movie ended I was exhausted and wanted the comfort of my bed. Wearily I stood up and felt lightheaded by the movement. I stumbled only to feel Liam's hand curve around my arm, steadying me.

"You alright?"

I nodded slowly. "Yeah. I'm fine. Just a dizzy spell."

He didn't let go of my arm until I looked up and met his gaze. He was watching me – no calculating me like I was this equation that he didn't know the answer to.

"Okay," he finally said, letting go. I picked up my discarded bag and headed towards the door, waiting for Liam to slip on his sneakers.

We walked down the hall silently with only the drone of the t.v. playing. Mr. Rowely was asleep on the sofas as we passed through and headed out the door.

"So I'll see you tomorrow?"

He nodded and gestured for me to follow him. "I'll walk you home."

I fell in step with him, letting a comfortable silence settle between us. I had come for specific answers pertaining to our Sunday rendezvous. Instead, I had discovered a secret that Liam had hidden for years. Then there was the whole issue with the magazines, but I imagined that he wasn't the only teenage boy who had a pile of them in their room.

We came to a steady stop in front of my house as the wind picked up around us. Liam dug his hands into his pockets and kicked a small pebble with the tip of his shoe, skidding off into Mom's garden.

"Well, now that you know the difference between Smeagol and Gollum – I think my job is done."

I smiled. "You didn't even say anything throughout the movie. I had to teach myself. Those aren't grounds for a good job."

"Maybe you'll give me a second chance," he said.

I crossed my arms over my chest and grinned. There was more than one meaning to his words and I wanted him to know the weight of my answer when I said, "I'm a huge advocate for second chances."

He smiled – not smirked, or grinned, but smiled.

Chapter 12

A nya

The rest of the week went without any further unexpected road blocks. Theater practice was running smoothly every day after school with only three weeks until opening night, and I had finally decided on the piece for my Julliard audition tape. Gemma grew ecstatic as the hype for the Winter Formal spread like wildfire. On Thursday, after two hours of pleading she finally coaxed me into attending the dance. I was not in the least bit thrilled about attending this rite of passage.

I didn't believe that being highly involved in school functions made a person have a complete high school experience. I believed that it was some sort of sell out created long ago to burn a hole in our pockets – or should I say, parent's pockets.

When Friday morning rolled around I woke up feeling strangely weary and nauseous. It passed when I arrived at school, but the feeling of uneasiness and dizziness was surfacing once more during passing period. Gemma and I were gathering our books for Calculus, while she went on about the dance, dresses, tickets; the whole shebang.

"We should check out the Cat's Meow later this weekend – see what they have in stock," Gemma signed.

"Mhm...sounds good," I said trying to sound seemingly interested. My stomach was doing acrobatics and felt like I was going to vomit my breakfast. "I'll ask my parents. Maybe they could drive us to Mobile. We could check out their stores there," I suggested.

Gemma beamed. "Great idea! And you said you weren't excited for this – look at you thinking ahead," she nudged my shoulder and grinned, sharing a secret smile with me that made her eyes sparkle.

I smiled back, but felt that it wasn't completely genuine; it was forced like I had to show I was strong when I felt the complete opposite. A migraine had begun to appear at the back of my head like a small jack hammer that became louder with each passing second.

"Anya?" Gemma said. Her voice was soft like a feather. My name sounded distant like it had long ago drifted away in the air. "Anya, are you alright?"

I looked up at the concern in her brown eyes and nodded. White, hot pain seared through my head – a blinding flash of light, followed by hazy, distorted shapes. My limbs felt of cinder, everything was stiff and heavy like I was trapped in quicksand in the middle of a burning hot desert. It took every ounce of my strength to take a step forward, but I soon regretted it as I felt the crashing sense that everything and everyone around me was fading. I felt a tight hand grasping my forearm to keep me upright as my eye sight became blurry and unfocused. My voice sounded far away even to my ears as I said, "Gemma. Get my dad fast. I think..."

The words were lost on my lips as my knees gave out beneath me. I waited for the fall, but it didn't come. Arms wound around me before I was lost in the bottomless depths of darkness.

Liam

She didn't look so good today.

Anya was having difficulty all throughout our morning classes to stay awake and focus. I saw her drifting off into space as she absentmindedly tapped her pencil on her desk in Government. Something was wrong, and like hell I was going to get to the bottom of it.

I shut my locker and headed down the hall where I saw Gemma's hand tightly wound around Anya's forearm. My steps quickened and I ran when I noticed the glaze look in her eyes as I bound closer. Her knees buckled, no longer able to support her body as she began to fall backwards. Gemma tried to hold her, but she was too small. I leaped forward, closing the gap that remained between us and caught her before she hit the floor.

Gemma cried out; panic rising like bile in her eyes. "Is she sick?" I asked her.

She nodded and began speaking words that I could not understand. Her words were pronounced differently and sounded strange to my ears. It was like she was a foreign exchanged student trying to speak English, but was not getting anywhere.

I shook my head. "I don't know what you're saying." Gemma let out a frustrated sigh and pointed down the hall.

"Nurses office?"

She gave me a loaded glance and hit her forehead. Gemma mouthed, duh, and rushed down the hall in the opposite direction.

I hurried down the hall with Anya in my arms. She was smaller than I had thought and disguised how fragile she was by the baggy clothes she wore. Even in the light purple dress she wore I saw that it was size to big for her small frame.

There were curious stares and whispers that quickly filled the corridor as I passed and entered the nurse's office. Mrs. Quinby jolted from her desk when she saw me and beckoned me to an empty padded bed to lay Anya in.

The next thing she did was bombard me with questions. "Did she faint? Were you there? Did she hit her head? Does her father know that-"

I held up my hands to stop the flow of questions. "Yes to the first two. Then no and yes."

She nodded and continued to assess Anya. I watched as Mrs. Quinby hastily walked back and forth throughout the room like she didn't exactly know what to do in this situation. Her low mumblings of "Oh dear," weren't helping to quench my uneasiness either.

The door opened, crashing into the wall as Mr. Vanchester walked in with frantic eyes and rushed to his daughter's side. "Phillip, she has a fever. It's not-"

She stopped and glanced in my direction quickly averting my gaze. My brows furrowed as I tried to make sense of the sudden quietness that stilled the room. Mrs. Quinby cleared her throat and looked back at Mr. Vanchester who eyed me wearily. "I'll take her home," he finally said. "Ellen can you talk to the secretary at front and see if they can find someone to cover the rest of my classes?"

"I can try Phillip, but-"

"Sir," I interjected. He turned his attention to me and gave me a loaded glance. There was no time to mend the rift I had caused between him and I – it was something to fix another time, if I could fix it. What mattered now was Anya. "I can take her home. It won't be an inconvenience to me."

He paused, thinking. He rubbed a hand at the back of his neck and said, "No, I suppose not...but I certainly won't allow my daughter on the back of a motorcycle in the state she's in."

He was right. She didn't have the strength to withstand the speed and velocity I'd be driving to get her home. I glanced over to where she lay with a cold cloth on her forehead to sponge the excess sweat her body was generating. She was pale and looked deathly sick. I felt useless – someone without a purpose in the room as I did nothing to help her.

When I looked back at Mr. Vanchester he was talking to Ellen, making arrangements to leave with Anya.

"I'll take your car," I said without thinking, but felt the surge of resolve in my words. "I'll leave my bike here and come back for it later." I was certain that it was a good plan. Mr. Vanchester could keep my bike for leverage for all I cared.

He shook his head. "No. No, that's not-"

"Daddy."

We all turned at the sound of the small voice coming from the corner of the room. Her mouth was parted as she searched for her Dad's eyes. Mr. Vanchester hurried to her side and ran a hand over her forehead tenderly. "Let him, daddy. You have work...I'll be okay."

"Honey, I don't think it's a good-"

Her voice was soft and strained when she said, "It's decided."

There was an understanding that passed through them in that one simple statement. It left me wondering the significance of her words as Mr. Vanchester turned and swiftly tossed me his car keys. I caught them and moved forward to gather Anya in my arms.

"I'll be home at exactly three," he said. "Her medicine is in the kitchen cabinet. It has her name on it – you can't miss it. Give her a spoonful. That should make the fever subside. Also be sure to keep an eye on her – don't leave her out of your sight. Got it?"

I nodded feeling the empowering feeling of doing something that had a purpose. "Yes, sir."

Out in the parking lot I located Mr. Vanchester's car and strapped Anya gently into the back seat. She had drifted off to sleep and was shivering in the 87 degree weather. Taking off my leather jacket I draped it over her shoulders, hoping that it would help the chills raking her body. I hopped into the vehicle and drove the ten minutes (it was actually six as I drove over the speed limit) to get to her house. I was lucky enough to not get a speeding ticket. I would have never heard the end of it from Mr. Vanchester.

Anya curled into my chest as I carried her up the driveway and opened the door to her house, tossing the keys on the small table beside the door and heading up the stairs to her room. Her bed was unmade, which made it easier tucking her in and pulling the moss green coverlet under her chin. Running down the stairs I found the medicine called Hydroxyurea. Her name was neatly printed on the bottle with Dr. Novak's (Hayden's dad) name on it. I wondered for a split second what the medicine was for and why she was seeing Dr. Novak. He was a hematologist (or something like that), someone who specialized in human blood.

I shook my head and grabbed a spoon from the dishwasher, letting my thoughts fade. I sprang up the stairs taking them two a time as I heard the pounding of my heart loudly in my head.

Anya was still as I entered the room and took a seat at the edge of her bed, twisting the child proof cap open. I set the medicine and spoon on the nightstand and softly asked, "Anya?"

She stirred and fluttered her eyes open. "Hmm?"

"I need to give you medicine." She nodded and tried to sit up. I saw the strain the effort caused on her body that I helped lean her back on the headboard. Her eyes were heavy and unfocused as she watched me pour a spoonful of dark brown liquid and opened her mouth wide, taking the medicine.

"Water," she said scrunching her nose in distaste.

"Is tap water fine?"

She nodded.

I went into the bathroom and found a glass in her medicine cabinet, filling it halfway. She slowly took a few sips of water, and handed it back to me. "Thank you."

"Rest," I said tucking her back into the covers. I touched the back of my hand to her forehead and felt the clammy hotness of her skin. She didn't protest as she sank back into the comfort of her bed. Her shaking had ceased a while after we got inside the house, but I could see that she was fighting something more than just a fever.

Anya fell asleep in a matter zof minutes, leaving me only to keep an eye on her. I don't know how much time passed by as I watched her sleep; her chest rising and falling as dreams moved behind restless eyelids that made me wonder what she saw in the depth of her conscious mind.

I remember when we were kids and Anya would fall prey to a cold or fever. She always had a hard time recovering, and I knew that this was another one of those instances. She was always so frail and small – that hadn't changed, but she was a completely different person. Even though she looked fragile she was anything but that. Anya had grown into a...feisty girl. There was a time where she wouldn't defend herself when kids would bully and say cruel words. That was the time when I was there by her side, defending and protecting her. She wasn't like that anymore. It has been years since I've seen her weak or defenseless. She was quiet but she was no longer taking my crap or anyone else's for that matter. She didn't need me to protect her anymore.

She hadn't needed me for a long time.

It surprised me, catching me off guard to see her standing before me on the first day of school. She looked fearless, standing up for the freshman that I was pummeling. My reasons weren't justified that day – I see that now. It was a good thing that something had awakened within her to approach me. She was being brave or try-ing to appear that way as she called me on my reckless, indignant bullshit. I saw the hint of fear or maybe it was nervousness twined in her eyes as she held her ground for something she believed in.

Anya stirred, the soft hum of content escaping her lips as she turned to her side and hindered her face from my view. She looked peaceful under the circumstances and hoped that this would pass and not turn into more than it ought to be. I couldn't bear to see her suffering, while I just stood by the sidelines – watching and not doing anything to make her better.

I stared at the purple neon numbers of her clock and grew restless with every passing minute. Only an hour had passed with my stomach growling from hunger. It was lunch time and I usually had a smoke during this part of the day. I knew it was a bad habit – something that I had picked up from my dad, but habits were pretty damn difficult to break.

Slipping out of her room I went down stairs to find something to eat. The only thing that I found that was edible to eat (to my liking) was a box of pizza rolls. Everything was frozen vegetables or mystery health meat. I honestly didn't know how people survived on that stuff. After popping the bag into a bowl for five minutes and ravishing my plate in two I headed back upstairs to find Anya still sleeping.

I was restless and began to walk around the room, keeping in mind not to wake her. Being patient was not in the list of acquired skills I'd come to master. – Her walls were plastered with posters of bands (I've never heard of before), movie posters, and sticky notes with quotes of various topics, but they were mostly about love, strength, and God.

I walked to her desk and found it neatly cluttered with passed exams and sheet music buried within folds of old assignments. There was a thick white page sticking out from the mess of papers that was not like the others. Curiosity tugged at the recesses of my mind and I pulled on the page, setting it loose from its place. My eyes widened in surprise as I read the letter from Julliard. She was a shoo in for music school; there was no doubt in my mind that she wouldn't be accepted. The letter was practically stating that she was guaranteed a spot.

Setting the letter down, my eyes lingered to a folded piece in her pencil holder. I quietly unfolded the paper and read that it was dated January 19, 2007. It was titled Anya's Bucket List and had a few things crossed off. I heard Anya stir and promptly set the paper down, taking my phone out and snapping a quick picture of its contents. Why would she have a bucket list? Isn't that sort of thing for ailing elderly people who only had a few months to live?

I stride forward and sit on her bed as she slowly opened her eyes. They were a swirl of light and dark brown hues with curiosity creased in the small frown of her forehead. "What are you doing here?"

"You don't remember?"

She shook her head and managed to sit up on her own. Her brown eyes lingered on my own as she waited for an explanation for my presence in her room. She looked better than she had before, but I noted that she was shivering under the covers. My hand involuntarily went up to touch her forehead and felt the coldness of her skin.

I flinched. "You're freezing. How is that possible? You had a fever only a few hours ago."

She shrugged and looked away from my questioning gaze. "I'm fine." Her voice was soft, but resolute. It reminded me of her words earlier in the nurse's office to her father.

I scoffed. "You were never a good liar."

She didn't say anything and I began to take of my shoes, climbing into bed with her. "What in God's name are you-"

"It's called body heat. You're shaking in your bones like you have hypothermia. The sheets aren't helping – might as well be of some use to you."

She protested and tried to squirm from my grasp as I pulled her close to me. "This is wrong. So wrong on so many levels."

"Saving your life is wrong?"

"I wouldn't call this saving my life. I've been sick before and have been fine without you. This is no different," she defended.

"There's one thing that's different," I said. Her eyes searched mine as she gnawed on her lip, thinking. It took all my self control not to kiss her in that moment even though it was the one thing...that I wanted. She looked...sexy biting her lip in a manner that was almost a tease.

"What's that?" she asked.

My brow furrowed as I felt caught in a mist of enthralling magic. When I looked – really looked at her – I saw a tinge of confusion that must have mirrored my own etched on her face.

"What were we talking about?"

She rolled her eyes and said, "I've been sick before. You being here doesn't make it any different."

"Oh, yeah..." I said remembering. I pulled her closer to me and she submitted, no longer protesting as I heard her sigh in resignation. Anya nuzzled her nose into my chest as I wrapped my arm around her abnormally cold body.

It was comforting and intimate, holding her in my arms. There was a sense of familiarity as she laid her head on my chest and listened to the sound of my heart beat beneath my skin. Never in my life had I held someone like I held Anya. She was the epitome of life, while I was dead; an empty shell that had been abandoned. Sex was the only thing that made me feel something – anything. Yet, Anya made me feel in more ways than I could possibly say.

It was a twist in the deceptive story I had constructed.

"This doesn't mean anything," she said, pulling me out of my reverie and breaking the comfortable silence that had engulfed us. "You're still a jerk."

I felt the smirk tug at the corner my mouth. "Wouldn't want you to think any less of me babe."

She punched me. "Don't call me babe."

"Hey easy there tiger! Don't want you damaging my livelihood."

She laughed – really laughed as she said, "So what? Are you some sort of escort or something? I didn't know you had a side job."

"Now that was just plain rude."

She giggled and buried her face into my shirt. "Sorry. You left the door wide open on that one – setting yourself up."

"Guess I'm rubbing off on you – in more ways than one." She detached herself from my arms and grabbed a pillow, hitting me with it.

"Hey, hey! Didn't we just talk about not damaging the goods?" I laughed. God, I hadn't laughed like this in ages. Being with her brought out a side that had long ago been forgotten, buried in the darkest of places and she was slowly digging it out with the proverbial shovel.

"Who would want to sleep with a jerk?"

I quirked my eyebrow and looked at her dumbfound. "Lots of girls. I guess it comes with the territory. Girls have a thing for bad boys. Kinda like you."

She scoffed and threw the pillow at me. "I don't like you," she said defiantly, her cheeks turning crimson. "You're a....jerk."

"That's what you keep saying," I leaned back on the headboard and put my hands behind my head. "I think it's just a defense mechanism."

She began to get out of bed, but I stopped her. "Hey," I said hearing the note of seriousness in my voice. "If you need something I'll get it. You're still sick."

All the light amusement and light teasing was gone from her eyes as she said, "If I'm able to argue with you then I'm fine."

I cocked my head to the side and eyed her warily – not believing a word she said. She was still shaking, slightly, but it was far from being better or worse. "I'll go get you something to eat. I'll be back."

"Liam wait...ugh!" I heard her say as I walked out the room, down the stairs, and into the kitchen. I discarded the dish I'd used into the sink and grabbed a pot, filled it with water, and turned the stove on. It took only five minutes for the water to boil, and I poured it into the cup. In the fridge I found cans of pop and Capri Suns. I took the latter and headed up stairs with the two in hand.

Anya raised her eyebrows and gave me a hard look as I entered her bedroom. "Cup of noodles? Seriously?"

I shrugged. "I can't cook."

"I hate this stuff. You could have a least brought me some pizza rolls."

"To bad, you're eating it. Also, there wasn't any more left...I sorta ate the last batch."

She shook her head and reached her hand forward for the cup. "Fatty."

I swiped the cup from her reach as she exclaimed, "Hey!" I tsked and saw the amusement lighting her eyes once again. I grinned. "Take it back."

She crossed her arms over her chest and insolently said, "No."

"Hmm...I guess someone isn't getting their food," I teased.

She huffed. "That's cruel! You're depriving me of food and going to let me die of starvation."

I shrugged but couldn't help the smile forming on my lips. "Pretty much."

She sank back into the bed and pouted. "You're more of a jerk than I thought."

I laughed.

By the time that Mr. Vanchester arrived home, Anya was once again fast asleep, curled against the warmth of my chest. He hadn't come home at three like he said, but found it oddly pleasing to have spent a few more hours with her than originally agreed.

It was almost six when I heard a car rev into the driveway, jolting me awake from the space caught between consciousness and sleep. Carefully, I unwound my arms around Anya and gently laid her head on the feather soft pillow. She settled into her bed and hugged the space spread before her. An unsettling and unfamiliar feeling coursed through my body as I looked back at the serene face that was lost in a dreamless sleep.

I headed down stairs and met Mr. and Mrs. Vanchester at the foot of the stairs. Mr. Vanchester had a pharmacy bag in hand while Mrs. Vanchester rushed forward with wide, anxious eyes and asked, "Is she alright? How is she?"

"She's better. I think the fever has passed." The tension in her shoulders sagged in relief and she briefly nodded, saying, "Thank you," and started upstairs.

I turned and saw Mr. Vanchester's red rimmed eyes. He walked forward and clasped a hand on my shoulder. "Good to know that we can trust you once again, Liam." His voice was completely devoid of disapproval and brusqueness. It was filled with the exact opposite, like he was...proud...?

"Go home," he said. "Get some rest, kid. You're welcomed to a ride for school tomorrow since your bike is still in the lot."

I was taken aback by the courtesy, and couldn't comprehend how one single act could change a person's perspective of another. It seemed too easy, and I was slightly suspicious. "No, it's alright. Thanks though. – Have a good night."

"You too, kid."

Walking out into the cool night air felt refreshing, and strangely calming. Today had been strange – out of the ordinary. Ever since I had said goodbye to my friendship with Anya I never once looked back, but things were slowly changing – twisting their way back into familiar terrain. It seemed like Mr. Vanchester no longer hated my guts and Anya was slowly letting down her guard around me.

It was kind of funny and ironic...because I found myself doing the exact same thing.

Chapter 13

L iam

Her list was simple, yet she hadn't done more than half the things written on the paper.

1. Go on a road trip
2. Send a message in a bottle
3. Sleep under the stars
4. Play in front of an audience
5. Visit a REAL haunted house at night
6. Go cliff diving
7. Experience a sunrise
8. Compose a beautiful and inspiring piece
9. Ride on the back of a motorcycle
10. Fall in love – real and true love
11. Go hiking
12. Kiss under a mistletoe
13. Ride a mattress down a staircase
14. Go to a drive in movie
15. Be at two places at once
16. Milk a cow
17. Learn how to surf
18. Dance under the moonlight

19. Go horseback riding
20. Be able to count all the stars in the sky
21. Make a difference in someone's life

The only things that were crossed off her list were numbers 4, 9, 11, and 14. I couldn't hide the smile that played on my lips as I read number 9 crossed off again. Ever since I went home last Friday night and read her list I couldn't stop myself from reading it over and over again when I was alone. I lifted my gaze from my phone and glanced at Anya sitting at a table a few feet away.

The sun shined on her hair, making it lighter than it actually was. She was laughing, her big brown eyes glowing with glee as she took a bite of an apple, and tried to suppress the laugh that played on her lips. There was no trace of sickness marring her face. She was happy, and looked better than I had seen her in a long time.

I looked back down at my phone, reading number 9 again. My mind itched with curiosity, wanting to ask if I was the one who had caused her to cross off that particular item in the first place.

"You and Vanchester, eh?" I startled, sliding my phone into my front pocket nonchalantly. When I turned I faced Collin's raised eyebrow and set jaw, his teeth grinding against each other.

"It's nothing."

He scoffed. "Right." Collin folded his arms before him and leaned his frame against the stucco wall. "It's never nothing, not when it comes to girls like her."

I rolled my eyes. Collin hadn't spoken to me once since I punched him the night I went out with Anya. We had silently agreed to stay out of each other's way, but that didn't refrain him from fueling the rumor mill with his snide comments and lies about her.

The only thing I did was grin and bear it, just as I saw Anya do. She was far stronger than I would ever be. There was more than one occasion that I wanted to find Collin and give him what he deserved. I knew that she wouldn't agree with my method of handling things, which is why I bit my tongue.

I forced a laugh, trying to lighten the strain between us. "What's your problem with Anya, did she turn you down, too?"

He scoffed again, but this time there was no trace of vehemently in his voice; his brown eyes turning from cold, hard pools of mud to reflecting a glint of mischief. "Weren't you there a few weeks ago? The girl practically ran away from me."

"I think she ran from both of us."

He laughed and clasped a hand on my shoulder; his eyes leveled on mine, serious. "Well, whichever it was are we good, mate?"

I nodded, clasping his shoulder in return. All the tension in the air disintegrated between us. He was my best friend no matter how much of an idiot and a complete ass he made of himself. "We're good."

Anya

"The color of our eyes, the color of our hair – even how you walk, or whether you can roll your tongue...who we are is determined by the genes passed down to us from our parents."

Mrs. Claemont walked between the tables, handing out a pack of test cards to each row until she was once again at the front of the room. "Okay, let's begin our blood type test." Her fingers clasped together tightly as she rolled on the balls of her feet, excitement evident in her dark brown eyes. "Use a needle to prick a drop – Jesse, cut that out–"

We turned our attention to Jesse Gray, where he mimed sticking the needle into his throat. You would think that that kind of level of maturity would be absent in AP Biology class.

"Now, as I was saying...oh, yes! Use a needle to prick a drop of blood onto the four fields on your test cards. I hope you've all brought samples of both your mother and father's blood. We are going to test your blood type. Some of you may even be surprised to find out whose side you carry."

I wasn't particularly excited for this lab. It wasn't that I was afraid of needles or got queasy at the sight of blood. It was just another painful reminder that I was different from my parents.

"This should be fun," Hayden said beside me. "I already know that I get most of my genes from my dad so I should have the same blood type as him."

"Should, is the key word." I said teasingly. "What if your blood type is from your mom? It would explain why you have girl lashes."

He slumped into his chair. "Ha-ha. You're hilarious, Vanchester. Don't quit your day job"

I laughed and playfully punched his arm. His face contorted into one of mock hurt before he smiled and got back to the test cards in front of him, taking two vials of blood from his backpack. I did the same, rummaging through my bag for my vials.

"Anya?" I looked up and saw Mrs. Claemont's steady eyes on me. "Can I see you outside for a second?" I nodded and stood from my desk, following her out into the hall.

She quietly closed the door behind us and said, "I will give you full credit if you don't want to take this lab. I understand that-"

"No," I said. My cheeks flushed at her sincere and genuine attempt to spare my feelings. All the teachers knew about my unique circumstance. I saw some of their sympathy on a day to day basis.

"It's alright. I want to take the test."

She flashed a small smile that didn't reach her eyes. "Okay, if it's fine with you then proceed with the assignment."

I nodded. "Thank you, though."

Forty-five minutes later I was peering at each of my three test cards. I must have done something wrong like put the wrong antigen and solution in each of their cooperative circles. None of my parent's cards matched with my own. When I looked at each card under the microscope I was able to identify that I was AB positive, matching the groupings of cells with the result card Mrs. Claemont had handed out earlier. Mom was O positive and Dad was A positive. I recalled from my readings that O positive was a universal blood type. I could either have had O or A, but to be AB positive? That didn't make any kind of sense.

I glimpsed at Hayden's cards and saw that he had been right. He was B positive just like his dad, while his mom was O positive. He was all done with the lab, and was cleaning up his station with only twenty-five minutes to spare before the bell rang and class ended.

"I think I did this wrong," I said.

He raised his eyebrow. "Hmm?"

Taking my cards from the desk I set them in front of him. "They don't make sense. I don't think I did it right."

His brows furrowed down the center as he analyzed the cards before him. He carefully shuffled the cards from one to the other, his eyes widening as the seconds passed by. Hayden must have examined each card at least four times before finally setting them down on the table. I looked at him curiously, wanting to know what he had realized.

His eyes were serious, green coals of newly blossomed leaves when he looked back up at me. The look he gave me sent a shiver down my spine like someone had dumped a cold bucket of water all over me.

"Anya...I think you should talk to Mrs. Claemont after class."

My brow furrowed in confusion. "Why? What is it?"

He shook his head, pushing the cards back into my hands. "I don't know. I-I might be wrong, which is why you need to talk to her."

I opened my mouth to say that he was being weird, but he quickly stood up from his seat and went to the sink to wash his hands. My shoulders slumped forward at his strange behavior and brashness. It was odd to say the least, and wondered what had caused his sudden shift in demeanor.

I turned my attention away from him and began to clean up my area, carefully setting the test cards on my chair. The way that Hayden was reacting sort of sent me on edge. What did he realize that I hadn't? I really hoped that he hadn't figured out my secret. There was no possible way that he would know by just looking at my card, but he would see that I was different.

When the bell finally rang, I picked up my stuff and made my way towards Mrs. Claemont's desk. Hayden didn't even wait for me like he always did, and I made a mental note to ask him what his problem was. He had carefully avoided me for the remainder of class, not even looking at me as he sat restlessly in his chair, waiting for the bell to ring.

If this is the way he treated me by noticing a slight difference in my blood – then what would he do once he knew of my secret? He probably thought that I was some sort of freak, wanting to get far away from me as possible.

"Mrs. Claemont?" I asked after everyone had left the room.

"Oh, Anya! How did the lab go?"

I smiled. "It went good. I actually had a question about it." She set her pen down and gestured for me to continue. "I think that I might have done something wrong during the lab. My test cards don't match with either of my parent's."

She pursued her lip, quirking her eyebrow. "Hm…let's see them." I handed her the cards and she put her glasses on to examine each one. A small gasp escaped from her lips and she muttered, "This is genetically impossible."

I leaned forward, wanting to see what she saw. Her reaction had been different from Hayden's alarming one.

"Are you sure this is your parent's blood? Did you leave it out to sit too long?"

I shook my head. "No. I followed the instructions on the hand out…"

My words faded on my lips as I saw the complete intrigue marking her face. She furrowed her brows, creasing down the middle as she set her glasses down. "It's not possible unless…" She looked up at me, her dark eyes watching me inquiringly. Whatever she had concluded made me feel small like an ant fearing for its life as it ward being crushed by a kid's foot.

"Anya," she said finally. "Are you adopted?"

I shook my head, felling the weight of her words sink into the pit of my stomach.

"No...that's not possible...I can't be..."

My heart thundered in my ears as the heartbreaking realization hit me like a massive tidal wave. Everything I had ever known came crashing down before me as I sank to my knees, tears brimming at the edge of my eyes, wanting to escape.

She wasn't wrong...how could something like this be wrong?

It was genitically impossible...I was...

Adopted.

Adopted.

Chapter 14

I was thankful that Mrs. Claemont had sixth period prep. No one saw my breakdown except for her, and it would have been utterly humiliating if anyone else did. What would I say? What would she say?

Anya found out she's adopted. Everyone keep calm, and give her space.

Yeah. Right.

It would be exact opposite of what people would do. They'd probably stare at me with huge bulging eyes and study me as if I was some unknown species from outer space.

Mrs. Claemont didn't exactly know what to do. I heard her calling my name, but it wasn't registering. Nothing made sense. It felt like I was in my own black corner of the world with the ground slowly dissolving around me until I fell into a dark bottomless pit; lost to the unknown before me.

A million questions filled my head, none lasting more than a few seconds. Who was I? Who were my real parents? Why didn't they tell me? Where they ever going to tell me? Why did they give me up? Did they not want me?

I gasped for air as if I was drowning. My breath came out in short, labored. I immediately knew that I was having an anxiety attack and I needed to pull it together. Mrs. Claemont sank down to her knees and was telling me to concentrate on the chair in front of me. I did as she said, and slowly everything came back into focus. Under her breath she muttered Dad's name, and began to take her phone out. That's when everything became clear and clicked.

I shook my head and laid my hand over the phone she held. "No, please. I'm fine." It was a lie. I was most definitely not fine. But I had to deal just like everyone else did when they when a terrible truth was discovered.

With my mind functioning properly and my bearings straight, I picked my crumbled self from the ground. I mumbled my goodbye to Mrs. Claemont, the door clanking shut behind me as my name echoed behind me. I marched down the empty hall with anger seething in my veins. Dad also had sixth period prep, and I couldn't see a better time to confront him. This couldn't wait until later.

He was surprised to see me as I stepped into the room, his eyes crinkling at the corners as he smiled. It was almost enough to stop me from unleashing my wrath on him. Almost.

I thought that when I spoke my voice would have had a note of fury or betrayal, but instead it was weak, hurt; like a small bird chirping the lost of its mother as it was left abandoned in a nest high up in a tree.

"Were you ever going to tell me?"

His brows furrowed in confusion as he set the eraser down, and patted his hands together to get rid of the residue. "What are you talking about, honey?" He peered at his watch and raised an eyebrow. "You're late to class. What's the matter?"

"You lied to me," I repeated. "How could you never tell me? Where you and Mom ever going to tell me I was adopted? Or were you going to keep it a secret for the rest of my life?"

His eyes widened in shock at the sound of my voice, rising with every word that left my lips. He took a hesitant step forward, and I matched his by stepping back – not wanting him near me. If he touched me I would break like a porcelain doll.

His eyes lingered to the cards in my hands. His eyes – they were the same shade of brown as mine. Maybe they were a little darker, but I definitely shared Mom's exact eye color. When we went into town there had been many instances where people said I looked like her. That couldn't have been a mistake on their part. How then...could I ever think I was adopted – that I didn't belong to them?

"Oh, sweetheart." He sighed, his shoulder slumping in defeat.

Is that all he could say?

"Why didn't you guys ever tell me?" I demanded. He didn't say anything. He just stood there with a hurt expression on his face as he took a seat on the edge of his desk, his hand rubbing the back of his neck restlessly.

Why was he hurt? I was the one who had been lied to for seventeen years!

"We'll talk about this with Mom at home, Anya. Not here."

I shook my head. My hands were shaking, and I felt like my breath had been stolen from my lungs. "No," I said. "No." In my anger I stepped forward and threw the cards down on his desk. "Forget it! I don't care what you have to say. You're not even my real father."

I turned on my heels and walked out the door with him calling after me. I didn't turn back. I couldn't. How could I look at someone who had purposefully lied to me all my life?

Newly, fallen autumn leaves crunched beneath my feet as I made my way down the road, away from the school, away from him.

I folded my green arm jacket around my torso as the cool October air sent a chill down my spine. There were signs of Halloween decorations on some of the houses I passed. One was decked out with a huge, fake spider that gave me the creeps. I hate spiders. Disgusting creatures they were. I often wondered why God created some of the animals we have. What was the point of them other than scaring us out of our skin, and being deathly afraid of them?

I didn't know where I was going all I knew was that I couldn't sit through two more class periods with the newfound development that had settled deep in the recesses of my mind. Everything I've ever known was falling apart as it was based on a lie.

I took out my iphone from my pocket and sent a quick text to Gemma.

Can't make it to practice. Tell Devino I'm really sorry. Will explain later.

Devino would no doubt murder me for not showing up a week before opening night. Memories of Juliet running laps across the aisles filled my mind as Devino made an example of her "not show-ing up" two days before opening night. It was utterly humiliating, and I prayed Devino would not inflict the same punishment on me.

My phone beeped in my hand and I read:

What's wrong? Hayden texted me saying you weren't in class. Where are you?

Hayden.

I should have known he would have said something. He was part of the reason why I decided to skip out the rest of the day. I couldn't bear the thought of him looking at me with pity laced in his green eyes. He knew. He had known the second he examined those cards that I was different, and he didn't tell me.

Locking my phone, I slipped it into my bag, and walked to the park, where I kicked my sandals off my feet, and dropped my bag on the edge of the playground.

Time did not exist when I was in my own world. Everything turned into background noise, except for my own thoughts. I couldn't turn down the invisible dial, and make them stop. My thoughts consumed my mind as I tried to think as far back as I could remember. There were no memories that I could recall of me growing up with other people. The farthest memory I could gather was when I was five, and I had fallen off a tree, twisting my ankle in the process. I was lucky that I didn't break anything. I knew now the severity that that would have caused if the accident had been much worse.

Dad had heard my cry, and rushed out the back door, picking me up in his arms. He was strong, and a hero in my eyes as he dressed my wounds. He put a Piglet bandage on the scrape on my elbow, and a Buzz Light Year bandage on my knee. I couldn't properly walk for two days, and he helped me up and down the stairs; getting my pj's for bed, preparing my breakfast, and playing in the yard with me – making sure that I did not hurt myself again.

He never once complained. He was my dad. That's the kind of things dads did, right?

He's not your dad.

I gulped at the unwelcomed thought. That little pessimistic voice in my head was right. Phillip Vanchester was not my biological father, but he was still my dad, just like Charlotte Vanchester was still my mom.

They weren't going to tell you.

No, they would have...eventually.

Face it, kid. They weren't going to ever tell you. You would have died not knowing who your real parents were.

I pushed myself off the ground and swung myself on the swing. I needed to shut off my brain, at least for a couple of minutes. How psychotic was it that I was arguing with myself? I didn't know what to feel. I felt angry and betrayed that they didn't tell me. But then I felt like they had a valid reason – whatever that may be. They wouldn't intentionally hurt me. They loved me and never treated me as if I was a burden they couldn't wait to get rid of.

The sun began to set over the mountain top, turning the sky into shades of various pinks and dark purples. I didn't get up to leave, and knew by the occasional ring of my phone that my parents, Gemma, and even Hayden were worried. I'd call them back...soon. I liked being here. It was like my own little corner at the end of the world where no one could come and take it away from me.

Shoot. I just jinxed myself.

I didn't turn back at the sound of footsteps behind me, and kept swinging nonchalantly with the air caressing my face. From the corner of my eye I saw Liam take a seat in the empty swing next to me.

"What are you doing here?" I asked. My voice was loud even to my ears, and I hoped that he didn't take offense.

"You weren't in seventh period. You're not the kind of girl who skips class."

My eyebrows shot up in surprise. "Really? Well, what kind of girl do you think I am?"

"The running kind."

I skidded to a stop, cocking my head to the side. What did that mean? He noticed the perplexed look on my face and smirked. Ah, there was the Liam I was getting to know. I dug my feet into the cool, squishy sand and waited for him to enlighten me with whatever smartass remark churned in his mind. No words came. Instead we sat their quietly, listening to the rustling of the trees as the wind blew my hair in my face. Agitated, I pulled it back into a ponytail and saw his bike parked on the side of the road. It was odd that I hadn't heard it come up in the deserted atmosphere.

"What did I miss in Calculus?" It was small talk, and I hoped that he would take the bait.

He didn't. I wasn't fooling him. He knew me too well from the past we shared.

"Why'd you skip school?"

I bit my lip, pensively. Could I tell him? I haven't told Gemma yet, and here I was contemplating in telling Liam Rowely. I never imagined that he would come back into my life. Did I hope for it? Yes. But now that he was here...well, I didn't know what to think. That seemed to be a reoccurring factor today.

Part of me wondered what he wanted. He was being nice – too nice for his own good. Why had he suddenly become interested in me? Why did it look like he actually cared?

I decided to play it safe, and not tell him the entire truth.

"Have you ever just needed to...?" I sighed, waving my hand before me, trying to explain. "I don't know...like escape? Get away for a few hours; take a breather."

He nodded, understanding flickering in his eyes. "All the time."

His response struck a chord somewhere inside the recesses of mind. "Can I ask you a question?"

"Sure."

I gnawed at my lip, wondering if I should ask. I was curious to know why he felt like he needed to escape all the time. Was his life literally like his own personal hell? Why was his Dad in this downward spiral? The last time I'd seen Mr. Rowley was a few days before I found out about my condition, and aside from his grief stricken state, he was okay – as okay as a person could be when someone they loved had died. Grief did one or two things. One, it could either bring people together, making them realize that life is short, and should be spent to the fullest – forgetting trivial matters that were non consequential. Two, grief could tear the same people apart, making them forget the meaning of life altogether, and fixate on the past – never letting their iron grip loosen.

The latter was what happened to Mr. Rowely, but why? What had happened in those years where Liam and I didn't speak? What else was happening in the Rowely household that I wasn't already aware of?

It seemed like my mind was on overdrive with a million questions. I narrowed it down to one. After all, only one mattered at this moment. "Is it because of your Dad?" I finally asked.

He didn't say anything for a long time. He was transfixed in his own thoughts, his eyes staring blankly ahead at the ground as he loftily swung his feet back and forth.

"Liam?"

"I said you could ask a question." His mouth quirked up at the corners in a half smile – that didn't reach his eyes. "I never said if I'd answer it."

I rolled my eyes, but couldn't hide the smile that tainted my lips. Leaning my cheek on the cold metal chain, I said, "Typical. Only you would find a loophole like that."

His eyes lifted to meet mine. There was a dangerous glint of amusement shining in the endless sea of grays and blues. What-ever he was thinking of made his entire facial expression change from vacant and detached to relaxed and pleased.

"Let's get you home," he said.

Home.

It was the last place that I wanted to go. I wasn't ready. Not yet.

I reluctantly hopped off my seat, and headed to where I left my discarded shoes and bag. Liam walked a few feet ahead of me, his hands lazily tucked into his front pockets. Slipping on my sandals, I caught up to him, and took the helmet he handed to me. I didn't protest like I had the first few times. This was fast becoming a norm in my life, and I hoped it stayed that way.

He revved up the engine, and I wrapped my arms around his torso, tightening my thighs around his waist.

"Ready?"

I shook my head, and remembered he couldn't see me. "I don't want to go home. Let's go somewhere. Anywhere."

He didn't question me, and I heaved a sigh of relief at the consideration. Liam revved the engine once more, and took off down the road – not knowing the destination that lied ahead.

Chapter 15

Anya

"Where are we going?" I asked, following him aimlessly toward an open field where patches of dandelions grew. He didn't answer, and continued to stride forward through the grassy plain; lost in his own thoughts.

I sighed and thoughtfully leaned down and plucked a dandelion from its place, bringing it to my nose as the seeds caressed my skin like the breeze that ran through my hair.

When I was a kid I used to make wishes on the weed whenever I found one growing nearby, which was rare. It was something that I just did. None of my wishes ever came true, at least not to my knowledge. But that didn't stop me from making them whenever I saw a lonely dandelion growing on the ground. It gave me hope that one day my wishes would come true, but in the meanwhile, I would blow softly on the weed, letting its seeds fly in the air until they landed on the soft ground; growing into more than just the one that had been there at first.

I twirled the flower between my thumb and index finger pensively as I looked up at the sliver of moon that hung above the treetops. What to wish for, I thought.

I withdrew my gaze down at eye level to see that Liam was several feet ahead of me. I skipped through the field, careful to not step on a patch of dandelions, and caught up to his even and strong gait. We were practically through the pasture, and heading toward the dense forest where the mountains laid.

There was a determined look on his face when I tugged on the hem of his shirt to stop him. I felt the strong set of muscles graze my fingertips, causing me to instantly drop my hand like his skin had burned mine. He paused, raising a strong brow as he looked at me with feigned amusement.

I put my hands to my hips, hoping that he did not see the blood pooling in my cheeks as I demanded, "Are you going to hack me to pieces?" Liam crossed his arms over his chest, and raised both his eyebrows. A sly smirk crept onto his lips that made my heart drum inside my chest. I wanted to just scream at my stupid heart and demand what was wrong with it. I couldn't very well do that. Not with Liam standing in front of me looking as if I was the most entertaining thing in the world – like a monkey tap dancing and reciting the ABC's at the same time.

Instead I defiantly said, trying to hide the beating of my pathetic heart, "If so you could have done it at the park. It was pretty isolated there."

He chucked, darkly (if I may add). "Ah. But you see, Anya." He leaned forward, his eyes sparkling dangerously with mischief. We were practically standing nose to nose, his breath cool on my skin when he said, "Someone would have heard you scream. No one would hear you scream here."

I eyed him warily – not letting my eyes waver from his. If I looked away it would be a sign of defeat. He sighed, racking a hand through his dark blond hair, and looking skyward.

Score! Point one for Anya. Check.

"Would I give you my diabolical plan if I planned on killing you?"

I thought for a second. "Well, it wouldn't matter anyway, because I'd be dead."

He rolled his eyes, grasping my hand in his. "Come on. I want to show you something."

I sighed in resignation. His hand was warm against my clammy cold one, sending my heart into another silent frenzy. I was suddenly very self-conscience as he led me towards the dark woods. The sound of twigs snapping beneath our feet made me look around every so often, thinking about all the horror movies I've seen where the couple gets slaughtered walking through the woods at night.

I gripped the forgotten dandelion between my fingers, and I grinned – knowing exactly what I would wish for now. Bringing the flower a few inches from my lips, I whispered into the still night air, "I wish that Liam doesn't kill me tonight."

He heard me, his mouth twisting into a smirk. I thought it was very clever. It was one wish that would definitely come true, at least, I hoped. I didn't picture Liam to be a serial killer, but then again I never thought he'd be smoker. I could very well be wrong about his secret homicidal tendencies. I was probably even his first victim.

I softly blew onto the dandelion, smiling at my outrageous thoughts. The small white seeds flitted through the air until they gradually disappeared into the moist ground below.

Liam

We walked into the deeper part of the woods, the glow of the moon our only light in the vast darkness. Anya clutched my hand as she tripped over rocks, and swore under her breath. It might have not been the best idea I've had (bringing her out into the forest when she was not properly dressed), but it was the only place I knew where I could forget about the world, and its many problems.

I abruptly stopped, looking over the sea of boulders we would have to cross to get to the other side. Anya collided into my back, stumbling backwards in the process. Instinctively, I put my hands on either side of her arms, steadying her as she mumbled an apology.

"It's alright. Just be careful."

She nodded; her eyes wide as she saw the rocks before her. "We're not going through that, are we?

"We are," I said.

"No...no...no...that's like a death trap waiting to happen. I am not going."

"Fine." I shrugged. "You can go back to the bike and wait for me."

I stepped forward and began to cross the boulders one at a time, checking that the rock was steady before I placed my weight onto it. Knowing that Anya wouldn't go back, I trudged slowly until I heard her call out, "Wait!"

Turning, I saw her climb upon a boulder and begin the journey towards me. I waited patiently; watching the awkward movements of her body as she cautiously stepped from one rock to another. When she finally reached me there was a sheen coat of sweat on her forehead from the exertion.

"That's not as bad as it looks," she said huffing.

I smiled. "Just takes practice. Come on – this way."

She warily followed; her steps slow and agile. For her sake, I slowed down and waited for her whenever the distance grew between us. She was a quick learner, knowing where to place her foot or retract it when a boulder was loose. I watched her as she bit her lip, and flipped her hair back from her face - concentrating on the rocks beneath her like they were the answer to her troubles.

The sliver of moonlight cast her soft locks in dark brown waves that masked her face as she treaded forward. There was something about her determination to get away that piqued my curiosity. What was causing her to run away from her problems? Whatever it was – it was something that she couldn't fight alone. The Anya I knew would have never run away. She would do one or two things: Accepts it or come face to face with whatever it was, and fix it.

I didn't have the right to ask her, and even if I did I would have waited until she told me on her own terms.

Coming to the end of the boulders, I jumped down the seven odd foot drop to the ground. I landed gracefully – like a cat on its paws – and wiped my dirty, sweaty hands onto the front of my jeans. When I looked up I saw Anya peering over the ledge, shaking her head in dismay.

"I'll catch you. It's not far."

She laughed, but there was no humor in it. "Ha-ha. Right."

"It's like jumping into a pool. That's how far it is when you jump into the deep end."

"There's only thing wrong with that scenario, Liam. There is no water to jump into."

Just wait until you see where I'm taking you. There is plenty of water.

Stretching out my arms, I could practically touch the ledge. "Trust me. I'll catch you."

She gnawed at the corner of her lip and loudly sighed, no doubt cursing my name. I saw her crouch down and sit over the edge, her arms angling towards mine. Then in one swift motion she pushed off, and I caught her, my hands tightening around her waist.

Her eyes widened in disbelief as I gently set her down. "I thought you would have missed and let me plunge to my death."

I clutched my heart in mock hurt. "You have so little faith in me, it hurts."

She punched me, playfully. "Shut up. Stop being a baby." She pulled her hair to the side and began to braid it into a low ponytail; her face softening as she focused on a point beyond my right shoulder.

All I could do was watch her as I tried to search her eyes for an indication of what she was feeling, but there was nothing I could read. She was a mystery that I wanted – no, needed to solve.

"Are we almost to your secret destination?"

At the sound of her voice I tore my gaze from watching her, and pointed north towards where a mass of trees accumulated just underneath a high ridge. "We follow this trail until we get up there."

She looked up, and shook her head. "You're going to be the death of me."

I chuckled. "I think you'll be in for a rude awakening. We haven't even gotten to the main course."

I knelled down, searching for a thick branch among the brush-wood to tear apart any spider webs we came across. "What could be more interesting than those rocks?"

I found a sizeable branch and stood, following the trail that lead to the ridge. "If I told you then it wouldn't be a secret."

She crossed her arms and huffed vehemently, gracing pass me as she made her way up the trail. I shook my head, smiling as I followed a few inches behind her. Anya was never one to like surprises, but I knew that she would like this one.

Anya

I stood, transfixed as I gazed down at the beautiful river before me. The crescent moon's reflection shone brilliantly on the black water's surface as the breeze caused waves to gently crash on the cliffs below. An owl hooted behind us, and I turned to see it perched high on a tree branch; its yellow eyes glowing unnaturally in the vast darkness. It was a bit creepy to say the least.

"What do you think?"

My gaze flitted to Liam, his thumbs nonchalantly hooked on the edge of his jean's pockets as he looked over the sight before him.

"It's beautiful," I said in awe. I wondered how many times Liam had been up here alone with the tranquility the woods had to offer. What did he think about while he was up here, if anything at all?

From the corner of my eye I saw him begin to take of his shirt. Wait. I turned and saw that that was exactly what he was doing! He tossed his black fitted t-shirt to the side, while he began to unzip his jeans.

"What are you doing?" I squeaked, my voice rising a few octaves in alarm. "What the heck are you doing?"

"You want to forget about your problem? No better way than an adrenaline rush." He dropped his jeans and tossed them on top of his shirt, along with his shoes and socks.

I covered my eyes at the sight of Liam standing bare-chested and only in his boxer briefs that snugged against him perfectly. My traitorous cheeks gave away how completely and utterly flustered I was. I could just die in absolute mortification.

Liam's warm hands seized my wrists and pulled my hands away from my face. There was nothing I could do, but gaze into his beautiful slate-blue eyes that could melt a girl into Jello. Oh my goodness. I'm becoming like one of those girls that fall over head over heels for him. There was no doubt in my mind that this was how he got them to fall in love with him. I mean, who could say no to those incredible sculpted set of abs?

I'll tell you who.

Me.

I shimmied away from him and peered over the cliff. "No way. It's too high."

He came up behind me and said, "That's the point. You forget."

I crossed my arms over my chest and turned to face him. "I can't jump fully clothed."

"Then take your clothes off."

I stared at him like he was insane. He said it so matter-of-factly that I could punch him.

"No."

He held up his hands in mock surrender and turned around, walking to the pile of his discarded clothes. He tossed me his black t-shirt, which I caught with my oh-so fast reflexes. "Wear that over your, uh," he gestured to my body, and turned around; giving me some semblance of privacy.

"You are unbelievable," I muttered. I heard the faintest trace of laughter as I began to wiggle out of my clothes. I imagined that Liam had this pleasing smirk on his face as he recalled my reaction to see him half naked.

That's not the reaction I get from most girls.

That's what he would have said. I was sure of it. And I was glad that I was not put into the "most girls" category. Who wanted to be most when they could be unique?

One by one, my clothes landed in a pile next to Liam's. I drew the shirt over my head, and got a whiff of his strong musk scent that was a mix of cologne and cigarettes. His shirt was big on my small frame that it was almost like a dress; the hem reaching a few inches above my knee.

I crossed my arms over my chest as the cool breeze nipped at my skin. I shivered, mentally slapping myself to ever have agreed to do this

"Okay," I said through chattering teeth. "I'm-m read-dy."

He turned around and walked over to me, his eyes traveling from the top of my head to my head. I hugged myself, feeling my cheeks turn crimson as I looked down at my bare, dirt ridden feet.

Liam's voice was low and gruff as he said, "I'll go first. When you jump I'll make sure you break the surface."

I snapped my head up, and met his intense gaze. "Alright?"

Closing the gap between us, I stood next to him and peered over the cliff. The water didn't look so inviting anymore, not when I knew I was about to plunge into its black depths. "No...no...I can't do this." I shook my head as fear stirred my erratic, beating chest into a wild frenzy.

"You can," he said, encouragingly taking my hand. "We can jump together if you'd like."

I nibbled on my lip, mulling this over.

Fear was only as deep as the mind allows.

It was a Japanese Proverb I had written down on one of my many sticky notes that grazed my bedroom wall. It was one of my favorite quotes as it signified that man was the only one who instilled fear in their own mind. That's exactly what I was doing. I was afraid because I was allowing myself to be frightened.

I swallowed back my fear, and twined my fingers with his. "Okay. Let's do this."

A small smile crept onto his lips and he nodded. "Alright. On the count of three, okay?"

I nodded, readying my body to make the jump.

"One."

I took a deep breath, letting it out in a big whoosh.

"Two."

My grip tightened around Liam's hand, and I felt him give it a little squeeze.

"Three!"

At the same time, we leaped forward as gravity pulled us down towards the deep, dark waters. Wind whipped past me, whistling in my ears. Everything became background noise as we fell. There was only the air biting at my skin, the overwhelming fear of drowning, and my stomach lashing up in my throat. The water loomed before me, crystalline water that went on and on for eternity. The sound of waves crashing upon the base heightened my fear of boulders beneath the surface.

Gravity infringed upon us, pulling the weight of our bodies fast and faster until we plunged the surface. My stomach rose into my throat and I felt like my lungs had collapsed by the impact.

Suddenly, I was no longer falling towards the murky depths of the water, but immersed in it. Liam had let go of my hand when we broke the surface, and was now tugging at my elbow, pulling me up with him. My heart thundered wildly in my ears as I kicked and swam towards the surface, sputtering water once I broke free.

"Hey, hey. You're okay. I've got you," Liam said, wrapping his arms around my waist.

We lulled there for a moment, me taking deep gasping breaths, while Liam held onto me. Once I got my bearings straight, the realization of my actions began to sink in.

"I did it. I actually did it!" I wrapped my arms around his neck, my body crashing into his. He seemed taken aback as it took him a few seconds to embrace me in return. "Thank you," I breathed into his ear. "I couldn't have done it without you."

He didn't say anything, and a moment later he unhooked his arms from my waist, letting me float on my own. His gaze didn't leave mine, and there was an intense look in his eyes; one that I had never seen before. When I only continued to stare, he leaned forward, until his face was only a few inches from mine.

I closed my eyes, my lips parting slightly as I waited for his lips to touch mine. I didn't know it until then how much I've wanted him to kiss me. But then, I was afraid that I would be bad at it if he did. His breath was cool on my skin, and for one heart-pounding moment I thought he would, but then I didn't feel his breath on my skin any longer. And when I opened my eyes he had put some distance between us.

There were no words to describe the complete and utter disappointment that crashed and set up camp at the pit of my stomach.

"We should get out before you catch a chill," he said, swimming towards the small beach.

My mouth dropped open in bewilderment. I couldn't believe this. I was mortified; more so than I had been up on that cliff. Reluctantly, I swam towards him. All I wanted to do was go home even if it meant facing the wrath of my parents that no doubt awaited me than face Liam after that humiliating display.

I mean, why would he want to kiss him? He probably thought I was a loathsome, disgusting creature; at least, that's how Karla had so nicely put it. I stood on my feet as I drew closer to the shore, and walked out of the river; water dripping in rivulets from his shirt.

"Wait here," he said disappearing into the woods. "I'll be back."

He was gone before I could utter a word, leaving me shivering in my knickers. Hmph. It didn't take long for him return with the pile of our clothes in one hand, and pieces of wood in the other. He looked like a lumberjack, except that he was half naked, and didn't have a fuzzy beard or wear a red plaid shirt with khaki pants and suspenders.

He set our things down and began to pile up the pieces of driftwood he had collected. "I'll get a fire going. It should warm us up pretty soon."

I walked over to a log that lay two feet away from where Liam built the fire, and watched as his strong hands handled the wood with such precision that I could only conclude that he had done this before. He flicked on the lighter, the small flame dancing in the breeze, and lighted the wood. The flames roared to life, and the heat was instantaneous.

Liam wiped his hands on the front of his jeans, and came to sit next to me, his thigh touching mine that I felt the now familiar heat pool at my cheeks.

I opened my mouth and said, "Thanks for-" at the same time that he said, "Anya, I-"

I shut my lips as I gestured with my hand for him to go first. He leaned forward, his elbows resting on his knees as he stared at the dancing flames before him. After a long awkward moment he said, "It was nothing. I just wanted to...say that you...did good."

My brows furrowed into confusion. That was not what I was expecting. I thought that he was going to say that he didn't mean to pull away, but had to because he was protecting my virtue or something like that. It would have been romantic, and at least, explained to me the reason he pulled away.

All I could say was, "Thanks," and leave it as that. When I woke up tomorrow morning, I would realize that this had all been a mistake, and that my feelings were only heightened because of the adrenaline rush. My hormones were all out of wack as Gemma would say.

Yeah, that's what it was.

Awkwardly, I asked, "How did you learn to build a fire?"

It seemed like he had also been searching for a change in topic because he answered nonchalantly, "Boy Scout."

I laughed at the memory that those words had begun to form in my mind. "I remember. You use to wear that funny looking hat with the raccoon tail hanging loosely to the side."

He softly laughed, picking at the fire with a branch. "Yeah. You made fun of my hat, but I think you were always jealous that you couldn't have one."

"I was not!" I nudged his elbow and he nudged back.

"It's true. I could just see the green-eyed monster in your eyes. It was scary."

"I did not!"

"Did too."

I poked him each time as I emphasized, "Did not. Did not. Did not!"

He seized my hand, capturing it in his strong one. Liam's eyes lost their teasing light as they turned intense and serious just like before when I thought he was going to kiss me. His lips parted and I saw his adam's apple rise as he swallowed. His blue eyes flickered from my eyes to my lips in a way that made me think he was ongoing an internal battle.

"We, um, should go. Your dad's going to castrate me."

A laugh escaped from my lips and I nodded in agreement. He still held my wrist, my skin burning beneath his hand. I was unable to tear my gaze away from his. My eyes lingered to where his hand gripped my wrist with such fierce conviction that only left my mind muddled with confusion. He gently let go and stood, running his hand through his hair as he walked towards the pile of discarded clothes, where he began to dress himself.

Once he was done he walked back towards the fire and began to put it out by scuffing dirt onto the flames with his foot. His back was turned to me and I took that time to quickly dress, holding onto his shirt so that it didn't get dirty.

"Ready?"

"Yeah."

"Alright," he said, walking over to me. Liam took his shirt back and drew it over his head, the fabric cold against his skin that he shuddered.

I bit my lip and turned, walking ahead of him so that he didn't see the mix of emotions that were clearly written on my face.

Chapter 16

Liam

It was nearly midnight when I pulled up to the curb of Anya's house and keyed the ignition. There were many scenarios that plagued my thoughts, while I drove down the familiar path to our neighborhood, of what actions Mr. Vanchester would make once he saw that I was the one who had kept his daughter out well into the night.

I expected Mr. Vanchester to march outside in a heat of anger once he heard the roar of my engine coming down the street. Or I expected him to lie in wait, hidden behind one of the many strawberry bushes that aligned their garden with a taser in hand. Whatever the scenario, nothing – and I mean absolutely nothing – could have prepared me for what awaited us.

Anya gasped and hopped of the bike, her hand running through her hair as she muttered, "I can't believe they did this."

My eyes flickered to the police cruiser that was parked on the driveway.

"Well," I said. "Guess being castrated is the least of my problems. Being hauled off to jail is way worse. Handsome guys like me don't fare well in prison."

Anya turned on her heels, and eyed me incredulously. "You don't actually think that...do you?"

I chuckled, bounding off my bike. Anya continued to stare at me dumbfounded, seeming to ask in the dark brown of her eyes if I wanted a death sentence, which is what I would get when we walked through the door together. There was nothing humorous about the situation, except for the worry lines that creased her forehead as her brows furrowed.

The smile that formed on my lips was of its own volition. There was something about Anya worrying about me that caused my mind to wonder if she felt the way I was beginning to feel about her.

I closed the gap that separated us, and stood in front of her. Anya didn't even bother to look at me, her eyes solely trained on the ground. I titled her chin, willing her to meet my gaze. When she did her eyes were two small brown pools with tears brimming on the edges, ready to spill any minute.

"Anya?"

"You don't know," she said, swallowing back the lump in her throat. "I can't face them. I don't know what I'll say."

My brows furrowed as I realized that she wasn't only talking about our outing, but something else altogether. I wondered if it was the reason that she wanted to get away for a few hours – to forget. And it had worked – the forgetting – but now those feelings were resurfacing, and there was no more room to run any longer.

She needed to face it, but by the tears and reluctance perceptible in her eyes – she didn't want to.

I moved my hand from her chin and rested it on her shoulder. With a fist she wiped at the tears that silently fell on her cheeks. It was then – seeing the obvious conflict on her face – that I wanted to ask her what was going on because it wasn't a small pebble that had cracked her reality, but a huge boulder.

But I didn't ask. Instead I said, "You don't have to do this alone," and offered my hand for her to take.

She slipped her hand into mine and we walked up the driveway, where the living room lights flicked on at the sound of our footsteps on the paved granite stones. Anya took out her keys and unlocked the door, sighing before she opened it to the empty foyer.

The emptiness didn't last for long as Mr. and Mrs. Vanchester marched into the living room, their worried faces dissipating as they saw their daughter. A second later Mr. Weatherly (still dressed in his chief uniform) and Gemma stepped into the foyer. Gemma's arms were crossed over her chest and had a look of utter betrayal written on her face as her eyes flickered to Anya and then me.

"Where have you been?" Mr. Vanchester demanded. "Do you have any idea what time it is?"

"Sorry. Lost track of time," she said detached.

Mr. Vanchester's eyebrows rose at the tone of her voice and stepped forward, only to be stopped by Mrs. Vanchester's hand on his shoulder. "Phillip." There was a quiet exchange between the two as Anya dropped her bag by the door and began to sign with Gemma, her hands rapidly moving as her mood darkened and became exasperated with each passing minute.

I had no idea what they could possibly be talking about, but futile glances were thrown my way by both parties that I could only guess they were talking about me. I stood awkwardly by the door, watching the display before me. All three adults had huddled together and were talking in low whispers that were inaudible from where I stood, leaning back on the wooden front door. They glanced ever so often at the girls as they continued on with their silent conversation.

By Anya's blazing eyes and Gemma's tight mouth – I knew without a doubt that they were fighting. The atmosphere grew stifling that I was sweating under my leather jacket. Gemma kept eyeing me with a cold, disdainful look that I physically cringed.

There's nothing worse than a woman's scorn.

I swallowed, my father's voice reverberating through my head. He was right, at least, that logic was right. I couldn't figure out what I'd done to Gemma. Last time I'd seen and talked to her (well you couldn't really call it talking) was when Anya had fainted at school last week. She seemed perfectly fine then, and didn't know what was causing the open animosity thrown my way.

"That's enough," Mr. Weatherly said and signed, his voice breaking through my reverie. His hands were on his belt, giving both girls a hard look that was intimidating. It was a look that I had come to know very well when he'd busted Collin and me breaking into private property a few months before, landing us both with forty hours of community service. They flinched under his penetrating gaze, clasping their lips shut and eyeing the badge under his right breast pocket. "Apologize to each other. Now."

Neither Gemma nor Anya made a move to be the first to apologize. Anya's eyes were hardened with unrelenting anger, while Gemma's brown eyes held a twinge of chagrin and anger that mirrored Anya's. Mr. and Mrs. Vanchester looked flabbergasted at the sight of their daughter's crude behavior.

"Anya," Mrs. Vanchester said softly. "Apologize. It's not her fault that she feels you..." she paused, her eyes sweeping through the room and lastly settled on me, a small frown forming on her mouth.

"She should understand," was all Anya said, her gaze unwavering from Gemma's.

Gemma's shoulders sagged in defeat and weary she signed something that made Anya's rigid, straight back relaxed. The next moment they were hugging much to my confusion. Mr. Weatherly looked pleased, and signed something to his daughter. She nodded and they both began to make their way towards the door. I stepped aside, but not before Gemma signed something to me, her eyes soft unlike the contempt that had previously been reserved for me.

No one bothered to translate for me, but I knew that she was offering an apology. I slightly nodded my head in recognition and she smiled. They left a moment after, Gemma waving goodbye and Mr. Weatherly saying, "You all have a good night."

When the door shut behind them I felt like there had been a cloak removed from the room, and with the tension had been unveiled in full force. Mr. and Mrs. Vanchester cautiously walked towards their daughter, but she stepped away from them and bumped her hip into the side table, sending a vase crashing to the floor.

"Dammit," she muttered leaning down as she rubbed at the pain on hip. Striding forward, I crouched down and helped her pick up the shattered glass pieces. Mrs. Vanchester left the room to grab a broom and dustpan; at least, that's what I thought she'd said –while Mr. Vanchester thanked me for bringing his daughter home. I was more or less taken aback. What did I expect? I'll tell you what – I definitely did not imagine Mr. Vanchester thanking me for bringing his daughter home at midnight. Something was majorly wrong with this picture, don't you think?

With the pieces picked up and discarded into the black trash bag Mrs. Vanchester held, I began to take my leave. Anya led me to the door as her parents went into the leaving room, giving us a few minutes to ourselves.

"I'm sorry you had to see that. It's just everything is…"

"Complicated?" I offered.

She nodded, opening the door open for me. She nibbled at the corner of her lip, uncertainty swirling in her eyes like a dark muddled storm. "I'll…explain…tomorrow."

The difficulty it took for her to say those words were evident by the way she wouldn't met my gaze. I leaned forward – like I had before, but this time I didn't tilt her chin. Instead, I leaned forward and gently kissed her forehead, caressing the side of her face with my hand.

"I'll hold you to it."

Anya

The moment Liam left was when my parents began to demand where I'd been. I just listened, perched on the edge of the sofa, while Dad read me the Riot Act – something I've never been privy too because I was a good kid. This was my first offense. Ever.

"Why should I tell you anything?" I asked through gritted teeth. "It's not like you guys were going to tell me I was adopted. Plus, you said I could do whatever I wanted with my time. A little teenage rebellion didn't hurt anyone."

I know I was being a petulant child, but I couldn't help the resentment I felt towards the both of them. What right did they have asking me questions when they weren't answering the one question I wanted to know? It was like everything I said went over their heads without a second glance. They didn't care what I said; Dad just continued to prattle on about responsibility and some other things that I tuned out.

My mind wandered to the events that transpired earlier this evening. I wasn't entirely sure what to think about Liam, except that he only cared about me as a friend and nothing more. He kissing me on the forehead was proof enough. It was a sign of implicit affection – like when I petted Mr. Cuddles and he purred in perfect bliss. Except, of course, I didn't purr that would just be strange.

I had made two mistakes tonight. The first had been allowing myself to feel more than I ought to for Liam. It was a hopeless cause to even think that he would like me. Even if he did like me, he would just go to another girl once he got tired of me. Isn't that the kind of thing he did? Wasn't Karla a prime example? I don't know about her, but I certainly would not want to be publically humiliated if he dumped me as he had her.

The second mistake I had made was fight with Gemma. She had every right to be hurt by my betrayal – or at least, what she thought was a betrayal. I put myself in her shoes, and saw that I would be just as angry at her if she did what I had. I shouldn't have ignored her calls – that was the least I could have done. She was worried as were my parents about my whereabouts. But her worry soon turned to anger when she saw who I'd been with all evening.

"So, he comes back into your life and you decide to ditch your friends?"

"You know that's not true. He has nothing to do with why I-?

"Then what is it? What is it that you couldn't even tell me – your best friend, Anya? You know you can tell me anything, yet you go off to God knows where with Liam! Do you not trust me? Do you trust him more than me, is that it? Because if it is; tell me now."

"That's not it at all. You know you are really starting to piss me off. It was your stupid boyfriend who-"

"Don't bring Hayden into this. This is between you and me and-"

"And what? You're supposed to be the understanding best friend and not some demeaning, psycho bit-"

That was roughly when Mr. Weatherly cut our conversation short, and I was glad he did or else I would have said something I would have deeply regretted. The fight had been transient. I couldn't stay mad at Gem, especially when she apologized for being callous and acting like a jealous boyfriend. I laughed at that and our brief fight was mended.

It wasn't going to be so easy restoring the tear that had shown itself right in the middle of a newly patched quilt.

"Anya. Anya!"

I startled at the sound of my father's booming voice. "Are you even listening to me?"

I rolled my eyes. "Not really. I tuned out after the first," cocking my head I peered at the clock above the fireplace. It was half past one, which would mean that... "I stopped at promptly one-ten."

He let out an exasperated sigh and said, "Charlotte, talk to your daughter."

Mom looked taken aback by his tone and chided, "Now, Phillip. I don't think that it's the best way to-"

Dad cut her off by demanding, "Then what is the best way dear, hm? She obviously doesn't care what I have to say."

"Damn straight."

"Anya," my mother scolded. "Watch your language."

This was ridiculous. I abruptly stood up and said, "You know what? Ground me. See if I care. I'm going to bed now because in case anyone has forgotten – I have school tomorrow."

I turned on my heels and ran towards the stairs, pounding up the stairs with Mr. Cuddles on my heels. I slammed the door shut and collapsed on my bed face flat, my body weary and my stomach growling as loud as Mr. Cuddle's meowing. Dinner had been skipped thanks to my little adventure with Liam, and now it was all catching up to me; the adrenaline fleeting from my veins with every passing minute.

Time was a mere illusion as I lay there, unmoving as I stared at the intricately woven leaves on my green comforter. Mr. C had fallen asleep, curled up on a pillow with his tail tucked around him like a shield. Quietly, I stood and grabbed my pjs from my dresser, changing and discarding my clothes into the hamper. My stomach growled, demanding to be feed that I thought it was loud enough to wake Mr. C. He didn't stir though, even when I tripped over my own two feet as I made my way out the dark hallway and down the stairs. That cat was gone, heavily induced with dreams of endless mice and stuffed rabbits to play with.

I pried open the fridge and was blinded momentarily by the bright yellow light. It took me a moment to adjust to it as I blinked back the black dots that clouded my vision. A sudden wave of vertigo quickly followed afterwards, and I clutched the handle of the fridge tightly – willing the pain to go away. I felt the acrid smell of blood before I tasted the hot, metallic on my tongue.

I brought my fingers to my mouth, and came away with them stained red. My heart began to pound loudly in my ears as I grabbed handfuls of napkins from the dining table. I was freaking out, and all I wanted to do was run to my parents and curl underneath the covers with them as they lulled me to sleep just like when I was a kid and complained about the hammering headaches I frequently obtained. But I couldn't do that. I was mad at them, and that would be declaring defeat.

I wasn't going to lose this because I was right and they were wrong. They shouldn't have kept the nature of my adoption a secret from me. Weren't they ever afraid of me finding out like I had today? Did that never cross their minds as the years passed by and I grew up? Did Mom or Dad ever look into my eyes and sadly think that I wasn't theirs?

Hot tears prickled down my cheeks before I could stop them. It wasn't fair. None of this was fair. All I wanted was to go back to biology class, and change my response when Mrs. Claemont asked me if I wanted to participate in the lab. If I had chosen to sit out; things would be different. I wouldn't be here crying in the middle of the night while my head pounded like a drill, feeling like my skull was going to split in half.

I don't know why things happen the way they do, but I wished to know the reason for this as I sank down to my knees and closed my eyes; for once welcoming the darkness that was all too familiar.

Chapter 17

G rounded.

The word was foreign, alien – as if it was a concept too complex for my feeble mind to comprehend. Maybe my inadequate understanding came from my expectation of what my grounding would implicate against the reality of it all. My first thought had been that I would have all my freedom revoked and become a prisoner in my own bedroom – like Rapunzel locked away for the rest of my life. Okay, so maybe that was a bit too extreme. My parents weren't that cruel. Sometimes, I wished they were. It would make hating them all the more easier.

A few days passed and soon a week had come and gone. I had carefully managed to avoid them, still angry, still feeling betrayal and resentment towards the secret they had kept from me. It was draining, harboring these dark feelings towards the people that I loved most. I missed talking to them about my day, telling them about the A I received on my AP Government test Friday or how Devino had called Karla's lip syncing, the most dreadful performance he's ever seen.

But I couldn't tell them any of that stuff because I had firmly told myself I was not going to be the first to concede. I think it was the same thing Dad had promised himself because he could barely look at me without the flash of hurt and disappointment reflected in his brown eyes – the same as mine.

No. I couldn't think that way. They were not the same. I didn't share any physical attributes from them. Nothing. I was someone else's kid. My parents were somewhere out there or maybe they were dead. Maybe that's why I came to an adoption agency, where Phillip and Charlotte found me.

Stop it, a voice reprimanded. Stop being harsh. This isn't you. They are your parents. Blood is not all that makes a family.

I hated my subconscious. It was that nagging voice that triumphed over my own always being right and taking pride over the fact.

The thing that bothered me about this whole grounding thing was that they didn't even take away any privileges from me. I still continued my daily routine of coming home late from theater practice and hanging out with my friends on our weekly Friday Movie Night. I honestly didn't understand this whole grounding thing. Was I even grounded? They weren't really talking to me (not that I was making it any easier for them to do so) and I had also taken to eating dinner in my room for three nights and they didn't even refute my decision.

It was maddening.

When I come late that Friday night, I was met with two suitcases propped against the stairs. I don't know why but I freaked out at the sight of the black leather clad baggage. Fear racked through my mind as I tentatively walked into the kitchen where Mom was preparing a cooler of food and Dad was walking out of his study, caring an armful of binders and stray papers.

"What's going on?" I asked. My heart was hammering in my throat. I had pushed them too far and now they were sending me away to some boot camp for unappreciative kids. Or maybe they were going to send me to some all girls academy in the middle of nowhere.

"We're taking a trip."

I gulped, fear clawing its way out and becoming a reality.

"Teacher Convention in Montgomery. We'll be back late Sunday night."

And just like that my fear slowly deflated like a balloon. They weren't going to ship me off to some unknown place, leaving me all alone because they had come to a consensus that they couldn't put up with me anymore. The overwhelming relief almost made me want to dissolve the resentment I still felt towards them both.

Almost.

"We need to get going now, Charlotte, if we don't want to be caught in traffic."

"Alright. Just a sec." There were various assortments of condiments spread out on the counter with dirty napkins tossed to the side. She hastily began to throw away the trash and zip up plastic bags that carried peanut butter and banana, turkey, and peanut butter and jelly sandwiches.

I stepped forward, depositing my bag on the kitchen table. "Don't worry about it. I'll clean this up."

She froze, a smile breaking through the weariness in her eyes. The sight brought a small smile to grace my own lips, shattering the cool front I'd carefully built the last couple of days. The atmosphere in the room was awkward, but what did I expect? I hadn't said a word to them since the night I found out I was adopted. I didn't want to talk to them yet, not until I got the answers I so desperately wanted.

I lowered my gaze from her and silently began to clean up the kitchen. From the corner of my eye, I saw Dad's shoulders sagged in defeat. He muttered something incompressible and exited the kitchen with Mom following him a few seconds later. I waited, listening to the sound of the door closing, signaling their leave but it never came. I fixed myself some pizza rolls, remembering that Liam was the one who ate the last box. Well, there went my dinner plans.

Five.....ten....fifteen minutes passed when I saw Mom standing in the doorway. She pushed her bangs out of her eyes and said, "We're heading out now. Dad left a fifty on top of the dresser in our room for food if you need it."

I nodded. "'Kay."

"Anya...there's," she bit her lip, mulling over her next words. I didn't understand why she was acting strange like there was something important she needed to tell me, but didn't know how.

After a few painfully awkward seconds she finally said, "There's something in the living room for you. Just know that..." her voice dropped down to a mangled whisper as she swallowed back the tears brimming in her eyes. I looked down at my feet. My heart constricted at the sight of her; vulnerable and fragile when all I've ever known is the woman who has been my rock, who has always kept me grounded and humble.

I hated myself in that moment. I hated that I was the cause of the pain she was feeling. I couldn't even imagine what I was putting Dad through.

"We love you, Anya. Just know that we love you."

Silent tears slid down my face. I couldn't do this anymore. I couldn't keep on pretending that I didn't care about them when my heart told me otherwise. "Mom, I love you-" My words ceased on my lips as I saw that she was gone. I ran across the room and headlights through the window as the car reeled out of the driveway.

I sighed, feeling the overwhelming weight of guilt churn in my stomach. I felt sick, my head spinning like a dancing table top. I padded to the living room and sat down, propping my feet on the coffee table. I closed my eyes, taking slow, even breaths as the pounding in my head receded to a low buzzing drone.

When I opened my eyes again I was met with encompassing darkness. I dug through my pockets for my phone and turned it on, the bright light momentarily blinding me. I squinted, reading that it was half past midnight and that I had two text messages. I turned off my phone and tossed it on the sofa as I got up and turned on the light.

My eyes adjusted to the bright yellow light and the first thing I noticed out of place was a beige folder perched on the edge of the coffee table. Was that what Mom meant was for me? I plopped down on the couch and slid the folder across the table. I thought that this was finally my punishment written down clearly in black and white. Mom and Dad must have worked on this handbook for days judging by the number of pages inside.

I opened the folder and was rendered speechless; the air knocked out of my lungs as if someone had punched me. It wasn't a rule book like I had originally mused. Instead, it was my adoption record.

There were countless of documents with names of people I've never heard of, signing the proper paperwork for my parents to adopt me. They had gone through background checks – the federal government required to provide a sound environment for the child in question to go to a good and stable home. My birth certificate was also among the pile of documents. The date of birth was the same – that hadn't changed, but my birth place was different and so were the names of my parents. I wasn't born right here in Fairhope, Alabama. Instead, I was born in Montgomery. The names that replaced Charlotte and Phillip Vanchester on the certificate were Madison and Ryan Reiner. It was plainly printed on the sea green paper that they were my true parents. My biological parents.

Anastasia Sophia Reiner.

That was my name. That was my real name. Tears prickled the back of my eyes and I willed them to go away, but it was no use. They flowed freely. I dug through the pile of documents frantically, trying to find the reason they abandoned me. I scanned the papers reading over birth dates and locations, educational levels, and medical history, but there was nothing that indicated a reason as to why they signed me over like I was a business negotiation.

Enclosed were pictures of my biological parents. I flipped through them; Ryan and I playing with blocks in my nursery. In another, I was only a few months old, smashing green peas all over my face. Disgusting. I hated green peas. No wonder I was playing with them instead of stuffing them in my mouth. Finally, there was a picture of Madison, holding me in her arms at the hospital. Her blond hair was tied back in a tight bun as she looked down at me. It looked like she cared....

Why would someone just willing give up their child? If she cared – if they both cared...why would they abandon me? Was I a burden to them? Was that it? Madison was only twenty when she gave birth to me, while Ryan was twenty-two. They were more than capable of taking care of me – so why did they give me up?

Why?

Anger boiled in veins like a kettle that had been left on the stove for too long. I shoved the photos back into the folder and grabbed it, throwing it across the room in a fit of rage. Papers fell out in disarray like an explosion had gone off. I heard the hard thump of something crashing to the floor and saw a bottle of red wine rolling away on the hardwood floor, slowly coming to a stop against the wall. I marched across the room and picked it up, feeling the coldness of the bottle beneath my palm. My first thought was to smash it into smithereens and watch as the small pieces of glass spread out across the floor.

But that wouldn't be enough. I wanted to feel numb. I didn't want to remember anything. I wanted to live in the moment.

I uncorked the bottle and brought it to my lips. There was a brief moment of hesitation; a distant voice in my head questioning if this was the right thing to do.

"Screw it."

I took a swig, tasting the bitter and acrid liquid as it spread over my tongue like fire. I swallowed and the sensation only grew worse as it burned down my throat. It filled my belly with a warm, fuzzy feeling that was alerting yet, new and thrilling. I took another swig and another and soon enough the bottle became empty. I broke into my parent's liquor cabinet and grabbed an armful of bottles, not caring what they were just that I wanted them. The effects of the liquor turned my world upside down in a kaleidoscope of beautiful, colorful pictures. The images were too distorted to distinguish, but it was pretty like a fast moving picture on a projector, leaving you breathless and guessing as to what was seen a second ago.

It all became blurred the more I drank.

And drink I did.

Drinking alone was boring and no fun. Liam knows how to drink. It's his forte. Maybe I'm doing it all wrong. On t.v. it's fun, letting yourself go. There was always more than one person. What was that saying? Two is a crowd and three is a party? I shrugged. I'll go ask Liam. He would know.

I padded towards the door and opened it. The air was so cold, prickling my skin like a thousand small needles all over my body. I walked out and shut the door behind me as I made my way towards his house down the street.

I stumbled, giggling as the world swirled around me in a whirl of bright lights and never ending darkness. It was lonely and I wanted to dance, awakening the dead space around me. I twirled around in circles, my hands over my head, feeling free – like nothing could stop me. I looked up at the sky where there were lots and lots of bright, shining dots filling the atmosphere.

Pretty.

It was all so pretty.

Liam's house loomed overhead as I stood and gazed up at the structure. His bike was parked in the driveway. Thank goodness! He was home! Time to get this party started. If luck was on my side he'd even have a few cases of beer we could down. I didn't know why I hadn't tried alcohol before. It wasn't at all like the horror stories I've heard.

I walked towards his door, stumbling forward as my heel caught a crack on the pavement. Phew! That was a close call. I made a mental note to watch out for that conspicuous crack for future references. There was no telling when I'd need to recall the incident when I made a phone call to the city council and demand them to fix the crack! Someone could get seriously hurt.

I didn't see another car parked in the drive and briefly wondered where Mr. Rowley was out this late. Maybe, he was out partying too! It seemed like everyone was out having the time of their lives!

My fists bang on the door, calling out his name. "Liiiiiiiiiiiiaammmmmm. Liiiiiiiiiiiiaammmmmmm." I spun around, the air caressing my skin like a secret kiss. I giggled, twirling around and around, feeling like a bird.

I sang like a bird would; singing from the top of my lungs as I spun around in circles. "OOPSS I DID IT AGAINNN. I PLAYED WITH YOUR HEARTTTT, GOT LOST IN THE GAME. OHH BABY, BABY....HIT ME BABY ONE MORE TIME."

I giggled, feeling like I could fly as the world became a blur. "OHH BABY, BABY....HIT ME BABY ONE MORE TIME." Stupid crack, I knew I should have made a call to the mayor as soon as I saw that it was a hazard. My heel got caught in the fracture. I lost my balance and fell backwards, scraping my elbow in the process. Tears welded up in my eyes as hot, searing pain shot up my arm.

My eyes flickered to my shoe and I gasped. "Oh, no! My poor shoe! Gemma's gunna keeeeeeeeeel me."

I crawled towards my shoe and cradled it in my arm like my own little baby. "It's going to be alright. We're gunna fix you right up. Auntie Gem doesn't need to know about this. It'll be our little secret."

I jerked my head up as I heard a creaky sound that belonged to a door opening.

Liam's door.

He walked forward, his hair messy and sticking up in disarray. He looked sleepy. He had been sleeping and I had woken him from a dream of rainbow bursting unicorns like in that Ke$ha video. I sucked. He probably hated me now. I know I would hate me if I was disturbed from a dream like that. C'mon, it was unicorns!

He kneeled down, his bare chest and legs exposed in the cold air. All he had on was cotton blue boxers. I know that he was cold. I was cold and I had more clothes than he had on.

"What the hell. Anya?"

He didn't sound angry. At least, I don't think he did. But his eyes no longer held a trace of sleepiness. They were alert and focusing on me.

"I fell...I broke my shoe. Can we give my shoe a proper funeral? It's only fair. Pleasssssseee?"

By answer, Liam scooped me up in his arms and took me inside where the warmth of his house was a drastic change of temperature. In his room, he gently tossed me on the bed, where the sheets were warm and rumpled from sleep.

"Alright. Stay here."

I shook my head. "But what about my shoe? It needs a burial. It was my fault. I killed it."

He stared at me for what seemed like hours until his brow began to slowly rise. There was a flash of recognition is his beautiful eyes that made me melt. God, he was so pretty. I just wanted to run my hands through his soft messy hair...

"Stay put. I'll go make you something to bring you down."

I pouted. "But I don't want anything. I just want yo-" I shut my mouth as both his brows rose in amusement.

"You've never been drunk before, have you?"

I leaped forward and crashed into him, putting a finger to his lips. "Don't say it out loud. Someone will hear you!"

His eyes flickered around the room. "You're silly. There's no one else here." I peered around the room and saw that he was right. He took my hands in his and said, "I'll be back in a sec. Go sit down."

Liam was gone before I could protest. I was left alone to stare up at the roof where I saw stars. Did his roof come off? Is that why I could see the stars? It was pretty neat. They weren't as pretty as the ones I saw outside, though. These were green and fluorescent.

"Sit up for me." I turned my head and saw Liam perched on the edge of the bed. "I want to see how bad your fall was." I sat up and leaned my back against the wall as I watched him dig around a medium size first aid kit. He handed me a cup of hot tea and I sipped it as he got to work on the cut on my elbow. His hands were rough and calloused as he carefully disinfected the scrape with a care and precision I couldn't help but compare to a doctor. After he was done, he handed me a pair of old sweats and a t-shirt.

He turned around and I quickly changed, noting for the first time that I was covered in dirt. I didn't remember falling into dirt...did I? Everything was so fuzzy.

"Alright, you dressed?"

"Mhmm."

He turned around, closing the gap between us. "Okay. I'm going to take you home, alright?"

"No....no...you can't." My voice trembled as I remembered there was something at home that I was scared of.

His brows furrowed in confusion. "Why not?"

"Because.....because there's...there's something......under my b ed....."

He frowned, taking my hand and leading me towards the bed where I sat down, tucking my legs underneath me.

"Where are your parents?"

I sucked on my lip. "Teacher's Convention."

"No one's home?"

"Do you think the boogeyman will eat me if they're not?!" My eyes widened and I clapped a hand over my mouth. In a hushed whisper I said, "Don't tell Mr. Boogey I said that they're not home."

He smiled, biting his lip. He was trying to suppress the laugh that bubbled up in his throat. I stared wide eyed as he openly mocked me. My reaction only seemed to press him further and he finally broke like a dam, overflowing with a fit of rumbling laughter.

"This is serious business, Liam! Serious seriousness!"

He laughed. "Better yet, leaving you home alone might not be a good idea. You'll probably hurt yourself. You can sleep in here, I'll take the floor."

"I can take care of myself..." Even as I said the words I knew it was no use. I couldn't go home! The Boogey Man was there, waiting to kill me!

"Fine. But I think we should take cover. He might come over and get us both."

He shook his head and leaned forward, putting his hands on both sides of my cheeks. His hands were warm, sending small waves of heat coursing through my body. "Nothing is going to hurt you. Not while I'm here. Understand?"

I nodded. He didn't let go and I didn't move away. He stared at me, his eyes growing intense by the minute. My eyes lingered from his eyes to the shape of his full curved lips. Without thinking, I crushed my lips to his. For a split second, he was taken aback – not knowing what to do – but then his hands wrapped around my waist, pulling me closer to him. The smell of wood and smoke filled my senses. My hand ran through the soft tousled waves of his hair as his hands slid up and down my back, pressing me to him.

The kiss grew feverish with a hunger that I had never known. He was the water I had been blindly searching for years on end, never knowing exactly what I was looking for. He was...

Liam began to pull away and I protested, fighting to keep holding on to him. But he was much stronger than I was.

"No..." His voice is husky, making me want to kiss him again. "We can't...we can't do this."

"Why?" I pouted.

"Because..." He ran a hand through his hair in exasperation. "Because you're drunk."

That doesn't seem like a very good answer to me. "Soooo....?"

"So, I'm exerting a lot of self control right now and if you keep doing that I won't be able to help myself and you'll hate both of us later."

I shrank back, realization hitting me like huge meteor rock. "You don't want me." I backed away from him, putting as much distance between us. I couldn't hide the pain in my voice at his rejection. It was clear what he wanted. It was clear what kind of girls he preferred. Blond and with a big bust. "If....if I was Karla you'd want me right now."

He shook his head, reaching forward but I cringed away. "You're not her. I wouldn't be taking Karla's virginity."

I crossed my arms over my chest. "What do you know?" I questioned. He didn't know me. He didn't know me at all.

"I know you're too good for any of the guys in our school, for one."

I scoffed. "Including you?"

"Especially me."

I looked up and saw the distorted image of him before me. I shook my head, trying to get rid of the sudden dizziness that fogged my head. I felt his arm wrap around my body and the feeling of his muscled chest beneath my hand.

"What's going on...? Why am I...?"

"Shh...no more talking. It's time for sleep. Go to sleep, Anya."

My eyelids were heavy and it was exertion just trying to keep them open. "I...feel....so...tired..."

"Shh....sleep, Anya. Sleep. I'll be right here when you wake."

His words were comforting, like the lull of waves crashing on the shore. I settled into the warmth of his embrace, letting the heavy pull of fatigue take me under.

Chapter 18

Anya

The sound of a blaring alarm in my ear startled me awake. I groaned, picking up my pillow and covering my head, muffling the annoying ringing sound. It was too loud and my head....oh it hurt tenfold. It wasn't anywhere near a jack hammer – like when I had my infamous headaches, but more like a bulldozer that just kept coming back with full force until I was crushed into a bloody pulp.

There was a grunt and the sound of sheets rustling on the ground followed by a sleep induced voice saying, "Anya? Will you turn that off?"

I lifted my left hand from under the covers and searched the nightstand for the maddening sound. My hand curled around the rectangular shape, my fingers searching the familiar snooze button. It wasn't there. I threw my covers aside and sat up, squinting against the rays of sunlight seeping through the blinds.

Blinds. Not. Curtains.

My eyes widened as I realized where I was. The steady pulse of my heart quickened as I saw Liam's curled form on the floor. How did I get there? What happened? Why was I wearing his clothes?!

As my hysteria grew, so did the pounding in my head and the sudden queasiness in my stomach. I untangled myself from the mess of sheets and perched on the edge of the bed. My toes grazed the cool, wooden floorboards. My eyes flickered to Liam, his back was to me and I couldn't see if he was sleeping or just pretending. Surely, he could hear my heart beating tenfold like it was going to fall out any minute.

I stood up slowly, the gnawing sick feeling in my stomach intensifying. I rushed to the bathroom, stumbling across the hall and shutting the door behind me. Sinking to my knees, I grasped the side of the toilet and heaved last night's continents into the shiny, white surface. Tears welded in my eyes as I retched, my back arching and constricting from the pain.

There was a soft knock on the door. "Anya? Let me in."

"Nooo..." My voice shook and I heard the rattling of the door knob before Liam opened the door and walked in.

"I'm f-f-fine. I'm just s-s-sick," I told him. He didn't leave. I swallowed, scrunching my nose as the bile slid down my throat. It only caused me to heave once more into to the toilet. Liam sat on the edge of the tub and pulled my hair away from my face, patting my back in a slow, soothing circular motion. I breathed in and out, trying to get my bearing straight. The shaking in my hands lessened after what seemed like an hour, but it couldn't have been more than ten minutes.

Liam handed me some toilet paper and I blew my nose and wiped my mouth free of any slimy residue. He silently left afterwards, only to return with a pair of jeans and fresh boxers in his hands as I washed my mouth clean with fresh water.

I saw him lean against the doorway, his reflection clear in the mirror ahead of me. "How much did you drink?"

My brows furrowed. Drink?

Distorted images of the night before flashed in my mind's eye. I remembered the first bottle I drank and then it got hazy; there was me walking to Liam's house and singing, awfully singing; his arms wrapped around me as he carried me inside after falling; the warmth of his arms as I lost consciousness. There was more…there was more that happened, but I couldn't remember.

"Anya?"

I looked up and met his gaze in the mirror. His eyes were unwavering, two misty blue pools of awaiting expectancy.

I turned around, leaning my body against the sink. A lock of hair escaped from my low ponytail as I turned and I tucked it behind my ears, unable to meet his eyes as I answered, "A bottle of wine…maybe two…I don't remember."

He shook his head, a sly smile on his lips. "You're a light weight of the worst kind."

I crossed my arms over my chest, hating the smirk on his face. "Of course, with my first time drinking and all, who wouldn't be?" I snapped.

He held up his hands in mock surrender. "You could kill a guy with that stare. I was just stating the obvious."

I shook my head, rubbing at my temple in a circular motion. This was all too much. What had I gotten myself into?

Liam cleared his throat and I looked up to see him coming into the bathroom and setting his clothes on top of the laundry basket. I took the hint and quietly exited, stumbling a little as my vision blurred. Liam's hand curled around my arm, while his other hand gently pressed itself on the small of my back, leaving a trail of heat in its wake.

"Easy there," he walked me across the hall to his bedroom and helped me sit down on his bed. The headache was returning, but instead of it being a bulldozer it was more like an annoying ringing that I couldn't turn off. Liam left my side for a few seconds and return with a bottle of water in hand.

"Thanks." I hadn't known how parched I was until I took a drink and guzzled the cool, fresh water like it was the last drop on earth.

"There's more in the fridge if you want more. So, I-" A sheepish smile curved his lips as he rubbed the back of his neck. "Stay here, okay? Just...I'll take you home before work, alright?"

I felt the furrow in my eyebrows deepen as I stared at him. Slowly and evenly I said, "I don't need taking care of."

He scoffed, obviously finding my response amusing. "Right." Liam crossed his arms over his chest and shook his head, his slate-blue eyes piercing as if his mind was calculating something – something that concerned me. I folded my arms in front of me, not liking the way he was looking at me. I felt vulnerable – like a work of art he was carefully examining.

Ha. A work of art. I really should consider a job as a comedian. I'd earn big bucks.

The sound of a door closing startled me out of my thoughts. When I looked up I saw that Liam was gone and heard the sudden start of water reverberating through the vents. I sighed and flopped backwards, looking up at the ceiling. In the light of the day the plastic glow in the dark stars were a ghostly white. There were so many of them that I felt compelled to count each and every one of them until I grew weary.

I tried to remember everything that happened last night, but couldn't. I don't know what logic brought me to Liam's house or what my brain was thinking to stay over. Did something happen? Surely, if something happened I would remember. Right? But even if something did happen – he wouldn't have done...

No. It wasn't possible. It was absurd to even think it.

I sat up abruptly and crossed my legs before me, bowing my head and interlocking my hands together. I closed my eyes, breathing in and out evenly until I felt relaxed and at peace; a feeling that I hadn't felt in a long time.

Softly, I came forward and uttered my plea for forgiveness. It wasn't just last night that I prayed to be forgiven for, but also for the way I had been acting towards my parents. I asked God to take away all the resentfulness I'd felt the passed few days and to help me find the strength to forgive them as He would forgive me. I poured out my heart, feeling the sting of tears in my eyes.

"I feel as if I have lost myself in light of everything. My momentarily lapse of judgment...and I just don't know what to do. I know they love me, Father, I know it...but why...why would my real parents give me up? Was it because of me? Was it because I was sick and they couldn't take care of me?" I wiped the tears that cascaded down my cheeks with the back of my hand; the pounding in head receding to a low hum.

"I just ask that you help me, Father. Give me strength to keep moving forward, to keep on living for as long as it is written in your hand. Thank you...thank you," I smiled looking up at the ceiling, "for always being there for me, for listening to me when I need someone to talk to or even listening to the silent unspoken prayers of my heart. Thank you, Father.

In Jesus' name, Amen."

I breathed out a heavy sigh of relief; feeling like a weight had been lifted from my shoulders. Standing up, I arched my back and stretched like a Cheshire cat. My eyes roamed Liam's room until I found my clothes next to his desk covered in dirt. I found my black leather boots, one of its heels deterred, broken.

I sighed, "Gemma is going to kill me. She bought them on sale just last week. I wonder if I can fix them with super glue..."

The sound of Liam clearing his throat put a stop to my mumblings. I turned my head and the sight of him made my breath caught in my throat. A towel was wrapped around his neck, soaking up the excessive water dripping from his hair. His face was unshaven, darkening the strong line of his jaw and upper lip. He looked rugged, undeniably sexy. Rivulets of water snaked down his chest to the vee of his...oh, goodness. I looked away.

"You know," he said. I could practically see the smirk sliding unto his lips. "If you wanted to see me naked, you could have just asked."

"Don't you ever get cold?" I asked exasperated, hoping that he didn't see the heat rise to my cheeks. "It's a bit drafty in here. You should definitely put a shirt on."

He chuckled. "That's not what you said last night."

I whirled around and gaped at him. "We didn't- we didn't do anything...?" My voice broke into a squeak as I saw him smiling and then wink at me.

"Most girls," he said taking a seat on the edge of his bed. He slid the towel off his neck and ran it through his hair casually with a grin playing on his lips. "Well, most girls come on to me when their drunk...you-" I held my breath. "You wanted me to orchestrate a funeral for your shoe and protect you from the boogey man."

I exhaled the air out of my lungs like a deflated hot air balloon. "And that's all that happened?"

He quirked an eyebrow, apprehension flashing in his eyes. Slowly he asked, "What do you remember?"

I eyed him suspiciously and shrugged. "Not much. It's all so...disconcerting. My head hurts trying to remember." Which it did. My head was beginning to pound just trying to recall last night's chain of events.

Pushing himself up from bed, he sauntered towards the closet and drew on a black v-neck t-shirt that hugged his body nicely. It looked like he was about to bust out of his shirt like the Incredible Hulk when he got angry or transformed. Except, Liam wasn't angry or (to my knowledge) the Incredible Hulk...his biceps were just bulging when he flexed and...

Oh, goodness. I had to stop thinking of him in that way. Snap out of it, Anya! It's not like you haven't seen him half naked before. It shouldn't be a seventh wonder of the world.

Liam's eyes focused on something behind me and I followed his gaze to the alarm clock and read that it 8: 24. Was it really that early? And on a Saturday for that matter! It should be illegal to be up this early.

"Let's get you home."

I nodded, feeling a drop of disappointment seep into my soul. I didn't want to go, but there were things Liam had to do. I couldn't overstep my boundaries no matter how much I wanted to feel safe and warm in his arms. At least, that was a good memory I recalled for last night before sleep claimed my weary mind.

We walked the short distance to my house, the cool autumn morning nipping my skin. He walked me to the door where the knob turned underneath my hand, vaguely remembering that I had just walked out the previous night. God, I really hoped no one decided to do a crime spree and hit my house.

"Try not to get into any trouble while I'm gone."

"Believe me," I said opening the door and stepping through the threshold. "It was a one in a lifetime gig. Never. Happening. Again."

He crossed his arms, his mouth tight as he tried to suppress a smile. "Whatever helps you sleep at night. I'll see you later."

I opened my mouth to refute his allegation, but he was already walking down the steps and heading towards his house. The last thing I saw before I closed the door was his hands in the front pockets of his jeans and his shoulders rumbling with laughter.

Liam

"Pretty light day of work, huh, son?"

I wiped a bead of sweat from my forehead with my arm and glanced up to see a wiry smile on Jimmy's mouth. There was a smidge of oil running on his forehead and an old rusty maroon rag between his hands as he cleaned the top layer of oil off his hands.

I grunted, twisting the wrench in my hands to get a bolt tightened around the compressor. "Yeah, hardly anyone's come in." My eyes racked the engine, checking to see that all was fixed and ready to go for pickup early tomorrow morning. To my satisfaction, I was finished and closed the hood. Jimmy threw me a rag (one of many that littered the shop) and I caught it, wiping my hands.

"You should get going, kid. It's a beautiful day and not meant to be spent in an ol' musty garage. Don't you got some pretty girl to take out?"

I forced a laugh. Jimmy was a middle aged man who still took his wife out every Saturday night for 50's Night at Darcy's. He gave me a hard time on the Saturdays I got called in to work, asking if I had a girl and if I was giving her the world in the palm of her hands. The old man was crazy – stuck in ye' olden days.

I shook my head. "No...there's no girl."

He stared at me, looking me over as if he'd found something he'd never seen before. "What's her name? And don't lie to me, boy."

My shoulders sagged forward and I breathed out her name. "Anya. Her name's Anya."

Jimmy's brows rose a meter. "Phillip's little girl?" I nodded and he whistled, a crooked smile lifting the corners of his lips. "That Vanchester girl. Goes 'ta my church. Sweet little thing, easy on the eyes for ya I bet."

"It's not like that," I said, throwing the towel into a bin. "She's...well, she's..."

His smile turned into a grin and was nodding his head like a broken bobblehead. "She's da reason 'yer were late this morning, ain't it?" I didn't answer because it was true. "From what I just saw the tone of 'yer voice says 'yer smitten with her."

I laughed. His accent was thick; reminding me how old the bat was; too old to be fixin' cars and whatnot. Teasing him I said, "What do you know, old man?"

Striding forward, he put his hand on my shoulder. He was a good two inches shorter than me, age welting his stature. "I was in 'yer shoes fifty years ago. Made her mine, never looked back, 'n never been happier."

"In case you've forgotten, old man," his eyebrows rose at my tone and he reeled back as if I had physically hit him in the heart with an arrow. I laughed, never getting tired of the old man's theatrics. "It's not ye' olden days. Things are different and…it's not like that."

"Sure it ain't. Just don't go breakin' her heart, pretty boy. Girls like this Anya don't come around oft'n."

I shook my head. It was no use arguing with Jimmy. He was stuck in his old ways. Back then it might have been alright for a guy to profess his love for a girl, but nowadays if a guy confessed his love for a girl he barely knew – she would take it as a joke or worse, run towards the hills faster than the Roadrunner.

"What are yer' still doing here?" I looked up and saw him smiling like a mad man. "Go on. Get outta here, boy! I'll see ya Monday."

He didn't have to tell me twice. I said bye to the old man and headed out the shop, hopping onto my bike and burning rubber. It was only five o'clock last time I checked and there were only two stops I needed to make before I went to see how Anya was doing. If luck was on my side, I hoped to find her well and not in harm's way. Who knows what kind of trouble she could have gotten into in the eight hours since I left her.

I rang the doorbell, my hair slicked wet from the quick shower I grabbed before heading over to her house with a box of Charlie's famous pizza in hand. There was no answer and after a minute I rang the doorbell again and again and again until the door opened.

Anya glared at me, an ice pack covered around a multiple array of paper towels held up to her head. "Will you stop that? It's quite annoying and loud."

She opened the door wider and let me through, closing it behind me. "Damn. You look like hell." There were deep circles around her eyes, her hair was in a messy bun and she was wearing a pair of old sweats and a tank top. Sweat beaded her forehead despite the coolness of the ice pack on it. I worried that she might have a fever or alcohol poisoning. God knows how much she took a liberty to drink last night.

"I feel like it."

She led me towards the kitchen, where I set the box down and grabbed two dishes from the cabinets. "I figured Gemma would be around, taking care of you."

She smiled, her eyes hazed over as if recalling a memory. "I scared her off."

I licked my lips, the deliciousness of pepperoni and cheese drifting to my nostrils. "I'm not surprised, I'm a little scared."

She stuck her tongue out at me and grabbed a plate that was meant for me. It was loaded with four slices. "That was mine."

She inspected the plate. "Really? I don't see your name on it." Anya dug in, taking a bite. "Mmm...this is so good. Thanks. I was starving."

"I figured. You sure you're gonna eat all that?" I asked around a mouthful of pizza.

She slowly slid the plate towards her protectively and eyed me warily. "Yes...yes I am."

I shrugged and we ate in silence. Anya practically ravished the slices and opt out for more. She was rubbing her belly and grumbling to show her discomfort. I knew she shouldn't have ate that much. She was small and there was only so much space that food could occupy in a small body.

I threw the box away in the trash while she picked up our plates and offered me a can of coke. The soda tingled my throat as I swallowed. I pursed my lips and heard Anya laughing. "What?"

"You make the weirdest face, like you just ate something sour."

My brows furrowed as I watched her, trying to figure her out. After the meal she looked better. Some color had return to her skin and I hoped that the alcohol had gone through and out of her system. There was only one thing that I questioned: Why did she do it? It just seemed...out of character for her to lower her guard and drink without having the intention to stop. What if she hadn't had the thought to come to my house? Who knows what would have happened then.

I took a shot and tossed my can into the trash, scoring. "Impressive."

I shrugged, nonchalantly. "Oh. I almost forgot," I said, remembering that I had something of hers in my bike. I walked hastily towards the door and heard her footsteps behind me. "Wait here." Marching to where my bike was parked in the driveway, I lifted my seat to grab Anya's forgotten and broken shoe. I had only found this one in my bedroom and looked for its pair, but it was nowhere to be found.

Closing the door behind me, I looked for Anya in the kitchen but she was gone. The next place I looked was in the living room. She was sitting on the loveseat with her legs folded underneath her.

"We need to talk."

Anya straightened up and asked attentively, "About what?" Her voice held a tinge of hysteria and I couldn't place why she was freaking out. What had I said?

I pulled out the shoe from behind my back and in the most serious tone I could muster in this kind of situation I said, "It's time to let go."

Anya lifted an eyebrow, her eyes flickering from the shoe to my face every couple of seconds. "Hilarious," she said without a trace of amusement.

Tough crowd.

"It's one of my many talents."

She rolled her eyes and pushed herself up from the loveseat, striding over to me and taking the shoe from my hand. "What are you doing?"

She strode into the kitchen and hovered the shoe above the trashcan. "Throwing it away. I've come to terms that it can't be fixed."

I snatched it from her hands and she exclaimed, "Hey!" Anya jumped, trying to reach it from my hands as I playfully toyed her with it like a cat wanting a ball of string. "You suck. You're way taller than me! It's practically cheating."

I tsked. "Sorry. Not my fault for the genes I've been given."

She gave up and put her hands on her hips, glaring at me. I laughed and turned on my heels, walking towards the back of her house, and opening the sliding door that lead to her backyard. I found a good patch of dirt and begin to dig a small hole, deep enough to bury her shoe.

"You can't be serious," she mumbled, sinking down to her knees to help me.

"You're the one who asked this of me. I am just holding up my end of the bargain."

"I was drunk! All the things I said or did are not liable. Drunk people can't be trusted!"

I laughed, not buying into any of that crap. I was more or less an expert on being intoxicated and when a person was drunk their inhibitions were down. It was a sober man's deepest desires uttered from a drunk man's lips. In this case, woman – but nevertheless...she didn't remember...she didn't remember that we kissed and I wasn't going to be the one to tell her.

But this? Burying her shoe? Well, I could definitely impart this small detail. When the hole was finished, I laid the shoe in the ground and pushed myself up. Anya followed my lead, dusting dirt off from her knees.

"Any last words?"

She hummed. "Other than...you're a jackass?"

I put my hand over my heart as if she had shot me. "I'm hurt."

"Right."

"It's true. I've seen the error of my smartass ways. I thought we were friends."

There was a smile playing on her lips but she tried her best to fight it. "If by friend you mean someone who'd just as soon drop an anvil on, then yeah...we're friends."

I gaped at her. "You don't mean that."

"Find me an anvil and watch me go."

I pouted. "You're a grumpy post drunk."

"Screw you."

I chuckled. "Name the time and place, babe." A second hadn't even passed before I uttered the words and she was already smacking my arm.

"Is that all you ever think about? Gees!"

"Nope. I think a lot about food and then its sex...then maybe cute little kittens."

She looked at me incredulously "Now you're just messing with me." Anya looked down at the ground, tapping her foot impatiently. "So are we going to do this or not?"

I motioned for her to go first and she sighed. "RIP Anya when Gemma finds out I broke you. At least, you're being given a proper burial. She won't bother with formalities. I'd end up in a ditch somewhere."

A breeze picked up and she hugged herself. Quickly I said my peace. "I didn't know you for long but you were a good shoe, very supportive, but ultimately destructive towards Anya's balance." She huffed and punched me. I rubbed the spot in mock hurt and slowly knelt, covering the shoe with dirt until it disappeared into the earth.

Anya shivered in her winter boots and we treaded back into the house, the warmth comforting in light of the cool night air. I stole a glance at a clock on the wall, noting that it was still early.

"Got any movies?" I asked, following her up the stairs and into her room. She grabbed a light jacket and drew it on.

"Yeah. Behind you."

I turned around and rummaged through her bookshelf. "Sweet. You have the original Nightmare On Elm's Street."

"Mhm...you know how I like my horrors."

I remembered. She had always hated the modern horror films; they didn't have the same air of fear that the 80's portrayed.

We shuffled downstairs where I popped in the movie and Anya went in search for some snacks. She came back with a bag of Redvines and two fresh cans of coke. She set our refreshments down on the coffee table and left again. I settled back into the sofa, propping my legs on the table and grabbing some licorice.

Anya returned shortly after with two sets of blankets in hand, setting them between us. I felt her weight shift on the settee as she wrapped a blanket around her lap.

The movie began, my attention wavering from Freddy Krueger mauling one of his victims with his razor sharp claws to Anya, stiffening in her seat and covering her eyes with the blanket. I found it amusing, yet interesting to say the least. She loved scary movies – that was a given fact, but she was frightened of them to the point that she was afraid to go to bed.

I remembered the first time we watched Nightmare On Elm Street. We were ten and Anya's parents were gone for the weekend, leaving her at my house for two days. We ate chocolate, popcorn, candy corn, and a bunch of other things that made us sick to our stomachs. She thought it would be a good idea to watch the movie, saying and I quote, "C'mon. What are you? Chicken? I bet you five bucks that it's not even scary."

Damn was she wrong. I don't think I got a wink of sleep that night as we strategized a plan to stay awake and not sleep or else Freddy would get us in our dreams. The only good thing I got out of that day was the five bucks she owed me.

Time passed and soon the movie was over. I offered to grab another movie and she agreed. When I came back downstairs she was nestled into the sofa like a small bird, warm and safe in a nest. She was still awake, barely – her eyes half closed as she feigned sleep.

Three episodes later of the first season of Supernatural and Anya hadn't said a word. Her chest rose in slow even breaths and she murmured something incomprehensible. Her face was serene, unmarked by the frowns that creased her forehead when she was thinking or the way she bit her lip, making my heart pound heavily in my chest. A lock of hair lingered on her face, hindering her small porcelain face. I reached forward, tucking the strand behind her ear.

"Anya?"

She didn't move. I don't know what made me do what I did next, but it felt right. My thumb traced the contours of her delicate face – embedding this moment clearly in my memory. I traced the outline of her brows, and left the feeling of her soft plump lips until last. Lips that tasted of sweet strawberries, lips that I had kissed last night, but she hadn't the faintest idea about what occurred.

"Will you stay?"

Her soft voice startled me and I reeled back, my heart pounding as I was caught red handed. Anya didn't open her eyes, and I didn't know if she was sleep talking or was asking me a question as she tethered between consciousness and sleep.

In a gentle whispering voice I asked, "Do you want me to?"

She nodded her head. She had been sleeping, but I had waken her. "Mhm. You have to protect me from the monsters...like old times."

A smile spread onto my lips, recalling all the times we camped out in our backyards; flashlights in hand and Mr. Cuddles between us as we warded of the monsters that watched us after the sun went down. We couldn't have been older than seven.

"Alright," I said.

I grabbed the blanket she'd brought for me and turned off the lights before settling into the sofa adjacent to her. It might have been a figment of my imagination but I could have sworn that I saw Anya slightly open her eyes, peering into the darkness to make sure that I was really staying. I wouldn't have left her, not now when she was in such a fragile state of mind.

She said I had left her when I believed that she was the one who abandoned me. I don't know what went wrong. It might have been a mistake made on both our parts and neither was wholly to blame. Whatever happened, it was all in the past. I wouldn't leave her again, not when she needed me the most.

I just wished she knew that.

Chapter 19

Liam

The rich, delicious smell of pancakes woke me from my slumber. I sat up, rubbing the sleep from my eyes. Shuffling into the kitchen, I saw Anya whipping up a fresh batch of chocolate chip pancakes like she intended to feed an army. Her hair was pulled to the side in a messy braid as she silently hummed a tune to a song I didn't recognize.

I leaned against the frame of the door, crossing my arms over my chest and watched her. There was an extra spring to her step as she sang and shimmied around like no one was watching. It was a different side of her; one where her guard was completely down and anyone could walk straight to the door and knock, knowing they'd be welcomed, knowing that they wouldn't receive the door slammed in their face and rejected.

Anya twirled on her toe and let out a shriek, reeling backwards with her hand to her heart. "You scared me!"

I ran a hand through my messy hair, a smile tugging at the corners of my mouth. "That's not the response I generally receive in the morning. It's more like 'oh Liam, take me now.'"

With an eye roll, she shook her head and wiped her hands on the Kiss The Cook apron she wore. "So," I said, stepping forward.

My eyes locked with hers as the thought of pulling Anya to me and kissing her played in my mind. She was undeniably beautiful, the kind of beauty that wasn't seen right away until you learn to appreciate it for what it's worth. God. How I wanted to kiss her and feel the softness of her lips on mine, the curves and warmth of her body as I pulled her closer. She must've saw something primal in my eyes, because with a shaky laugh, she gestured to the food.

"Um...you want some pancakes?" she asked, turning her back to me. She stacked four on a plate and slid it across the counter effortlessly like she was an experienced chef.

I grabbed a fork and dug in, moaning at the mouthwatering goodness. "These are good. I didn't know you cooked."

She turned the stove off and grabbed a plate, sitting across from me. There was a twinkle in her eye when she said, "There's a lot you don't know about me."

"Like?"

"Like that I want to be a ninja."

I smiled. "I don't believe you."

"It's true! It's my life's goal to reach that level of awesomeness." She laughed, taking a bite and washing it down with milk. "What about you?"

I took a drink of OJ and said, "I'm an open book. Guess."

She scoffed. "Yeah. Right. Hmm...in that case." There was a glint of mischief in her eyes. "You secretly want to be a...girl."

I ran a hand down my mouth. "That's exactly it. Then I could look at myself naked. Like in that Scooby-Doo movie where Fred switched-"

"You hated that movie."

I smirked. "Daphne was fine. The things I'd like to-"

She held up her palm. "Okay! Forget that we ever had this conversation." She gave out a shaky laugh and got up from the stool, proceeding to wash her dishes.

I stuffed the remaining pieces of delicious fluffiness and washed it down with juice. Visions of a 1950s America television show starring Anya as the little woman, home cooking, and me as the man out earning a paycheck flitted through my head. It was a bit surreal. She swiftly came around and slid the plate and empty glass from their place in front of me and washed them in ten seconds flat. She was like a superhero. Maybe she did have what it took to be a ninja.

"So, umm...what are you doing today?"

I shrugged. "Nothing. Why? Can't get enough of me?"

She rolled her eyes and threw the dish towel at me. I caught it swiftly and she stuck her tongue out at me.

"Very mature."

"Shut up."

My eyebrows shot up in amusement. "Feisty."

She pressed her lips together, trying to suppress the smile that edged its way unto her lips.

"I was thinking," she began, balancing back and forth on her toes, "that we could maybe go into town and you could...help me with something?"

I arched an eyebrow, seeing the tiniest amount of hope, hesitation, and embarrassment all swirling together in her eyes. My interests piqued, wondering what she had brewing inside her head. One thing was certain – if she thought I would bail she was sadly mistaken.

"What do you have in mind?"

The bell jingled, signaling our entry into the empty shop. Mr. Edison turned, his grim expression turning into an ear to ear grin.

"Anya! Liam! What a pleasant surprise!" He rushed over and enveloped Anya and me in a bear hug. We shared a conspiratorial look, smiling at the old man's kind heart.

"What brings you in on Sunday?" he asked Anya.

"I wanted to ask you for a favor."

He laid a gentle, weathered, old hand on her shoulder. "Go ahead and use the piano. Sunday's are usually slow. I take it that's what you're here for."

She nodded. "Then go for it kid."

Anya hopped with excitement and kissed the old man on the cheek. "Thank you!"

He chuckled, crossing his arms over his chest as we watched her run to the other side of the room, taking her place on the bench.

"What I'd give to have her lay one on me."

Mr. Edison turned towards me, his gray brows hitched upwards in complete and utter shock. I hadn't realized that I said that out loud and felt the blood rushing to my face. I coughed, clearing my throat. "Sorry."

"Mhm." He patted my shoulder, striding towards the counter. He turned around, inclining his head for me to follow. I did, setting down the black case that held Hayden's video equipment. My job for today was playing cameraman for Anya's application/audition tape.

The harmony of chords filled the room as Anya warmed up. Mr. Edison leaned forward, and in a low tone said, "It can be done."

My brows lifted in inquiry. "Really?"

"Yes. It's won't be cheap, kid. What you're asking...it's more than a pretty penny."

"How much?" I asked.

"About two hundred."

I dragged a hand down my mouth, feeling the scruff from not shaving. "When will it be here?"

"Depends. Have you got a song yet?"

I nodded. My ears perked, hearing the very song I had in mind playing. I turned, watching Anya as she played the melody with the same fervor I had seen in the dark, empty theater. She became one with the music, her hands flying over the keys; the notes twisting and winding to form a story, warping into words, pictures.

"Liam?"

I turned back around and faced Edison's knowing smile. "Ah. River Flows In You. It's one of her favorites, you know. It's modern, harmonious, melodic, beautiful...Yet, it has that classic vibe that draws you right in like a mouse to a square piece of cheese."

I chuckled. "You're hungry, aren't you?"

He patted his round belly. "You bet I am. Haven't had breakfast other than the loaf of banana bread I got an hour ago."

"That's not very filling."

He chuckled. "You got that right, son."

The music abruptly stopped and we both turned our attention to Anya, who was openly eyeing us warily. "What?" we said simultaneously, which only made us even more suspicious. She shrugged and resumed to play a different tune – this time it was classical.

Once we were positive that Anya's attention was solely on her music, Edison and I proceeded to our business arrangement. "So, River Flows In You?"

I nodded. "Have you finished the diagram?"

He beamed, his gray eyes shining with excitement. He crouched down, taking out the ring of keys from his pocket and finding the right one that lead to a safe, hidden beneath a secret compartment in the glass show case. He unrolled – what looked like an old piece of parchment – over the glass counter. My eyes racked over the drawing, finding that everything was better than I had hoped to imagine.

Anya

They were up to something, and I didn't like it.

I needed to get to the bottom of it – do some sleuthing later on in the day.

But for now, I needed to concentrate on the first piece I'd chosen from Bach. I closed my eyes, feeling Liam's gaze on me as he filmed me playing by memory. The piece was light, articulate in every way possible with a meticulous rhythm that I was familiar with. As the song progressed, it became heavier, the notes lower in range and pitch. There was another change, the composition slowing down to a hauntingly beautiful melody – like something you'd hear being played at an opening gala back in the early 1800's.

I played the piece at least a dozen times, my heart swelling with each note that escaped the piano. Time seeped right through my fingers. I lost track of reality, lost in my own world where music was the air that I breathed with every fiber of my being.

There was a change in the atmosphere, breaking my concentration for the slightest fragment. I opened my eyes and saw Liam sitting next to me on the bench, his slate-blue eyes solely trained on me. I paused for a moment, giving him a side glance.

"What?"

"I think we've got enough footage."

I completely stopped, sighing. His hands were free and from the corner of my eye I saw the video camera propped to the side, the green light that signaled recording was off.

"What time is it?"

"Almost four."

Grabbing my music from the stand, I silently began to pack up. I took a quick look around the shop and noticed that Mr. Edison was nowhere in sight. Liam must have guessed what I was thinking and said, "He left about an hour ago. Said you'd be here awhile. The man was not joking."

I twirled the ends of my hair around my finger, feeling a little embarrassed. "I-I...you could have gone home too. I wouldn't have minded." I flashed a small smile. "Plus, I bet you stopped filming hours ago."

"I did. But it's not the reason I didn't leave."

I cocked my head to the side, my eyes focusing on anything but the lingering look he cast when I asked, "And what was that?"

He stepped forward, tilting my chin so that I had no choice but to look at the intensity in his eyes. My skin grew warm at his touch – like a fire slowly spreading to my cheeks. I knew he saw the blush, but he didn't make a joke or even an offhand comment about it. He was serious, which only made my heart beat loudly in my ears like a thundering war drum.

"Selfishness."

The word alone stirred confusion, my brows knitting together as I tried to understand. A sliver of a smile formed on his lips, his eyes becoming softer, losing their note of seriousness. He grazed his thumb over my brow and I closed my eyes, melting under his touch.

"I wanted to be with you."

I slowly opened my eyes, afraid that I'd imagined those words. I expected to see a smirk on his face, signaling me that he was pulling my leg. But instead I was met with two soft pools of gray, filled with a sincerity I had thought was gone forever.

The boy I had known was back.

He was truly back, and didn't have plans on leaving anytime soon.

I smiled, taking his hand in mine, feeling the roughness that marred his strong hand as I grazed my thumb along his palm. He pulled me to him, and I nestled my head against his chest, still holding his hand.

"And here you are," I whispered, my voice muffled by his shirt. "Here you are."

Chapter 20

By the end of the day, I decided to tell Liam about my adoption. I'd been thinking about it since we went to Billy's Ice Cream Parlor after leaving the music shop. We'd split a large waffle of Rocky Road dosed with sprinkles and miniature marshmallows. It had been like old times, sitting in the parlor listening to Frank Sinatra's jazzy hits. I had to fight him in order to get any ice cream myself. The boy was a monster when it came to sweets, ravishing spoonfuls of deliciousness, while I had to fend for myself. At one point I even hogged the waffle and took several bites. But that failed miserably. The next second I was assaulted with a brain freeze and Liam's ringing laughter.

I don't know what changed between us, but I glad that it was this way. I just hoped that it wouldn't end once school began first thing tomorrow morning.

I told Liam to stay put in the living room, while I fetched the folder from Dad's study. I clutched the file to my chest; memories of Friday surfaced in my mind as I saw the documents flutter to the floor; anger blinding rationality and logic.

Shuffling back into the room, Liam's gaze settled on me, his eyes shifting downward to the file in my hands. I took a deep breath, settling into the seat next to him. My fingers drummed on the folder, doubt surfacing in my mind. What would he think? What would he even say? There were no words of consolation to say to something like this. I hadn't even mentioned the folder to Gemma when she came over yesterday. We were too busy cleaning up the mess I made on the kitchen floor. It was then that I vowed never to drink ever again in my life.

Gemma left shortly after as I was in no condition to talk about anything in particular – though I did remember the distinct look of disappointment and resignation in her eyes.

"The suspense is killing me, babe."

I bit my lip, turning my attention to him. "What did I tell you about calling me babe?"

His voice was terse when he said, "I don't know. I wasn't listening."

I grunted in annoyance.

"I'm joking, babe."

I threw my hands up in the air. "Stop saying that!"

An easy going smiled slipped onto his lips. He covered his ears with his hands and took on a look that only a ten year old could master. "I can't hear youuuu."

I grabbed the nearest object in close proximity to me (which was a throw pillow) and flung it at him. "Hey! Careful with the cargo!"

I rolled my eyes. He was such a jerk.

Liam chuckled, sighing in mock defeat. "Okay. So what's this about? The suspense is killing me. Please don't tell me you have like three months to live. It would explain the..."

He trailed off, his eyes flickering to the floor.

My eyes had widened at his assumption, but only because it was painfully close to the truth. But then…"What are you talking about? Explain what?"

He rubbed the back of his neck, his voice gruff and low when he said, "I-It's nothing…so what's in the folder?" His hand reached out to grab it from my hands, but I snatched it away. I stood up, hands on my hips as I looked down at him with a look that made him flinch.

"Okay, okay," he said. He breathed out a deep sigh, leaning forward to rest his elbows on his thighs. "Remember when I stayed over to take care of you when you fell sick at school?" I nodded, remembering that day clearly. "I had some downtime and I couldn't help but notice the list on your desk."

"You read my bucket list!" I accused. "How…what…" I closed my mouth, unable to form a coherent sentence. His mouth lifted into a crooked smiling, finding amusement in my incredulity. I paced the small area, until a light flickered inside my mind.

I turned on my heel, squinting at him. "Is that the reason you took me cliff jumping? Because you knew I wanted to do it?"

He rose, coming to stand right in front of me. He brushed away a lock of hair from my cheek and gently tucked it behind my ear. His touch alone made my knees grow weak. I inwardly chided myself. I was becoming one of those girls, and I hated myself for it. Liam wasn't….he wasn't…anyone special. He was just a guy.

He's just a guy, I told myself –repeating it like my very own mantra. Just a guy. Just a guy. Just a guy.

"You still mad at me?"

I shrugged, looking down at my feet. Words weren't very reliable in this moment. I felt like my tongue was stuck at the roof of my mouth or a cat had caught it in its, making it impossible to speak. "Anya." He tipped my chin upward, and suddenly the choice to avoid his gaze was taken from me.

I gulped, swallowing back the lump in my throat. "No," I said, finding my voice. "I'm not mad at you. It's hard to feel that emotion around you when you do that."

He cocked his head to the side, dropping his hand from my face. "Do what?"

I pointed at his face. The complete and utter confusion and innocence written in his slate-blue eyes was priceless. I laughed, finding enjoyment in his bewilderment. I now understood why he found it funny when I was at a loss for words. All the amusement suddenly died in my throat when he looked at my lips, his eyes trailing painfully slow, until his clouded gaze met my eyes. My heart throbbed in my chest. Pressed against me, I knew he could hear it, especially when the edge of his lips lifted into a smirk. That smug bastard.

"That," I breathed.

He raked his hand through his hair, his brows knitting together. He played innocent (and he did it so well) when he knew exactly what he did to me. That smirk alone sold him out. Frustrated, I took his hand in mine, leading him back towards the sofa, his low chuckle reaching my ears. I pushed the folder into his hands, thankful to be rid of the burden.

Despite everything we've been through, I wanted him to know. Even the last couple of minutes hadn't changed my mind on the matter. Underneath that thick layer of arrogance was a different side to him. There always was. I had been wrong. I thought that it had completely faded away, eroded and weathered by time and harsh climate. But that side of him had just been carefully hidden deep underground in a land mine.

"There's something you don't know about me, something that I didn't even know till recently." He didn't open the folder, waiting for my signal to do so. When I gave him the okay, he slowly flipped the cover over, uncertainty laced in his eyes. In instant, uncertainty was replaced by a blank slate as he slowly let the words on the documents sink in.

Liam had left an hour before my parents came home from their weekend in Montgomery. I was in the kitchen, aimlessly flipping through a Cosmo magazine and awing at the beautiful and chic styles the celebrities wore when I heard the click of the lock.

I sprang from my seat, running to the door. "Anya we're-" I skidded to a stop, Mom's words died on her lips as she saw me and not a second later I wrapped my arms around her.

"Sweetie, did you miss us that-"

"Dad!" He walked through the doorway and I tackled him. He caught me, the bags he was carrying dropping to the floor in a heavy thud.

"Woah...what's going on?" he said, setting me down.

I helped them with their bags, shouldering Mom's carry on and dragging their suitcases down the hall. I ignored Mom's perplexed look and Dad's raised brow as I dashed into the living room and grabbed the my adoption file.

I slapped it on the dining table, their expressions morphing into something that I could only call grim and weary – like they knew this was inevitable, and were waiting for this exact moment.

But if they thought I would ask questions about my real parents and about the adoption process, well, they were going to be utterly shocked.

Liam had convinced me to not ask questions tonight, and instead insisted that I tell them how much I loved them.

They need to hear it, and you need to say it no matter how much you think you don't. You do.

I realized he was right when tears began to brim in my eyes and he tugged me to him, silently letting the tears flow down my cheeks. He rocked me in his arms just like when we were younger and I'd be teased by the other kids in our grade. Their words hurt me more than I could say, but Liam was always there.

He was just there.

"I-" I took a deep breath, willing the trembling in my hands to seize, and the lump in my throat to disappear. I looked at them, their brown eyes assessing my own. "I'm sorry for the way I acted the past week," I began. "I was just angry and felt betrayed that you guys never told me about this. But I shouldn't have acted like you guys did it with a malicious intent. I see now that it was because it didn't matter. Because I'm your daughter..." my voice caught in my throat, hot tears welling in my ears. "Because I'm your daughter either way. Because you treat me as such, and you've never treated me like I wasn't." I closed my eyes, letting out a whoosh of air. "I couldn't...I couldn't have asked for better parents than you guys. I'm lucky. No." My voice rose in fierce conviction. "No...I'm not lucky. I'm blessed. God gave me two great and loving parents. And I'm happy that it was you guys instead of some crazy people who would treat me as their ticket to free government money."

My mom laughed softly, while Dad's mouth quirked into a smile that lighted his eyes. I caught my reflection in the mirror hanging over Dad's shoulder and seeing myself – red eyed, messy side ponytail, and runny nose – made my breath hitch in my throat. There was so much emotion swirling inside of me that I couldn't keep it at bay any longer.

"I love you both so very much. I'm so sorry...I'm sorry..." I sobbed, feeling Dad's arms wrap around me the next moment.

"Shhh...don't cry Bug. Shhh." His soft, lulling voice only made me cry even more. Mom's hand ran through my hair, and I shifted my body to her outstretched arms.

"Sweetie, it's not your fault. We should have told you sooner...but as the years passed; it just didn't matter anymore. You are ours," she said. I looked at her through bleary eyes and saw her own tears brimming on the edges.

"Blood alone does not make people family," Dad said, standing beside Mom and taking her hand. His eyes were rimmed red as he struggled to be strong and not cry. I bit my lip, afraid that a sob might escape once more.

"It's about the strong bonds that are made," he reached out his hand towards me, my small hand engulfed by his. Mom and I locked hands, sharing a watery-eyed smile. "They hold people intact through thick and thin, never once leaving your side when the waters get rough."

He kissed my forehead tenderly, wrapping one arm around me and Mom and bringing us in for one of his infamous bear hugs. "I love you both and don't either of you forget it. Got it?"

Mom and I shared a look, smiling up at Dad. My heart swelled at the unconditional and irrevocable love reflected in their eyes when they stole a glance at each other. When they looked back at me, I hugged them closer, feeling complete and utter peace and joy for the first time in days.

Chapter 21

Every night for the next week I asked Mom and Dad a question about my adoption. One question was enough for one day as I let their words sink into my head, trying to understand, trying to arrange the puzzle pieces until it all made sense.

I no longer felt like Madison and Ryan had abandoned me. What I had gathered all week from my parents was their untold story, a story that couldn't be written down in all those official documents regarding my adoption.

The low drone of conversations buzzed all around me as Gemma and I took a seat at our usually table for lunch. Hayden wolfed down his burger, slathered with extra ketchup, mustard, and mayonnaise. It was surprising that he hadn't had a heart attack yet with all that sodium in his system. Gemma scrunched her nose as she took a seat next to him, scrunching her nose in disgust.

I raised my eyebrow; my facial expression completely wasted on him as he paid no mind to us. She shook her head in dismay, a small smile breaking at the corner of her mouth.

"So ready for tonight?" she signed.

Hayden's head perked up from his plate and with a mouthful of food asked, "What's tonight?" Gemma slapped his arm, giving him hard look. "Oh, right. The play."

She rolled her eyes and he chuckled, wiping his hands on a napkin. "I was kidding. My body would be at the bottom of the bay if I'd really forgotten." He wiped his mouth with the back of his hand, a sudden mischievous glint in his eye.

"I'd like to propose a notion." We eyed him warily and when neither of us objected he continued. "No more horror movies for our movie nights. I don't want you two getting any ideas."

I chocked on my coke as I wide smirk spread on his face. Gemma grinned, leaning forward and wiping at the corner of his mouth where a smidge of ketchup stuck to his scruff.

"Hilarious," I deadpanned.

He shrugged, smiling. "I try."

Continuing with my regularly scheduled lunch, I took a bit of my apple. I chewed, my eyes lingering to where Liam stood with Collin smoking a joint. It never ceased to amaze me how they never got caught. As if he felt my eyes on him, Liam turned away from Collin. Even though I couldn't see his eyes as they were obscured by the pair of aviators he wore, I could still feel his cool, steady gaze on me. I smiled, lifting my right hand in small wave. Gemma and Hayden turned to see Liam wave back and when they turned their expressions mirrored one another's.

I sighed, wishing for not only the first time that I had someone like Gemma has Hayden. No wonder they were so perfect together. They practically were the same person.

"I wonder when he'll ask you out," Gemma said thoughtfully. "I mean, he obviously likes you. What's taking him so long?"

"Gemma, he-"

Hayden cut me off by saying, "He does like her. Remember how long it took me to ask you out?"

Gemma smiled, her eyes hazing over at the memory. I wasn't present the day Hayden finally asked Gemma three months after they first met. She texted me immediately after it happened and I couldn't help but squeal in delight.

It was about damn time.

Those were my exact words as I texted Gemma back. Except, there had been a gazillion exclamation points and three smiley faces.

Someone shook my hand as the sound of my name penetrated through my thoughts. "Yeah?"

"Were you thinking about Liam?" Gemma teased. "Cause yano...it'd be totally understandable."

I felt heat rise to my cheeks and I batted her hand away. "Actually," I leaned forward as Gemma and Hayden did the same. "There's something I need to tell you both."

Reeling back, I saw their fixed gaze set on me – Gemma's knowing brown eyes, which made a small smile form on my lips, and Hayden's green apprehensive ones.

"Alright." I clasped my hands in my lap, absentmindedly twining my thumbs in a circular motion. "It's about my parents...my real parents..."

I took a sip of coke in intervals as I retold all that I had learned about Madison and Ryan to Gem and Hayden.

I started at the beginning with how they had met in Africa while they were both in the peace corp in their early years of college. Madison had only been eighteen while Ryan was twenty. He was in the middle of his undergrad program studying at the University of Alabama. Madison and Ryan were assigned in the same unit and lived in the same housing site in a small city outside the coast of

Somalia. It wasn't until two months into their service that they had met as Madison was taking a swim in a small private alcove.

She told him to go away, of course. But he wouldn't leave. Angry, she swam back to the shore and left in a fury. After that day she stayed clear from him, carefully avoiding him around the camp. Ryan took notice of her behavior and one night after a bonfire he had cornered her, demanding to know what was her problem.

One thing lead to another and Ryan had kissed her. And that small kiss lead to something else entirely.

For the rest of their service, Ryan and Madison became insepara-ble, spending most (if not all) their time together offering medical service and freshly grown fruits to malnutritious men, woman, and children That was only some of what their service entailed.

When their two year service was over they flew back to the States where Ryan proposed two weeks later. They had a small wedding ceremony where my parents were a few of the guests attending. They actually were the best man and maid of honor.

Gemma's eyes widened, while Hayden muttered, "And the plot thickens."

The shrill ringing of the bell ended my retelling. They both frowned as simultaneously they said, "We'll talk later." They shared a smile and he kissed her temple whispering something that was incomprehensible.

I left the two love birds alone and threw my trash in nearby bin as I walked to AP Bio without Hayden. Gnawing at my lip, I thought about how I was going to tell Hayden my secret. I couldn't keep it from him any longer because the secret was the reason why Madison and Ryan died.

"Penny for your thoughts?"

I lifted my gaze from the ground and saw Liam walking beside me, a hand leisurely wrapped around a strap of his book bag. I flashed a small smile, unsure of what to say as he followed me down the corridor, leading to the science rooms.

"Hey," he laid a hand on my shoulder, stopping me in my tracks. "You okay?" His slate-blue eyes steadily assessed me. From my peripheral vision I saw the strange and curious looks being thrown our ways. Liam didn't seem to notice, his gaze solely trained on me.

"I'm fine," I finally said.

He eyed me warily. "You were never a good liar."

I sighed. I could never get anything passed him. I could never get anything passed anyone. My eyes betrayed my emotions.

My.

Stupid.

Beady.

Eyes.

He took a step forward, closing the gap between us. My eyes widened in alarm as his hand reached out, his fingers grazing the tip of my ear, tucking away a pesky strand of hair. Heat rose to my cheeks as I said through tight lips, "Liam, people are staring. What if-"

"I don't care what people think."

His voice was resolute, firm. They mirrored the hard set of his eyes when I finally met his gaze. The shrill sound of the bell startled me, breaking the intense connection between us.

"I have to go. I'll...umm..." I shuffled my balance from one foot to the other, slowly but surely, meeting his eyes once more. "Are you..umm...coming to the play tonight?"

His eyes softened a little. "School functions aren't my thing."

"Oh." I could hear the disappointment in my voice and I mentally slapped myself for it. "Okay. Well, I'll just see…"

The words died on my lips as I saw a smile glinting in his eyes. "I'll be there. But only for one reason."

"And what is that?"

He smiled, shaking his head and walked off – leaving me more confused than ever.

"Alright," Devino called, clapping his hands together. "We've got a full house tonight. All those grueling hours full of blood, sweat, and tears have led to this very moment. If you're nervous – for all you first timers – take long deep breaths. Center yourself. Relax. Forget about everyone else except for you and the character you're playing. Go into your bubble."

I looked around our makeshift circle and saw a few of the cast members close their eyes, taking slow steady breaths as they emptied out their mind of everything but their role they were about to perform.

I took a deep breath myself, willing the sudden nerves that had sprouted in my hands like a bothersome weed.

A hand clasped around my shoulder. "You ready kid?"

I nodded. "More or less." Devino smiled and gave me a small push towards the drawn curtain.

"Two minutes!" I heard him call.

I drew an opening in the curtain and stepped through to see the theater packed with people in the aisles searching for any available seats in the first four rows. The lights dimmed and I hurried to the piano along the left side of the stage. When I was settled and ready to go I skimmed the opening song, reading over notes that were as familiar to me as Mom's restaurant floor plan was to her.

"Anya," someone whispered to my right. "Anya."

I turned to see Hayden sitting in the second row with Gemma next to him grinning and waving wildly. I returned the gesture, only to find myself scouring the crowd looking for my parents and...

Liam.

Seeing him among the crowd of patrons caused my breath to hitch in my throat. He was two rows behind Gem and Hayen, sitting lazily in his seat. When he met my eyes he straightened up in his sight, obstructing the view of whoever had the luck of sitting directly behind him. An easy, natural smile tugged at the corners of his lips, changing the bored look in his eyes into one of interest and wonder.

"Break a leg," he mouthed, or at least, that's what I thought he'd said.

The lights over the theater dimmed, casting the audience in a low shadowed light until they flickered off completely. The sound of the curtains being drawn drew my gaze back to the ivory keys before me and with a final calming breath; I played the music that accompanied Karla's lone figure entering the stage.

As the play unfolded, I found myself yearning to see Liam. He was too far back to see through my peripheral vision. The only way to see him was to turn my body a full 90 degrees and that would have been blaringly obvious.

I chided myself for feeling that way about him. Just because we were slowly becoming friends didn't mean that there would ever be anything other than friendship between us. He made that very clear when I thought he was going to kiss me in the river.

There was only a glimmer of hope that my stubborn side clung onto like a lone piece of driftwood in the Gulf. But the more logical side of myself wanted these newfound feelings of him to fade and never come again. I couldn't bear the thought of Liam falling in love with me, while I knew that it might not last because of my affliction.

I couldn't be selfish. Not with him.

Silent tears streamed down my cheeks as the final scene of the play came to a close. My feelings aside, Karla was a great actress along with Jason Dean playing the Beast/Adam. They were the reason why I was crying by the end, making the notes in front of me a watery haze.

The audience burst into thunderous applause as the curtain closed only to reopen a few seconds afterward with the entire cast taking a bow. I stood too, hollering Adam and Janie's name. The spotlight beamed suddenly shined on me, momentarily blinding me.

"And to our extraordinary pianist."

I searched the stage to find where Devino stood, his voice coming clearly over the speakers and the roar of the audience. I bowed after my failed attempt at finding him.

"Wohoooo Anya! Woooooo!"

I smiled hearing Gemma and Hayden hollering my name with the spotlight moving once more to the direction of the stage and the cast. The applause lasted less than five minutes with the onlookers slowly treading out of the theater. I collected my music and headed backstage where I was assaulted with a hug from Janie and Adam.

"You guys were great! Janie, your voice was beautiful. And Adam! You made me cry at the end."

He waved away my praise. "Not as good as you, Anya. Your playing practically made this production! It always does."

I blushed. "It does not."

He smiled, running a hand through his hair. Janie was still beside us, talking animatedly to her sister Lila. "So you going to the after party?"

"Oh!" Janie broke away from her conversation with Lila and said, "You have to go, Anya! Everyone is going to be there."

"I still have to ask my parents. I was planning on staying in."

Janie scrunched her face. "It's Friday night! Live a little. I'm sure Gemma would agree. Right, Gemma?"

"Right."

I turned to see Gemma behind me with Hayden in tow. She smothered me in a tight hug and said, "You have to go...unless, you have plans?" I pulled away from her to see the smile playing in her brown eyes.

"What are you-" She spun me around quickly in the opposite direction. "Hey, what is-" The words faded on my lips as I saw Liam make his way through the crowd. Karla saw him too and stepped in front of him. He easily side stepped her like she was just a bump in the road.

There was a bouquet of soft violet lilacs in his hands. "I bet those are for you," Gemma whispered.

"They aren't. I bet they are-"

"Who else would he give them too? Karla? Ha. He likes you and it's time you stopped denying it to yourself."

"I'm not-" She put her hand up, not wanting to hear whatever I had to say. Gemma hugged me one last time and sauntered off to where Hayden stood talking to Adam and Veronica.

"I hate you!" I called after her.

She turned and signed, "I love you, too."

"Yeah, right," I muttered.

"Am I interrupting something?"

I turned to find Liam standing right in front of me with the flowers separating the few inches between us.

"No, I-" He's just a boy. Just an ordinary boy, I told myself. "You came," I said, mentally cringing at how lame that sounded.

"I told you I would," he said smiling. "Here." He handed me the bouquet and I saw for the first time a small white card sticking out of one of the stems. "These are for you. Mr. Edison helped picked them out."

I brought the flowers to my nose and smelled the sweet aroma. "Their beautiful. Is he here?"

Liam dug his hands into his pockets. "No. He picked them out before the play. I was in town and..." He trailed off, running a hand through his messy blond hair.

The grin that spread on my face was irrepressible. A crooked smile grazed his lips and he said, "You're cruel, you know that?"

"I think it's quite amusing actually. Do you do this often?"

He eyes glinted with mischief. "Only when I know what I want."

My face flushed under his steady slate blue eyes. What in the world did that mean?

"What are you doing tonight?" he asked.

I was grateful for the change in subject. This I could answer without feeling like words were suddenly out of reach.

"Nothing in particular. Why?"

"If I told you, it wouldn't be a surprise."

I bit my lip, thinking about his proposition for a moment. "Alright. Can you at least give me a hint? I'm going to have to tell my parents something."

"It involves food." He laughed, leaning down to press a kiss to my temple. In a gruff whisper he said, "I'll meet you up front. Don't forget your jacket."

I nodded, turning on my heels to find my parents waiting in the lounge. After I had their permission I rushed backstage to grab my stuff and headed towards the entrance to find Liam casually leaning against his bike.

His face was cast in shadows, like a mask pulled over his features. When I approached, Liam handed me his helmet and I hopped on, revving the engine. I wrapped my thighs around his hips, weaving my arms around his waist, ready for the forward jerk of the bike that always made my stomach drop.

Chapter 22

Liam had the evening all figured out, while I was kept in the dark.

He had walked into Le Bistro's Italian Cuisine five minutes ago with an order to stay put. If we were going to have dinner, wouldn't it consist of me going into the restaurant with him? Why was I still out here in the freezing cold if that was the case?

I tapped my foot on the concrete, patience waning thin as the seconds ticked by. The glowing red sign seemed to mock me as its lights flickered out for a split-second before charging back to life. People filtered in and out, jazz music escaping through the open door.

I groaned, my stomach growling in assent. I wanted to march right in there and look for him, but that would just ruin his plans; whatever those were. He was being secretive and it frustrated me. But on the opposite side of the spectrum I was also intrigued.

Stop whining. It's a surprise! Of course he's not gonna tell you what it is.

I sighed. Texting Gemma was the only thing keeping me from going insane while I waited for Liam. I wondered if he was some-how trying to contrive a plan to steal some food from the kitchen. He'd come out of the restaurant in a frenzy, telling me to get on the bike while the manager or one of the cooks yelled at him to come back and pay for the food or they'd call the cops. Or maybe he was working his charm to get us good seats, but the host was not so easy to persuade.

What do YOU think he's up to?

I tapped my thumb on the screen as I waited for a reply, absently pacing back and forth. She responded a minute later.

Idk something romantic? You should be bursting with joy! You're finally on a date with him! :)

It's not a date. It's just food.

Ha. Mkay. Keep telling yourself that, An. Still on for dressing shopping tomorrow, right?

"Sorry to keep you waiting. That took longer than I expected."

I whirled around to see Liam carrying a picnic basket. It was the strangest thing I had ever seen. Wait, no. That was a lie. The strangest thing I had seen involved a donkey and a trapeze artist, but that was an entirely different story. The basket looked foreign on his person against the stark leather of his jacket, like it didn't belong.

I slid my phone into my pocket, making a mental note to text Gemma back later.

"We're going on a picnic?"

"Not going to tell you."

I huffed, crossing my arms over my chest. "I'm not moving from this spot until you tell me what you're up to. It's all very suspicious here, pal."

His eyebrows shot up in amusement. "Fine. You can stay, while I go and eat all the food in here." He tapped the basket for good measure and shrugged, crossing the street.

In the end curiosity got the better of me, and I followed him towards the dock. Plus, the rumbling and grumbling of my stomach pleaded with me to concede and follow. I couldn't let my stomach down. I had to take one for the team.

The night was peaceful and beautiful with only a steady breeze rustling the trees to break the silence that stretched between Liam and me. I glanced at him every so often, wondering what he was thinking. His face was relaxed while his eyes danced with amusement. I caught sight of a faint smile on his lips. Shivers ran down my arms, but it wasn't because of the chill in the air. I bit my lip and looked away, focusing on the rifts in the water from the wind. The moonlight's reflection shone brilliantly on the surface, casting iridescent rays to dance across the water.

Liam put the picnic basket down at the edge of the dock. He took out a blanket from the inside, unfolding it and spreading it over the cold wooden boards. Once he was finished I took my place, tucking my legs underneath me and helping him spread out the continents of the basket.

"You didn't have to go through all this trouble." I set down the plates to the side, searching for the utensils next.

"No trouble at all."

"Hmm...what are you up to, Rowely?"

"Can't a guy just take you out to dinner without some suspicious motive?"

I laughed. So maybe Gemma was right. I was overreacting, but that didn't mean that I was wrong. The light in his eyes begged to differ.

"Dammit," he mumbled.

I leaned forward. "What?"

"I forgot the candles."

My heart leapt in my chest as Gemma's words echoed in my mind.

You're finally on a date with him!

I gulped. Was it a date? How could it be a date when he hadn't said it was a date in the first place? Did he say it was a date when he asked me? No, he didn't. I would have remembered if he did! I ran a hand through my hair and smoothed out the nonexistent wrinkles on the front of my black slacks. I frowned as I looked down at my sheer blue top. This was no first date attire! I looked like I was going in for a job interview. No, worse. I looked like my mother when she was on her way to a business meeting.

I watched as Liam served a heap of pasta onto our plates followed by a serving of calamari. There was a bowl of tossed salad and cheese bread sticks with marinara sauce. The smell of garlic engulfed the air as I saw Liam placing the delicious bread slices on a platter. The glass plates covered every inch of surface on the blanket. My eyes didn't know where to look. There was so much food! My mouth watered as the last item was pulled from the basket – Le Bistro's famous caramel covered cheesecake.

I squealed in delight.

"Everything looks yummy! Can we dig in?"

He smiled, nodding. "Be my guest."

For the first time tonight I didn't object.

"For a small person you sure can eat."

Heat flushed my face. I let my hair fall over my face, covering the blush that burned my skin.

"So can you," I replied.

He shrugged. "But I'm a guy."

"So?"

"Sooo. It's in our nature."

I smiled. "I was hungry! Can you blame a girl?"

"No. I like a girl with a hearty appetite."

I averted my eyes, trying to hide the wide grin on my face as he took the plates from my hands and began to load everything back into the basket. The evening was slowly coming to an end just as soon as it had begun. I stared out at the water, the sound of waves filling me with a sense of peace and beauty. I pulled my legs up to my chin, closing my eyes as the world fell away. I took in the pure salty air mixed with the sweet scent of pine trees. The wind caressed my skin, whispering infinite secrets that the universe alone knew. I wanted to give a secret to the world even if I wasn't ready to admit it myself.

The tide below intensified causing the waves to crash violently on the shore. I felt Liam scoot closer to me, his arm grazing mine.

"What are you thinking about?" he asked quietly.

I opened my eyes, glancing in his direction. His eyes were locked on mine, curiosity shining through deep pools of gray.

"A message in a bottle. I've always wanted to send one out there and-"

"Hold that thought."

I cocked my head as I stared at him, perplexed. He sifted through the basket, taking out the half-full bottle of apple cider. Uncorking the top, he leaned over the pier and dumped out the liquid.

I lunged forward, scraping my knees on the wood. "What are you doing? You're polluting the bay!"

"People piss in the ocean all the time I imagine the cider tastes better. The natural cycle will wash it all away, right?"

I shook my head, exasperated. "That's not the point, Liam."

He ignored me until the bottle was empty. He took a napkin and dried the interior as best he could and then proceeded to tear a jagged corner of one of the menu's that came with our dinner.

"A pen...do you have a pen?"

I patted my pockets, finding the pen I used earlier for my scores. "What are you going to do?"

"It's not me who is doing anything." He handed me the bottle and torn paper. "It's you."

"Me?"

He gave me an incredulous look. "Yes, you. Write your message and send it out to sea."

"Did you get that from a fortune cookie?" I teased.

He bumped my shoulder, his smile sending my heart on a rampage. "Ha-ha. Very funny."

I looked down at the paper, gnawing on my lip. "Hmm...I think I know..." I flattened the paper on my thigh, beginning to write my message when I saw Liam hovering over me, trying to get a peek.

"Uh-uh," I covered the paper with my hand, sliding away from. "You can't look. It's a secret."

"C'mon. At least give me a hint."

My mouth quirked into a mischievous grin. "It wouldn't be a secret if told you, would it?"

He shook his head in disbelief. "Unbelievable."

I gave him a playful nudge as he turned his attention to the water. Quickly, I wrote out my message and rolled it up, fitting it into the bottle. "Where's the cork?"

He silently handed it to me, his eyes lingering on the paper inside wanting to know the words scrawled on it.

"Do you really want to know?" I asked as I threw the bottle into the water. It floated on the surface, its glass body shimmering from the light of the moon.

His voice was low, gruff when he spoke. "Only if you want to tell me."

I looked up at the moon, looking for the answer in its vast beauty. Unfortunately, I didn't find it because I already knew the answer myself. I lay back on the blanket, seeing the sky covered in million of small celestial dots.

"Do you remember when we would count the stars? We never passed twenty because we'd lose track on which ones we already counted."

Liam followed my lead, tucking his hands under his head. "Yeah. We'd just start over until we practically fell asleep on the lawn."

He shifted beside me, his arm coming around my shoulder until I was safely tucked against the warmth of his body. It felt natural, like two pieces of a puzzle finally fitting together. The steady beating of his heart conquered all other sounds. I closed my eyes, hearing the unwritten melody within. I felt the rise and fall of his chest as he breathed in the cool air. The familiar smell of smoke and cinnamon reached my nostrils as I buried my face into his chest.

"I remember when we swam half naked in the same kiddie pool."

I groaned but couldn't hide the smile playing on my lips. "I remember when I threw a mud pie at your face and you cried."

He chuckled. "It stung! I never would have thought that mud would hurt that bad. Plus, I was – what? Five?"

"Sounds about right."

Time ceased to matter as we laid there at the edge of the dock. It didn't feel like we were on the pier at all, but instead tucked away at a faraway corner of the world where no one else existed but the two of us. If there was anything that I had missed the past few years it was this, being close to Liam – feeling like everything in the world was going to be okay. There was absolutely no reason to think of anything else but the moment we were captured in like a work of art, forever an imprint of a time and place.

"Can I tell you a story?" I asked, breaking the comfortable silence.

"What kind is it?"

I smiled, tears prickling at the back of my eyes. "A good one," I whispered, "filled with love and sacrifice. It's about my parents. My real parents."

"Okay." His voice was soft. "Tell me about them."

I told him exactly what I had told Gemma and Hayden earlier; how Madison and Ryan had met in Africa, their dislike towards one another quickly turning into love; the wedding where my parents were the maid of honor and best man.

But I didn't stop there.

After the wedding, Ryan whisked Madi away to the town that came to be my home. Fairhope. He'd only visited the town when he was a kid, taking weekend trips with his parents until he was sixteen. They stayed for a few days, relishing in the beauty the small town offered.

They had only been home for two weeks when they both went back to Africa, taking on an extra two years in the Peace Corps. Being married had its perks in the organization. It assured them that they were to be stationed in the same place without the fear of being separated. They were assigned to the small city of Wajir in Kenya.

They lived a happy life together, aiding the people of Wajir with housing developments and food produce. Spending so much time in the sun lightened Madi's hair while it darkened Ryan's skin. Mom and Dad said that they even began to learn the native language when they would call their best friends back home and delve them with their adventures.

A year passed when Madi learned that she was pregnant. They couldn't have been more overjoyed about anything else in the world when they heard the news. At least, that's what both my parents said when Ryan and Madi called them about the news. That same day they decided to name Phillip and Charlotte my godparents even if they were not married or together. They were honored and readily accepted all that was entitled with the job. They couldn't wait to spoil me to no end.

Little did they know that they would have to do a lot more than just spoil me.

"They raised you in the end, didn't they?"

I nodded, burying my nose into his jacket that smelled like old cigarettes. I would have scrunched my nose in disgust if I hadn't already gotten use to the lingering smell that was him.

"It's kind of a funny story though."

"Your parents?"

"Mhm."

I closed my eyes, remembering the gleaming look in Mom's eyes when she talked about Dad and how she absolutely detested him. I recounted their words to Liam, feeling the low rumble deep within his chest as he laughed quietly. At first, Charlotte was attracted to

Phillip when they met at Madi and Ryan's wedding. Dad also stated that he found Mom attractive, but that was it. There was nothing more between them until I came into the picture.

"And how did you come into their life?" he inquired.

"Patience," I said. "It is not a story that must be rushed."

I fell silent, losing myself in the rhythm of his beating heart. His healthy and warm heart. I played with a shiny button on his jacket, seeing my distorted reflection on its surface. Liam nudged me, bringing me back to the tracks that I had momentarily derailed.

I took in a deep breath, mentally bracing myself for the next part. The words were slow as they rolled off my tongue. Liam's hold tightened around me in reassurance. His strength gave me the courage to let everything I've gathered come pouring out like long overdue rain in the desert.

I was a month early, but before that even happened Madi fell sick with yellow fever for at least a week and half before I was born. She didn't know and even if she did her sickness would only have been due to the pregnancy, at least that's what a doctor would say. The first stage of symptoms usually developed three to six days after the infection is contracted. Symptoms included headaches, muscle joints, and vomiting. Madi fell sick to a fever while she and Ryan were on route to the outskirts of Wajir, delivering fresh goods to the people who resided there.

They stayed in the town overnight as guests in a home as Madi was lost in feverish dreams. She complained of sharp pains in her sides as the hours went by. Ryan went in search of a doctor and was directed to a makeshift hospital. Along the way, Madi's water broke. It was unexpected as I was an entire month early, but I was coming that night. And if it wasn't that night then it would be in the wee hours of the morning.

There were complications with the labor. They had to operate a C-Section since Madi couldn't go through the stress of the labor. She was delirious in the end. The picture I found in the file was taken right after I was plucked and cleaned from her belly. She only had me for an hour and then she was gone.

Liam tensed beneath me, his hand stilled when he had absent-mindedly been weaving his fingers through my hair.

"I was put in an incubator because I was premature and that is where I stayed for a week. Ryan couldn't see me and even if he had then I would have ultimately fallen to the same fate that Madi was dealt." My voice dropped to an incoherent whisper as a lump formed in my throat. Tears blurred my vision and I gripped his jacket, wanting something to tangible to hold on to as the life I could have had was ripped away from me.

"It would have been the same fate that a week later Ryan fell prey to. He died of yellow fever contracting it about a week after Madi. They never got a chance to even be with me and I with them. If I had one wish it would be to have one day with them, to have one solid memory of who they were."

I broke into a sob, unable to contain the lost and sadness I hadn't known I locked away. Liam held me, murmuring in my ear to calm the wrenching cries that racked my spin. He didn't say anything. He didn't have to. Sometimes, all a person needed was to be held, to feel safe without questions or judgment. That's what Liam was – that's what he always had been as long as I could remember.

"The only reason," I started, fighting the lump in my throat. "The only reason I know all this is because there were reports written down of Madi and Ryan's death. They were given to my parents after the American Embassy brought me back to the States. Phillip and Charlotte were summoned to Montgomery where a social worker briefed them on what had occurred to their friends. It was then that they were given the choice to raise me or I'd be put into the system, awaiting the day until someone else came to claim me as their own.

"Mom was the first to speak up, unwilling to let me go even if Dad didn't want anything to do with me. He was hesitant at first, but decided that his friend would have done the same for him if the roles were reverse. That day they signed all legal documentation and went to the nursery where I was taken care of and took me back to Dad's apartment in the city. Mom stayed for a few aggravating days (as she put it) at Dad's place. She wasn't frustrated at me, but at Dad because they couldn't come to a consensus on where they would live.

"In the end, Mom stayed at a hotel – unable to live under the same roof as him. There wasn't a time that he couldn't agree with her more on the matter. They were two entirely different people. And that initial attraction quickly faded as they began to know each other and butt heads over simple things like how Dad left his shit all over the place and how Mom was anal."

I laughed, remembering my surprise at their language. It was definitely something they did not say often and even if they did it wasn't in front of me.

"So they hated each other?"

"Yeah. Big time. Mom would rather have jumped off a cliff than continue to see his infuriating face."

"What about your dad?" he asked trying to suppress the laughter in his voice.

"He would do anything to get 'that woman' out of his life."

"Harsh words. Wonder what happened to change their minds."

"I have no idea what changed. They didn't want to divulge me with details until I knew Madi and Ryan's story in its entirety. All I know is that they both hated each other's guts at the beginning. Mom said he was arrogant and reckless, but he was sure nice to look at."

Liam chuckled, "But your mom fell anyway?"

"She couldn't resist his charms apparently."

He flashed a crooked smile, "And neither can you, huh?"

I gaped at him, my face burning with mortification. "You wish." I untangled myself from his arms and sat up, staring out into the water. My eyes flickered to anything within radius, anything that didn't concern focusing on him.

"Do you believe that things happen for a reason?" I asked. My thoughts were muddled as I tried to forget about what Liam had said and the story I was almost finished with.

I saw him shrug from my peripheral vision. "Never really thought about it, why?"

I played with my hands in my lap, twiddling my thumbs to and fro in a circle. "Madi and Ryan – they believed that everything happened for a reason; even something like that. It's a concept that Mom and Dad also believe in. If it wasn't for me they never would have found each other or fallen in love. Mom says that I'm a blessing in disguise because she can't have children and I'm all that she's always hoped to be."

A skittered breath escaped my lips as I leaned back on my hands.

"It's something I believe in too. But sometimes I wonder – especially now – the what ifs, yano?" I glanced at him and saw that his eyes were downcast, lost in his own thoughts.

"Things didn't turn out so bad though, right?" He turned his body towards me, one leg idly swung over the edge of the pier. There was no trace of the haze in his eyes as if that brief moment of memories had never happened. Were the even memories that I saw in his eyes?

"Anya?"

I snapped away from my thoughts and turned my attention to him. "No, I guess not."

He took my hand in his, warmth shooting up my arm. "You're lucky you have people in your life who love you unconditionally. Not many people have that."

There was a swirl of emotions in his eyes that hinted at something deeper than just me. He quickly looked away, his eyes roaming to the sky.

"If Charlotte and Phillip didn't care, a person would be able to see it from a mile away. You'd be different. Plus, your father is very overprotective of you when I'm concerned."

I let out a shaky laugh. He was right.

"Then there are Gemma and Hayden. Could you have asked for better friends?"

I shook my head. "Their more like my surrogate siblings. Hayden is like the brother I never asked for while Gemma is the sister I always wished to have."

"See." His hand lifted and caressed my cheek; the slightest touch of his thumb grazing my skin raised gooseflesh on my arms. "Not so bad."

I felt a million times better. Telling him all that I had learned in the past week was liberating in ways that were indescribable. The closest I could explain it to was like a weight being lifted from my shoulders. I didn't have to keep that part of my life from him any longer.

I fiddled with the hem of my top, a thought flashing through my mind. He hadn't mentioned himself. How does he fit into my life?

"What about you?" I asked quietly, not looking up at him.

He tilted my chin, his eyes softened as he leaned in; close enough that his lips were tempting to be kissed. I inwardly shook such thoughts away, my heart betraying what my mind would not acknowledge.

"I'll always be here. I'm not going anywhere."

Chapter 23

Liam

My eyes traveled across the hall where Anya and Gemma loitered after school, gathering their books for tonight's homework. It was Wednesday and I could only imagine that they were talking about the dance this weekend. It was virtually what every girl in the building was babbling about.

Normally, I wouldn't give a damn about plays or school dances. But things had changed. I found myself thinking about scavenging through Dad's closet for a tux or even going into town and renting one. My interest in attending school functions hadn't piqued whatsoever. So why did I suddenly have the urge to attend the stupid Winter Formal?

It was one word – or rather it was person, a girl.

Anya.

Just thinking about her made me smile and seeing her a few feet away only made the smile widen. I probably looked like a psychopath, grinning like a jackass.

"You gonna ask your girl to the dance any time soon?"

I rolled my eyes, turning away to face the asshole who was my best mate. He always seemed to appear at the most unnecessary of times. His brows were raised in curiosity and expectancy like he already knew what I was going to say even if it was the opposite of what I wanted to do.

"Not going," I shrugged.

"You sure about that? Dean's already got a head start"

I froze, doing a double take at Collin's face and seeing the arrogant smirk. "Who?"

He crossed his arms over his chest and leaned his shoulder against the metal lockers. "Why don't you turn around and see for yourself."

I practically had to stop myself from spinning on my heels to see what the hell Collin was going on about. Pulling a mask over my features I let Collin see that his words didn't worry me at all. That was easier said than done when I turned around and saw Jason Dean talking casually with the girls. His hands were stuffed in his front pockets, his whole demeanor signaling nervousness. Words were exchanged and Gemma excused herself, nearly skipping to the exit.

That just left Jason and Anya. Alone. It took every bit of my self control to not march over there and haul her away from him. I didn't like him. I didn't want her to like him.

Tearing my eyes away from them I turned and shut my locker, shrugging on my book bag and striding towards the exit. Collin didn't bother to follow me as I walked through the semi-empty parking lot towards my bike.

My teeth ground against each other with such force that it sent a dull ache along my jaw line, like I had been punched in the face. I relaxed my jaw, taking a deep breath to calm down. There wasn't anything to be worked up about. At least, that's what I kept telling myself. But it didn't matter what I told my feeble mind to do. My thoughts kept on drifting back to Anya.

I hopped onto my bike, securing my book bag over both shoulders before turning on the ignition. The engine roared to life; music to my ears in this decrepit place. It was the only thing still a constant in my life. But now, Anya was one of those things too. Resignation flooded through me as I strapped on my helmet and revved the engine.

"Liam!"

I lessened my hold on the clutch, my whole body relaxing at the sound of her voice. I looked up and saw Anya striding towards me, a huge smile lighting up her face. The sting of jealousy was brief, but it was there, lurking in the depths of my soul. She was probably ecstatic over the fact that Jason Dean had asked her out.

What girl wouldn't be? Isn't that the kind of things that sent girls over the railing?

"Did you forget?" she asked, stopping right in front of me. Her eyes were shining bright with expectancy. I felt like a total asshole not knowing what on earth she was talking about. She read the confused look on my face, her face falling as disappointment settled on her full lips.

"The hospital – you promised the kids Saturday that you'd make it today."

Shit. I had. We were supposed to head to the hospital right after school. But those thoughts had been derailed the moment I saw her with Jason Dean. Damn it. It was all I could fucking think about.

"I can't." The words made whatever hopes she had disintegrate into nothing. Her shoulders slumped and I felt like a complete dick, but what else was I supposed to do? I couldn't be near her without knowing what went on with her and Jason. And that would have made me look like an overprotective, jealous...

I shook my head, getting rid of those thoughts.

"I got called in at work," I lied. "Tell the kids I'll make it up to them next time. I gotta go."

"Oh," she breathed out. "Okay. I'll...umm...I'll see you later then."

She gave a disheartened wave and walked passed me towards the sidewalk; her shoulders still slumped in disappointment.

I revved the engine and jolted forward, heading to the garage; a place where I could find a semblance of solace. I would bury myself into work and if Jimmy didn't need me then I'd just help organize his stupid office. God only knew how much Jimmy needed to see the surface of his desk. But I didn't do any of those things when I arrived. Instead I found something that I wasn't looking for but needed.

Anya

I looked back at my reflection in the mirror and wiped off the layer of cake batter slathered all over my face. I looked like one of those trashy jersey shore girls on TV. Pathetic. Dabbing on makeup removal to my face, I scrubbed my face clean and started over.

My spirits were low. I didn't even want to go to the stupid dance in the first place. But alas, I promised Gemma that I would attend. Plus, I couldn't just bail on Jason after he had asked me out. He had been really sweet and a nervous wreck. It was the first time I had seen him at a loss for words. He was usually very confident and charming, kind of in the same way that Liam was, but in a totally different sense.

Thinking of Liam only sent my mood plummeting into a gaping dark hole that I couldn't crawl out of. He had been distant the past couple of days, not really here on earth but somewhere else. It felt like we had taken five steps back instead of moving forward as we had been doing so rather successfully. I knew that there were things still unsaid and I wished that he could confide in me as I had in him. I wanted to know what was wrong. I wanted to ask him. But that had always been one of our unspoken rules. We would share what was troubling us to other when we were ready.

I hoped that he would come to the dance. There was thirty percent chance that he would show up unexpected. The other seventy percent likely showed that he would be spending his night somewhere else or with someone else.

The door bell rang and I stood up so quickly in my seat that I banged my knee on the vanity table. I yelped in pain and massaged the spot.

"Anya!" Mom called. "Jason's here!"

I did a quick once over in the mirror and saw that not a hair was out of place. Mom had done a really nice job at curling my long hair in soft waves and pinning the front strands back so that I looked like a Greek goddess in a floor length lilac empire waist dress. I completely fell in love with the dress as soon as I saw it in a store front window in Montgomery. My love for the dress only grew when I put it on. It was unbelievably perfect.

I dashed down the hall and slowed my gait when I saw that Jason was standing in the entrance talking to my parents casually. I let out a sigh of relief as I heard bits and pieces of their conversation. I thanked God that Dad hadn't decided to give him the third degree. I don't think I could have stood the humiliation.

"Wow. Anya, you look..."

"Beautiful," Dad finished, taking my hand as I reached the end of the stairs.

"Yes." Jason cleared his throat, a crooked smile lingering on his lips. "Very beautiful."

Heat rose to my cheeks. "Thanks. You don't look so bad yourself."

He flashed a charming smile and stepped forward, opening the plastic box that contained a white tulip corsage. I thought they were stuff of legends. I've never seen one before in my life except for in old 80's movies. The light of a camera flashed and I turned to see that Mom had captured the moment.

"Alright," she said. "A few more and you kids can be on your way."

At first the air was tense and unfamiliar between Jason and me as he wrapped his arm around my waist. His smiles were carefree while I realized that mine were forced. I hoped that when the pictures were developed that I didn't look like I was in pain. It had nothing to do with Jason and everything to do with Liam.

From the corner of my eyes I saw Dad's watchful expression. He was leaning against the doorframe, not really seeing me as if caught in a memory or assessing some complicated math calculation.

"Jason, will you take one of Anya and us?" Mom asked.

"Sure thing, Mrs. Vanchester."

Mom handed him the camera and he readily took it with skillful fingers. I smiled at him from behind the lens, recalling that he was a member of the school paper as their photographer. There weren't many things that Jason couldn't do. I wondered then why he had asked me out of all the girls at school. It was unexpected but sweet.

Dad came to stand on my left awkwardly, while Mom took to the right; casually wrapping an arm around my back.

"Will you relax," I muttered to Dad. "You look so brute like Thor. Whoever crosses my daughter shall never see the light of day again."

Mom stifled a laugh and bumped my shoulder. "Good one, honey."

"Ha-ha." Dad screwed on a face of mock annoyance, but it quickly cracked when he smiled at me.

"Okay. So you guys ready?" Jason asked.

"Yeah." I put on a smile and looked at the camera as Jason counted backwards from three.

"What happened to Liam?" Dad whispered thoughtfully.

I looked away from Jason and gave dad a questioning gaze when the flash from the camera went off.

Great.

I had ruined the family picture. I could only imagine what I looked like when that picture went in to get developed.

The blaring speakers drummed with a steady rhythmic pulse as we entered the extravagantly transformed gymnasium. There were giant snowflakes hanging from the ceiling and an ice sculpture where the refreshments were being served by teachers and chaperones. A DJ had his own platform pushed up against the bleachers in the middle of the room where he skillfully scratched on a record to Rhianna's Disturbia. We shimmed through the crowd of dancing students – occasionally stopping as Jason greeted his friends. They gave me a once over, silently wondering what he was doing here with me.

I couldn't help but wonder the same thing.

"Anya! Jason!"

I turned my head in the direction I heard my name come from. Peering through the crowd I saw Hayden waving us forward.

"I think they saved us a spot," Jason said near my ear. He engulfed my hand in his and led me through the crowd. His touch raised gooseflesh up my arms, the gesture casual yet intimate.

Gemma stood up from her seat when she saw me and wrapped her arms around me in a short but warm embrace. "You look great!" she signed. It would be useless to try to talk to one another with the music blaring all around us.

"Thank you. You look amazing, Gem. Bet Hayden drooled when he saw you."

She waved away my teasing. "Well, maybe a little."

We laughed and took our seats as the guys left to get us some sodas and finger food. The beat of the next song was catchy and I found myself nodding to the rhythm. My eyes traveled to the doors where I looked for a specific person to appear out of thin air like magic.

Gemma tapped my shoulder to garner my attention and began to sign.

"You okay?"

"Yeah. Why wouldn't I be?"

She gave me a dubious look. "Anya, hun." She shook her head. "So how is Jason?"

"He's great."

"Just great?"

"Yes, Gem. He's great."

"But?"

My brows furrowed. "But what?"

I didn't get the chance to know what she was talking about because at that moment the guys came back. Jason handed me coke and passed me a plate with an assortment of brownies, cookies, and cupcakes! It was going to be my mission for the night to find out who chipped in to buy all of these! They were incredibly delicious.

"Hey, Jason. You should take those away from here before she eats them all."

I looked up to see Gemma elbow him in the gut and sign that he was an asshole. Fortunately, Hayden knew the word all too well and looked sullen after the fact. I stuck out my tongue at him and pushed my plate forward.

"What did she say?" Jason asked.

"She called him an asshole."

"Ah." He was quiet after that, talking to Gemma and Hayden casually while I absentmindedly tapped to the beat of the music. When I looked up at the clock I read that only an hour had gone by.

I inwardly groaned.

"Want to dance?" Jason asked.

I looked to Gemma for guidance and saw that she and Hayden were gone. Great. Just when I needed my best friend she was MIA.

"Sure."

We stood up and entered the cramped dance floor full of sweaty bodies. Jason's hand on my shoulder was warm and clammy as he led me to a space on the left side of the floor. The upbeat music ended just as we began to dance. It was like that cliché moment in all those teen movies. I didn't know that kind of thing happened in real life, but I was mistaken again.

"This is for all the couples out there," the DJ said. He played a slow, melodic tune that I'd never heard before.

"May I have this dance?" he asked.

I smiled. "Yes, you may." His left hand curled around the small of my back and brought me closer to him with only a few inches separating our bodies. He was significantly taller than I was, my nose aligning itself with his breast pocket. I glanced around me as we swayed, my eyes flickering to the door ever so often. He was a very good dancer. I didn't have to worry about him stepping on my dress or him accidently sending me spinning into another couple. It's not something that I could say about Liam.

Just saying his name in my head caused my heart to sink. I was hoping that he would show up. If tonight was filled with clichés wouldn't he be here? He'd show up unexpectedly and ask Jason if he could have a dance. Jason would be polite and agree and Liam would send me spiraling into endless happy bliss.

But life isn't a movie. That kind of thing doesn't happy and I was delusional to think that it had a minuscule chance of happening.

"Go ahead, go find him."

I looked up at Jason, confused. "What?"

"I don't mind. I can't say I'm good company. I really wanted to go with Layla Bond, but Erik beat me to the punch. I figured that Liam wouldn't come, and thought since both of us would be alone, we could come together."

I dropped my hand from his and stared at him, dumfounded and surprised. His honesty brought a grateful smile to my face and he relaxed, his shoulders losing the tension that had settled at his confession.

"So I was your second choice?" I teased.

"Aren't I yours?"

"Touche."

I leaned forward and went on my tippy toes to kiss his cheek. When I reeled back, a small smile lifted up at the corners of his mouth. "Thank you."

He nodded and turned around, walking back to our table. I headed towards the exit and sprinted down the long corridor that led to the crisp November air.

My first thought was to head directly to his house. He would be in his room, lazily watching a really bad TV program, bored to death. But then this was Liam we were talking about. Why would he stay in on a Saturday night?

His house was the only lead I had so I followed it until I reached the park before our neighborhood. I stopped in my tracks as I saw the outline of a silhouette sitting idly in the middle of the bride that connected the jungle gym. I knew who it was before I walked closer and confirmed it. Call it intuition or a sixth sense. There was no denying that the person who was out here alone was Liam.

I had forgotten how the park was a place of refuge for the both of us. We'd come to its safe haven whenever we needed to get away from others and have a few hours of quiet solitude. Eventually, we'd break each other's isolation and patiently waited until the other was ready to talk.

The last time that Liam and I had been at the park was three days after his mom died. Her death had been hard for all of us but it had been the hardest for him. When I finally showed up he wanted me to leave, but I wouldn't let him push me away. It was the first time that he cried while I held him instead. I tried to be strong but I ended up crying too. I remember thinking at that time how strong he really was for all the times that I had cried in his arms.

I warily walked forward, afraid that he'd tell me to leave like he had those many years ago. He lifted his head when he saw me, a faint smile perceivable in the darkness.

"Hey," I said. "Mind if I join you?"

He sat up straighter looking through one of the blue bars, his face too big for the opening. His eyes were wide with wonder reminding me of a four year old finding a shiny dime on the street. "Anya," he breathed out. "I-I...you're beautiful."

I looked down at my feet and clutched a piece of material in my hand. "That's what everyone keeps saying. I think it's the dress."

He chuckled and inclined his head for me to join him. I kicked off my heels, relief flooding from my feet I hadn't realized how much they hurt from those dreaded contraptions. I positioned my hands on top of the rope ladder and began to climb up.

I folded my legs underneath me, carefully minding my dress. Dirt didn't matter but if I ripped it Mom would have a coronary.

"How was the dance?" he asked nonchalantly.

I shrugged. "Boring. I left early and walked here."

His brows rose. "Jason didn't drive you? What a dick."

I shook my head. "No, no. I left. He's actually really sweet."

Liam scoffed and rolled his eyes, leaning his head back on the bars and looking up at the array of stars littering the sky.

"Figures you'd fall for a guy like that."

That got my attention. "A guy like what?"

"Sweet, as you put it – tall, athletic, a drama geek. He's got it all, right? You're perfect dream guy."

I didn't like the direction of where this conversation was going. I also didn't like the contempt in his voice. It was harsh, reminding me of who he used to be. We didn't just make progress all these months to only have him backtrack. What was the point of being his friend if he was just going to revert back to his old ways. I didn't want that and deep inside I knew that he didn't want to be that way either.

I opened my mouth to defend Jason, but Liam turned his gaze to me; his penetrating gaze snapping my mouth shut.

"I'm sure your parents are pleased," he scoffed. "Going from no-future high school playboy to Harvard bound four-point-oh theatre club geek."

"You are such an idiot." I couldn't believe what he just said. He was admitting that he liked me but at the same time he was degrading himself. I got up from my perch and towered over him. "You don't know what I want or need so don't pretend like you do."

Angrily I stalked down the stairs and fished for my shoes from where I had left them. There was shuffling behind me and a light padded thump. I swirled around on my heels and saw Liam behind me. He had jumped over the bridge.

"Don't talk to me," I said, stepping onto the cool grass. I would cut through the park and walk the rest of the way home barefoot.

"You know...you are such an insufferable bastard. You want me to feel sorry for you and say 'Yes, Liam. I could never fall for a guy like you because frankly you are a disappointment to society.' Is that what you want me to say?"

He didn't say anything, his footsteps right behind me. "Right. Figures you'd just shut down after-" His hand curled around my elbow and he spun me around. "Let me go you stupid, arrogant jerk. I don't want to be friends with someone-"

He didn't let me finish. He cupped my face and pressed his lips against mine. The fight died inside of me as I sank into the kiss. It burned a path right through my very soul. My shoes fell out of my hands as I snaked my arms around his neck. His arms slid from my face, down my bare arms, settling on my hips as he pulled me into him, closing whatever gap still existed between us. I felt like I was on fire, his kiss deepening with feverish hunger.

Flashes of another kiss penetrated through my mind, a kiss much like this one but different. We were in his room – it was the night when I decided to get drunk – and I...Oh, God.

My eyes flew open and I pushed him with such force that he stumbled. I touched my lips incredulously as I looked at him. There was a dazed look in his eyes as if he couldn't believe that he had kissed me and that I had kissed him back.

"You stole my first kiss, yo-you...thief!" I stalked forward and closed the gap between us, smacking his arm in anger. He'd known all along that we had kissed and he never once told me! I would think that that would be a good thing to recount after a night of debauchery.

He blinked as if clearly focusing on my anger. A wiry smile lifted the corners of his lips and he chuckled, amusement gleaming in his eyes. "You stole mine ten years ago, Anya."

I gaped. The memory surfaced in my mind, but I willed it to go away. Now was not the time for technicalities.

"That didn't count!"

"You kissed me that day out by the docks."

My cheeks flushed with heat as I gnawed on my lip. This couldn't be happening. How could this be happening?

"I did not kiss you."

"You did." His eyes glinted with condescending pleasure. "And you enjoyed it, then and now."

I shook my head. "That was thievery!"

He smirked. "You're cute when you're flustered. I took your breath away. Admit it."

I let out a shaky laugh. I slowly inched away from him. His proximity was intoxicating. Everything in my mind screamed at me to run far away from him. This was a dangerous ground we were treading.

I was fool to think that I could escape him so easily. He knew me as easily as he knew the engine of a car. He didn't let me get two feet away from him before he was on me like a lion closing in on its prey. The amusement had faded in his eyes replaced by complete and utter seriousness.

"You know that's how it should be, you and me."

"That isn't how it's supposed to be."

He shook his head, gently laying his hand on my cheek. The touch alone knocked the wind right out of my lungs. I looked away from him, concentrating on a point in the grass. It was taking all my will power to not faint. This was too much. He couldn't be serious. He just couldn't.

"Anya, look at me." His voice was low, husky. My gaze met his steady, warm eyes; soft yet full of conviction. "I don't just want to be your friend. I want more. I want you."

There was a part of me that didn't believe his words. Part of me couldn't believe them. But then I looked into his eyes and the honesty in his voice rang true.

It still didn't stop me from asking him the question that sprouted doubt.

"Why? So you can sleep with me and leave like you have done with every other girl?"

"If you were every other girl I wouldn't be trying this hard. Just give me a chance."

"Why should I?" I whispered.

"Because I'm asking."

"Liam, I..." I was at a loss for words. The way that he was looking at me with such patience and warmth caused my heart to flip flop in my chest. This was everything that I had ever prayed to happen. But this was also what I couldn't let myself have. I couldn't hurt him. He still didn't know the whole truth about me. If he knew he wouldn't be confessing his feelings for me.

"No," I finally said. His eyes widened with the blow of my words. "I can't. I just can't. I'm sorry."

I stepped away from him and backed away, turning on my heels and running the rest of the way home.

Chapter 24

G emma was furiously signing at me, her eyes blazing with anger and frustration. I couldn't blame her. I was pretty angry at myself too. But what could I do? It's not like I purposefully ran away from Liam Saturday. Did I want to run away from him? No. But under the circumstances I couldn't let him get that close to me. I wouldn't.

It would be a week tomorrow since we'd last spoken. We'd both gone back to awkwardly ignoring each other at school, acting like the other didn't exist. I knew that it wasn't exactly like that per se. I saw him sneaking a glance my way during class when I would sneak a peek at him. It was childish, I know. But I couldn't bring myself to talk to him. And judging from Liam's behavior he couldn't exactly work up the nerve to approach me either.

"Go talk to him. Now." Gemma signed, lightly nudging me in the direction where Liam stood, the door to his locker open as he absentmindedly stuffed books inside.

I shook my head. "No." She had been trying to get us to talk to each other all week; all her devious plans failing. She'd even recruited the help of Hayden. To my surprise he had been 100% on board. He even took the initiative to talk to Liam personally, which must have been awkward since they haven't spoken since their falling out last year.

"C'mon!" She threw her hands up in the air, garnering a few stares in our direction. "You're miserable. He's miserable. Why don't you just explain? It's easy."

I shut my locker door in resignation and shouldered my bag, walking towards the exit. Gemma followed me and we began to make the familiar path to her house for our usual Friday movie night. But in light of Hayden's absence (due to a weekend trip to Montgomery with his parents), movie night was turning into girl's night. We hadn't had a sleepover for a couple of months and I was in dire need of one. I couldn't wait to drown myself in Ben & Jerry's and watch sappy sad romantic movies that broke my heart.

Yeah. It was definitely going to be one of those nights.

"Gem, it's not that easy," I signed. I felt like a broken record saying the same thing over and over again, but Gemma wouldn't listen. She believed that it was easy and that I was the one making it complicated and difficult.

"You're the first person who's really cared about him in a long time," she said quietly. I was taken aback, physically halting mid-step in the middle of the road. A car honked and I sprinted, getting out of the way before I was flattened into a pancake. The driver rolled down her window and yelled some vulgar profanity that I did not wish to repeat as she sped away.

"What did you say?" I asked, breathless.

"You heard me," was all she said.

We walked the remainder of the way in silence, her words churning in my head. Was I really the first person who cared about him in a long time? Didn't he have Collin? He hadn't been completely alone since our abrupt friendship ended that long ago summer. I doubted that Collin didn't care about Liam. They were best friends like Gemma and I. Weren't boys' friendships the same as girls'?

This was obviously way too complicated for my feeble mind.

"Gem?" I asked as we headed to her room. We dumped our school bags haphazardly on the floor and flopped down on our usual spots: Me on the purple bean bag chair and her on the bed.

"Yeah?" came a tired reply.

"He has Collin," I measly offered.

She slowly sat up and glared at me and then flung a pillow at me. "Hey!" I threw it back at her and she deflected it.

"What are you, stupid?"

I gaped at her. She'd never ever used that tone with me like I was a person who couldn't understand the simple fact that the sky was blue.

"You're just afraid to admit that you might actually have feelings for him," she said. "Wait, no. Knowing you, you do have feelings for him but you are denying it because you're going to die. It's pathetic."

I was astounded at the cruelty in her words. That wasn't true. The image of the message in the bottle flashed through my mind. I had admitted it, but she didn't know. I hadn't told her. I wanted to keep that secret between Liam and me. It still didn't give her the right to say those hateful words. She knew how I felt about it. She knew.

Tears sprang to my eyes and I buried my face in my hands. I heard the squeak of the mattress give under the absent of her weight and felt her arms curl around my neck.

"I'm sorry," she muttered. "I shouldn't have said that. I'm sorry, An."

"But you're right," I said through a lump in my throat. "You're right."

"Then why don't you just tell him, kid? You told Hayden and me everything. No more secrets between us. Why not tell Liam too?" Her arms unwound from my neck. She laid her hands on my shoulders, giving them a small squeeze. "He's changed these past few months. Surely you've seen it. I think everyone has seen it. What he feels for you is no pretense, if that's what you're afraid of."

I was. But I had come to rationalize that it was just an excuse to prevent myself from being with him. Just like my illness was another.

"I was going to tell him that day, Gem." Fresh tears sprang to my eyes as the memory surfaced in my eyes. I saw Gemma nod, understanding flashing in her soft brown eyes. "But he stopped caring, Gem. He was too busy partying with the new crowd that he forgot about me. He became a person that I hated. And even if it's the opposite that I feel now, I can't help but think that he'll do it again."

She leaned forward and wiped the tears from my cheeks with her thumb. "He won't. He's said he won't, right?"

I weakly nodded. "But it doesn't stop me from thinking that-"

"You always think too much," she interjected. I let out a small laugh. "If you can't tell him at least tell him that you still want to be friends with him, Anya. Please? I can't stand to see him so...crestfallen and wounded like a small little bird whose wing has been broken."

I laughed, shaking my head in amazement. "Gemma. Seriously?"

She shrugged and laughed. "It's the truth! That's what he looks like. You broke him when you ran away from him while he was weak and vulnerable."

I groaned and buried my face into my hands. Gemma, ever so gently (not), pried my hands away from my face. There was a meaningful look in her eyes when I met her gaze. It was the kind of look that was full of understanding, yet, there was also reproach at my actions for the last few days.

"You need to talk to him," she said. "Now."

She was right. But did it have to be now? As if seeing the protest on my face she lifted one perfectly arched brow. "No buts."

"Gemma," I groaned. "I can't. He's works today, I think. Tomorrow. I promise I'll talk to him then."

She shook her head. It was impossible to argue with her once her mind was made up. I was regretting bring up Collin earlier. If I had just kept my mouth shut we would have never stumbled onto this topic of conversation. We could be watching one of Nicolas Spark's movies and eating pounds of ice cream!

"You're going to go and talk to him later tonight. I will personally walk you to his door and leave you there myself."

I don't think I've ever hated anyone as much as I hated Gemma at the moment. Okay, so maybe I didn't hate Gemma per se. But I really disliked her for leaving me alone on Liam's door like I was an abandoned kitten in a basket. I saw her form retreat into my house where she was sleeping over for the night.

I wasn't below going back on my word. I had the good sense of walking to the park and staying there for a few hours only to let her think that we'd patch everything up.

You'd be a coward if you did that, a voice whispered in my head. I inwardly groaned. Plus, you'd be breaking a promise to your friend.

I hung my head in dismay. If I had a pillow I would let out a smothering scream. Words could not describe how conflicted I was feeling. In the end, I raised my hand and knocked on the door, praying against all odds that he was sleeping.

The odds were not in my favor. The worst part of it was that Mr. Rowely answered the door smelling like he'd taken a swim in alcohol and later rolled in acrid cigars. He glared at me, his mouth set into a grim frown.

"What'd ya want girl?"

I gulped, curling my fists against my side. I found that my hands were shaking and I didn't want to give him the satisfaction that I was nervous and maybe a little bit scared to stand in his presence.

"Is Liam home?"

The frown curled into a sly grin. "Come right in." He opened the door wider and stepped to the side, allowing me to enter. He closed the door behind me and led me towards his room across the hall. As we got closer the dull resonate sound of rock music reached my ears. "He's in one of his moods," Mr. Rowely said. "Don't know what's the matter with him." He lifted his hand and pounded Liam's door with his fist. "Turn that shit down!" I flinched, stepping away from him. Maybe this wasn't such a good idea. I was going to kill Gemma when I got back.

The music was lowered but it could still be heard through the paper thin walls. I swear that the walls shook as an angry scream boomed from the speakers.

"You've got a visitor," Mr. Rowely bellowed. He turned his head to look at me, his eyes hazed over. "A pretty one from what I can tell."

I turned my eyes away from him, focusing on the peach nail polish on my toes. It was the beginning of November with the temperature dropping as the days went by. I loved winter. I loved the cold. My feet had a high tolerance for the cold climate, but I felt my skin prickle despite the warmth of the house. It was Mr. Rowely's unflinching gaze that made my toes chill to the marrow.

I was relieved when Liam opened the door, his steely gaze landing on his father first and then flickering to me.

"No funny business." His voice held a note of seriousness for a second and then he broke into a sputtering laugh, leaving me alone in the hallway with Liam. He ushered me inside, practically pushing me into the safety of his humble abode. The door was shut and the radio turned up a few dials louder.

I took a seat at his desk, thinking that his bed was too comfortable, too familiar. Liam leaned against the frame of the window, close enough so that we could hear each other above the blaring speakers.

"What are you doing here, Anya?" The note of resignation was enough to break my heart into a million pieces. Gemma said I had broken him and seeing him in front of me with half dark shadows under his eyes, mouth drawn in a line that was on the verge of a frown, and hair messily tousled like he'd ran his hand through it a hundred times – well, I didn't know what to say to him. My mouth went dry and I averted my eyes to my lap where I played with the hem of my shirt.

Words couldn't express how deeply sorry I was. What I wanted to do was wrap my arms around him and feel his arms wrap around my waist, feeling the warmth and safety I had come to associate to him. He'd tell me that everything would be okay and I'd believe him because in the end things always worked out the way they were always meant unfold in the first place. This was just a bump in the road and we'd go over it just like we went over pervious troubles. The place where we were at – it was always the hardest. It was always difficult and never simple.

"Anya?" I hadn't notice that he had knelt in front of me. His eyes were filled with concern, which only made me feel even worst. I didn't deserve his worry. But here he was, giving it to me like I hadn't just stepped on his heart and left it out to dry.

"Do you hate me?" I asked, unable to meet his gaze.

I was met with impenetrable silence. The only sound I could hear was the pounding of my heart in my ears. Not even the music could compete with the loud hammering that had taken over. I lifted my eyes to see Liam rubbing the back of his neck, the hem of his shirt lifting to expose the bare skin of his hip. I looked away quickly, my face flushing.

Liam turned down the music to a low drone and said with his back turned to me, "No, I don't hate you."

The words should have washed relief over my body. But it didn't. It was what he didn't say that caused me to become hyper-aware of my surroundings.

"But?" I pressed.

The muscles on his back contracted, becoming hard and rigid like he was exercising extensive force. "Why are you here?" His voice had lost the note of resignation and instead it was cold and distant.

"I-I came..." I bit my lip at a loss for words. This wasn't particularly going how I imagined. Liam turned around, his face a mask of pure stoicism. There was no trace of evidence to prove that concern once marred his features a minute ago. He was putting on a brave front because of me.

How could I even explain to tell him how I felt with him like this? It would be impossible.

Not impossible, a small voice whispered. Just listen to your heart.

"I don't want us to stop being friends, Liam." His shoulders relaxed one tenth of an increment. It was a good sign and I continued. "I've been miserable the past few days and Gemma says that you have too." A small smile tugged at the edge of his lips. "I miss you. But I can't be with you."

The smile quickly disappeared from his mouth. I was taken aback by how sudden it was. "Give me a reason why you can't."

"Because of me," I whispered.

He crossed his arms over his chest, his eyes patiently waiting for a better answer. I let out a whoosh of air. He wasn't going to make this easy.

"I don't want anything to ruin our friendship. I can't bear to lose you again, Liam. After years of not having you in my life..." I stood up from my seat and approached him. "You don't know how sorry I am for running away from you Saturday. I shouldn't have, but I freaked out. Apparently it's what I do."

Something flashed in his eyes, but I couldn't read what it was. He was silent for a long time. His eyes were unfocused as he took a seat on the edge of the bed, leaning forward and resting his chin in his hands. I didn't know what to do. I felt useless just standing there in the middle of his room and trying to evade my eyes from him. He looked like he was lost in his thoughts and wouldn't be surfacing any time soon. It was strange seeing him in that sort of stage where he looked like he was caught between dreaming and waking.

After a few minutes, I began to make my way to the door but his voice stopped me in my tracks.

"What happened to us?"

I looked back and felt a wave of vertigo wash over my body. The image of a twelve year old Liam briefly flashed in my mind's eye. It was only for a fragment of a second – his words bringing me back to that year. It was something that I've always wanted to know and he'd share the same sentiment. I felt the warmth of his fingers circle my wrist, righting my balance as the image faded and my vision cleared.

"You alright?"

I blinked, focusing on the blue of his eyes. "Yes. Thanks."

He nodded and led me to the bed, his eyes racking over my body, making sure that I was okay in every way. It was the sort of look that a parent gave their child when they'd just fallen off their bike and scraped their knee. For some reason it made my heart sink.

"Liam?"

"Hm?"

"What happened to us?" I asked, mirroring the same question he'd ask before I had my dizzy spell. I was grateful that I hadn't blacked out. That wouldn't have gone very well.

"I don't know, you tell me."

I bit my lip. His voice was once again back to its resigned note. I was really starting to miss his sarcasm. "You said that I abandoned you just like everyone else had," I quietly said. "What did you mean?"

He ran a hand through his hair and let out a tired sigh. He didn't look at me when he spoke. Instead his words rushed out like he had wanted to say them for a long time. "I made stupid decisions that summer and you never once came to knock some sense into me. You were disappointed in me and just cut me off when you were the only person who could have kept me grounded. Dad wasn't – well you see how he is. I never imagined that you'd just check out like he had. But you did."

"You're right," I said. He looked up at me, pain flashing in his eyes. "I was disappointed in you, but not because of what you did." I took his hand in mine. He hesitated for a brief second before he gaze my hand a small squeeze. "You ditched me at the park and I felt betrayed even more when I found out what you had done that day. The next day you didn't even come to apologize and I waited for you until I figured that you didn't want to be friends with the poor little sick girl anymore."

"Anya I never–"

"I know that now," I cut in. "Judging from both sides of our stories, if we'd just gone to each other then the long stretch of absence never would have happened."

He nodded, a glint of mischief surfacing in his beautiful eyes. I held my breath, anticipating his words. "If you weren't so prideful maybe we'd always be friends."

I gaped at him and smacked him in the arm. He feigned mock hurt. "Me? Prideful? Hilarious."

He chuckled. "I don't know about you but I'm glad we got that out of the water."

"Me too."

I hopped of the bed, feeling a million times better. There was a happy grin plastered on my face and I wasn't going to be a fool to hide it. Liam let down his guard, his shoulders were completely relaxed and judging from the smile on his face he was better too.

"Friends?"

A muscle in his jaw clenched but he quickly pulled me into a hug, answering my question. I sank into the familiarity of his arms wrapped around me, letting out a breath full of relief.

"I should go," I said as I disentangled myself from his warmth.

"I'll walk you out."

I wasn't sure what time it was by the time I got home. Dad was in the living room reading a book by the dim glow of the night stand. Not wanting to disturb him I walked across the threshold. My foot was on the first step of the stairs when I heard him call my name.

"Yeah, dad?" I backtracked, shuffling into the room.

He gave me an apprehensive look. "How did things go?"

I groaned. "Did Gemma tell you?"

He chuckled, sliding a bookmark to keep his place and closing the book. "She did." He patted the arm chair and I obediently took a seat. "I think she's still up. She could hardly contain her excitement when you left so I asked what was up and she readily gave your mom and me the details."

I shook my head. I was going to kill her when I go upstairs.

"Everything is good now. Nothing to worry about, Dad."

He beamed. "Good, bug. I am proud of you for taking the first step. If Liam was anything – well, never mind that."

"No. What were you going to say?" I really wanted to know and nothing could hide the curiosity in my voice.

"Nothing," he said smiling. "You should head on up. It's late."

I sighed and kissed his cheek. "Night, Dad."

"Night, sweetie."

I trudged up the stairs and was bombarded with Gemma bouncing up and down in excitement.

"Well?" she inquired. "How did it go?"

"I should kill you right now."

She smiled and let out a high pitched squeal. "C'mon! Tell me!"

I flopped back onto the bed and told her everything with a smile on my face.

Chapter 25

The minute the final bell rang; Liam hastily sprang to his feet and marched out of the class. My brows knitted together in confusion as my gaze travelled between the empty seat beside me and the door. It left me completely frazzled as I packed up my things and filed out of the classroom with the rest of the students.

The week had gone by terribly fast. I felt like time was being stolen from me as the days became unrecognizable. Thanksgiving was next Thursday and that meant our annual Thanksgiving dinner with the Weatherly's and Novak's. I couldn't wait to eat Mrs. Weatherly's famous pumpkin pie or Mrs. Novak's homemade chicken pot pie. Then there was Mom's delicious turkey that she made every year. Unfortunately, the men in the family – including Hayden for that matter – just sat in the Novak's den and watched a football game. Sometimes, Gemma and I would sneak away from the kitchen to join them for a while. A girl couldn't miss a football game – especially in the Vanchester/Weatherly houshould –no matter what. Cooking could be put on hold for an hour...or two.

I was invested deep in thoughts of turkey, mash potatoes, and football – my mouth practically watering at the imaginary table I'd conjured in my mind – that I abruptly stopped when I saw Liam talking to Gemma by her locker. The person behind me crashed into my shoulder, sending a sharp, dull ache down my arm.

"Hey!" the girl said, her eyes flashing with annoyance. "Watch where you're going, freak."

"Sorry," I mumbled. My reply must have satisfied her, but before she sauntered off she rolled her eyes as if my presence alone caused her great affliction.

I veered to the side, trying to analyze ex-best friend talking to my current best friend. Liam's hands were stuffed in the front pockets of his jeans, his gaze intently trained on Gemma. I squinted my eyes in their direction, noting that she was talking to him.

Gemma was talking to Liam.

In public.

What in the world could they possibly be talking about? Is that the reason why he practically ran out at the end of Calculus, to talk to my best friend? If that was the reason, well, it made sense. If he wanted to talk to Gem alone then he'd have to ditch me. The question was: what did he need to talk to her about?

I felt the anxiety settle at the pit of my stomach as I crossed the hallway and headed towards them. My eyes widened in disbelief as I grew closer and saw Liam signing. He was lightly tapping the right side of his temple with his right fist. His eyes were focused on Gem as he repeated the sign three times with a faint smile on his lips. There was a sly, cunning smirk on Gemma's face which only made what he was signing even more confusing.

I came to a stop beside Gemma, cocking my head to the side. "Why are you calling my friend an asshole?"

His hand fell from his temple, his brows knitting together in confusion. "What?"

Gemma laughed beside me, her eyes shining with amusement. "Think of it as a hazing ritual."

I laughed, a wide grin plastered on my face as I saw Liam run a hand through his hair as if the motion alone could dispel his embarrassment.

His brief moment of humiliation was quickly replaced with a small smile. "I'll have to use that on an unsuspected bystander next time."

Gemma beamed. "Definitely. You'll get a kick out of it too." She turned towards me, lifting her hand and beginning to sign.

"I like him." Her eyes momentarily flickered to Liam and then back at me. So this was the reason she switched to signing. She would never have said those words in front of him. Sign language was definitely handy when it came to being secretive. "He's good just like I figured. He was just lost and needed you like you need him."

I shook my head. "Gem..."

"Okay, okay. I'm sorry. Just..."

She didn't get to finish her thought because Liam chose that very moment to clear his throat. "I'd love to continue this stimulating conversation that I wasn't invited to, but I have to head to work. So I'll see you guys later."

"How rude," Gemma muttered.

Liam's brow rose, his hand flying to his chest in mock indignation. "Me? Rude? Never."

"Try always," I quipped.

Liam shook his head, his bright eyes betraying the straight face he was trying to accomplish. A moment later his face broke into a crooked smile and he winked at me. I smiled and looked down at the floor, playing with the ends of my hair as my stomach flip-flopped in giddiness.

"Anya," he said. "I'll see you later?"

I nodded. "Usual time?"

"Yes. I'll come get you."

I bit my lip, anticipation already coursing through my veins at his words. "Okay."

He gave a slight nod and turned on his heels, heading towards the side exit that led to the parking lot. Gemma nudged my shoulder as we watched him disappear around the corner. "He's not giving up, An. You know that, right?"

My shoulders sagged forward, the thrill of seeing Liam quickly fading as I let out a long breath full of resignation and guilt.

The day before Thanksgiving, Liam and I spent it at the hospital in the children's ward. It had become one of my traditions – that every Wednesday before the holiday I would come and spent the entire afternoon with the kids. It filled me with an unexplained sadness, seeing and knowing that the children who were too sick to go home couldn't experience Thanksgiving. I just wanted to take them all home with me. There would be enough food for everyone and absolutely nothing would go to waste. Most of all, I wanted to bring Madi and Jon's family to the Novak's tomorrow. They'd have a blast, running around their townhouse, exploring every nook and cranny.

But they couldn't leave the hospital. Their families would come and spend a few hours with their children like they did every year and then they'd leave to enjoy the rest of the evening with friends and family. There were a few exceptions like Katie, Griffin, and Kyle's parents, who would stay until visiting hours were over at six. I wished that there were more people like that. I loved their parents for spending as much time as they possibly could with their children. They treasured every second of every day, never knowing if tomorrow was guaranteed.

"Anya?" Jon tugged on the hem of my shirt. "Are you okay?"

I looked up at him, his eyes filled with concern. His small hand was frozen in midair as he was about to finish the castle he'd intricately built from the small Legos scattered in front of us.

I nodded, not trusting my voice. A lump in my throat formed as Jon crawled to me, wrapping his small arms around my neck. I smiled, rubbing his back soothingly. "What's this for, kiddo?"

"A hug always makes someone feel better. You said that to me, remember?"

"Yes." I bit my lip, holding back the tears that threatened to spill. My heart was heavy, filled with impenetrable sadness. I needed to go and take a few minutes to pull myself together before I upset the whole ward.

Jon unwound his arms around me and gave me toothy smile. "Better?"

"Better," I lied.

He crawled back to his place, triumph lighting up his face. "I'll be right back," I told him. "Don't let Liam get into any trouble."

Jon flashed me a bright smile as our eyes travelled to him across the room, reading a book to Griffin, Sophie, Todd, and Jeff. I walked out the door, closing it quietly behind me, not wanting to alert my absence. I should have walked straight to the bathroom without pause. I shouldn't have turned back to gaze through the window at the kids all happily playing together in groups or individually like Jon. Madi was playing dress up with Katie and Amy; her eyes shining with enthusiasm as Katie said something, triggering an idea.

A sob escaped my lips and I covered my mouth with my hand, running towards the bathrooms at the end of the hall. I locked myself in one of the halls, bringing my knees up to my chin, letting the tears fall down my cheeks.

Life wasn't fair.

It wasn't.

I hated it.

Why did it seem that the good people in the world were always the ones who had to deal with the hardest things that the world was plagued with? None of those kids deserved to be sick. None of them. I hated how most of their parents had given up hope, not even wasting their time to visit their own children. It broke my heart, seeing the sadness that lingered in their eyes at times. It would come and go, but never fade. I would never know fully how they felt because my parents cared. They loved me with all their hearts, and they'd do anything to keep me with them for as long as possible. But just imagining how it felt made my chest heavy.

Just one day, I prayed. Give me one day.

I waited expectedly, silently; afraid that I would miss His voice. But nothing came. I was met with the low hum of the air conditioner above me. Defeated, I buried my head in my knees and cried. I don't know how long I cried for but it seemed never ending. Just when I thought it was over a new tremor of sobs would break through and then, the process would start all over again.

A soft knock on the stall brought me back to my sense. "Sorry," I croaked. "Busy."

"Anya, let me in."

I couldn't believe it. Liam. How had he found me? I lifted my head from my knees, my eyes locking on the dirty and worn converse on the other side of the door; a stark contrast to the gleaming white tiles. His blond hair toppled over the stall and if he wanted too, he could even peek over the door to see if I was okay.

"What are you doing in the girl's bathroom?" I asked instead. Swiftly, I unrolled a line of toilet paper and blew my nose. I needed more than just a couple of sheets, and possibly some ice cream. I'd have to ask Liam if we could make a stop at the parlor before we headed home.

"Anya."

I sighed and reached forward, sliding open the lock. The door voluntarily swung inward and Liam took a hesitant step forward, crouching in front of me. His eyes shone with concern as he laid his hand on my knee. My heart melted when he reached out his hand and brushed the strands of hair from my face, tucking them behind my ear.

"Why did you leave?" he asked.

I shook my head. "It's stupid."

"Hey." The warm touch of his fingers on my chin brought my attention to him. His eyes were intensely steady as he said, "Whatever it is can't be stupid. You wouldn't cry over something mundane, Anya. I know you."

When he said those words something inside me broke. Before the tears began to fall from my eyes, Liam pulled me into his chest, enfolding me in his arms. I nestled my face into the crook of his neck and breathed in the lingering scent of smoke and cinnamon. In a strangled voice I told him about how I felt, pushing through the lump in my throat and the tears in my eyes. He listened without interruption, occasionally reaching forward and tenderly wiping the tears from my cheeks with a calloused thumb.

He didn't need to say anything afterwards. The understanding in his slate blue eyes as we walked back to the ward was enough to show me how he did know me. Words were limited at times, but actions burned fervently with all that needed to be said.

Before we went into the play room I tugged on Liam's forearm. "Wait. I need to ask you something."

"Okay," he said. "I'm all ears."

I smiled. "What are you doing tomorrow for Thanksgiving?"

His brows furrowed. Something flashed in his eyes, but quickly faded as he crossed his arms over his chest. Just by his composure alone I could read that Thanksgiving was a subject he rarely discussed or even thought about. Thanksgiving was something foreign since his mom passed and Mr. Rowely drowned himself in spirit. It made me angry and guilty that I hadn't thought about what I was proposing sooner.

"Don't know." He shrugged. "I'll probably head out of town for a few hours. Why?"

"We have Thanksgiving dinner every year with the Weatherly's and Novak's and if you want you're welcome to join us. It'll be fun. There will be lots of food and football."

His lips quirked into a lazy smile. "You had me at food and football. Count me in."

"I knew you wouldn't be able to resist."

He smiled and we headed back into the room where we were met with Madi and Jon wrapping their arms around our legs; their smiles bringing forth one of our very own.

Chapter 26

Liam

I had the disconcerting feeling that I was marching into a war zone as I trudged up the familiar path to Hayden's townhouse. There were two other cars aside from Hayden's '67 Chevy Impala parked in the driveway. Mr. Vanchester's old and beat up Ford Taurus looked out of place to the Impala's immaculate black exterior, the surface shiny beneath the sun's rays. The other was a '06 Ford F150 dark blue truck which I could only guess belonged to the Weatherly's.

Balancing the store bought apple pie to my left hand, I rung the doorbell, and waited. My nerves were shot as I impatiently drummed my fingers on the plastic surface of the pie covering. A muffled "Coming!" reached my ears and a second later the door opened.

"Hey," Hayden said. He opened the door wider, revealing a red foam finger cover his right hand with a big #1 printed on it. His eyes narrowed and asked, "Alabama or Auburn?"

I shook my head, aghast. "My loyal to the Crimson Tide has yet to change."

He nodded and stepped aside, allowing me to come in. "I'll let Anya know you're here." I nodded as I shrugged off my leather jacket, hanging it on the coat rack by the door. "Anya!" Hayden hollered. "Liam's here!"

"Thanks for that introduction."

Hayden chuckled, clasping a hand on my shoulder. "It was a bet between Gem and I. She'll owe me five bucks later when I win."

"What's the bet?" I asked curiously. His mouth quirked into a sly, knowing grin as his eyes fixed on a point behind me.

I turned around and saw Anya striding forward, dabbing her hands on the yellow apron she wore. There was a smudge of powder on her nose that I wanted to gently wipe away. But it was neither the time nor place. I was acutely aware of Hayden's eyes flickering back and forth between me and Anya; a lazy smile plastered on his face.

"Hey." She smiled and quickly looked at the ground when she caught Hayden's gaze. When her eyes flitted to me again I noticed the rosy tinge to her cheeks. Hayden crossed his arms over his chest and suppressed a laugh as Anya flashed him a hard look.

"Isn't there somewhere you need to be – like, I don't know..." She shrugged and bit her lip, her mind churning for an idea. Hayden waited expectantly, amusement apparent in his green eyes. I could practically see the light bulb flash on in her eyes when she said, "I heard Auburn made a touchdown on my way over here."

The grin on Hayden's face slowly turned into a mask of horror. "What? You've got to be kidding me!" He took a step back and began to retreat down the hall, muttering underneath his breath, "Damn dirty Tigers." As a last minute thought he pivoted on his heels and added, "You remember your way to the den, Rowely?"

"Yeah," I said. "I'll be there-"

There was no point in finishing my thought as Hayden waved his hand and continued down the corridor, disappearing around the bend.

Turning to Anya I said, "That was a good way to get rid of him."

She laughed. "Yeah, well, that's Hayden for you. He can make a situation turn awkward with the snap of his fingers. I have no idea how Gemma deals with him."

I chuckled and handed her the pie. "So when's dinner?"

She smiled, shaking her head. "Is that the only reason you came, for the food?"

"No, I came for football too."

"Is that all you care about?"

I shrugged. "I'm a guy."

She rolled her eyes but there was a faint smile pulling at the corners of her plump pink lips. "Typical. Well, go watch your football," she shooed, putting her hands on the small of my back and leading me towards the hall. "Do you want anything to drink? We have water, coke...beer?"

"I'll have a coke."

"Alright." She removed her hand and I found myself missing the warmth she emitted whenever she touched me. "I'll bring you one. It's probably time to bring fresh rounds to everyone anyways."

"Okay."

She turned and walked back towards the foyer, her heels clicking on the cherry wood floorboards. My footsteps echoed along the empty hall as I made my way towards the den at the opposite side of where the kitchen was where I imagined Anya scurrying around, preparing for the dinner that would take place a few hours from now.

I glanced at the few paintings and family portraits that littered the walls on my way. Everything was placed exactly where it had been since the last time I'd stepped foot in Hayden's place. The memories of cheap beer and video games filtered through my mind's eye, lasting only a fragment of a second. I realized, as I reached the room and saw Hayden perched on the edge of the sofa (intently watching the game without blinking) that I was a fool to sever all ties with him.

After all, wasn't I chasing the same thing that he had found in Gemma?

"Looks like we got a newcomer."

I blinked; the voice breaking through my reverie. All eyes were on me as I warily stepped forward, unsure of what the men would think of my presence here. Mr. Vanchester was the first to break the prolonged silence as he stood up and offered me his hand.

"Good to see you, Liam. I'm sure you're acquainted with everyone here?"

"Yes," I said. My gaze lingered on Mr. Weatherly longer than anyone else. Even dressed down to plain black dress pants and a blue buttoned up shirt he still radiated an air of daunting authority. The man probably hated me for all the late nights he had been dispatched for an offense I'd committed. His brown eyes assessed me, trying to read my mind – which I didn't doubt was a secret super power he'd acquired after years on the force.

Mr. Novak, on the other hand, flashed me a courteous smile, bringing up the hand he was holding his beer as acknowledgement.

"Thanks for having me, Mr. Novak."

"No problem, kid. You're always welcome here."

I smiled and took a seat beside Hayden on the sofa. Turning to my right I extended my hand to Mr. Weatherly and said, "It's been a long time, sir."

The grim frown on his mouth twisted into a grin. He took my hand and shook it, his eyes softening. "Good thing too, son. You've come around. It's not something I see every day."

I was taken aback by his words. They weren't something that I expected to hear in a million years. All I could mutter was a simple, "Thank you, sir," and those words alone couldn't express the gratitude that stirred deep inside the recesses of my chest.

After we got settled, Anya and Gemma came shortly after with cold sodas and a few bottles of beer. They didn't stay for more than a few minutes, their gazes lingering on the twenty inch plasma screen mounted on the far wall for a few seconds before leaving.

The girls didn't return until the fourth quarter where Alabama was in the lead against Auburn 27-14. Anya settled at my feet, leaning her back against the sofa as she cheered on Dee Milliner's 35-yard interception return early in the fourth quarter.

"That was beautiful!" she exclaimed. "The Tigers are going to have a hard time coming back after that one."

She was right as the game continued. Auburn managed to hold on for three quarters, but once Milliner intercepted Moseley's bad pass everything changed. The Tigers made small mistakes that cost them the game and as the ending reared, the game only grew fiercer with a penalty to Frazier for overthrowing a receiver.

"Good eye, Ref," Gemma said, earning a proud smile from Hayden.

The aggression was practically steaming from the screen in perpetual waves as Auburn tried to make a comeback, pushing back the Tides a few yards but not getting very far.

"They aren't ever a match for Bama. They always screw up in the last two quarters," Anya said, taking a sip from her coke.

"They've got a good defense," Mr. Vanchester said. "But they have to take Moseley out if they want to have successful passes."

"Agreed," Mr. Weatherly said. "That boy is screwing up. I wonder why Gene Chizik doesn't pull him out of the game now."

There was a collective assent as we continued to watch the remaining ten minutes left of the game. Anya idly tapped her fingers on her knee and squirmed around, unable to sit still. I remember making a joke a few days ago about her having ADHD. It was early Tuesday night and we were watching Spiderman 3. She was lying on her stomach, absentmindedly swinging her feet back and forth, getting up and re-positioning herself on the pillows, and drumming her fingers on the comforter every few minutes. It was distracting and if I didn't know any better I would have thought she was doing it on purpose.

"Touchdown!" The rooms booming cheer jeered me back to reality. On the screen I saw Jalston Fowler in the recap making a 15 yd run, earning the Tides a 27 point lead.

"We're so winning!" Gemma exclaimed. "C'mon Shelley, make that kick baby."

My face broke into a smile. Never would I have imagined that Gemma (or Anya for that matter) loved football with a fiery passion. Both girls squealed in delight as Shelley made the field goal.

In the end, the Tides swept the Tigers out of the water. The final score: 42-14.

"Alright, let's get this dinner underway," Mr. Novak said, setting down the remote on the coffee table. "But first a toast."

We stood, grabbing the remainder of our drinks. Anya flashed me a secret smile, her eyes dancing brightly under the warm light emitting from the lampshade. "To Bama," Mr. Novak began, "for their strategic and well played game. They are a perfect example of what a team made up of heart and soul can accomplish."

"To Roll Tide," we chorus and raised our glasses, taking a drink. Anya scrunched her nose as the cold lemon tang of the Sprite she downed burned her throat. For some unknown reason it made me smile. She radiated vigorous warmth, reminding me of a bright morning star at dawn.

"So who's hungry?" Gemma asked.

We looked at her dubiously and broke out into easy laughs, filing out of the den and towards the kitchen.

When we entered the Novak's opulent dining room I was assaulted with the delicious smells of cooked turkey, bacon, mashed potatoes, and lasagna. They were the only aroma's that were distinguishable among the array of other dishes spread out on the dining table. The crystal chandelier that hung in the middle of the ceiling sent a kaleidoscope of colors dancing along walls. The lights around the room made Anya's dark brown hair a lighter shade, matching the brilliant hue of her eyes.

"This is wonderful girls," Mr. Vanchester said. "Anya, where is-"

The side door that led to the kitchen swung open as Mrs. Vanchester walked in carrying a hot pan of bean casserole. She set the dish down on the table and tugged off the oven mitts. Mr. Vanchester came around and planted a kiss on his wife's temple. Mrs. Weatherly and Mrs. Novak walked into the room a few minutes after with no aprons or mitts in sight. All the women wore simple but elegant dresses their hair pinned up in an elaborate do. I felt like I was in a 50's Thanksgiving Special as they all welcomed me with open arms. I wondered what the guy would do in the show. Would it be a comedy where the minute dinner began he'd run away? Or would it be a heartwarming episode where he'd learn some valuable lesson?

I stood to the side, watching everyone else take their placed seats. Mr. Novak sat at the far end of the table with his wife and Hayden on either side of him. Next to Hayden, Gemma took her seat while her parents sat across from her next to Mrs. Novak. Anya sat next to Mr. Weatherly and Mrs. Vanchester sat directly across from him. Mr. Vanchester took the opposite end of the table, leaving the seat across Anya vacant. I slid in as stealthy as I could and grabbed the napkin intricately folded in front of me, laying it on my lap as everyone else had.

"Phil," Mr. Novak said. "Will you lead us in grace?"

Mr. Vanchester didn't reply – instead, he reached out his hand to Anya and me, joining hands all around the table causing a domino effect. Everyone bowed their heads and closed their eyes and I mirrored their actions, unsure of what I was supposed to do other then listen.

He recited a simple prayer, his words lost to my ears as the memory of the last thanksgiving dinner I remembered flashed through my head. I saw Mom smiling and laughing, her blue eyes crinkling at the corners at something that Dad had said. He looked younger and healthier without the scars of grief and spirits marring his face.

"Amen."

I blinked my eyes open, the room hazy for a moment as the disconcerting feeling of the memory grew faint until it was gone.

Anya's soft brown eyes were the first thing that came into focus. Her eyes assessed me, curiosity clearly visible in their depth.

"Are you okay," she mouthed as everyone began filling their plates.

I nodded. It was all I could do to let her know that I was fine. Absentmindedly, I filled my plate with two slices of turkey, a large spoonful of mash potatoes and lasagna. I dug in, stifling a moan that crawled from my throat. It was mouth-watering. I couldn't remember the last time I had a good home cooked meal. I should have been able to remember, but those memories – that time – they were hard to grasp. All I could associate with that period was Mom dying and everything going up in flames because of it.

I got lost in my own thoughts as all around me the low drone of voices buzzed around me. Laughs broke through my musings for a fraction of a moment, but I quickly sank into my own deprive once more. I kept thinking about my mom in those last few months were her will to survive was the strongest form of fortitude I had ever seen. She was frail; barely holding onto a thread, but her hope spoke volumes to anyone who saw her. Dad tried to be strong for the both of us, but it was hard seeing the woman he loved slowly deteriorate to someone he barely recognized any longer.

I was angry with him the day he renounced his will two days before Mom passed. I found him unconscious on the living room floor, the smell of alcohol pungent in the air. I didn't realize then that night would be the first of many where I'd have to clean up the mess that Dad had gotten himself into.

I never told Anya any of it; afraid to shed light of the burdens I carried. It proved to be too much for a fourteen year old to handle because I turned into my father that summer, taking in the solace that a bottle had to offer..

I wondered how things would have turned out if I'd just told Anya. How much would things be different? How much would our lives have ended up the same? I couldn't turn back time and change the past, but I could change the course of my future.

"Liam? Hey, Liam."

Snapping back to reality, I looked down at the hand that shook my forearm. Anya's eyes were laced with worry, and as I glanced around the table I noted that everyone wore a similar expression.

I mustered a smile and said, "Yeah?"

"Mom was asking how you like the food," Anya said, retracting her hand from my arm. She leaned back in her seat, gnawing on her lip in concern.

"Oh, the food!" I put my fork down, clearing my throat of the false vibrato my words were laced with. I turned my attention to Mrs. Vanchester, her brown eyes mirroring the concern that I had seen in her daughter's. "It's spectacular. This has far exceeded what I had expected."

"What did you expect?" Gemma asked.

"Honestly?"

"No, lie to us," she muttered.

I chuckled and said to Anya, "I see now how Gemma deals with Hayden."

Anya broke out into a fit of giggles. Everyone else smiled, the tension in the room dissipating as Gemma and Hayden tried to grasp the joke. Mr. Novak clapped a hand on his son's back and said something like "Let it go." Gemma harrumphed but Anya quickly dispelled any hard feelings by signing with one another across the table.

Gem smiled and retold the story to Hayden. When he finally got the joke after five minutes he said, "Ha-ha. Good one, Rowely. Quit a knee slapper."

"You're just jealous you didn't get it," Anya quipped. "Everyone else seemed to. Talk about being slow on the tracks."

"Anya!" Mrs. Vanchester exclaimed.

She shrugged, trying to stifle the giggles that were proving to be difficult to stop. "It's true!"

Hayden crossed his arms and feigned mock anger. Mrs. Novak stood up from the table, an armful of empty dishes in her hands. She set them down on the marble island and ruffled her Hayden's hair on the way back to her seat. "Isn't he cute when he's angry?"

"Mom!"

"What?" she asked. "You know, when he was younger and he didn't get his way he would beat his head on the floor and throw a tantrum. I think I have a picture of him doing that somewhere..."

"Oh, God," Hayden muttered. "Kill me now."

Laughter filled the room as we all found amusement at Hayden's expense. He took it all good naturedly, adding his own quips as the attention switched to Mrs. Novak and her love of art to Mr. Weatherly's elaborate story telling skills as he recounted past cases.

The time passed quickly after that as someone took over the role of story teller. Dessert was served and eaten as the atmosphere in the room changed to a friendly and familiar vibe that I rapidly became a part of. Whatever fears I might have had today were promptly squashed as I caught Anya's sparkling eyes. Happiness emitted from her body, encasing her in reverent warmth like an angel sent from above. For a moment, it felt like we were the only two people in the room, basking in each other's nearness.

As dinner came to a close, everyone gathered their plates and filed into the kitchen, depositing them in the sink. I wondered if it would have been polite to stay and help, but Anya tugged on my elbow, signaling me to follow her down the hall and towards the foyer.

"You made quite an impression," she said. Her words were etched with praise and wonder. I couldn't see her face, but I could imagine a carefree smile on her soft lips.

"I thought I'd be flayed alive, but it wasn't so bad."

"You're so dramatic." She turned; halting in the exact same place she had been when I entered the house. The lights were dim in this part of the house. Slivers of light filtered through the drawn velvet curtains, casting her face in shadows. I stepped closer, the smell of her perfume filling my nose. She smelled like crushed roses in the wee hours of the morning when I cruised by Leighton Street on my way to school.

"I'm glad you came." Her voice was barely above a whisper.

"Me too," I said. "Thank you for having me. You were right – you did have enough food to feed an army."

She smiled. "I'm happy you liked it. – Hey, you never did answer Gemma's question."

I raised my brow. "Which one?"

"The one about your expectations."

"Ah, that one." Voices resonated through the hall as the others approached. Anya's face contorted into an annoyed and resigned expression, her shoulders hunching forward. She ran her hand through her wavy locks, letting out a sigh. Her emotions reflected the ones that stirred within my chest.

She walked me to the door, taking my jacket from the coat rack and handing it to me. The cold winter air bit at my skin with its icy fingers as I stepped through the threshold. The half moon gleamed in the sky, its rays offering light to the dark world below.

"Drive safely, okay?"

I nodded and leaned in, pressing a soft kiss to her temple. It was a bold move; a risk that had wanted to take since I kissed her a few weeks ago. I wanted to kiss her again, but I couldn't push Anya to feel the same thing that I felt for her. That wouldn't prove anything other than confirm her suspicions about me. All I could do was show her that she meant more to me than anything or anyone else in my life.

"I'll be careful," I finally whispered. "Have a goodnight."

Her cheeks were flushed when I pulled away, but I couldn't tell if it was from the cold or the kiss.

Chapter 27

The days following Thanksgiving quickly turned into weeks and those turned into two months. Again, I felt like time was being stolen from me with the finality that my life was coming to an end. But it was the opposite of how I felt. Everything was finally settling into place – just like I'd always prayed it to be. Liam and I spent countless hours together – much of the time in his room, watching all our favorite movies and remembering all the precious moments we shared when we were kids.

Other times we would lay there basking in comfortable silence, on opposite sides of the bed; me with my knees propped up against the headboard, lost in thought; his face inches from mine, draped across the lower half the bed. After long days at work, Liam would come home exhausted and he'd fall asleep beside me. Those days were my blissful secrets as I watched him peacefully slumber. There were no lines of worries on his face or the sharp edges of his jaw. He was beautiful with his golden tousled hair, reminding me of an angel who had lost their way.

Our blossoming relationship wasn't the only thing that had changed. Within the past six weeks my health had drastically changed directions. I was stronger and vibrant, full of energy and everlasting hope. Dr. Novak wanted to know what I had changed in my daily routine, but I couldn't give him an answer. I kept taking insulin and medicine in the morning just as I had my whole life.

I was overjoyed with the news and so were my parents. There was still hope that I would live to be at least fifty. It was more than I was guaranteed when I was fourteen, but it was something. I wasn't going to give up.

Not now.

Not ever.

"Anya."

I jumped, startled by the sound of my name. Mom's soft chuckling brought a smile to my lips as I turned in my chair to see her standing at the door. There was a brown packaging envelope in her hands. On the packaging label there was a giant red PRIORITY stamped haphazardly across the mailing address. The sight of it made my heart leap in my chest.

"Is that...?"

Mom smiled and crossed the room, taking a seat on the edge of my bed. I jumped out of my seat and settled next to her, taking the package from her hands. "Wait, where's Dad?"

"Downstairs."

I gave her a dubious look and she smiled sheepishly. In a really loud holler she called, "Phil! Get up here. Now!"

I counted five Mississippi's before I heard Dad's loud footsteps up the stairs. When he entered my room he was rumpled and out of breath. His eyes were wide as he looked around the room, assessing every corner as if he would find something out of the ordinary – like an alien or a half naked Liam. I'm not sure which would frighten him more.

"What's the matter? Are you hurt? Did something...?"

Mom and I burst into a fit of giggles at his disheveled and alarmed appearance. He blinked and scratched his head, confused for a minute before concluding that nothing was amiss.

"Okay," he said. "If nothing is wrong then what is?"

I smiled broadly and held up the package for him to see. It was all I needed to do for Dad to get on the same boat Mom and I were in. He strolled across the room and sat next to me, his eyes shining brightly with anticipation.

"Alright," I said, letting out a whoosh of air. "Here it goes."

I tore open the packaging and gingerly shook out the papers that were inside. My eyes widened and I squealed in joy as I skimmed the letter from Julliard. I rocketed out of my seat and jumped up in down in pure elation. Mom and Dad grinned, a knowing glint in their eyes as they enveloped me in a hug.

"They liked my pre-screening audition tape and live auditions are the first week of March!"

"That's great, honey!" Mom hugged me again, her eyes glassy with tears threatening to spill. I looked at Dad and saw that his expression wasn't far from Mom's. His eyes were shiny and he clenched his jaw, trying to hold the tears at bay. Looking at the happiness and pride in his eyes caused a lump to suddenly form in my throat.

I untangled myself from Mom's arms and went to Dad's. I stood on my tip toes and rested my chin in the crook of his shoulder as he patted my back tenderly and whispered, "I knew you'd always make it, Bug. I'm so proud of you."

I grinned, swallowing back the tears that wanted to be unleashed in the moment. Pulling away from Dad I turned to both of them and said, "Okay. You guys need to go 'cause you're both making me cry."

They chuckled and I smiled as they shuffled out of the room and closed the door. When they left I grabbed my cell from the vanity table and texted Gemma, Hayden, and...

I stopped at Liam's name, an idea surfacing in my mind. I sent a quick text to both Gem and Hayden telling them about the news. I didn't wait for their reply. Instead I tossed my phone on the bed and headed out, stopping at my parent's bedroom and letting them know I'd be back in an hour.

I shivered in my coat as I brought up my fist and lightly tapped Liam's bedroom window. He appeared in an instant, drawing the curtain and opening the window. He shuddered as the cold air licked his skin and stepped aside to let me in. Sneaking into his house (if I could even call it that) had become one of our secrets in the past month. He didn't like the way his father leered at me so entering through his window had become the norm for us. I straddled the sill and swiftly hopped off, closing the window behind me.

"Guess what?" I asked, balancing my weight on the balls of my heels.

Liam narrowed his eyes, assessing my face, trying to read what I had not voiced. A smile curled the edge of his lips as he said, "It's something good, isn't it?"

"Duh! Do you think I'd be here at," I peered down at my wrist watch, quickly reading the time, "nine forty-seven p.m if I it wasn't something good?"

He chuckled and folded his arms. "Eh, you've come here before for no reason. So..."

Hastily, I closed the space between us and playfully slapped his arm. "This is different," I smiled. "Guess. C'mon, Liam."

"I have no idea. Tell me."

I grinned. "I got a package from Julliard."

"And?" he pressed, his smile curling up even farther. He knew what was coming, but he wanted to hear it with his very own ears.

"I'll be going to New York in March for the live auditions," I squealed.

Liam engulfed me in his arms and picked me up, swinging me around in a small circle. I let out a surprised gasp, clutching the folds of his t-shirt to hold on. It felt like I was flying as crazy as that sounded. I was like a bird in the sky. The warmth of Liam's breath brushing my cheeks sent me reeling into a haze of beautiful and vibrant colors.

The feeling didn't end when he gently set me down, our laughter filling the empty room with life. If it was even at all possible I bet that our happiness would have sprouted flowers beneath our feet. I couldn't breathe with all the giggling and squealing I had done and his arms around my waist were not helping at all.

"I can't breathe," I wheezed out like a broken vacuum cleaner. That sent me into another fit of giggles.

"No?" he teased. Liam hugged me tighter, ignoring my protests. I squirmed in his embrace, trying to get away. But that wasn't such a bright idea as my foot caught around his and we stumbled backwards. Liam took the worst of the fall as I landed on top of him, my feet tangled around his like I was a fish in a net.

I laughed and smacked his chest. "See what you did!"

"Me?" He leaned his head back and let out a rumbling laugh that resonated deep within his belly. His hold around me tightened and

I buried my nose into his chest, drinking in the fresh smell of his Irish mint shampoo.

We laid there for what seemed like hours, but in reality it couldn't have been more than five minutes. Liam broke the easy silence between us as he reached forward, grazing the pad of his calloused thumb on my cheekbone.

"You'll get in," he said. "There's no doubt in my mind that they won't even consider you. They'll fall under your spell once they hear you play."

I smiled. "Hmm....a spell, huh?"

He gave a small nod to his head, but whatever he was thinking of was far more compelling than the teasing tone in my voice. As the second passed, my cheeks flamed under his intense gaze. I couldn't bear it and I stepped back. This wasn't the first time that he'd lost himself – or I for that matter. Being with Liam, spending time with him – was becoming harder with each day that passed. There were times in the past two months that I found myself wanting to kiss him when a moment like this happened. We just got caught up in the moment, forgetting about the wall we'd unconsciously built around that subject.

I slowly backtracked towards the window and said, "I should go...I'll see you-"

"Anya, wait." I stopped in my tracks and met his eyes. "When is your audition?"

I tilted my head back, looking up at the ceiling as I recalled the date I read on the letter. "March 9th."

His brows furrowed in thought and he marched forward towards me and veered to the left where his desk was. Scrambling around the mess of papers on the surface he dug up a florescent green flyer. "That's the last day of school before spring break."

"That's cool," I said slowly, uncertainty clear in my voice. I had absolutely no clue where he was going with his revelation.

"Are you going on a plane or driving up there?"

"Driving." There was no hesitation in my voice. I couldn't go on a plane for medical reasons. Now that I thought about it, I definitely was not looking forward to the twenty plus hours it would take to drive from Fairhope to New York City.

He rose a perfectly arched eyebrow and ran a hand down his face in thought. "Hmm...."

"What?" I asked curiously.

"Maybe," he muttered. "Don't know if you're parents would agree though. I'll have to ask and see...things need to be planned..."

I sauntered forward and shook his shoulders. "What are you talking about? You're talking like a mad man. You're starting to remind me of Smeagol now."

He blinked away his muddled thoughts and smiled. "What would you say to a road trip?"

"To where?" I was still not following. Maybe my mind's slowness had to do with how late it was. I couldn't expect my brain to function as well as it did during the day. God knew how lost I got when I was tired, hungry, or both.

He gave me an incredulous look, shaking my shoulders like I had done to him a minute ago. "New York. For your audition."

Now it was my turn to stare at him incredulously. "You're kidding, right? Liam, I couldn't ask you to..."

He held up his hand to silence my thought. "You're not asking me to do this, Anya. I want to do this. Let me."

"You're...amazing." I smiled. A warm fluttering feeling filled my stomach as his eyes crinkled and lit up like a bright star in the sky. "I don't know what to say, Liam. This is...thank you."

He beamed. "We've got a few more weeks to figure this out and that's if your parents agree."

I nodded. "Right." He was thinking ahead. I really liked that. I couldn't remember the last time that I'd seen Liam full of anticipation and excitement. He held his emotions at bay. It was only in those rare moments where he revealed what he truly felt. Those moments scared me sometimes. But not this one; not this time.

"So are you game?" he asked.

I lifted my eyes to meet his and grinned, nodding my head like I was a broken bobble head.

"Oh. I'm definitely game."

Chapter 28

On a slow Saturday afternoon a week later, Liam came ready to ask my father permission. It would be an easy sell – or so I thought. Mom was easy to convince, as she always is. She never denies me anything – even something as carefree and spontaneous as a road trip. Dad on the other hand...

"Absolutely not," he said, leaning forward in the armchair and resting his elbows on his knees. His penetrating gaze settled on mine across the room where I sat next to Liam on the loveseat. I gulped and looked away, finding a sudden interest in a hangnail on the corner of my forefinger. Liam slid forward, resting his arms on his lap and interlocking his hands together.

"Sir," he said politely. I looked up and he glanced at me. His flashed me an easy smile that seemed to say Don't worry. I got this. I shot a panicked look at Mom and she returned it with a reassuring smile. She knew Dad better than I did, but when it concerned me...well, I didn't exactly know what he'd do or say. Dad turned into an overprotective alpha wolf, whose main objective was to take care of his cub.

"I'll take good care of her, Mr. Vanchester. I won't let any harm come to her. We researched which would be the safest route. I've got a car..." I raised my eyebrows in surprise. This was the first that

I've heard he had a car picked out for the trip. Was it a rental? Was it his Dad's beat up Sedan? Was he borrowing Collin's blue pickup truck? We hadn't discussed any of those details yet because we first needed to get passed the parental units.

"...should consider." I didn't catch what she was saying beforehand, but I quickly snapped back to attention. "They're right. I can't miss work for two weeks; you know how it gets busy during the spring. And you can't deviate your lesson plans a week early with your AP students."

I could have high-fived Mom at the moment. She caught my gaze and winked. I beamed and nudged Liam. "Mom's got it in the bag," I whispered as Mom and Dad were too enthralled with their argument to pay any mind to us.

"They're fighting," he stated. "It's not what I intended."

I reached forward and squeezed his forearm. "They aren't fighting," I said. I glanced in their direction and saw Mom's cool composure thwarting Dad's tight set of his jaw. He was losing the argument and he knew it. Dad didn't like to be wrong, and he knew better than to go up against the mighty force of Mama Bear.

"Just watch," I said.

Liam directed his gaze across the room where Mom and Dad were by the fireplace, speaking in hushed tones. Dad's shoulders were rigid as he spoke, his eyes flickering to us every few minutes. Liam squirmed in his seat and I found his behavior amusing. Liam was bigger than my dad, towering over him by 4 inches, and he was afraid of him. I didn't know if I should find it reverent or hilarious.

Part of me liked that he respected my parents, especially Dad with all the hard times he gave him. It wasn't always like this, reminding me of Thanksgiving dinner, and how everyone had welcomed him with open arms. I didn't know when Dad changed his opinion about Liam. It seemed like a century ago when I listened to Dad having a coronary when he found out I'd been on Liam's bike that first time.

I knew Dad liked Liam, but I was still his little girl and he wasn't going to let me go gallivanting to New York with him – or any boy for that matter.

"So what car did you get," I asked, leaning towards him.

Liam averted his eyes from my parents, his face a mask of complete and utter seriousness. "Hey," I said, running my thumb over his drawn brows. His face relaxed, flashing me a tight smile. "This happens all the time," I reassured him. "Mom always wins in the end."

He laughed uneasily. "So I guess your mom wears the pants in the relationship."

"You got that right. We Vanchester women are independent and stubborn. Plus, we're always right."

Liam flicked my nose and smiled, leaning in close and stealing a quick kiss on my forehead. "I wouldn't want to lose that sort of bet."

"Nope," I said, popping the "P". "Don't ever go to Vegas."

He chuckled. "Where did that come from?"

I shrugged. "I'm random; you should know this by now. Try to keep up, will you?"

"I'll keep that in mind." His eyes shined brilliantly with an unspoken secret that I wanted to desperately be submerged in. He interlocked our fingers together, the pad of his thumb lightly grazing the top of my hand, sending a fiery warmth coursing through my veins.

An urgent and maddening cough shattered the blissful moment between me and Liam. I looked up and retracted my hand from his, missing the reassuring warmth the next instant. The absence was short lived as my eyes connected with Dad's steady brown ones. He gave Mom a look, but she did not falter, shrugging nonchalantly. With his undivided attention back to us, Mom sneaked us a smile and gave us the universal Ok sign.

I smothered a smile and pinned my hands underneath my knees, waiting for the verdict.

"Alright," Dad said, striding forward and halting two feet in front of us. I glanced at Liam, his eyes unwavering from Dad's. For a second, Liam reminded me of a Greek soldier, bracing himself for the wrath that was to come from his commanding officer – my Dad. I saw the unsheathing of swords when the decision was the one that Liam could not accept. The sound of horses and shouting were drowned out by clamor of metal against metal.

"Liam."

Just two syllables. That's all it took to yank me away from my daydream, causing it to burst like a soap bubble. His name – it made an effortless smile form on my face whenever I said it, but coming from Dad - it instilled fear in the merriest of souls, and that was saying a lot. It sure was what it did to me. Dad also said it in his authoritative voice, the one that all parents acquired the moment they had a child.

It scared me because I hardly heard Dad use that tone. It meant business and I wondered how Liam was handling it. Beside me, he straightened and answered, "Yes, sir?" like a warrior waiting for orders on the brink of an onslaught.

"Do I have your word that you will ensure my daughter's safety?" he asked like I was some fair maiden from the Middle Ages. It was an indication that he read too much classical literature. I wondered what he was reading now that was influencing this sort of behavior. Plus, I could take care of myself! I learned Jujitsu when I was twelve.

Okay, so that was a lie – but I could take care of myself. I had a can of pepper spray and a small switch blade in my bag. Dad knew that – he's the one who purchased them for me.

"Yes," Liam said. His next words were full of conviction, awakening the sliver of butterflies in my stomach. "I won't let anything happen to her."

Dad gave a curt nod, accepting and believing Liam's words. He looked over at Mom, who also nodded and said, "Alright then, it's settled. You two can go. But," I held my breath, hopping it was a good but and not a bad one. Knowing Mom it'd be the former rather than the latter. "Both of you will work on all the assignments you will be missing when you're not traveling. I expect everything to be done the night before school starts, understand?"

I nodded vigorously and I Liam said, "Will do, Mrs. Vanchester."

"Good," she said. "That's all from me."

I jumped out of my seat and enveloped Mom in a hug. "Thank you, thank you, thank you!" I gave her a big sloppy kiss on the cheek and she laughed, kissing my forehead.

When I disentangled myself from her arms I looked over at Dad who was silently sulking. I flashed him my best puppy dog face and the frown immediately turned upside down. "Come here," he said, inviting me into his arms. I didn't hesitate and I slipped into his embrace, the steady rhythm of his heart drumming beneath my ear.

"Oh, and Liam?" I glanced up at Dad, his eyes glinting with benign...mischief?

Liam raised an eyebrow, his eyes flickering to mine for a second before settling back on my father.

"I just want you to know that if my daughter comes back without her virtue intact, I will hide your body where no will ever find it. I watch CSI."

My mouth dropped open and I sprung away from Dad only to punch him in the arm. "Dad!" I turned to Liam, my face flushing in a matter of seconds, and saw the glinting amusement in his slate gray eyes.

I couldn't believe this. Dad had threatened him and he found it funny! I could have punched him too if I wasn't so at a loss for words. That was that – I was going to end up forever alone with twelve cats in an even smaller town where WIFI was virtually impossible.

I.

Would.

Die.

"Now that you're done threatening Liam," I shot a look at Dad and he put his hands up in mock defense, "we're going upstairs. If you need us, you know where to find us."

I took Liam's hand and hauled him towards the stairs. When we were halfway up, I paused and quickly said, "I'll be right up. You go ahead."

Liam nodded and I turned on my heels running back down the steps towards Dad. I skidded to a stop and hugged him. His arms snaked around me after taken aback momentarily. "I love you," I breathed out., "Even if you are overly protective."

He chuckled. "I know, Bug. I love you, too." He ran a hand through my hair and patted my back soothingly. "Now," he said, setting me at arm's length. "Go on before I change my mind."

I grinned and kissed his check before I sprinted back upstairs to Liam.

When I entered my room, Liam was holding a piece of paper in his hands, entirely absorbed in it. It wasn't until I approached that I saw what he was looking at that my heart kicked into overdrive. Closing the space between us, I snatched the paper away from his hands.

"Hey!" he exclaimed. "I was reading something important."

I stuck out my tongue at him, hiding the paper behind my back. "Liar. You've already read it, if I remember correctly."

He smirked, his eyes dancing with familiar, swirling mischief. "So who's the lucky guy?" he asked.

"What are you talking about?"

He lifted his brows, his eyes shining with infuriating enjoyment. "Is it Hayden? Must be a bummer to be in love with your best friend's boyfriend."

I shook my head. "Are you delusional? Did you hit your head while I was gone? I didn't know I needed to keep an eye on you 24/7."

"Feisty."

"Shut up." I cracked a smile zond gave up. "Okay, so what on earth are you talking about?"

Striding forward he swiftly took the bucket list from my hands and said, "This. Number ten is crossed off. So who was it if not Hayden?"

I rolled my eyes and punched him, trying to hide the blush that crept onto my cheeks. "It's not crossed off, it's scratched off."

He shrugged. "Same thing. What's the difference?"

I sighed and took the paper back from him, folding it thrice into a small square big enough to fit in my pencil holder. "It's not that I fell in love. It's that I...it's that love...it's not..." I couldn't find the right words to say. Things had changed since I scratched out number ten from my list. It was around the time where I truly believed that Liam and I could never be together even if there was something between us.

But the tables had turned once again. I could possibly fall in love and be with him for years before death claimed me. I wouldn't leave him unexpectedly like I had believed four years ago. But it was all circumstantial. There was still a fifty percent chance that I could fall asleep and never wake up again. I couldn't do that to him...not after he'd lost his family. I couldn't be another person that he loved and lost.

Tell him, a voice whispered in my head. He needs to know. Tell him.

I closed my eyes and let out a breath I didn't know I was holding. Slowly, I turned around and faced him; the smirk that was on his lips quickly fell as he walked forward, tilting my chin upward. "Hey," he said tenderly. "You alright? Anya, I was only..."

"I know," I whispered, taking a step back. This was it....it had come down to this moment. I bit my lip and played with the end of my braid. I took a chance and glanced in his direction – his clear gray eyes were mesmerizing as he looked at me, trying to understand some hauntingly, and beautiful poem in Dad's class. It only made my secret that much harder to say.

"Liam, there's something that I-"

The blaring sound of Ellie Goulding's voice singing Lights cut through the room. Liam sighed and stepped back, shaking his head like he was in a daze.

Hastily, I marched across the room, following the sound of the ringtone. I fished out my phone from underneath a pillow and picked up two seconds before it could go to voicemail.

It was Gemma.

I picked up only to be told, "Answer your messages!" then she hung up. I stared at my phone and muttered, "Well, that was rude."

"Who was it?" Liam asked, making himself comfortable on my bed.

"Gem," I answered at the same time I was replying to her text messages. She wanted to know how it went with the parentals and I briefly told her what happened.

In the back of my mind, I didn't know if I should take Gemma's call as a sign. It had conveniently occurred just when I was about to reveal my secret to Liam. Part of me felt relieved. Maybe it wasn't time yet to divulge or plague him with something that was irreversible. I wouldn't want him to seek for a solution, churning his mind day in and day out to something that didn't exist.

Her call was a sign from above. It put a stop to whatever I might have said. I believed that wholeheartedly.

Maybe, my conscious said. But you'll have to tell him sooner rather than later.

I was already tethering on later. What was a couple more weeks...or months?

If I was lucky, I could have years.

Chapter 29

"You're going to Tybee Island with Hayden?" I couldn't believe it. Mr. Weatherly would never let Gemma go out of the state with Hayden let alone on spring break. "What happened? Did your Dad go Terminator on his ass?"

"Anya!" She gaped at me and I smiled sheepishly. It had just slipped. Never in a million years would I had uttered such a thing like that. But well…I was spending way too much time with Liam as of late, not that I regretted it in any sort of way.

"I'm sorry," I said, trying to suppress the smile that tethered on my lips. "When did this happen? Spill."

Gemma flopped onto my bed as I sat down next to her, picking up my suitcase and dumping it on the floor. Packing for tomorrow would have to wait. Hearing Gemma's story could not.

"He came over earlier. I didn't even know. And as luck would have it Dad had just gotten off at work." I raised my eyebrows and shook my head in bewilderment. Oh Hayden…men. They had such terrible timing. "When he asked Dad if I could go with him to Georgia – I swear that I saw Dad's fingers twitch to his gun strapped at his belt."

My hands flew to my mouth as I covered my surprise. "What happened next?" I asked eagerly. I imagined that Gemma's encounter was ten times more mortifying than mine ever was. Dads. Why did they have to be so mortifying and overprotective?

"He read Hayden his Fifth Amendment rights."

I stared at her blankly. "Madness," I whispered in a horrible attempt at a British accent. "He's positively mad!"

Gemma giggled. "Don't ever do that again." I bumped my shoulder to hers and she fell backwards onto the bed, staring up at the ceiling. In a slow easy breath she let out, "I wanted to die, An. It was worst than when Hayden came to pick me up for our first date. I thought that my heart was literally going to jump out of my chest. Hayden handled it all well – it was more than I could say for me."

I smiled. It reminded me of how I felt about Liam those weeks ago when he faced my father. Seeing the new sparkle in Gemma's eyes reminded me of the newfound respect I had gathered for Liam just as she had for Hayden. They were brave men for surviving the inquisition.

"So when are you guys leaving?"

"Next Saturday. I wish you were coming with us."

"I wouldn't want to be the third wheel, Gems."

She propped herself up on her elbow and peered at me mischievously. "You wouldn't have been. Liam would have been coming with us too."

"And how do you know that?" I countered.

Her lips quirked into a sly smile. "I know a lot of things that you don't."

"Like?" I pressed, curiosity getting the best of me.

" Like...howyou'remadlyinlovewithhimbutyou'retostubborntosayitevenwhenitsobviousthathefeelsthesameaboutyou." She said it all in one breath and by the end she was gasping for air.

I stared at her with wide eyes like some owl that had completely gotten lost in the woods. "What? How....not that again, Gems."

She held up her hands in mock defense. "I just tell it how it is."

Without any hesitation I grabbed one of my pillows and threw it at her. She caught it effortlessly and I harrumphed. Why did everyone have to be a secret ninja? That was supposed to be my job.

"So what's your first stop tomorrow?" she asked as she hopped off the bed and picked up my suitcase. "Probably Greensville or Montgomery, right? You'll reach Montgomery then go to Atlanta from there."

"That's what I'm thinking," I said. "But I honestly don't even have a clue." I didn't have the slightest idea where would stop for the night or if we'd take a detour along the way. All those technicalities were being taken care of by Liam. He was leaving me in the dark on purpose and for once I didn't mind. Some secrets were better kept hidden until later. And knowing Liam I had a feeling that he had a few tricks up his sleeves.

I just knew it.

"Have you asked him?" Gemma asked, heading to my closet. She picked up my favorite blue capped sleeve dress and brought it to me.

"Not really. All he said was that it was a ghost route. Whatever that means."

Gemma grinned. "Mysterious."

I rolled my eyes and continued to pack all my clothes into my suitcase. Once that was full to maximum capacity, I took out a purple sports duffle bag from underneath my bed as an added bonus. Gemma cranked the volume on the speakers hooked up to my laptop, filling the room with a random playlist on iTunes. She lost herself in a book she'd picked off from my bookshelf, while I gathered my belongings into place. By the time that I was satisfied with all that I was going to take I realized that I might have accidently packed my entire room.

"Overpacking is good, right?" I asked over Katy Perry's voice singing Thinking Of You.

She didn't hear me and I threw Mr. Cuddles squeaky toy towards her to garner her attention. It worked. Her head jerked up and she blinked, her eyes focusing in my directions. I signed what I had asked earlier and she smiled, signing back, "You never know what you might need."

"Alright. Are you hungry?" I signed, patting my stomach. "I'm starving."

She nodded and left the book upturned, not wanting to lose her place. Taking a glance back and squinting, I noted that she had begun to read The Luxe by Anna Godbersen. As we made our way towards the stairs, a familiar voice resonating from below halted my steps. Gemma flashed me a puzzled look. I pulled her down and we ducked behind the far wall.

"Liam's here," I signed.

Gemma's brows drew together as her hands spoke the complete perplexity written all over her face. "Okay. Why are we hiding?"

Now that was a very good question. Why were we hiding? More importantly – why did I have the strong sense to hide?

I shrugged. "He's talking to my dad about..." I cocked my head in their direction and only heard cut off phrases and muffled replies. "Well, I don't know but why is he here? Why didn't Dad call me down if Liam came over to come see me or hang out?"

After a long pause, Gemma replied, "Okay. You've got a point."

We were silent and stealth-like as I listened in on their conversation as best I could. I would then transfer my findings to Gemma via signing. It was ridiculous and at one point I almost gave our spot away by laughing. Gem attempted to crawl across the hall unnoticed, but epically failed when a frayed end of her blouse got caught on the banister.

She quickly crawled back to my side and the talking downstairs came to an abrupt stop. We were certain that we had been caught but after an agonizingly long heart beat, Dad and Liam commenced their conversation.

Dad: "....plan. Really good. Take it. You'll need it."

There was a short pause followed by Liam's voice saying, "I couldn't....idea, sir. I've got it....to worry."

I inwardly groaned in frustration. Why couldn't I be born with superhuman hearing like Clark Kent? It would have come in handy at times like these.

"How long are we going to stay like this?" Gemma asked. "What about food?"

My stomach growled in assent. Sighing I signed, "Okay, let's go down."

Gemma smiled in relief and we emerged from our hiding place. We acted casual, talking about how hot Bradley James was on Merlin. When Liam and Dad spotted us we waved courteously and went straight into the kitchen. I didn't dare look at Liam, fearing that he'd know in a moments glance that I had been spying on him. I didn't even think about Dad; he'd know the second he looked into my guilty eyes.

As Liam had pointed out many times: I was a terrible liar.

"So what should we eat?" I asked Gem, opening up the fridge and scrunching my nose. There absolutely nothing in the fridge. It was Sunday. Mom and Dad always went shopping on Monday nights, which meant that Sundays were deemed for takeout.

"Chinese?" she suggested.

I grinned. "Great minds think alike."

Taking my iPhone out of my pocket I walked into the living room and asked, "Liam, will you be staying for dinner?"

Liam glanced at my father, some secret message passing between them. I wanted to squint my eyes in suspicion but I wouldn't let anything in my face give away the thoughts running through my head. Turning back to me Liam said, "What are we ordering?"

My lips broke out into a smile. He knew. He knew Sundays were takeout nights. How could I ever have thought that he'd forgotten? "Chinese," I replied. "I'll order us some."

"Thanks, Bug!" Dad called after my treating form.

I dialed the number and ordered dishes full of fried rice, crab ragoons, choimen, orange chicken (Liam's favorite), teriyaki chicken and beef, and lastly fried shrimp dumplings. A half hour later our food was delivered and we sat around the table, passing around plates and sharing the carton of delicious food.

In the back of my mind I kept recalling Dad and Liam's guarded behavior. There was nothing in their eyes that gave away the slightest hint of what had transpired between them. Had they been talking about me? Did Dad call Liam over to talk one more time before we set out for New York tomorrow? Had Liam come over of his own free will to talk to Dad? Only God knew what had happened and I waged my little soul that I was going to ask Him about it tonight.

"You're quiet," Liam whispered as Dad and Gemma welcomed Mom home. I mumbled my hello as I played with my food.

"Just thinking."

"About?"

"Stuff."

I could practically hear the whoosh of air let out by his lungs at my pathetic answer.

"Are you nervous about tomorrow? I promise that I'll protect you, Anya. You're dad will castrate me if anything happened to you. You'll be safe with me, got it?"

I shook my head in dismay. "Please tell me that he didn't tell you that."

He flicked my nose, his gray eyes brightening to a dim ocean blue. "Now, there's the Anya that I-" His words came to an abrupt stop, my eyes widening. He cleared his throat, adding quickly, "Have you gotten your things all straightened out?"

I nodded, relaxing my shoulders. "You?"

"Not yet. There's a few more things I need to see to."

"Like what?"

His eyes regained the flicker of light that had snuffed out, the awkward moment passing between us. A curved smile wound his lips, contagious in its nature.

"You'll see tomorrow."

I dropped my fork, landing in a loud clattering thunk. I bit my lip and looked around the room, noticing that it was empty. Everyone else had made their way into the living room, leaving Liam and I alone.

"How many hours approximately to New York?"

"21.5."

"So we should be there by Friday morning at the latest?"

"Late Wednesday night or early Thursday morning. We could tour the city if you want."

"Will we be stopping in Montgomery tomorrow?"

Liam raised his dark brows. "Yes, why?"

"Just asking."

"Did you know that you're very inquisitive?"

I flashed him my best grin. "Knowledge is power."

"What about love?"

My grin faltered and I peered at him questioningly. "What about it?"

"Well isn't that the drive in most books and movies. That whole love conquers all motto."

I pointed at him in mock accusation. "Have you been sneaking into my room and stealing my cheesy romance novels?"

He chuckled. "Never."

I shrugged, picking up my dishes and heading towards the sink. "It's okay if you do," I teased. "I'll still be your friend if that's the case."

"I've been hanging around Gemma for too long. Her romantic ideals have rubbed off on me."

I whirled around on my heels. "What has she been saying?"

He shook his head, amusement lighting up his iridescent slate-blue eyes. "Nothing you'll find interesting."

I let out a groan. "You both majorly suck with your secrets. Fine. Don't tell me. See if I tell you both anything anymore." I turned back around and began to scrub my dishes clean. What had Gemma been telling Liam? What did Gemma know?

Ugh. They were impossible.

Warm familiar arms snaked around my waist. Instinctively I relaxed, breathing in the mint and gasoline smell he seemed to carry these days. He no longer smelled like cigarettes, the scent that had clung to his skin was practically non-existent. It made me smile, knowing that he'd gotten rid of the nasty habit.

"Do you trust me?" His breath was hot against my ear, sending shiver down my spine.

"Yes," I answered without hesitation. I trusted him wholeheartedly. There weren't many people in the entire world that held such power.

"Don't worry then. Trust in me." In a swift and graceful motion he turned me around to face him. "I'll see you tomorrow. Get a good night's rest. We've got an early start."

"How early?"

"Four a.m."

I scrunched my nose in distaste and groaned.

Tomorrow would prove to be a very long and surprising day.

Chapter 30

"Anya, honey. It's time to get up."

I groaned and pulled the sheets over my head. Mom's heavy sigh reached my ears and the next second she was yanking the covers from my hands. My eyes slowly fluttered open, heavy with sleep.

"Liam's already waiting outside."

His name was like cold water dumped all over my body, jolting me awake. I scrambled out of bed and headed to the bathroom only to let a small whimper escape from my lips. My hair was a frizzy mess looking like a lion's mane that was beyond salvaging in only a couple of minutes. I brushed my teeth and washed my face quickly, while I heard Mom gathering my suitcase and taking it downstairs. Since there was no time to straighten my hair I pulled it back into a side braid and rushed out the room, shimming out of my pj's and throwing on an old t-shirt and yoga pants.

My eyes roamed around the room, trying to think of anything else that I might have forgotten. It was then that I remembered to pack my toothbrush, brush, and make up into my bag where my medicine was, which was also something that I needed to take before I left. I went into the bathroom with my bag slung over my shoulder and dumped my toiletries inside. Once that was done I filled a cup full of water and swallowed down the pills.

A car horn outside hurried my movements out the door and down the stairs. The front door was wide open to a dark world outside where Mom, Dad, and Liam stood around a silver car. The frigid air licked at my skin and I shivered, wishing that I had had the sensibility to have brought a light jacket with me.

Liam was at the rear of the car, loading our luggage when he muttered, "Looks like she packed her entire room."

Dad chuckled, shaking his head and shrugging. "You should see them when we take weekend trips. It looks like we're going away for a month instead of a few days by all that they bring."

"Women."

Mom rolled her eyes and brought me in for a hug. "You ready?" she asked. It was a simple question. It would have been if I was a normal girl, but I wasn't. Those two words held more weight than anything else at the moment.

I nodded and sunk into her embrace. Even in the early dawn she smelled like rich cocoa butter and lavender.

"My turn?"

We turned, my eyes falling to Dad's open arms. I drew away from Mom and went to Dad. "You sure you got everything you need, Bug?"

I smiled. "Yes. Pretty sure I've packed everything." He chuckled, his breath coated with caffeine. It was just like Dad to have his cup of coffee every morning when he woke up no matter what time it was.

The engine roared to life and I broke away from Dad's arms. Liam was settled into the driver's seat, rubbing his hands together; the friction warming them from the coldness of the steering wheel. I opened the car door and settled in, dropping my bag by my feet.

"Call us when you get to Montgomery and whenever you can, alright?"

"I will. I love you."

He smiled and leaned in to kiss my cheek as I did his. "Be safe. God is always with you, remember that."

I smiled. "I know."

"Take care," Mom said as I shut the door. Dad slung and arm over her shoulder. She waved with a wide grin that was contagious as it was warm. "Both of you have a safe trip!"

We waved goodbye as Liam pulled out of the curb and shifted the car into drive.

I dozed off only to wake up a few hours later with the sun beating down on my face and the quiet hum of the car. Car rides always made me drowsy and in a matter of minutes I would welcome sleep like an old forgotten friend.

"Hey, sleepy head."

I yawned and stretched my arms in front of me, glancing over at Liam. "Hey. Where are we?" I glimpsed outside the window and saw the desolate land of lush green trees and endless grassy plains.

"Union City. We'll hit Atlanta in an hour."

I gaped at him. "I've been asleep for almost...five hours?"

He chuckled and gave me a side long glance, while still managing to keep his attention on the road in front of him. "I tried to wake you when I stopped in Auburn for gas but you were sound asleep."

"You should have woken me up. I'm missing everything!" I sat straight in my seat, determination settling deep in the core of my chest. I was not going to sleep for the rest of the day and miss the beautiful scenery all around us. That was such a waste and I wanted to mentally slap myself for falling prey to unconsciousness without a fight.

"Please don't let me fall asleep," I said. "If I do you are free to hit me or something."

"I'm not going to hit you. There are better things to do."

"Like what?" I raised my eyebrow questioningly as I saw a knowing smirk sliding onto his lips.

He shook his head, his shoulders shaking with laughter. "How about some music?" I nodded and he turned on the stereo, turning the dial whenever we heard crackling static.

"I don't think we'll find anything...oh wait!" I leaned forward and grabbed my bag, rummaging inside. "I burned some CD's a few nights ago. I know I have them here..."

The car filled with an abrupt and unexpected old soulful classic. Liam and I traded an ear to ear grin as I snapped my fingers to The Temptations' My Girl.

Liam suddenly belted out in song in a horrible off key tone and I stifled a giggle. I couldn't even believe that he knew the lyrics to one of the greatest hits of the 1960's. He sang to me as the second verse began and I tried not to blush as his eyes were bright and carefree with glee.

I don't need no money, fortune, or fame

"Please stop. My ears...Liam!"

I've got all the riches baby,

One man can claim

He ignored me and flashed me one of his charming smiles that made me melt in my seat. He might have been a terrible singer but

I was completely serenaded by the complete and utter easiness that surrounded him as he sang.

Well, I guess you say, what can make me feel this way?

My girl (my girl, my girl)

Talkin' bout my girl (my girl)

I shook my head and continued to snap with a stupid grin on my face. Liam shook my arm with such zeal that I couldn't deny him any longer. I sang with him as the song neared its end, cracking up with giggles as Liam belted out the tune in mock microphone fisted hand.

I've got sunshine on a cloudy day with my girl

I've even got the month of May with my girl

Talkin' bout, talkin' bout, talkin' bout

My girl

Wohooooo my girl (my girl)

"You are..."

"Incredible? Sexy? Multi-talented?"

I scoffed but it quickly turned into laughter. "I was going to say crazy but maybe delusional is a better word."

He dramatically brought his hand to his heart, giving me a long side-long glance. "Your words sting, babe."

Reaching forward I punched his arm playfully. "Just keep your eyes on the road, rock star."

He gave me a lazy smile and I grabbed a CD and popped it into the stereo. The first song was Substitution by Silversun Pickups, which I had discovered was one of Liam's favorite bands. I never heard of them, but after listening to one of their albums I completely feel in love and concluded that he had good taste in music. It wasn't one of those heavy metal bands which I detested, but a beautifully crafted alternative with lyrics full of captivating metaphors.

Liam softly hummed to the songs he knew, drumming his fingers precariously on the steering wheel as he maneuvered through the speeding highway. I stared out the window, listening to some of our favorite songs as the scenery changed from country and suburban life to the bustling and horn induced city life.

"What do you want to eat?"

I bit my lip, pensively. "Hmm...how about Subway?"

"Subway it is."

He merged into the right lane and took the next exit down a winding ramp. Before I knew it we were parking into a busy Subway restaurant with other tourists walking into the packed establishment. I opened the car door and swirled around on the balls of my feet. Across the plot was a Mickey D's restaurant and I suggested we go there instead. Liam concurred and we trudged along, mindful of the cars eagerly pulling in and out of parking places.

Liam held open the door to Micky D's and as soon as I stepped through my mouth watered and my stomach rumbled with hunger. We quickly ordered our burgers and grabbed seats in an empty middle part of the restaurant.

"How are you feeling?" I asked him as he slid the aviators off his face and set them beside him on the table. "You look really tired."

He shrugged, leaning back in his chair. "Don't worry about me, babe. I'm fine."

"I could drive for awhile, just give me the directions. That way you could rest for an hour or two."

His brow crinkled as he leaned forward with his elbows propped on the table. "You can drive?"

I stared at him incredulously. "Of course I can drive."

"I've never seen you...

I shrugged and heard our order number. "I prefer to walk." Liam gave a small shake of his head and swiftly stood up, bringing our food over a few seconds later.

He unwrapped one of the five McMuffins and dug in like a ravished wolf. I raised my eyebrows as I watched the breakfast sandwich disappear in 5.2 seconds.

"What?" he asked. It came out muffled and sounded more like "Wut" with all the food in his mouth.

"You're getting really familiar with that burger, aren't you."

He let out a laugh. "I like food way more than girls."

I took a bit of my hash browns and washed it down with orange juice. "I'm sure that burger has been the longest relationship you've ever had."

"I've had relationships!" he exclaimed offended.

I rolled my eyes and took a bite of my sandwich. "I'm sure you have. Name one."

His lips parted as he searched for a name through his muddled mind. I waited, patiently, my face clearly speaking all the words that I was thinking. He couldn't even remember one girl. One girl. That was all I asked.

I raised my eyebrows smugly. "See."

He glowered and took a bite of the sandwich. "McMuffin-a is a better girlfriend than any of the girls at school would be. She never lets me down."

I laughed almost spitting out the mouthful of OJ all over him. He raised his eyebrows and winked as I finished my meal and he wolfed down the fifth and final McMuffin. Boys. I would never fully understand them. Once Liam was all done with his food we headed out. My belly was fully satisfied as I fished my sunglasses from my bag and slid them on.

"Where'd you get the car?" I asked as we crossed the lot.

"I borrowed it."

"From who?"

"The shop."

I halted in my tracks. Liam stopped and turned back. "You stole it?!"

"I didn't steal it. I borrowed it. I'll bring it back."

I gaped and covered my mouth with my hand. "Oh my goodness! You're making me a thief!"

"Me? You're the one who dared me to steal a lollipop when we were six."

"I did not."

"Yeah you did." He chuckled and sauntered forward, taking my hand in his. "You were convinced that we would be on an episode of Cops."

I shook my head, not wanting to belief him but the vague memory of the moment drifted into my mind, playing out like an old film projector. I was such a strange little kid. First I kissed him and then I offer to go on a crime spree. What was wrong with me?

After filling the tank with gas we were on the highway again heading towards Columbia, South Carolina. With just two hours on the road I felt myself drifting off to sleep again as noon approached.

"Don't doze off on me again," he chided. "Keep me awake."

I smiled and lifted my head from the side of the door. "I did offer to drive, you know."

"Ask me something."

I titled my head and searched his face for something, anything. His eyes remained on the road and after a long pause he dragged his eyes from the windshield. "What?" A lopsided smile lifted at the corners of his lips as his eyes crinkled at the edges.

I shrugged. "Nothing. Hmm..." I churned thoughts in my mind and finally settled on one that is a big part of my life. "Do you believe in God?"

The lopsided smile fell and was replaced with a sinking frown. Immediately I regretted ever asking something that I felt was simple with either a yes or no answer. But I should have known. Nothing was ever simple and it was as much as Liam said.

"I don't know," he said. "After my mom died things just...took a turn for the worst. Dad started to drink and shit happened. It's like He abandoned us the moment Mom fell sick and things never got better after that."

I was quiet. I didn't know what to say. He had as much a reason to not believe in Him as much as I did believe.

"What kind of stuff happened?" I asked trying to deviate away from my question.

He sighed. "You don't want to know."

I sunk into my seat, feeling the strong pull of guilt taking me under. Why couldn't I just ask him what his favorite action movie was or something to that degree? I always had to ruin a perfectly good moment with something serious and disconcerting.

"You still believe in God after all the shitty things that go on in the world?"

"Yes," I answered without any hesitation. "It's not God's fault for the things that happen. Humans – we cause death and destruction and pain. We're blinded by those things and think there is no God and are so soon to reject all the good things that He's given us."

"Like what?" he challenged.

A lot of things, I said quietly in my head. A lot of things. I wanted to show Liam that life was full of beautiful moments but right now wasn't a great example. Instead I said, "I'll show you some time. I promise."

His right hand curled around mine and he weaved our fingers together, resting on my lap. "Something like this?" he asked, his eyes slate-blue gaze lingering on my face. I looked down at our joined hands and smiled, feeling the fluttering of butterflies beating frantically in the pit of my stomach.

"Exactly like this."

By one we were in Columbia with the day still ahead of us. We didn't stop and drove on for another hour which only aggravated me because I couldn't feel my butt anymore. I could tell by Liam's weary eyes that he wasn't faring so well either and after a long and agonizingly painful hour we stopped in Rock Hill, South Carolina.

It was breathtakingly beautiful as we drove to the central part of the town and parked near a quaint little coffee shop. The sky was covered with soft overcast clouds with the warm air caressing my skin as I stepped out of the car.

"Where to, miss?" Liam came around the front of the car and offered me his arm. I looped mine through his, smiling up at him.

"How about a walk?"

"A walk it is."

We settled into a comfortable pace, my eyes roaming all the small shops that littered through the old Victorian town. The smell of freshly cut grass filled my nose and sighed pleasantly, leaning in towards Liam.

"Pretty neat, right? I never thought I'd get out of Fairhope and here we are on our way to New York. Can you believe it?"

I smiled at the note of utter incredulity in his voice. "Me either. Who would have thought there was a whole other world other than Fairhope."

We came across a small park and aimlessly walked its lush grassy plain, sinking down on its grassy bed and looking up at the sky. Liam pulled me into him and I laid my head down on his chest, hearing only the sound of his beating heart.

It was a nice change of scenery from where we'd begun. Everything was so surreal that I thought this was nothing but a dream and one false step would shatter all that I had come to know. But Liam was the anchor that held me grounded. He was the person that made me believe that the last few hours since the start of our day were tangible and concrete. They weren't going to disappear if I suddenly blinked my eyes no matter how much I did think they were.

"This is one of those moments," I said as I felt the soft breeze of the wind caress my cheeks. "It's beautiful in its simplicity. It's these little things that are given to us. It just takes time to treasure each and every last one of them."

He ran a hand through my hair and pressed a kiss on the top of my head. "Is it to late to start now?" he asked softly.

I shook my head and buried my nose into the folds of his dark blue shirt. "No, it's never too late."

I bit my lip as he absentmindedly played with my hair. It was inevitable. In that moment I realized that I was falling slowly in love with him, and I couldn't stop my heart no matter how much my head pleaded with me not to.

He was a rough piece of stone with jagged edges that had softened as the time passed by, turning into something more beautiful than I could ever have imagined.

After grabbing a cup of coffee, hot chocolate, and two pieces of cheesecake we were on the road again. The sun had begun to set, setting the horizon into a blaze of wonderful warm oranges and reds. We had spent four hours in Rock Hill, losing track of the time as we lost ourselves in our own little corner of the world.

I sipped at my hot chocolate and looked out the window as we passed a sign that read:

Now Leaving South Carolina.

Liam began to pull to the side of the highway and parked, taking off his seat belt.

"What are you doing?" I asked, following his lead.

"C'mon." He opened the car door and got out, shutting it behind me. I placed my cup of hot chocolate in the cup holder next to his and slid out of the car.

"Okay, what are we doing?"

He took my hand in his and dragged me a few feet forward, the beaming lights of the car illuminating our way.

"Place your feet shoulder length apart, like this." I looked down at his feet and mimicked his posture as he held both of my hands in his.

"Okay. Now what?"

He flashed me a dazzling smile and let go of my hand, pointing at something behind me. I turned my head and saw another sign.

Welcome to North Carolina.

"Now you're in two places at once."

I beamed and closed the space between us as he took me into his arms and swung me around once in a small circle.

"Was this always part of your plan?" I asked with a wide grin on my face as he set me down.

He disregarded my question and slid his phone out of his pocket. "Smile." I moved a bit closer to the sign and pointed it at it with a goofy grin on my face as he snapped the picture, the light momentarily blinding my eyes and leaving black spots behind.

"So was this your plan?" I asked again, wanting very much to know the answer.

We walked back to the car and he threw me a sly smile. "I don't have the slightest clue of what you're talking about."

"Oh you know," I said as I got into the car and put my seat belt on. "You know but you just won't tell me."

His eyes glinted wickedly with the last rays of the setting sun disappearing over the mountains. He smiled to himself and I desperately wanted to know what he was thinking as he put the car into drive and continued down the dark, desolate road.

"What else do you have up your sleeve?" I asked after a few minutes of quiet solitude.

"If I told you, it wouldn't be a secret now, would it?"

I shook my head.

He reached forward and cupped my chin with his right hand all the while keeping perfect control of the car. "Some secrets," he said as he flickered his gaze between the windshield and me. "Some secrets are better kept hidden until the right time calls for them."

"So there's more to come?" I could hardly contain the excitement in my voice. What did he have in store for me – for us?

He nodded and retracted his hand from my chin. I instantly missed his touch and wanted nothing more than for him to hold my hand again; to feel the rough yet warmth of his skin.

"There's plenty more." He smiled and glanced my way. "And we're just getting started."

Chapter 31

Nearly three hours later, Liam took the exit ramp to Greensboro and drove until we found a Holiday Inn close to the freeway. I climbed out, stretching out my legs in front of me. I pulled my arms one at a time behind my head, stretching my muscles from the stiffness they'd have to endure today. From across the roof of the car I saw Liam roll his shoulders as he made his way towards the back of the trunk and unloaded our suitcases.

"God," I heard him huff as he set down my luggage. "What do you have in here, a body?"

I rolled my eyes and grabbed the handle of my suitcase as he shouldered his duffle bag and led the way to the entrance. "You are so cranky when you're tired," I teased.

He flashed me a crooked smile and greeted the concierge, asking for a suite with two beds, and handing over a credit card that looked oddly familiar. I hadn't noticed it before, but in the dim lighting of the lobby – the questions that I had had before our trip suddenly clicked. I opened my mouth but before I could say anything Liam shook his head, his eyes seeming to say, Later.

With the room ready and paid for, we received two room card keys and were ushered towards the elevator. It was a slow climb to the fourth floor, feeling like we would both just crumble in a heap from fatigue and exhaustion. Liam's steps were heavy with weariness as we made our way down the hall to room 423. All I wanted was a shower and a soft, fluffy bed where I could lose myself in a dreamless sleep.

Finally reaching our destination, Liam opened the door to our suite and flicked on the light, flooding the rich colored room with warmth. The soft click of the door shutting reached my ears as I ventured further into the room and took the bed closer to heavy draped windows. I lifted my suitcase – with much difficulty – on top of the fluffy cream coverlet.

Liam wasn't too far behind, throwing his keys onto the night-stand between our beds and flopping back onto the covers, shielding his eyes with his forearm. He practically took up the entire bed with his tall stature. He hadn't even bothered to remove his old, dirty Converse or change out of his jeans, exhaustion surpassing even the smallest detail.

It couldn't have been more than five minutes that had passed when I heard the soft, distant sound of snoring. I flicked my eyes towards where he lay, his chest evenly rising and falling with every breath he took. I smiled and quietly headed towards the bathroom with my toiletries and pajamas.

I turned the knob to the hottest degree and shimmied out of my clothes. I grimaced as the boiling water scorched my skin for the first few seconds before it became accustomed to it. I knew that I should have brought my own shampoo and conditioner when the little samples they left in the room were barely enough for my thick and long hair. Closing my eyes, I bathed under the rivulets of water, wanting to stay for an eternity like this. It felt so good after a long day on the road.

But all good things must come to an end. The hot water turned luke warm and before I knew it, coldness had crept onto my skin. I turned off the faucet and grabbed a towel, drying myself off and putting on my favorite pink polka dot pajama bottoms and the Doctor Who t-shirt that I had begged Gemma to get me last Christmas.

Brushing my teeth and grabbing my clothes I headed back out into the room where Liam was still sound asleep. I tip-toed across the floor and dumped my dirty clothes by the window. As quietly as I could muster, I picked up my suitcase and set it on the floor. It was an epic fail. I lost control of the handle and it landed with a heavy thud. I bit my lip as Liam shifted his weight on the bed, his body facing me. My eyes widened and I held my breath, not wanting to wake him from his slumber.

After what seemed like a century, I resumed my activities without any further interruptions. He didn't once stir as I unmade the bed and tossed the excess pillows to the floor. I was ready to settle into bed and turn off the lights when the image of him lying still caused a small smile to form on my lips.

I kneeled down at the foot of his bed and unlaced his shoes, setting each one down underneath the bed. He was such a heavy sleeper, nothing could ever disturb him. A war could be going on outside right by our window and he would never realize it until morning when he'd see the soot and destruction.

Okay, so maybe that was a bit extreme. But it was the truth. He was a rock that was impossible to move once he'd succumbed to unconsciousness.

Taking one of my sheets, I draped it over him, tucking it right under his chin. My hand involuntarily reached out towards him, running the pad of my thumb across his dark brow. My eyes flickered to his slightly parted lips, and as hard as I could I tried to remember how it felt to feel his lips on mine. But I couldn't remember. All that I could see in my mind's eye was the heartbroken look on his face when I'd rejected and ran away from him.

A small sigh escaped his lips and I backed away faster than you could say "A dirty llama riding a bicycle."

Settling into bed I flicked off the last light, sending the room into a dark abyss. I smiled to myself and buried my face into my pillow. I sneaked one last glance at Liam and closed my eyes, welcoming the sleep that swept me under like a lolling ocean wave.

"Anya...Anya..." Shaking. Someone was shaking me; the image of a girl bleeding and damaged gathered in the arms of a boy fading into darkness. I opened my eyes and found Liam leaning over me, the sunlight from the window illuminating his body like some sort of angelic being. His hair was sleek wet, making it a shade darker than natural; while his eyes were a clear ocean blue, laced with utmost urgency, jolting me awake.

"What's going on?" I asked, untangling myself from the sheets.

"We overslept." He helped me out of bed and I quickly gathered a change of clothes from my luggage.

"Does this throw of the schedule?"

He ran a hand through his hair as he crossed the room to his duffle bag, searching for something. "Just by a few hours. Can you be ready in half an hour?"

I nodded. Seconds passed before I realized that he hadn't seen me. He turned his attention towards me and assessed my eyes, searching for an answer. I wanted to slap myself for being mentally incapable in the morning.

Yeah," I croaked out, scurrying into the bathroom.

Twenty minutes later I was ready to go. We hustled out of the suite with our belongings and headed down the lobby. Liam was practically bouncing with an enigma that was oddly comforting.

We checked out in less than five minutes; a new record that we were setting compared to all the times I'd been on the road with my parents. From what I gathered, I guessed that there would be no time for some much needed R&R, unless it involved sleeping.

But that was the thing about Liam. I thought one thing and in the end he proved me wrong.

"When's the next town?" I asked casually after we'd been on the road for a half hour. He'd been unusually quiet like there was something plaguing his mind.

"Hm?"

I flashed him a dubious look which he didn't see and asked him again.

"Oh. We should be in Durham in another half hour, but judging from the traffic it'll be maybe an hour."

I groaned.

"Hey, it's not my fault. You're the one who slept in."

"Me?" I exclaimed incredulously. "Well, if you were up so early why didn't you wake me up?"

He didn't say anything, but there was an amused smile tugging his lips. "Ha. I win."

"Didn't know we were playing a game."

I smiled, looking out at the lush countryside. "I've been keeping score for months now."

"Really?"

I turned to him, meeting his lingering gaze. His eyes were tinged with mischief, and I reached forward and flicked his nose like he did to me. His smile turned into a carefree grin.

"Yeah. And so far I'm winning."

We reached Durham in an hour, stopping for gas and food. My belly was practically upset with me for neglecting it nourishment for two hours. Liam was famished by how much he ordered at the 7 Eleven. I didn't even know where he put it all. I'd be concerned for his health if he wasn't so fit; which made me wonder what he did to work out because those arm muscles of his did not just appear out of thin air.

He ordered three quarter pound hotdogs and a Big Gulp Coke slush, making my Turkey sandwich and Kiwi Strawberry Arizona look like a happy meal.

Saying our thanks to the cashier, we grabbed our food, and were on the road again. I ended up being Liam's personal assistant, handing him extra ketchup and mayonnaise he'd grabbed from the dispensers. He'd also entrusted me in holding his slush because it didn't fit in the cup holders.

"I'll tell you right now that I will not be held liable if this spills all over the car."

He chuckled and shook his head. "Unbelievable."

"What?" I asked, setting the drink between my thighs and taking a bite of my sandwich.

He shook his head biting into his hotdog, while leisurely keeping his left hand on the wheel and his eyes on the road.

"So…"

"So," he repeated, averting his eyes from the road for a split second and asking for his drink. I handed it to him and I waited patiently, watching his Adam's apple move up and down as he gulped down the slushy goodness.

"Alright, so what's in Richmond?"

He handed me back the drink and I took it, barely able to contain the excitement running through my mind. What was in Richmond that had Liam racing towards the beautiful city?

"Lots of things," he said ominously.

"Obviously." I could have told him that. It didn't take a genius to know that there were lots of things in Richmond.

"Feisty."

"You know what I mean. What are we going to do?" I shook his arm and he laughed. "Tell me. Pleaseeeeeee. The suspense is killing me."

"Don't you go with that saying, you know...the one about a cat or something."

I furrowed my eyebrows. "Curiosity killed the cat?"

"Yeah, that one. If you were a cat you'd be dead already."

"Fortunately for me, I'm not. Now," I twisted in my seat and faced him, "stop changing the subject and tell me."

He flashed me an infuriating coy smile and I groaned. He was not going to tell me no matter how much I pestered him. Giving up, I sat back in my seat and crossed my arms over my chest. I might have been acting like a petulant child but it wasn't fair! I really wanted to know where and what we were doing.

He had been exhibiting some strange and reserved behavior since morning, and I could only conclude that there was something he'd planned in the city. It was the reason why we were out of Greensboro in such a hurry. Plus, I hadn't forgotten what he'd said last night. Add that with my mountain of suspicion, and I knew there was a mystery to be solved here.

"C'mon. Don't be like that."

"Like what?" I grumbled.

He reached forward and cradled my chin with his hand. "Like that."

"Can you at least give me a hint?"

"Nope," he said popping the P.

"You are so infuriating."

He let out an easy laugh and reached for the trash bag by my feet and dumped the empty hotdog cartons inside.

"Where do you put it all?"

"What?

"The food."

His brows furrowed down the middle like they did when he was trying to figure out a difficult math calculation.

"Umm...in here?" He patted his stomach, a triumphant smile displayed fully on his lips.

I shook my head and smiled. "You are such a dork."

"You love it. I remember when we were eight and you were oh-so fascinated with my Pokémon collection."

I gasped. "That's because they were awesome. You had like every known Pokémon in the planet. Do you know how huge that is?! How could I not be interested?"

"I had a feeling that's why you remained being my friend. You just wanted my Pokémon."

I rolled my eyes. "Cocky much?"

A devilish grin tugged at his lips and he wiggled his eyebrows suggestively. "Not cocky. Confident."

"Ha-ha. Sure, whatever helps you sleep at night."

"And it sure does."

I giggled. "What are we doing?"

He shrugged, unable to hide the wide grin on his face. "Don't know. But Richmond is just half an hour away."

It wasn't half an hour. Okay, no, let me rephrase that. We did reach Richmond in half an hour, but it wasn't where we were going. It was another hour before we reached our destination at 4:47 exactly. My eyes had been practically glued to the dashboard where the minutes ticked by an agonizingly slow pace. Traffic had been a horror, and once we parked in the lot, I practically jumped out of the car with uncontainable elation.

I breathed in the cool, salty air and ran towards Liam where I kissed him spontaneously on the cheek.

"Thank you, thank you, thank you!"

He chuckled and spread his arms out, "Welcome to Yorktown Beach."

I beamed. "This is...amazing." I was completely at a loss for words as I stared at the vast blue ocean in front of me. A few bodies lingered on the shore; kids running around and splashing in the water, women scattered on the sand sunbathing, and men of various ages taking leisurely strolls or playing volleyball.

Shielding my eyes from the penetrating rays of what was left of the sun; I saw the distant outline of a bridge, looming around the town. It was massive; nothing like I had ever seen before. To my left there was a dock, much like the one we had in Fairhope. It brought a smile to my lips, wanting my family and friends to be witnessing what I was. But whatever they were doing I knew that they were having the time of their lives like I was with Liam.

"How about we make the most of the day we have left."

I turned my attention to him and saw a green plaid blanket tucked under his arm.

I smiled. "What do you have in mind?"

"Eeek! Liam!" My voice raised an octave as he chased me towards the water, discarding the blanket in a heap along with his shoes, car keys, and phone. Hastily, I unzipped the light black sweater I wore and discarded it near the shore, toeing off my sandals in the process.

"No!" I whirled around, my breath labored as I put my hands up in defense. He was a few feet away, a dangerous glint in his eyes. "Don't come near me," I threatened, backing away slowly from him. The back of my feet brushed against the waves and I shivered from the freezing temperature.

"It's so cold! Don't do it!"

He grinned, mischievously and ran forward. I squealed and trudged into the water, cringing as the coldness prickled my skin. Liam caught me, wrapping his arms around my waist and swinging me around.

"That's no fair!"

"And how's that?"

"You are stronger and faster. The waves practically swallowed me up."

He chuckled and set me down. "All's fair in love and war."

I grinned and splashed him, running as far away as possible from him. I didn't get very far and when he reached me I was assaulted with water. We were both soaked to the marrow when we submerged from the watery depth and laid out on the sand, the blanket forgotten.

"Stay here," he breathed out.

"Where are you...?"

He trotted off into the distance and I smiled lazily, looking up at the clear blue sky as it turned into a sea of vibrant pinks and oranges. I was alone, the peace and tranquility surreal as I lay back, hiking up one of my legs. I closed my eyes, taking in the sweet salty water and burying deep into the warmth of the sand.

It couldn't have been anymore perfect as I felt the cool spring breeze on my skin. The sound of crashing waves centered my being, and I felt weightless; like I was floating away in my very own soap bubble.

The space next to me was soon occupied, but I didn't need to open my eyes to know who filled it. I was hyper aware of him, my brain somehow remembering the cinnamon scent that he carried even when he was drenched in salty water.

A shadow cast over me and I pried my eyes open, my heart in my throat as his dazzling blue eyes paralyzed me.

"Don't move, alright?"

"Why? Is there a sea urchin..."

He shook his head. "No." I let out a breath I hadn't realized I was holding and glared at him.

"Don't scare me like that."

He flicked my nose and moved to my right. I tilted my head in his direction and saw that there was a pile of sea shells in front of him.

"Where did you get all those?" There were all sorts of colors, the last rays glinting on top of their smooth surface.

"Found them around the beach. Where did you think I'd gone?"

"I don't know...maybe to go get us some ice cream?"

He smiled. "We'll get ice cream after it's what you want."

I nodded. "Yes. Oooh and maybe a burger. I'm starving. You?"

"Now that you mention it..." He was fully preoccupied with intricately placing the seashells around my frame like an outline of a snow angel. I watched him in awe, his lips slightly parted in concentration reminding me off the night before when he slept peacefully. The wet t-shirt clung to his body, outlining the muscles underneath.

His hands were nimble, swift, and strong. They were capable of harming someone's jaw and knowing their way carefully around an engine. They could also be tender, as soft a feather as they caressed my skin.

"What are you thinking of?"

"Hm?"

"You're smiling."

I bit my lip. "Can't a girl smile without being questioned?"

He looked down at the ground and back at me, a smile fighting on his lips. Slowly as if his movements were unsure, he loomed over me, closer than when he'd come back from his scavenger hunt.

My breath caught in my throat. We gazed into each other's eyes, the light of the sun dimming as the seconds passed by until his eyes were no longer a cool blue but shining gray.

"Anya."

It was one word. My name. It was about the only thing that could cause my heart to rapidly thud inside my chest. Liam leaned forward, his hand caressing my cheek. I leaned into his palm and closed my eyes. Anticipation coursed through my bloodstream as I waited for the feel of his lips against mine. But when all I felt was the warm press of his lips on my forehead, I couldn't help but be disappointed.

Once I opened my eyes again I found Liam sitting next to me, staring out at the dark ocean. I sat up, mindful to not destroy the display of seashells around me.

We sat in silence for a long while, neither wanting to disturb the calmness of the sea. In the distance, the bridge was aglow with lanterns strung across its metal hinges. No other living soul was left on the beach, but the sounds of people laughing and enjoying their night were carried from afar.

"Can we stay here?" I asked.

He turned to me and cocked his head. "Here? Like on the beach?"

I nodded. "We could sleep under the stars or," I titled my head across the beach where some sort of party or festival was being held, "we could join them."

He weighed my words and then pushed himself up, brushing off the sand that clung to his skin. His eyes were shining with a secret smile that was contagious. I didn't know what he was churning around in his mind, but whatever it was I knew that I would follow him until the ends of the earth because being with him was where I wanted to be.

Chapter 32

We danced under the moonlight, enjoying the cacophony of gleeful squeals under spirits and the light-hearted music resonating beneath our feet. It felt like we had just traveled back in time to an era where dancing was done carelessly like in the roaring 20's or jazzing 50's. They played all sorts of music; Frank Sinatra being one of my favorites.

I hadn't known that Liam knew how to dance or the fact that he was a good dancer. He was light on his feet, twirling me around with such precision that I had never known he held. We traded secret and merry smiles as the evening wore and the moon was high in the black canvassed sky. It was all a never ending blissful dream – one in which I never wanted to find myself woken up from.

But we weren't creatures of the night and soon sleep settled into the marrow of our bones. We waved goodbye to the new friends we'd made within the last few hours and trudged down the beach, the cool sand squishing between my toes.

We settled at a spot far off to the coast with only the sound of the crashing waves impenetrable to our ears despite the party we'd just left in the distant. Liam laid out on the blanket first and I crawled in after him, curling my body close to his. The chill in the air seeped through my sweater and I shivered. Liam hugged me closer to him, wrapping an arm around my waist. Our legs twisted together, giving off resonating warmth that spread through my veins like a steady flame igniting my whole being.

Sleep soon gnawed at my very core, pulling me under with only the sound of the lulling waves crashing on the shore, and the steady beating of Liam's heartbeat in my head.

Feeling the cool icy fingertips of the wind on my skin I slowly rose from the land of the dead. I lifted my head from the warmth of Liam's chest and nestled my face into the folds of his shirt. He stirred and a second later his eyes fluttered open.

I smiled. "Morning."

He blinked. Once. Twice. His eyes were hazed over like I was a mere image his mind had conjured out of the valley of waking dreams. One moment his face was a complete mask of awe and the next it transformed into a loving smile.

"Good morning."

I bit my lip and sat up, running a hand through my tangled waves and looked down at him and his infectious smile.

"What?"

He raised his brows and put his hands behind his head. "Nothing. Just thinking about how I could get used to this in the morning. "

I looked down at the ground and smiled, wanting to hide how much his words affected me. The soft caress of his hand on my chin brought my eyes to his slate-gray ones, speaking volumes of endearment in that one look.

"The sun's about to rise."

"Did you come up with that startling conclusion all by yourself?" I teased.

He flicked my nose. "Smartass."

"So I've been told."

Liam shook his head, amusement dancing in his eyes as he took my hand in his and pulled me towards him where I sat in front of him, his legs sprawled out on either side of me. He looped his arms around my waist and rested his chin on my shoulder.

"Have you ever seen the sunrise?" His breath was hot in my ear, sending shivers down my spine. I gulped, unable to properly think about anything except for the pounding sound of my heart rushing in my ears.

I shook my head in response. From the corner of my eyes I saw the slight tug of a smile on the corner of his lips.

"Relax, alright? I just..." I turned my head slightly and looked at him. He loosened his grip around my waist and I tried to hide the absence of their strong, reassurance off my face. His lips were mere inches from mine and I did my best to keep my eyes on his instead of them diverting south.

"I just like being near you. That's all."

I smiled and cupped the side of his face with my hand, feeling the roughness of the five o'clock shadow he was sporting.

"I do, too. You're...well, there's no need to go making your head bigger than it already is."

He gaped and clutched his heart with a mock expression on his face. "You really know how to strike an arrow through a guy's heart, babe."

I shook my head and hit his arm. "What did I tell you about that word?"

"Sorry." He wrapped his arms around my waist again and pulled me against the lean muscle of his chest. "Force of habit."

"I'll forgive you this time, but next time you won't be so fortunate."

We sat in comfortable silence for a few minutes, enveloped in the cool morning beauty that surrounded us. The sky was a violet gray, streaking over the vast horizon in a hue of dark blues and purples. The ocean was strangely calm, with only the sound of the tides rolling to the shore in a peaceful lull. I closed my eyes and leaned back into Liam, his arms immediately responding and tightening around my waist.

I listened to the low, caressing rustle of the palm trees somewhere nearby; their branches singing a harmonious and sweet melody. When I opened my eyes once again the sky had changed into a rosy pink, where the sun was beginning to rise over the sea's surface. I glanced around the beach and saw no other living soul on the premises. Even the bodies from last night had disappeared, leaving no trace of a party every occurring on the front steps of the shoreline.

We were alone; blissfully alone as the sun slowly crawled over the horizon, setting the water into a fiery blaze. Orange hues mixed with rosy pinks until all the pinks, purples, and blues disappeared from the sky; leaving only soft, glowing ambers in the sky.

"I missed this when I was sleeping?" I softly asked, my voice caught between a mixture of incredulity and awe. "I can't believe..."

"Shh." He rested his chin on my shoulder, his breath warm at the nape of my neck when he spoke. "It was nothing like this."

"Promise?" I asked, tilting my head to look at him. His eyes were a cool gray just like the color of the waves before dawn.

"Promise."

With the early morning still upon us we set out for the road. I smiled at the sea, saying my silent goodbye to its beauty. I rolled down the window as Liam drove, feeling the morning air cool on my skin. The ocean air grew dense the farther away we drew from the beach until it altogether faded in the wind. It was soon after that vast ocean canvas disappeared in my review mirror.

I hit the switch and pulled my window up. Even though we were miles away from the sea, I could still smell the salty air that clung to our skin. It was like a gift from the ocean itself, asking us to never forget.

Smiling, I settled back into my seat and looked out my window, watching green pastures pass along by. A few houses stood erect along the road, weathered and abandoned. Others were beautifully built estates that left me staring back long after we'd driven by.

An hour had passed since we'd left Yorktown Beach when I found myself trying to stay awake. The road had become desolate with only a few stray cars on the highway, their passengers starting out their day. The scenery was beautiful, but there was only so much greenery that could fascinate me until I grew bored, falling prey to car drowsiness.

I was in that state between sleep and consciousness when I felt the car roll to a stop. I fluttered my eyes open and cringed from the sudden bright rays of the sun. Keys rattled the unfastening of a seat belt drew my attention to Liam getting out of the car. He appeared at my side in a moment's noticed and opened the door for me, climbing out on shaky feet.

"Where are we?" I asked, shielding my eyes from the sun's strong rays.

"Baltimore. You really are a heavy sleeper."

"Me? You're the one who..."

I stopped my tongue from saying anymore than needed to be said. I couldn't very well go spilling out my secrets like they were candy. Liam raised his eyebrow, searching my eyes; like he was trying to figure out my thoughts.

Lucky for me, he wasn't a mind reader or else I'd be mortified beyond belief.

Instead of getting usual fast food, Liam settled for a quaint small diner he'd stumbled upon. It wasn't until we were through the door that a sudden panic attack settled in my throat.

My bag.

Words were exchanged between the hostess and Liam, but I paid no mind to them. All I could think about was my bag inside the car and what contents I needed from it.

"Anya."

I blinked and looked up at Liam, his head cocked to the side as he motioned for me to follow. I stood transfixed for a moment, debating my options. There was only one of two things I could do:

1. Don't get my bag and suffer the consequences.

Or:

Get bag but face possible embarrassment.

"Hey," Liam said, turning his body towards mine. The hostess gave me a loaded glance and crossed her arms over her chest, tapping her foot restlessly. I hadn't noticed the interested look in her eyes before or the way that Liam seemed to cast her aside. It filled me with an unexplained giddiness that was soon quashed with the thought of what I was about to do.

"You alright?"

"Yeah." I waved away his concern and took his arm, pulling him to the side. "I just...forgot my bag. Can I have the car keys?"

"Breakfast is on me. You don't have to worry about it."

I sighed. "I know. But I need it...I have..." I couldn't find the right words to say, whilst my stomach began to twist into painful knots. The longer I stalled the more suspicious Liam seemed to get. His eyes were a cool gray, calculating and imploring. I was hoping that he wouldn't ask any questions, but things were never that simple.

"I need my stuff. It's a girl thing, you know? Girl stuff."

"Oh," he said. His concerned expression faded into a face stricken with abject horror, making me want to go dig a hole and bury myself alive in it.

He reached into his pocket and handed me the car keys, my cheeks flaming with utter humiliation. It was just something that he did not need to know even if it wasn't true. I guess my pride could suffer rather than him knowing the real truth.

"Press unlock twice to open and once to lock it."

I nodded and said, "Got it," and dashed out of the diner before he could say anything else. It took less than a minute to get in and get out, heading back inside towards the bathroom and into one of the empty stalls. My hands were shaking by the time that I opened the medicine bottles and poured out its contents. Feverishly, I popped them into my mouth and took a long drink from my water bottle.

Once I was finished, I dumped my belongings back into my bag and shrugged it across my shoulder. I felt undeniably better, but my reflection said otherwise. White lips, pale face, and tired brown eyes stared back at me. My eyes were sad, undoubtedly mixed in with cold realization.

I couldn't be with him. I couldn't be with anyone. It would mean bringing what I carried – who I was into whatever semblance of a relationship I wanted. Gemma and Hayden were different – they were my friends – and even then I saw the concern in their eyes every day I wasn't feeling well or looked it. My parents had to endure it ever since they chose to take me in as their own, knowing full well the consequences of caring for a baby with an untreatable sickness.

But with Liam it was different. I wanted to protect him from this as long as I could even when my heart wanted the opposite.

Liam

Anya settled into a quiet and withdrawn state when she met me at the table a few minutes later. I had ordered our drinks for us – orange juice for her and coffee for me – knowing that I would need all the caffeine I could inhale for the last few hours before we hit NYC. An old and codling waitress came by and took our orders. She flashed cheeky smiles and winked at Anya, her eyes roaming back and forth between us suggestively. Anya's cheeks flamed and she took to absentmindedly playing with the napkin in front of her, avoiding my gaze.

I didn't have much of an appetite when our food arrived. A looming darkness had settled between her and I that made it impossible to think of anything else. Anya muttered a simple thank you and dug in with quiet reverence. She remained lost in her own thoughts, not once looking up from her plate.

We left shortly after we were both done eating, none of us trading more than a few casual words. As soon as I began to drive again, Anya fell into a quiet slumber. The grassy plains of Maryland were barren with endless fields of tall stalks and trees. I didn't blame her for being a horrible passenger. If I was in her position I'd probably knock out for most of the trip.

Driving, on the other hand, wasn't so easy. There were instances when weariness settled over my entire body, wanting sleep more than anything else in that moment. I fought it, keeping it at bay by turning on the stereo and popping in one of Anya's made CD's. An easy smile quickly spread on my mouth whenever I heard a Silversun Pickup song in the mix of songs she'd carefully chosen.

All Anya ever did was listen, storing away the information for a later date. Her knowing one of my favorite bands was proof that, not to mention all the other things she remembered about me; past and present.

Sometimes, I felt like she was a mirage while I was in a middle of a desert. She was still here with me despite all the fucked up things I had done. She didn't resent me for it as much as I believed I deserved it. I was an arrogant ass who only cared about myself and didn't give a shit about what anyone else thought. The more time I spent with Anya the more I began to realize how pitiful the life I had been living was. I was tired of feeling sorry for myself and blaming everything on Dad. He had made his decisions and I had made mine. That was one thing that Anya had taught me. I could change my life if I wanted too.

I did.

"Dammit," I swore, hitting my palm against the steering wheel and honking the horn.

"What happened?" Anya exclaimed, looking around frantically.

I shook my head and waved away her concern. "Nothing. This dumbass cut me off. We haven't been in the city for five minutes and already it has changed me.

"The city?"

I glanced at her, keeping my eyes simultaneously on the road ahead. The traffic was horrible with car horns beeping every other minute and impatient drivers cutting off one another. It was just our luck that we had gotten into the city at rush hour.

"We're in the city!" Anya shook my arm, excitement evident in the squeakiness of her voice. I smiled at her, glad to have my Anya back.

"This is terrible," she mumbled, wiping away the sleep from her eyes and staring out the windshield.

"Tell me about it. People don't know how to fucking drive around here."

"Woah. Someone's a little grumpy."

"Look at the bright side. We're here! Finally! After three days of endless driving, we're here."

"Endless driving? How about endless sleeping."

She punched me and I exclaimed, "Hey! Don't hurt the driver."

"I don't recall that ever being a rule in Driver's Ed."

"It's not. It's one of my rules."

"Who says I have to listen to you or your rules," she retorted.

I raised my brow and looked her way where she was sticking her tongue out at me.

"Very mature."

She beamed. "Thank you."

Two hours later the traffic had thinned, and I exited at 10th Avenue, heading for our hotel. Anya was completely enthralled by the lights and sky scraper buildings we'd passed on the highway. It was unbelievable – the sights and sounds; everything. I'd never seen anything more full of life than the city. It seemed that everything and everyone had somewhere to be with not enough time to get there.

The place I arranged our stay at was called Liberty Inn. It was only a half hour away from Julliard, but in the quiet part of New York City. As we stepped out of the car and grabbed our luggage, Anya was practically bouncing with uncontainable joy ready to escape at any given moment. The concierge eyed Anya and I suspiciously, but after finding my name in the list of booked guests, he set the key cards on the counter while I dug into my jeans for my wallet.

Anya covered her hand with mine as I was about to hand over the credit card to the concierge, and took it from my hands.

"I knew it. No wonder it looked familiar," she mumbled. "Why didn't you tell me?"

I shrugged and took it back from her, handing it to the small man behind the counter. "I didn't think it was important."

He charged the room and hand it back to me, leaving us to be on our way. The lobby was quiet with only an old woman sitting loftily in a purple armchair reading a book. She looked up at us as we passed along and I smiled at her. Her eyes crinkled at the corners and she let out a sigh, getting back to her book.

"That's why you were at my house, wasn't it? Dad called you over to give you his card."

I pressed the call button for the elevator and immediately the doors clattered open. "Yeah." Anya passed through first and I followed, pressing the closed button to shut the doors. "He insisted, telling me that he didn't want us to spend either of the money we'd saved up."

She leaned her head back on the cold metal wall and looked up at the mirrored ceiling; a small smile tugging on the corners of her lips. "It sounds like something he'd do."

A high bell-like ding signaled our floor destination, followed by the doors clattering open. We made our way to Room 358, finding it at the near-end of the hall.

"Let me," she said, holding her hand out for the key card.

"Be my guest." She smiled as I gave her the card and took her suitcase in tow. There was a low beep, the red button turning green, and an audible click. Anya pushed open the door, holding it out for me as I walked into the small suite. The door closed shut behind me as I set our things down in the middle of the room.

"It's small but cozy. I like it."

"You should see the view."

Anya turned on her heals, her eyebrows raising in a question. I waved her forward and she walked across the room, tearing the sheer curtains apart with such force that I thought she'd break them.

"Oh my...It's beautiful."

Before us was the view of the Hudson River. The water was dark and vast with tall buildings rising in the distance. The lampposts cast the river in dark blue shades against the twilight. Cars whizzed passed on the darkening road, but the river remained still. Tranquil.

"You never cease to amaze me, you know? What's next? Dancing with penguins?"

I laughed, sinking my hands into my front pockets. "Don't know. Guess you'll have to wait until tomorrow. We do have a full day to ourselves until your audition."

Her brown eyes mirrored the smile that spread on her lush lips. She closed the space between us and threw her arms around my neck. "Thank you," she whispered, "for everything."

I wrapped my arms around her waist, only for her to pull back a second later.

"Umm..." She ran a hand threw her hair and looked down at the ground sheepishly. "I bet you're tired. I'll just let you sleep and I'll..." Whatever she was about to say faded as her eyes focused on something behind me.

I turned and saw what she was looking at; a queen sized bed framed against purple colored headboard. Anya came around and sat down on the plush olive green coverlet, running her fingers over the duvet. Her brows were strewn in concentration like she was debating something with herself.

"I'll go talk to the manager," I said, taking a few steps backwards towards the door. "I'll fix this."

"No. No." She stood up from her perch and walked towards me. "It's fine. There's no need to trouble him. Mistakes happen. Plus, I'll take to the sofa. You need it more than I do. I slept along the way and I am pretty wired."

I shook my head. "Don't be silly. There's plenty of room for the both of us. It's not like we haven't slept together."

Anya let out a small laugh and looked down at the ground, playing with a non-existent fray at the hem of her shirt. I knew what my words might have meant to her, but I was stating only fact. We had slept together a handful of times on this trip and nothing had happened, if that was something she was afraid of. Nothing was going to happen because I didn't want Anya in that way. I wanted her in wholly different way that I didn't even entirely know how to explain.

She had settled into the yellow sofa chaise lounge that ran around the edge of the walls and flipped on the television, absent-mindedly flipping through the channels. I plopped down beside her and toed off my sneakers, reaching underneath the coffee table for the room service menus.

"How about some grilled steaks and mashed potatoes for dinner?"

Anya leaned towards me, peering at the pictures on the menus. "Mmm," she said, pointing at a picture of cheeseburger. "That looks good."

"I'll ring up our order."

She smiled and diverted her attention back to the t.v. "Oh! If Only is on."

"What's it about?" I asked as I dialed the number. I was immediately answered and I gave the man who answered our order. He told me it would be up in ten minutes and hung up.

"It's about a guy who doesn't appreciate the girl he has in his life until she dies."

"Sounds morbid."

"It's not. Well, I guess it depends on how you look at it. Its heart wrenching. The first time I watched was with Gemma and we ended up crying our eyes out."

"Please don't tell me we're going to watch it."

Anya smiled mischievously. "Oh, we are. You have no say in the matter."

"I do if do this." In a swift motion I pried the remote from her hands. She leaped forward and attacked me, trying to get the remote back.

"That's not fair! I had it first."

"I had it second."

"You're such a little kid."

"I think it's an enduring quality."

She huffed and punched my arm. She was all over me, trying to get the remote but it was out of her reach as I feigned her off with my other hand. Anya was not below tickling as I had gathered the moment she began to strike.

"Now that's not fair." I squirmed out of her reached and she raised her eyebrows, smugly.

"Well to bad; shouldn't have taken it from me. Now, you must suffer the consequences."

We didn't stop feigning off each other until there was a knock at the door. Anya and I were tangled up on the floor, her hand reaching over my head for the object that was stretched out of her reach. I had to give her an A for effort. Other girls would have given up and tried to seduce me.

But not Anya.

I found it enchanting like she was weaving a spell every time that she just smiled at me.

Fuck. I sounded like one of those sentimental fuckers.

Another knock at the door brought us to our feet, our fighting ceasing as I opened the door to reveal a delicious aroma over-whelming my senses.

"Room service." The waiter looked to be around our age as he strolled in with the cart, holding the dinner that I couldn't wait to dig into. Not eating much at breakfast had been a mistake and I was just running on splurged caffeine.

"Here you go," Anya said, handing him a five dollar bill. "Thank you."

He shook his head and waved away the tip. "I'd rather get your name."

I raised my eyebrows and stood in front of Anya. The guy, whose name tag read Jesse, raised his brow in turn. He was inept if he thought that Anya would so easily give him her name.

"Thanks for the food. I'll be sure to write a review on how it is."

Jesse's eyes searched for Anya's, but when she didn't respond he took the hint and exited with a tail between his legs. I locked the door behind him only to find Anya smiling coyly when I turned around.

"What?"

"Nothing," she said, taking her plate and settling down on the sofa. She propped her feet up on the coffee table and took a bite of her burger, unable to hide the smile that tugged on her lips whenever she looked at me.

"What is it?" I asked, taking my seat next to her with my own plate.

"Nothing."

"That's not a nothing nothing that's a something nothing."

She laughed quietly. "You have such a way words, did you know that?"

"No, but thank you for that startling observation."

She rolled her eyes and ate a French fries.

"So what's with the smiles. Don't tell me that you actually wanted to give the guy your name."

"No. But someone was jealous."

"Who?"

"You."

"Me?" I sounded like a fucking owl. I put my plate down on the coffee table and turned my full attention to her. An easy smile was playing on her lips, melting the hint of annoyance that had crept into my mood.

"It was sorta cute. Guess it's just another one of your endearing qualities, right?"

"What is?"

"Being protective. Jealous even."

I shook my head and ran a hand through my hair, tugging on the ends a little. "I was not jealous."

"Alright. Whatever makes you feel better."

We ate in silence and somehow during dinner Anya had won, getting the remote and changing it to the movie she had chosen in the beginning. As the movie progressed, Anya and I slowly inched our way to each other until she was curled up in my arms. Her whole body shook with silent tears as Jennifer Love Hewitt's character breaks down in the hospital with only her best friend to be there for her.

"This was a terrible movie to watch," I said softly as the credits rolled.

"Why?" she asked, wiping around the tears on her cheeks.

"Because it was sad. He gives her the best day only for him to die and leave her scarred for life."

"She's not scared for life," she argued. "Look at what he did for her at the end. He inspired her to sing, and she will never forget that. She'll miss him as we all miss someone who has left us, but at the same time, she is thankful to have known him."

"She'll never love again and she'll be alone forever."

"When you look at it that way of course it's sad. But life isn't about dwelling on all the bad things. I think that's something that most people forget. It's like those bad things are imprinted into our souls like a disease, making us forget all the good things that happened before the sickness."

She spoke with passionate conviction, making me second guess my own thoughts. It didn't matter what she had said, but the way she said that captivated me. She could have been talking about how shellfish were the most delicious aphrodisiac in the world and I would have believed her. Her eyes were steady and warm like liquid fire, holding firmly what she whole heartedly thought.

Anya lost herself when she spoke of something she was truly passionate about. It was something that I loved about her.

I loved her.

It was in that moment that I realized what I wanted from her. I hadn't known before; hadn't put the pieces together.

All I wanted was for her to know that I loved her and for it to be returned.

Fuck. I was becoming one of those sentimental fuckers.

Chapter 33

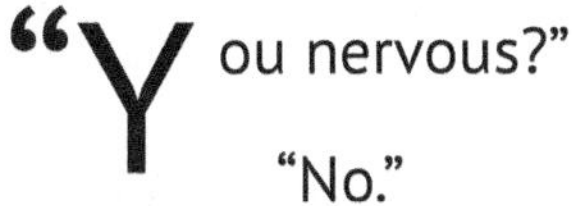

"You nervous?"

"No."

"Anya."

I turned away from the girl on stage, who was playing a beautiful rendition of one of Beethoven's Sonata's, and looked up at Liam.

"They want you here and you'll be here in the Fall."

"How do you know? Have you been consorting with the Mystics?"

He flashed me a charming smile, the kind that made my legs feel like gelato and my heart quicken inside my chest.

"No, but I've heard you play and it's…" His words were lost on his tongue as he took my hands in his. My heart thudded wildly in my ears, and I hated it. I wanted to shout at my stupid heart to stop, but no matter my protests, my heart would hear none of them.

"Vanchester. Anya Vanchester."

We both turned to the source of the voice; a woman dressed in a casual business suit with four inch stiletto heels. Her eyes searched the crowd for the face of the name on the clipboard she had just called.

"I'm here." I waved my hand in the air, garnering her attention. Her heels made a click-clackity sound on the wooden deck as she approached, the rhythm synchronizing with the erratic heartbeats in my eardrums.

She halted a foot away from us, her eyes flickering to Liam's, giving him a once over. Gathering that he was not auditioning she said, "Guests are to wait and observe in the theater."

Liam shrugged absentmindedly and leaned in, brushing a kiss on my temple. "Break a leg," he whispered. My breath caught in my chest as I watched him saunter off towards the stairs at the edge of the theater floor.

"You will be after Ms. Woosley is finished with her performance. Your name will be called and that will be time you will take the stage. Any questions?"

I shook my head. I knew all this. Ms. Woosley's performance wasn't the first that I had seen nor would it be the last. Maybe I was a little peeved that she had so rudely dismissed Liam. But at the same time I was surprised and pleased that he had not raised a riot. The old Liam would have bitten her head off, demanding to know what her problem was. For that I was entirely grateful.

Before she left she handed me my sheet music, the words APPROVED were stamped in red at the top right hand corner of the papers. I breathed a sigh of relief, sending a silent prayer of thanks to God for having everything running smoothly so far.

As I waited my turn to take the stage my mind drifted to yesterday. Liam had taken me to Central Park, where we had a picnic under the shade of the giant Hornbeam trees by the lake. We spent the entire afternoon there, soaking up the rays, getting lost with the simplicity around us. The cool March air nipped at our skin, sending small spasms of chills down my spine. Liam pulled me to him, spreading his legs on either side of me. I leaned back into his chest, wanting to say the only word that I had come to associate with him.

Sweetness.

We talked about the past most of all, remembering times that we had forgotten, but the other had held on to, not willing to let go. He talked about his mother, Layla. His voice grew quiet and husky as he replayed the memories of her in his mind.

"I remember the first time I met you."

"You do?" I asked, trying hard to find the memory but coming up blank. We had been so young, the memory lost to years of knowing each other, to memories that I truly treasured with us.

"It was when you feel off your bike and scarped your knee really badly. No one was around except for Mom and me."

I furrowed my eyebrows, trying but failing to conjure up the memory.

"She went to you and helped you up, examining the injury. All I could think about was the blood and how much that must have hurt."

"I didn't take you to be squeamish," I teased.

He laughed faintly. "Neither did I."

"What happened next?"

He leaned his chin into my shoulder and somehow I leaned back, closer than we were before. His hands around my waist warmed my bones to the marrow. My cheeks flushed and I was glad that he could not see my face. He couldn't know how he made me feel. Ever. But it was getting harder and harder with each passing day. I felt like a dam that any moment could crack, unleashing a tidal wave of feelings that could no longer be kept at bay.

"You had strayed from the neighborhood. Going farther than you had even realized. As luck would have it, Mom knew who you were and so did I as I remembered seeing you around, playing outside. We took you home, while I rode your bike. You did not like that at all."

The memory was slowly resurfacing as I remembered a blond little boy riding my bike. "I told you to get off."

"You did."

I titled my head to the side and sucked on my bottom lip. "I remember...that was you?"

He slowly nodded. "Yep. You were feisty even then; a testimony that people don't change."

I elbowed him playfully. "Shuddup. I remember what you did afterwards."

"And that would be?"

"Anya Vanchester."

I perked my ears at the sound of my name, my heart suddenly thumping wildly in my chest. The memories dispersed, crawling back into the depths of my mind. Taking a deep breath, I went into my bubble as I walked towards the stage, ignoring the eyes that followed me.

Emerging from the red, velvet curtains I took the stage. I breathed easily. In. Out. In. Out. My heart felt like it was going to explode with how loud it was thundering, madly in my chest. As I took my seat on the bench, I set the music on the stand and flipped to the first piece of music I would play, followed by the order of other great works I would perform.

Closing my eyes, I let all other sounds fade into the background. I was in my bubble and with that came tunnel vision. All that mattered, all that I needed to concentrate on were the notes in front of me; notes that I knew as well as the lines engraved on the back of my hands.

Nothing else mattered, except for the music.

I started with Back's Fugue No. 10. The notes were light, sweet, floating. My nerves quickly grew faint until there was nothing left. As the tempo progressed so did everything around me. The word spun in a series of beautiful colorful leaves. Greens. Blues. Browns. All colors imaginable clouded my vision. At the same time I was highly aware of the music being released from the piano, engulfing the very nature of time.

It all happened so fast after that. I played the wonderful pieces of music that had been masterfully created by artists who had once been like me. I lost myself in Mozart's 331 Sonata, andregained my composure when it came to Chopin's mesmerizing and dark Nocturne in C sharp Minor. I played another piece by Chopin titled Chopin Etude No. 10 No. 12 (which was one of the hardest pieces I had ever played) followed by Debussy's Claire De Lune. Lastly, I played Beethoven's Moonlight Sonata, its captivating and low lull a resonating contrast to Chopin.

When I was finished, I was greeted with thunderous applause. I shyly bowed and calmly walked off stage, which was the last thing that I wanted to do. I wanted to run and hide behind a tightly sealed door where I could scream at the top of my lungs.

I had done it!

By the end of the stairs I wasn't met with a door I could safely hide behind, even though it was a musing that I was certain of only seconds before. Instead I was engulfed with something entirely better.

"It was amazing. You were amazing," he breathed out.

I clung to him for what seemed like ages, like an island surrounded by the vast and tremulous waters. For fear of letting go would surely lead to drowning.

But it was what we did in the end as he led me to a seat in the audience. Silently, we watched the rest of the auditions – Liam absentmindedly listening, while I nervously played with a napkin I had whipped out of my bag. At one point, Liam covered my hand with his, stopping the obsessive habit. I smiled sheepishly and he returned it with a crooked smile. For the rest of the time, we sat there, hand in hand, which was a long time indeed.

"Finally," he said once the final curtain was drawn. Over the cacophony of clapping and voices Liam said, "Let's get out of here. I'm starving."

"Where are we going?" I asked.

"There's a restaurant across the street. I believe it was Italian."

I grinned. Italian was my favorite. I could use a good plate of ravioli right about now.

"Okay. Let's go."

I grabbed my bag and shouldered it, following Liam in the beeline towards the large, wood paneled double doors.

"Excuse me?" said a voice from behind. I turned, sure that the voice couldn't possibly be for me.

The voice belonged to a man in his early 20's with inquisitive light eyes and shaggy yet well kept brown hair.

"Anya Vanchester?"

I stopped, fully turning my attention to him and calling for Liam to wait. The man ushered me to the side, away from the throng of people in the aisle.

"Hello, I'm Anya," I said, extending my hand towards him. I wasn't the best at meeting new people and the Lord knew that I wasn't the most sociable.

The man took my hand and shook it. "I'm Bastian DeRoux," he said.

By the way he said his name he was hoping that it brought some recognition. It didn't. Unfortunately. He looked familiar, but I couldn't put my finger on it. Surely I would have remembered him if I had met him, but nothing came to mind – that is, until Liam found us, hitting the arrow straight to the heart – metaphorically speaking of course.

"Your performance was –for lack of a better word – beautifully done. My wife," his gaze traveled to a woman with beautiful long silk hair and tanned skin standing a few rows from us, talking to one of the music directors I'd met earlier. "She agreed and it's why I'm here."

I furrowed my eyebrows not quite sure where he was going with this. I looked behind my shoulder and saw Liam, his arms impatiently crossed over his shoulders, waiting for the last remnants of the audience to shuffle out and allow him a path to me.

"Thank you." It was all I could think of to say.

"I want to privately fund your tuition. Julliard is an expensive establishment and it is not to say that you won't get the scholarship. You were one of the best – if not my favorite – performance that I have seen to date. Music speaks to you and it's–"

"Wait. You can't be serious." This could not be happening. "I don't even know who you are. Why would you..."

"Woah." I turned and found Liam's wide eyed gaze transfixed on Bastian. "You're the guy from Highway to Hell!"

Bastain's cool composure melted as an easy and appreciative smile lifted the corners of his mouth. They clasped hands like old friends as I was left completely dumbfounded.

An actor? An actor wants to privately fund my expenses for school? What in the world was going on? This seemed like something that would happen once in a blue moon. They talked about the movies he'd been in and about motorcycles which I completely was at a loss. Most of the things that they were saying just went in one ear and out the other. Everything was happening so fast.

Until Bastian's wife joined us.

"You played wonderfully, sweetheart. I felt like...well I felt like I was reading your story while you played. Only one person has every made me feel that way." She glanced at Bastian, sharing a secret smile between each other. Bastain wound his arm around her waist and kissed her cheek. She smiled, a dreamy haze clouding her warm brown eyes.

"How about we talk about this matter over dinner?" Bastian suggested.

"That's an excellent idea, honey. What do you guys think?"

Liam and I looked at each other, he nodded enthusiastically. He couldn't be more happy than a kitten with a ball of yarn. I, on the other hand, felt like I was an alternate universe. This could not be happening. Could it?

At last, I found my voice and said, "Sure. We would love to."

Bastian took out a business card and wrote something on the back of it, giving it to Liam while his wife and I traded formalities. "I'm Ridley," she said. "Sorry I did not introduce myself at first. But I honestly thought that you were wonderful."

"I'm Anya," I said, smiling. "And thank you. You're too kind. I don't even remember how..."

She put a delicate hand on my shoulder and said, "We come to this event every year for the past 3 years and you are the first to have caught my attention from the start."

"Really?"

She smiled, her brown eyes shining with modesty. I had just met her and already I liked her. There was something comforting about Ridley that set me at ease, where Bastian had sent me off the rails in a matter of seconds.

Weird.

"So we'll see you both at 9 at the Plaza."

Ridley gave Bastian a hard look. He responded, "What?"

"Don't you think it's a little too extravagant?" she said, looking at my expression that must have been like a broken bobble head with its eyes inhumanely sticking out of its plastic head.

"I don't think it is."

"Yeah, it's like Burger King with caviar."

My eyes flickered from Ridley to Bastian as they engaged in their own private bantering session. I knew in an instant that Ridley wasn't of his world. She had come to terms with the lifestyle because of her marriage to him. She hadn't lost her sensibility, which I admired undoubtedly. It was easy to get lost in the glitz and glam, or so I heard.

"It's not too flashy," Bastian said through gritted teeth. "I want to do something nice for her, for them and you think..."

"They are..." Liam's words died on his lips as he tried to find the right words to describe them. I crossed my arms over my chest as their conversation fused into the background. They reminded me a little of...well, of Liam and I. We would sometimes find ourselves squabbling over the most mundane things that proved to be important to us.

Ridley thought it was extravagant.

Bastian did not.

I wonder if everyone around Liam and I thought it were as cute and ridiculous at the same time whenever we publicly fought like Bastain and Ridley were doing now.

Just for game keeper's score, I was on Ridley's side.

Not too extravagant?! – that was Bastian's concrete argument. I scoffed. It was the world famous Plaza Hotel. Of course it was going to be extravagant. It was solely for the rich and no peasant like me would ever have dreamed to set put in a place built for bold and the beautiful.

"It's good I packed a suit, then," was all Liam said as we watched them take their leave, waving goodbye as they disappeared through the doors.

An hour and half later, Liam and I were walking into the most beautiful hotel ever created on the face of the earth. Chandeliers, beautiful and intricate glass ceilings, and marble flooring were in every room we walked into. I was in complete awe and judging by the look on Liam's face, so was he.

Ridley and Bastian were waiting for us outside the grand ballroom. Upon seeing them I felt completely out of place. Ridley wore a sweeping blue empire waist dress that looked especially made just for her. Her hair was intricately swept back into Grecian twisted braids, embodying the very essence of that time. Bastian looked like a dashing prince while from a faraway land standing next to her. He was dressed in a black tailored suit with narrow lapels.

"I feel...underdressed," Liam muttered.

I glanced at him and smiled. For some reason his words put my doubts and uncertainty to an end. "Diddo. But I don't think they care."

"Glad to see you guys found the place. We were getting worried," Bastian said.

I smiled, while Ridley shook her head and said, "He thinks he's a comedian." He shrugged, an easy smile tugging on his lips. "I told him not to quit his day job."

Liam and I traded a smile.

We followed Ridley and Bastian through the grand ball room, my footsteps stopping repeatedly that Liam had to practically guide me through the room. I wanted to capture everything in my mind's eye, recalling the memory whenever I saw fit. Round tables covered with white cloths were scattered around a wood paneled stage floor on one side of the room. There was a band setting up quietly as all around people elegantly dressed dined and veiled in low drowning conversations. The ceiling ledge was arched, giving the room a curved appearance. A crystal dome chandelier occupied the center of the room, illuminating the space with sheer warm light. Three small candles were displayed on the tables, the flames dancing carelessly in the round glass holder.

Liam pulled out my chair just as Bastian pulled out Ridley's. I muttered a simple and impressed "thank you" and he nodded, taking his seat next to me. Bastian ordered for us once he gathered and we explained that we did not know what a single thing on the menu meant. It looked like French mixed with Slovakian.

Okay, so I was exaggerating. The menu was in plain English, but it was filled with things like shallot vinaigrette, wild arugula, and almond romesco. I honestly did not know what any of those things were along with three-fourths of the menu. My only protest was that I was not having caviar. Liam seconded my motion. There was something about eating fish eggs that was vile and turned our stomachs.

I won't even talk about the price for a plate. It was more than I would ever see in a pay check once I started working.

Bastian ordered a Pappardelle Pomodoro for me and a Piedmontese Rib Eye for Liam. Ridley had a Maine Lobstair Cocktail and Bastian ordered a second Piedmontese Rib Eye. For side dishes he ordered Mac N' Cheese, Parmesan Fries, and Risotto "tater tots." I had a feeling that he did it solely for mine and Liam's benefit, but when the waiter brought the dishes, I found out that it was to appease Ridley. It was still fancy food but it had a sense of normalcy.

Liam didn't hide his hunger as he reached across the table and seized the bowl of Mac N' Cheese, heaving a nice pile into this plate. I grinned up at him, and he smiled, sheepishly – almost bashfully, as if he was remembering his manners.

"No, no," Ridley said, waving her hand as Liam slowly began to put the plate back down. "Help yourselves. It's all on Bastian, right, honey?"

His eyes grew into slits, internally sulking at what a hard time his wife was giving him. To us, he flashed us a charming and dazzling smile. "Eat as much as you want. We can always order more."

Bastian certainly did not have to tell us twice. I followed in Liam's footsteps, digging in with a hunger that was incomprehensible to me. I didn't remember the last time I felt this hungry, like I was going to stop breathing at any moment with all the mouth watering food in front of me.

When the main course arrived I barely had enough room in my belly to take 10 bites. Bastian had chosen wisely with our food. It was absolutely heavenly divine. I'd never tasted anything so rich and delicious in my life. This was the food made fit for a king!

"So, Anya," Bastian began. "Now, that we've gotten acquainted..." Ridley rolled her eyes and winked at me. I tried to stifle my giggles, but failed as Bastian noticed and raised a perfectly arched brow. Liam gave me a reprimanding side long glance and I couldn't help but to think how alike Bastian and he were.

"You don't have to be so formal," I said, digging my fork into some Mac N' Cheese. Ridley flashed me a grateful smile and traded a secret telepathic conversation with him. She was definitely giving him a hard time, but he was a good sport about him. My likeness for him grew as the night commenced.

"Oh, alright. So what do you say, Anya?" He loosened his tie a bit and leaned his elbows on the table. "I will personally fund your expenses for all four years at Julliard. You won't have to worry about living expenses or meal plans. Everything will be taken care of by me."

I looked up at him and met his eyes across the table. His eyes, I'd noticed, were blue. A darker blue than Liam's but lighter all to-gether. They were sincere and trust worthy and I briefly wondered if Ridley had fallen for those baby blues.

I shook the thought away and looked down at my plate. I was hoping that the answers would be right there, strewn about and written on the cheesy yellow noodles. But that's not how things worked. I had to make this decision – like others I had come across – by myself.

"Why would you do this for me?" I asked. "Why would you do this for a person you hardly know?"

"Because it would be a shame to see a great musician like you, miss an opportunity because of money."

I let his words sink in. That was the second thing that was stopping me: money. I would never choose to go to Julliard if it meant a difficult time for my parents while I was at school. They'd do it in a heartbeat, but I wouldn't allow it. I'd go to school at the University of Montevallo and be happily content with that outcome.

"We want to do this," Ridley said, taking her husband's hand. Bastian smiled faintly at her, glad to have her take over the conversation. "I was telling you earlier how only one other person has ever captured my heart like you did tonight." She glanced at Bastian and I knew right then and there that he was also a musician, a pianist. "The music you play comes from within, making it come alive all around you. You have a gift and that gift should be treasured and cared for."

"They're right," Liam added. "Your music is…beautiful. Spell binding. I remember the first time I…" His words trailed off, a hazy look clouding his eyes. He shook his head and focused at a point in the distance. He faced me, but he wasn't looking at me. It made me want to desperately know what he was thinking. What was he about to say before he thought better of it?

"You deserve this." Ridley reached forward, taking my hand in hers. A hot, prickling sting arose at the back of my eyes. A second later I realized that they were tears.

"I don't know what to say," I breathed out.

"You don't have to say anything," Bastian said. "I'm happy to be doing this for you. I will make the arrangements tomorrow."

My heart swelled. "Thank you so much. This means the world to me. I won't ever forget this."

He stood, coming over to my side of the table. I quickly got out of my seat and met him half way, where he embraced me, tenderly like a child he'd immediately taken a liking too. My eyes burned and I hastily excused myself.

I couldn't have found the bathroom sooner than I did. It was empty and I let the tears fall freely down my cheeks. They were happy tears, my heart crying for the incredible and blessed thing that had just happened. I never asked for this, yet God had done it. He'd given me a way to go to Julliard no matter what.

It filled me with a newfound strength. I was going to be here, in New York, in a couple of months. Graduation would come and go. My last summer in Fairhope would be a faded memory by the time that I walked the historic halls of Julliard. Liam would...

Liam.

The door opened immediately and I turned on my heel to find Ridley. Taking some tissue from the black marbled counter, she dabbed at my cheeks, a small smile tugging on her lips.

"He's in love with you."

My brows furrowed. Those were not the first words that I expected her to say. I didn't know if it was her way of getting me to stop crying. Either way it worked.

"Who?"

"Liam. He's in love with you."

"What?" I took a step back and caught my reflection in the mirror. "That's crazy. He drives me crazy."

Ridley gave me a knowing smile. She looked towards the door and I knew that if Bastian was anywhere in sight she would be looking at him. "He drove me crazy and look at us now."

I shook my head. "He'd never going falling for a girl like me. He's had other girls. Prettier girls. Girls that aren't..." I snapped my mouth shut and stared at my reflection. My eyes were blotchy and red, black running mascara framed my eyes. I knew that I should have worn waterproof mascara. What was I thinking?

"That's the same thing I told myself about him." A laugh escaped her lips and she shook her head. "Just don't let him get away. Whatever happens, be with him because true love only comes once in a lifetime. And once it leaves, it will never be the same again."

"But I don't-"

Ridley shook her head and gently turned me to face her. She dabbed around the skin of my eye, soaking up the black liquid with the warm paper towel.

"You do. You know you do but you're afraid to let him in. I know that look in your eyes, the kind of look a girl only gets when she's looking at someone she loves but tells herself she can't have him."

I bit my lip. She was sounding a lot like Gemma.

"How do you know all this?" I asked.

Her focus had been mainly on my cheeks, dabbing away at the mess I'd made. The moment the question escaped from my lips she looked up and met my eyes. Her eyes were like liquid gold as she smiled, knowingly.

"Because I was in your shoes once."

Ridley's words kept replaying in my head for the next few days. It was all that I could think of on the long drive back home. Liam's behavior hadn't changed towards me, at least, I didn't think so. He was playful and sweet. The sarcasm that he'd always bend at his will was still a part of him. There was no sign of what Ridley had said. How could she possibly know when she hardly knew him like I did?

The days mingled together until I lost track of time itself. I slept for hours on end, while Liam drove, listening to low hum of the stereo. He didn't disturb me, which I was grateful for. My bones were heavy with fatigue, pulling me under with an iron grasp. I wasn't able to stay awake for more than a couple hours at time while we were in the car. With the fatigue came the loss for appetite.

Liam was worried; I knew that much by the concern look in his eyes whenever he looked at me. I assured him that I was fine, but he didn't believe me.

I leaned my head against the car door and curled my body against its frame, watching the scattered signs along the dark, desolate highway pass on by. The sky was littered with small pinpricks of light with the waxing moon illuminating the dark space around it. It was vast, never ending. It was times like these that I realized that everything in the world was so small compared to the sky above.

"Seventy miles to go," Liam said. I turned my head and glanced at him. "We're almost home."

I smiled. "Finally." I looked at the dashboard and read 7:54. "Pretty good timing considering how bad traffic was in Montgomery."

"Well you've got an excellent driver behind the wheel."

I rolled my eyes. "You're so conceited."

"I like to call it confidence."

"You say potato, I say poe-ta-toe."

He shook his head, a faint smile on his lips.

"What?"

"You-" He didn't get to finish whatever he was about to say because at that moment there was a strange flopping sound coming from the back. His eyes shifted to the rearview mirror and he muttered, "Dammit."

"What was that?" I asked as he pulled to the side of the highway, turning off the ignition and unbuckling his seatbelt.

"Flat tire."

He got out the car and I followed, shivering from the frigid air. Liam kneeled and examined the left back tire. "Can you pop open the trunk for me?"

I immediately did as he asked and went back to him. He had already taken out a flashlight from the trunk and was shining it down on the incriminating piece of evidence. A nail had embedded itself on the side of the tire, tearing open a small but very detrimental hole.

"Can you fix it?" I asked.

"Yes," he said, pushing himself off the ground, "If I had a spare tire."

I hung my head back and closed my eyes. This could not be happening. We were so close to being home. So. Very. Close.

"I'll call my dad," I sighed, heading back to the front of the car. "I've got to call him anyways."

"He'll worry," he said, trailing behind me. "Let me call Hayden. He should be home from his trip with Gemma, right?"

I nodded. "But where is he going to get a spare tire from? Jimmy's is closed. Unless he..."

Liam ignored me, already dialing Hayden's number. Our very good and reliable friend picked up in a couple of seconds and Liam gave him a brief explanation of our car trouble, ending the conversation with, "Okay, we'll see you in thirty." He slid the phone back into his front pocket and turned off the flashlight, tossing it into the trunk.

"So, now what?"

"Now we wait." He leaned against the side of the car, crossing his arms over his chest. I wanted to tell him we could wait in the warmth of the car, but there was something serene about his composure that bade me to not say a word.

Silently, I settled next to him, resting my back on the cool metal. We were quiet for a few minutes until Liam broke the silence, turning to face me.

"There's something I want to give you."

I swallowed, my heart giving a sudden lurch inside my chest.

"What for?"

He didn't answer my question. Instead he went to the back and rustled around in the trunk for whatever it was he was going to give me. In those brief but agonizing seconds my mind went through a million possibilities – none being concrete and not one last more than a couple of seconds.

I was practically dancing on the balls of my feet with unfeigned curiosity and panic when I saw two squares of drastically different sizes in his hands. One was a small red box while the other was a medium sized, wrapped around shiny purple gift wrap.

"What's it for?"

"For making it into Julliard."

"But I haven't been accepted."

He smiled and reached forward, cupping the left side of my cheek with a free hand. "There's no doubt in my mind that you didn't get in. They would be crazy to not have accepted you."

I looked down at the ground and bit my lip. When I looked back up, there was uncertainty laced in his cool gray eyes. "Will you open them for me?"

I nodded, unable to form any words. He handed me the bigger of the sized presents. I smiled as I tore the paper and dropped it on top of the hood. An irrepressible smile formed on my lips as the outline of a journal easily became distinguishable. The cover was a solid lilac with my name engraved on the bottom right hand corner. I ran my thumb over the silver lined letters and then found that on the binding the words Let Music Free Your Soul were engraved in cursive. Lastly, I noticed that there was a heart shaped lock.

I turned over the paper on the hood, but didn't find the key among its wrapping. Thinking that I must have dropped it on accident while I tore open the paper, I glanced down at the ground but didn't see anything.

"It's beautiful," I said. "But..umm...how am I supposed to open it?"

As if he was waiting for me to ask that, he smiled and handed me the small square box. "With that."

"This is highly suspicious," I said, putting down the journal on the hood and taking the small box from his hands. "You could have just kept the key with the journal. You just wasted a perfectly good box."

He chuckled. "Just open it."

I did just that and felt my heart skip a beat.

Inside was a beautiful heart shaped silver locket with a small eight note right in the center of it. The minable light the night had to offer shinned down on the diamonds embedded around lining of the heart.

It was worth much more than a key ought to have been.

"Liam...I can't..." I looked up at him and saw that the smile that had been etched on his lips was beginning to falter. "I can't take this from you..it's..."

"Anya." The way he said my name stilled my heart. I wanted to cry. "I got this for you. No one else has..." A small sigh escaped his lips and he ran a hand through his hair. "Anya." He closed the few inches of distance between us and looked down at me, his blue-gray eyes vibrant and steady.

"Anya, I love you."

My breath caught in my throat and I shook my head. "No. No. You...you can't."

"I do."

I took a step back from. "I won't let you."

His brows furrowed and he scoffed. "It's kinda late for that."

"I'll make you hate me."

"Impossible."

I held my hand out, stopping his stride at mid-step. He did, his brow lifting in a challenge. The calmness that surrounded him at the beginning had long ago faded replaced with radiating heat.

"I want you to stop this inappropriate feeling immediately. Squash it. It's for you own good."

He let out a shaky laugh and shook his head. "I've never done things that were for my own good."

"It's not too late to start now."

"It is," he said simply.

I opened my mouth to retort with something witty, something to quickly defuse this moment. But nothing came to mind. I was completely at a loss for words; my heart beat beating wildly like a set of hummingbird wings.

Liam took a wary step towards me, like if he took a wrong step it would detonate a live bomb planted right beneath our feet.

"Tell me you don't feel something for me, Anya. Tell me and I'll never mention it again."

"I can't," I said. It was about the only thing that I could say. His eyes went completely still, a look of dejection crossing his features.

My heart sank and I went to him without a second thought. I was tired. I was tired of hiding how I felt for him because I was scared of what might happen. I'd been living in denial, afraid of being hurt because of uncertainty.

It all became clear as I took his hand in mine and held it to my heart.

"I can't say that I don't feel something for you because I do." He lifted his eyes and a swirl of hope danced across his eyes.

"Yeah?"

I nodded, my face splitting into a smile.

This was right. It felt so unbelievably right to be able to say what my heart had so long known.

"I love you."

He caressed the side of my face and held my gaze. His eyes travelled to my lips and I closed my eyes as he brought his lips down to meet mine. It was sweet. Delicate. Simple. It was unlike the other kisses we'd ever shared. It wasn't driven by a crazed, impulsive nature, but of love.

Pure, unadulterated love.

A blaring honk broke through a moment that seemed to be frozen in time. Everything had been quiet and still but the noise had brought us back down to earth. I turned and was blinded by car headlights.

"Well, it's about damn time!" hollered Hayden, rolling to a stop beside us on the road. Next to Hayden Gemma was clapping, an ear-splitting grin on her face.

"What took you guys so long?" Gemma asked, climbing out of the car.

Liam and I traded a look and smiled. He wrapped an arm around my waist and I leaned into his solid chest.

"Everything," was all Liam said.

I couldn't have agreed with him more.

Chapter 34

L iam

The next morning I drove the car to Jimmy's. The old man was in his office but when I pulled into the garage he met me outside. The skin around his eyes crinkled as he brought me into a bear hug, patting my back affectionately like he hadn't seen me in years rather than two weeks.

"Good to have yer back. You reckon we missed yer around here."

I chuckled and stepped back to look the old man right in the eyes. "Doubt anybody missed me but you old man."

He swatted my arm, his expression devoid of humor. But in the next second his mask cracked and the light was back in his brown old eyes.

"So how'd it go? Tell me all about it."

Jimmy leaned against the car, wiping his grease filled hands with a rag. He waited patiently, the wrinkles around his mouth deepening as the seconds ticked.

"What?" I asked, crossing my arms over my chest. I leaned against the door of his office and crossed one foot in front of the other. "Why you smiling old man? Something happen while I was gone?"

He raised his brows and shook his head all the while keeping a crooked smile plastered on his face.

"You told her you love her, didn't you."

I straightened and eyed him warily. How did he know? How did he always know things that he couldn't have possibly known? I wondered if he had a spy out there keeping an eye on me or something.

"The look on yer' face says it all, boy."

"What look?"

"That look," he pointed at my face and I shrugged, not knowing what in the world the old man was going on about now.

"There's a sparkle in your eye and you have an extra spring to your step."

What? I chuckled and shook my head, vying for cool composure. Jimmy saw through the façade.

"C'mon, amuse an old soul. Start from the beginning."

I cupped the back of my neck and looked up at the ceiling. Where did I even start to tell Jimmy all that happened?

From the beginning, genius.

Right.

Running a hand through my hair, I smiled and recounted the events of our trip. I skipped over the boring details of the twenty-plus hour drive and gave little facts of the seven grueling hours spent completing our homework. I couldn't give a damn about any of it. But Anya made a good point about not passing, which meant not graduating, and it was something that I couldn't afford. I needed – no. I wanted to graduate high school. At least with a diploma I could do something – like leave this town behind and start fresh.

When I came to retelling how Anya did at the audition, I felt like I wasn't making any kind of sense. I waved my arms around, trying to find the words to explain how her music moved me. It was like the first time I heard her play in the empty theater at the beginning of the school year.

Enticing. Captivating. Spellbinding.

Jimmy beamed when he heard the news of a private sponsor funding her tuition. "A true blessing," he said.

I agreed.

When I came to telling him about the night before, I stumbled over my words. It was harder than I had thought to delve into my feelings. Everything else had been like telling a story second hand. But how I felt about Anya was...me. No one else could tell how I felt about her, except, me.

I sounded like a completely moron.

Thankfully, I dodged a bullet. Jimmy saved me from my psycho babbling. He squeezed my shoulder and smiled up at me, his brown eyes glistening.

"It's good to see you happy, son. I haven't seen you like this since..."

My throat constricted. Jimmy gave me a small smile and looked down at the ground. He didn't need to explain. All that he felt and wanted to say was written across his face.

"Have you talked...?"

I shook my head. "No. I came home and it was the usual routine. I doubt he even noticed I was gone."

Jimmy gave me a sympathetic look and I just waved his concern away. I had come to terms with my father's behavior a long time ago, knowing that he would never be the man I'd learn to respect and look up to when I was young. Somewhere in Jimmy's thick skull, he knew it too. It was a lost cause to hope for something that would never see the light of day.

"How'd the car run?" Jimmy asked, circling the vehicle he'd let me borrow. He had to pull some strings, but he got the car available from a guy he knew in Mobile for a reasonable rate.

"I had no problems with her," I said, tapping the hood of the car. "Which reminds me," I dug out an envelope from the back of my pocket and handed it to Jimmy. "That is the last of the payment."

Jimmy shook his head, pushing the envelope across the hood to me. "I've already got it covered, kid. Think of it as an early graduation present."

I stared at him, keeping my gaze steady with his. The old man could win an old classic staring match with anyone any day. But today he would not be triumphant. I could not take his money. It was Jimmy. He was...well, he was like a long lost uncle that had appeared when I needed him the most, taking me in of his own accord.

"You ain't winning this, kid; might as well take it. No need to be worrin' about nufin."

"But I–"

He held up his hand, not wanting to hear another word. "Save it. You'll be needin' it for college, right? Which I hope you've been thinkin' about as a possibility."

I slowly nodded.

"Then it's settled. Now," Jimmy straightened and walked around the car until he came to stand in front of me. "Don't ya got somewhere to be, son? I reckon it's a lovely Saturday and there's a girl out there to spend it with."

I clasped his shoulder and smiled down at him. "Thank you...for everything."

"Don't mention it kid."

With one last smile, I sauntered forward to where my bike rested at the far end of the garage. I hopped on and turned on the ignition, revving the handles. The engine roared to life, welcoming me back from the long separation we'd endure.

"Liam!"

I looked up and saw Jimmy holding Anya's bag in the air. He set it on the hood of the car and said something that I didn't catch over the sound of the engine. I pretended that I understood and with a slight nod, Jimmy turned on his heel and went back into his office.

Slowly weaving my bike through the garage, I drove next to the rental car and grabbed the bag from the hood. But I grabbed it at the wrong end. The force caused some of the continents from the bag to tumble onto the floor in a noisy affair.

"Dammit," I muttered.

I turned off the engine and set the bike on its kick stand, crouching down and retrieving all of Anya's things that had fallen. I picked up dozens of pens among the array of CD's she'd burn for the trip. There was a book she'd brought that she never read once, at least, to my knowledge. Her iPod and cell phone were among the fray and I prayed to whatever God was out there that they hadn't broken. He must have been listening since not a scratch seemed to linger accusingly at me.

With everything picked up I looked under the car to make sure I hadn't missed anything. It was good thing I double checked or

I would have missed a pen and what seemed like a bottle of Ibuprofen.

It wasn't at all Ibuprofen. It was a prescribed drug. Whatever she was taking, she took it often as the bottle only had about half a dozen tablets left. I held the small bottle in my hand, clutching it as an unsettling thought dawned on me.

My stomach sank, my mind going through the worst scenarios that a person could ever be plagued with. She had always been sick – that wasn't a secret. But the severity of how sick she was, even when she was a little kid, had always been unknown to me. I always figured that she had a weaker immune system than a normal, healthy person.

But...

No, I told myself. No. I can't think like that.

Dropping the bottle into her bag I made sure it was closed tightly before securing it around the back of my bike. I hadn't planned to go directly to her house after I'd dropped the car off, but the sudden urge to see her, to make sure that she was okay, filled me with a determination that was unlike anything I'd ever experienced before.

I rang the door bell once and after a few minutes had passed, I rang it again. Mr. Vanchester was home as was his Ford Taurus, parked in the driveway. It felt like hours had passed as I waited for someone to answer the door. My heart was pounding in my chest like it was ready to jump out of my body at any moment. When the familiar sound of the locks shifting on the other side reached my ears, I let out a long breath that I hadn't known I'd been holding.

Anya opened the door, her eyes gratefully awaiting the person who she had been expecting.

"Liam. Hey...what are you doing here?" Her eyes were unfocused as she looked up at me. "I thought we were going down to the pier with Gem and Hayden later?"

"I-I...yeah. I just," I looked down, suddenly remembering that I held her bag in my hands. I thrust it towards her and she grabbed it, holding it to her chest like a wounded animal she'd just found. "You left it in the car. Jimmy was the one who found it."

She nodded, her eyes slowly focusing on my face. "I also wanted to see you," I added.

The corners of her mouth quirked up into a smile. She leaned forward, but her movements were slow and uncertain. She swayed and I reached forward only to grace my hand along her arm as she leaned on the doorframe to regain her balance.

"You alright?" I asked.

She measly nodded and began to retreat back, sliding her hand against the frame of the door. "I have to go, but I'll see you later?"

My eyes traveled down her body, surveying her pale face and strained eyes. "Yeah," I said, digging my hands into the front pockets of my jeans. "I'll come by at six."

"M'kay," she replied, beginning to close the door.

At a last course of impulse, I jerked my hand forward and stopped the door. "Wait." Anya peeked over the side of the door and opened it once more. I leaned forward and held her brown eyed gaze as a lingering question swirled within them.

"I forgot something."

"What?" she asked.

"This," I took her face in my hands and kissed her forehead, feeling the feverish heat radiating from her skin. It caused a pang to course through the recesses of my chest. As I let go, all my previous thoughts before coming to her house whirled around my mind like a benevolent storm.

"Hmm...you know, if I didn't know any better, I'd say you're becoming a romantic."

I tried to smile but it felt forced. Even though, I knew she wasn't feeling well, Anya caught the sudden change in my mood.

"What's wrong?"

I shook my head. "Nothing. I was just...thinking."

She eyed me suspiciously, but let it go. I reassured her that nothing was wrong by waving her concern away and plastering on a smile on my face. "I'll see you in a few. Try not to miss me too much, babe."

She rolled her eyes and huffed. "Just because I told you I love you doesn't mean you can go on calling me babe whenever you wish."

I chuckled. She was never going to let that go. It made me momentarily forget about the dread that was slowly creeping and settling into the core of my stomach.

"Alright, alright," I said, putting my hands up in defense. "I'm going."

"You better." With those last words she smiled and shut the door behind her.

The smile I had feigned dropped as I walked back to my bike. It took least than a minute to park and walk through the door of my house, my movements rushed and paralyzed all at the same time. Booting up my computer, I waited impatiently, drumming my fingers on my desk.

It felt like I had been waiting for hours, the dread of the possibility that I might find my worst fear weighing heavy on my shoulders.

When the system was up and running I typed in Google's search engine Hydroxyurea. I was uncertain if I'd remembered the spelling correctly. The Google search came back with no suggestion spelling and I felt a small feat of triumph course through my veins. The feeling was short-lived as I began reading what Hydroxyurea was used for, the anxiety that I had already been feeling tripling as I clicked on every link on the first page.

Her secret burned on the tip of my tongue that day. I wanted to ask her when we went to the pier with Hayden and Gemma later on in the evening. What I'd discovered was seared in the back of my mind. Nothing else mattered.

I went through the motions of everyday life for the next couple of days. There never seemed to the right time to bring it up. In the blur of Spring Break ending and classes resuming, Anya was happy – happier than I had ever seen her. There was a light in her eyes that never seemed to fade. It seemed like the stars themselves had found a new place to reside. Her happiness was infectious. We all felt it. Whenever she looked at me in that way of hers I felt a pang run through my chest.

The feelings that I'd built inside stayed there until Thursday afternoon. After school I took Anya into town, where we walked along the boardwalk hand-in-hand. The stares weren't as frequent as they had been that Monday. People whispered as we passed by them in the hallways, wondering what Liam Rowely was doing with Anya Vanchester, of all people.

In a small town such as Fairhope it didn't take much for the direction of attention to switch from Anya and I to Karla's wild escapades Monday night. Anya felt guilty, feeling partially responsible for her errant behavior. I tried to qualm her thoughts, but they were to no avail. At lunch Tuesday afternoon, Anya took Karla aside and talked to her. Anya wouldn't tell me what they talked about, but it stirred the rumor mill once more.

To say that I was over this high school bullshit would be a severe understatement. Graduation couldn't approach any more quickly than it already was.

We walked towards the pier, the stillness of the water sending calm ripples coursing through my entire body. Anya let go of my hand and sat down at the edge of the dock, dangling her feet above the water. I sat down next to her and looked out into the Bay with the sun still high in the clear blue sky. Cold air swirled around me; the trees rustling behind us as the wind traveled on through.

The tranquility made me calm – as calm as the water beneath my feet. But the prickling thought of talking to her floated at the edge of my mind. There was no escaping it, and I knew that this was a good time if any.

What happened after wasn't at all what either of us expected.

Anya

It was a beautiful day to be out on the town. The sky was a cloudless blue with the sun shining down on us. The water rippled beneath my feet as the wind jostled down and interrupted the stillness of the surface. Birds chirped a few feet away, singing a song that only they were privy to as the trees danced in the wind.

Liam was quiet beside me, his mind somewhere else as it lately had been. He was different and not in the way that could be misinterpreted of it being bad. But there was something lurking beneath the smile that seemed to shine in his eyes these days, something troublesome.

We sat in comfortable silence for a long time, neither disturbing the others thoughts. I liked being with him this way. Sometimes people did not need words to fill an empty space. Just another person sitting next to you was enough.

I don't know how much time passed before Liam spoke, breaking the quiet between us.

"Are you sick?" he asked.

I turned my head and looked at him, my brows furrowed at his choice of words.

"No," I said slowly, "I feel..."

He shook his head. "I googled what Hydrea means. That's what it's called, right?" He didn't wait for my response, instead he just barreled on through like he needed to keep going, needed to say whatever it is he found out. My heart beat increased, thundering loudly in my ears. "It was all about Leukemia and anemia and...do you have cancer?"

It felt like someone had kicked me in the stomach, knocking the wind out of my lungs.

"You had no right," I said, standing up on my feet. "How did you even...?"

"That's not the point." He stood up, towering over me with his eyes hard as steel. "Were you ever going to tell me?"

I looked away. This was not how I wanted him to find out. This was not how I wanted to tell him. If I had it my way he never would have found out. "It's not something you should know," I said, projecting my thoughts out loud.

He laughed but there was no humor in it. "You don't think I have the right to know?" His voice was hard, fighting to unleash the anger boiling inside.

It sent me off the rails. "No. You don't. It's my burden. I didn't want you to worry. I didn't want you to look at me with pity because I'm sick. Is that it? Is that what you wanted to hear?" Tears caused my throat to tighten and rise. "I've been sick with sickle cell anemia all my life, Liam. It didn't just happen. I didn't just wake up one morning and find out that I was going to die in a few years. It had been predicted. I've known for a long time."

"Did Gemma know? Did Hayden?"

I closed my eyes and nodded. When I opened them again I saw the betrayal and hurt in his eyes.

"You were never going to tell. What did you think? That'd it be better to keep me in the dark to spare my feelings?"

I bit the inside of my check, begging the tears to stop. I couldn't cry. Not now. "That's why I fought so hard to not fall in love with you. I didn't want to leave you in the end if something were to happen. You had no right to..." I angrily wiped the tears that matted my cheeks with a fist. The sudden realization of how he'd found out dawned on me then. "My bag. You looked through my bag!"

I began to retreat down the pier, not wanting to know the answer. He'd look through my bag. He invaded my privacy. We had built an unsaid bond of trust and he'd breached it because....because I don't know.

"That's not the point here," he said again.

"So you did look through my bag?" I retorted.

"No," was all he said.

"Then...?"

He shook his head. "It doesn't matter."

I searched his eyes but he wouldn't look at me. His jaw was set, his eyes focused on a distant point on the horizon. I let out a shaky breath and walked away, my hands shaking with anger and betrayal and dejection. The uncertainty of where that left us broke my heart most of all.

The rest of the week passed without any sight of him. Everyone told me to give him space. I did, but it hurt not knowing how he was. Hayden put into perspective how he would feel if Gemma had kept something that severe a secret from him.

"Betrayed. I'd feel like I wasn't important enough to know."

"But that's not how…"

"I know," he said. Hayden reached out and squeezed my hand. "But that's how I'd see it and it's probably what's going on in his head."

I nodded. I understood but it didn't mean that I liked it.

After a week went by, I sought him out. First stop was at his house, but I knew it was a lost cause when I saw that his bike was missing from the driveway. I continued anyway, trudging up the familiar steps to his house and knocking on the door.

Mr. Rowely answered a couple of seconds later, his body pungent with the smell of spirits and cigarettes.

"Liam's not home," he said brusquely.

"I know." I looked down at the ground. His gaze always sent shivers down my spine, reminding me of a rapacious wolf. "Can you tell me where he could be?"

He grinned but it was feral. "Why would I do that, sweetheart?"

His frivolous manner made me angry. I gritted my teeth and balled up my fist. "It'd be the nice thing to do," I retorted.

Mr. Rowely's eyebrows shot up in surprise. "Well, I didn't know my son caught a lively little fish."

"Look," I said, leaning forward and pressing my hand on the doorframe. "I don't have time for this, sir. I apologize for saying this but you need to get your act together. It's been years since Layla's been gone." He flinched at the sound of his wife's name as his eyes steadily narrowed at me.

"We all miss her, sir. But she wouldn't want her memory to be purged with cheap liquor every day. Your son needs you – he has needed you for as long as I can remember, but you're too selfish to notice."

He clenched his jaw and began to close the door, but I jammed my foot in the way. "You run and you hide," I added, unable to stop. The surge of courage to stand up to Mr. Rowely came from my desperation to find Liam. I didn't care about the consequences that would meet me later.

"What would Layla say if she saw you like this? What would she think about her son? Do you even know what's going on with him lately?"

He held my gaze, hard and unflinching. "No, I guess not. – Your too busy drowning yourself in misery and grief to pay attention to him or care for him like a father ought to."

"You're just a foolish girl," he muttered. "You don't know anything."

I shrugged. "Maybe. Maybe not. But at least I know that self-indulgence never solved anything." I let out a sigh, the bravado escaping through my bated breath.

Sadly I said, "I looked up to you too, Mr. Rowely. You couldn't think of Layla without thinking of you too. Everyone I know still speaks of you with the highest regard. The man who breathed beauty into metal – they call you – but with that title comes the lingering whisper of the tragedy."

He didn't say anything for a long time. The four years of walls he had carefully built were beginning to crack in light of my words. I pressed my lips together and turned on my heels. Behind me I heard the click of the door close and I smiled with the satisfaction that it had not slammed.

I walked the thirty minutes into town, heading to Jimmy's shop. When I got there I was met with a jubilant smile and sinking disappointment.

"What can I do for you, Anya? How are yer' folks?"

I smiled. Jimmy was always so sweet just like Mr. Edison. I wondered for a moment if they were friends. If they weren't I couldn't imagine a better bromance than the two of them.

"My parents are doing well. I...um...I was wondering where Liam is. Is he here, possibly hiding out back?" I craned my neck and looked around the shop but saw only another young man, dressed in greasy blue overalls, leaning over the engine of a car.

"He's a church."

"No," I said shaking my head with increduality. "He can't be there. Liam doesn't go to church."

Jimmy's brows wrinkled. "He's been goin' everyday to talk to the Rev for the past couple of days. Now that you mention it – I reckon it's been nearly a week."

"How long ago did he leave?" I asked.

Jimmy turned his head and looked up at the clock that hung above the door to his office. "'Bout twenty minutes ago."

"Thank you," I said, leaning in to lightly press a kiss on his cheek.

"No problem, kid. When you find him, tell him that I was right."

I cocked my head to the side, wanting to know more of his ominous message but he didn't say anything else.

I smiled and waved goodbye, heading towards the street once more. "Alright," I called back, "I'll give him the message! Thank you again!"

The church was quiet when I entered, closing the heavy oak doors behind me as silently as I could. There was no sign of Reverend Phillips anywhere, and I figured that he was in the back in his office, probably practicing his sermon for Sunday. There was however, a lone soul sitting amidst the presence of God on a bench in the middle of the room.

On light feet I made my way towards him and took a seat right next to him. "Hey," I whispered, glancing at him before my eyes traveled to the stage.

"How did you know I was here?"

"It wasn't easy. I had to rely on some good old fashion detective work."

"Meaning?"

I smiled and elbowed him playfully. "A good detective doesn't reveal her secrets."

The faintest quirk of a smile appeared before it sat grim again. "Liam, I-"

He turned his body towards me and looked at me for the first time in days. I let out a small gasp of incredulity as my heart sank into my stomach. Dark shadows rimmed his eyes and he was scruffier than I had ever seen him. To say that he looked tired wouldn't be enough to describe how he must have felt.

"Liam," I began again, reaching out my hand to caress the side of his face. He stopped me, taking my hand in his instead.

"Let me say this first and then you can say whatever it is that you want to tell me." I nodded, holding his gaze while searching for any sign of what was to come.

"I've been looking for answers and I found them here of all places." His lips lifted up into an unbelievable smile. "I wanted to know why bad things happened to good people. That concept never made any sense to me, and I realized that it was the core of my reasoning for being angry with Him and even hating Him ever since my mom left us."

I looked down and bit my lip. "I blamed Him for it. I blamed Him more than I resented my dad. It wasn't until Reverend Phillips should be a scripture in the bible that things became clear."

Liam let go of my hand and reached underneath his seat where he picked up a copy of the bible. He opened the book to Ecclesiastes and began to recite a verse that was very dear to my heart:

There is a time for everything, and a season for every activity under heaven: a time to be born and a time to die…a time to weep and a time to laugh, a time to mourn and a time to dance…

When he finished reciting the entirety of Ecc 3: 1-8, I found that there were proud tears brimming at the edge of my eyes.

"Everything happens for a reason," he said. "I get that more now than I did before. We may not know why, but it has a purpose that we'll come to see tomorrow or thirty years from now."

I nodded, my heart swelling at his words which rung with clear conviction and dawning realization.

"I'm not going to leave you," he said, closing the book and laying it on the other side of the bench. "If that was what you were afraid of. I've never felt this way about anyone else and I'd be damned if I were to walk away because I was afraid of losing you."

I smiled a watery smile. "You aren't afraid?"

He reached forward and padded his thumb across my cheek. "Terrified. But I'm not going to live in fear."

"Me either, not anymore, at least."

He took my hand in his, lacing his fingers through mine. "We'll get through this together. One day at a time. How does that sound?"

I squeezed his hand and smiled up at him. How could I have been so blind and full of doubt to see that he wouldn't just walk away from me? My anger seemed unreasonable. Keeping my secret seemed foolish, but in this moment none of it mattered because he'd said all that I could ever have imagined.

When I replied, I conveyed all my love into one word that couldn't even begin to describe how immeasurable or how greatly lived our story would be.

"Perfect."

Epilogue

8 years later.

My fingers grazed the name embedded into the gravestone, lightly sinking into the chiseled dents that spelled out her name. It had been five years since I had last seen her, since I'd last felt her embrace.

Those last few days had been the hardest of my life, but they had also been filled with an indisputable happiness that could rival the sun itself. The last few moments of my time with her flashed through my eyes – her tiny hand go limp in mine, her tired eyes drifting shut, and the tiniest smile on her pink lips.

My chin quivered slightly as I looked down at the ground, hot tears burning behind my eyes.

I was still hers, completely and utterly. I always would be. I tried to move on, tried to find her in every girl I passed on the street. But it was impossible. Anya was it, she was everything.

Tearing my eyes away from her name, I met the warm brown of Phillips; eyes that I associated with her, even if there was no blood relation. They were Anya's eyes. Despite my watery gaze, a small smile played on his lips.

"She'd be proud of you, Liam." The whispered comment brought goose bumps to my already chilled flesh despite the sticky Alabama humidity.

I didn't respond. The silence that spread between us spoke volumes as we were caught in our own private thoughts about what she'd say and how she'd react to the news. After a few minutes passed, Phillip put his arm around my shoulders awkwardly, and we walked back to his car.

Charlotte and Hope were playing outside in the front yard when we pulled up into the driveway. I had only stepped out of the car when a small purple blur dashed towards me and attacked my legs.

"Daddy!" she chirped. Her eyes were bright, searching my own as she tugged on the hem of my shirt. "Nana and I planted flowers, wanna see?"

"What'd you plant?" I asked as she led the way across the yard. She plopped down on the ground and pointed to a fresh plot of dirt, her movements remind me of her mother when she was young. But instead of planting flowers Anya had been famous for killing bugs.

"Orc-kids," she replied. "Nana said they'd grow in four years. That's so long!"

I crouched down and took her tiny hands in mine. "Just you wait and see. Those years are going to pass on by faster than you expect."

"Really?" she eagerly asked.

I nodded and she leaped forward, wrapping her arms around my neck. I picked her up and met Charlotte and Phillip's glistening eyes. Hope nestled her face in the crook of my neck, gripping the collar of my shirt with her tiny fingers, clutching herself to me like a baby Rhebus monkey.

Her birthday was just a few short weeks away, and with each passing day everything that at one time made Anya perfect – that still made her perfect was shining through the brown eyes of my little girl.

"Daddy?" Her tiny voice caught my attention, and I marveled at the pure innocence of her gap-toothed smile. "Did you see Mommy?"

I smiled. "I did, baby. She loves you very much."

"Daddy," she peered up at me through her lashes, "I wanna go next time. Pwease?"

I dabbed her nose with my thumb and she beamed. "She'll love that. She misses you."

"I miss her too," she whimpered, burying her face in my shirt, "but we'll see her soon, like Nana said. Right?"

"Yes," I reassured her. My eyes ventured towards the sky, savoring the sunset and the way it complimented Hope's fair skin as I tucked her into the car-seat of my car despite her protests that she was a grown-up big girl. My motorcycle still sat in the garage at my dad's place, a faded reminder of simpler days.

"Daddy?" She asked hours later as I tucked her into bed and double checked under the bed and closets for her.

"What is it, baby?"

Her dimpled smile brightened up her face in the dimness of her bedroom. "Tell me the story again. Of you and mommy?"

I kissed the crown of her head, the fractured beams of light casting shadows of stars along the walls, and began.

www.ingramcontent.com/pod-product-compliance
Lightning Source LLC
Chambersburg PA
CBHW070736190726
48292CB00002B/287